George Crooks

Life and Letters of the Rev. John M'Clintock

George Crooks

Life and Letters of the Rev. John M'Clintock

ISBN/EAN: 9783337149789

Printed in Europe, USA, Canada, Australia, Japan

Cover: Foto ©Raphael Reischuk / pixelio.de

More available books at **www.hansebooks.com**

Yours affectionately,
J. Mc Clintock

REV. JOHN M'CLINTOCK, D.D., LL.D.,

LATE PRESIDENT OF DREW THEOLOGICAL SEMINARY.

BY

NEW YORK:

NELSON & PHILLIPS.

CINCINNATI:

HITCHCOCK & WALDEN.

1876.

PREFACE.

———·———

IN the narrative here presented the author may have been partial, but has certainly been sincere. Care has been taken, however, to let Dr. M'Clintock himself tell the story of his life, and to this end his diaries and correspondence have been freely used. His charming letters need nothing more to set them off than to be placed in proper connexion with the events of which they are the best interpretation. His diaries are the fullest record remaining of his studies, and show with what eagerness Dr. M'Clintock devoted himself to the accumulation of knowledge. These sources of information I have supplemented from my own recollections, drawn from an intimacy which extended over many years, as well as from the recollections of other friends.

I return my thanks to the correspondents of
Dr. M'Clintock who have placed their letters in
my hands. I am also under special obligations to
his son, Mr. Emory M'Clintock, whose admirable
arrangement of his father's papers has greatly
aided me in the preparation of this volume.

For the young men of the Church, whether of
the ministry or the laity, the life which I have endeavored to portray has many and valuable lessons. The example of a simple, Christian faith,
firmly held by one who explored nearly every field
of human knowledge, will, it is hoped, not be without its effect. With all his growing, Dr. M'Clintock never outgrew the creed which he inherited
from his fathers. His highest aspiration was to
be a Bible Christian. For him the announcement
that "Jesus Christ came into the world to save
sinners" had a meaning which neither philosophy nor improved theology could for a moment
obscure.

CONTENTS.

CHAPTER IV.

THE TRIAL ON THE CHARGE OF INSTIGATING A RIOT.

CHAPTER V.

RESIGNATION OF COLLEGE PROFESSORSHIP.

CHAPTER VI.

CHAPTER VII.

CHAPTER VIII.

CHAPTER IX.

LIFE IN PARIS—PASTORATE OF THE AMERICAN CHAPEL.

CHAPTER X.

LIFE IN PARIS—PATRIOTIC ACTIVITY.

CHAPTER XI.

LAST YEARS OF LIFE.

CHAPTER XII.

TRIBUTES TO THE MEMORY OF DR. M'CLINTOCK BY HIS FRIENDS.

LIFE OF DR. M'CLINTOCK.

CHAPTER I.

JOHN M'CLINTOCK, JUNIOR, the second son of John and Martha M'Clintock, was born in the city of Philadelphia, October 27, 1814. The father, John M'Clintock, Sen., came from County Tyrone, Ireland, to America in the year 1806, and in the year 1807 married Martha M'Mackin, who was also a native of Tyrone. For many years he was a member of the St. George's Methodist Episcopal Church, Philadelphia, in which he held the offices of class leader and trustee. Mr. M'Clintock was a man of unusual intelligence, alert in movement, irrepressible in temper, persistent, tenacious, and altogether a man of mark in the religious community in whose fellowship he lived. His wife, the mother of the subject of this memoir, was a woman of very clear intellect, placid spirit, and deep, though unobtrusive,

piety. Five sons and three daughters were born to
John and Martha M'Clintock, all of whom lived to
mature age.

The family in Ireland was originally Presbyterian. The
earliest member of whom the home record makes mention, William M'Clintock, (born in 1717,) is described as a
farmer, in County Tyrone, "a very quiet, pious man."
His son James (born in 1740) was both a farmer and a
county physician of some repute. He is the first Methodist who appears in the family, and was a class leader
in the period of the beginnings of Methodism. From
James descended John, the father of the Rev. Dr.
M'Clintock. Thus through his father, grandfather, and
great grandfather, Dr. M'Clintock inherited the blessings
of religious thought and habit. His ancestors were, no
doubt, a substantial, godly people; fit representatives
of the Protestant Irish stock, which has contributed so
much to the vigor and energy of the English-speaking
race in America.

The home life of the M'Clintocks in Philadelphia was
simple and unostentatious. The father carried on a re-
tail dry-goods trade for many years with various success.
Store and home, as was then the almost universal practice, were in the same building. Here was dispensed a
hearty hospitality, the itinerant preachers being among
Mr. M'Clintock's most frequent guests. The faces of
Solomon Sharp, Ezekiel Cooper, Beverly Waugh, Dr.
John Emory, and others of the itinerants known to fame
in that day, were familiar to the younger members of
the family from childhood. The household held to the

Church by the closest tie; their Church-life was a very large part of their entire life.

The Methodist society to which the father and mother belonged, the St. George's, was the oldest in Philadelphia. After many renovations of its interior the homely edifice still stands, with its gable looking upon the street, and bearing without much change the same appearance as fifty years ago. Nearly opposite, on Fourth-street, is the St. Augustine's Roman Catholic Church, which, like its Methodist neighbor, has always been strong and populous, and has had an eventful history of its own. One cannot but feel that the two edifices, standing over against each other, have been types of two antagonistic systems of faith, brought by a singular coincidence face to face. St. George's was noted for the enthusiasm of its worshippers, and its crowded congregations. It was the fruitful mother of a great progeny of Churches scattered throughout the city and county of Philadelphia. The leading preachers of the connexion held it an honor to be appointed to its pulpit. Its roll of pastors includes such men as Henry White, Levi Scott, Joseph Holdich, George G. Cookman, Charles Pitman, and others of later fame. It was naturally, therefore, for long years, a centre of Methodist influence and power.

Into the life of this fine old Church, young M'Clintock, we may say, was born. He knew its hard, uncushioned benches, its arched ceiling, its over-jutting galleries, its crowded aisles, well. In the year 1825, being eleven years of age, he was placed by Dr. Holdich, then pastor, in a catechetical class of the children of the congregation, and on October 9, of that year, was received as a probationer in the Church. Of this fact of young M'Clintock's life, Dr. Holdich gives us the following interesting reminiscence :—

In the year 1825, being the fourth year of my ministry, I was stationed at St. George's Charge, in the city of Philadelphia. The Charge then consisted of five Churches. My colleagues were the Rev. Charles Pitman and William Barnes. During this year it was that George G. Cookman arrived from England, and, having some previous knowledge of each other through common friends, he naturally sought me out, and finally took lodgings in the same house with me. It was at the house of my senior colleague, the Rev. Charles Pitman. He joined St. George's Church as a local preacher, and at once began to preach with great acceptance and popularity.

During the course of our joint-pastorate that year, (1825,) we formed the children belonging to St. George's Church into a catechetical class, and met them once a week. Besides the catechism, we had singing, prayer, and exhortation. I do not know which of the ministers organized the class, but I know that we all, including Mr. Cookman, took part in it, and with this class young John M'Clintock became connected. I remember the hope he enkindled in us as to his future, and the gratification he afforded us by his punctuality, and his earnestness and zeal to enlist others in the same cause. He showed a good deal of talent, and was apt both in remembering and in communicating what he knew. I cannot say that he professed to enjoy experimental piety, but we had great hope of him, believing that he would, if he lived, grow up to be a useful and distinguished man. But he was only a boy, and liable to a boy's exposures and temptations. If he was not always faithful to his early convictions, I believe he never entirely lost them ; and the profession of religion which he subsequently made while in New York was, I believe, only the actualizing and carrying into practice the impressions he received while attending the catechetical class.

In the year 1822, the eighth of his age, he was placed in the Grammar School of the University of Pennsylvania, and began the study of Latin and Greek. Dr. S. B. Wylie, a famous old Grecian, was the principal. The school was formed upon the English model; the study of the ancient classic languages was the chief occupation of teachers and scholars every day. For this method of training Dr. Wylie was admirably qualified. Profoundly versed in both languages, especially the Greek, he appreciated the value of patient drill. He was among the earliest of American classical teachers to adopt the more philosophical method of deriving the parts of the Greek verb from a single root form. His Greek Grammar, first published in 1838, is a fine specimen of compact workmanship. I have heard Dr. M'Clintock say, that when his old preceptor became Professor in the University of Pennsylvania he would hear his classes in Homer without any use of text-book; his memory had treasured up the text line by line.

Young M'Clintock soon became a favorite with the good Doctor. He must have been an apt scholar, for I find the following note to his father under date of July 24, 1826:—

Mr. M'Clintock:—

Dear Sir:—John tells me you design to send him to the country to-day with the family. I am truly sorry for the arrangement. I beg, if at all consistent, that you will postpone the trip till next week. Our examination will be on Friday. John will make a first-rate figure. Why should you deprive either himself or us of the

2

honor—more particularly as the class at such a time (close before holidays) is usually thin? I will take it as a particular favor, should you not take John away till after that event.

Very respectfully, your obedient servant,

S. B. WYLIE.

Boy as he was, young M'Clintock did not, at this early age, shrink from high questions of metaphysics. The Rev. T. J. Wylie, a son of Dr. Wylie, tells this incident:—

During the time he was at school he was noted for proficiency in his studies and excellent behavior; though I have heard that sometimes the great questions of

" Foreknowledge, will, and fate,
Fix'd fate, free-will, foreknowledge absolute."

were very warmly discussed, during school-hours, between him and another pupil, (Mr. Benjamin B. M'Kinley, at present a member of the Faculty of the Deaf and Dumb Institute,) a staunch Calvinist, of the old true-blue, Covenanter kind, and now, and for many years, a respected member of the United Reformed Presbyterian Church of this city. I cannot say what effect these arguments may have had in developing the intellectual power of our dear friend, or in producing the respect which he has so eloquently expressed for the great Genevan Reformer; but the immediate consequence was correction, more or less severe, from the teacher, who probably supposed that his young pupils were talking about tops or marbles, but had no idea whatever of the true nature of the subjects which formed the themes of such earnest conversations.

It must not be inferred from this record that our subject had no genuine boy-life. He was a boy to the end of his days. Fun was perpetually bubbling up from his inner nature, and revealing itself in pleasant effervescence. Philadelphia was in that early day a boy's paradise. It had not become overgrown, and boys had not yet been put in strait-jackets by innumerable police regulations. The Delaware on the one side and the Schuylkill on the other invited to swimming, boating, and skating. The broad expanse on the north-west, then known as Bush Hill, made ample room for bands of ball-players. To the south of the city the marshes of the "Neck," crowded with reed-birds in the early fall, gave the youthful sportsman many an hour's exhilaration. Adventurous spirits could find their way to the Wissahickon, and spend the long sunny days on the slopes of its hills. Few cities have such surroundings, and, being yet small, the open fields were near at hand on every side. We may readily imagine that the school-boy's Saturday was improved by young M'Clintock. He was well up in all boyish sports, and always spoke of them with zest in his later life. Though his intellect was alert almost to precocity, there was nothing in its vigor akin to disease.

In after life he took more than usual care to preserve the memorials of his school and college work. I have a number of his exercise books before me, the earliest dated 1826, when he was still a mere boy. They show the thorough manner in which he was trained, and the closeness of his application to study. The earlier exercises were, as may be supposed from the character of the school, in Latin and Greek. All is written out with most minute attention to detail. In analysis, transla-

tion, scanning, every point of etymology, syntax, prosody,
mythology, and history was examined, and the fact or
rule stated.   This was the method of Dr. Wylie's school,
and in this exact discipline the foundation of Dr.
M'Clintock's culture was laid.   He did not leap to excellence, but rose to it by honest exertion.   Rapid and
brilliant at all times, he did not disdain what most young
men call drudgery.   His college note books show evidence of activity in every department of knowledge.
In the neatest of hands are preserved digests of lectures
on chemistry, mathematics, philosophy, and constitutional law; sketches of problems in the calculus; draw-
·ings of parts of the steam-engine, and of philosophical
instruments, with descriptions; in fact, nothing seems
to have come amiss to him.   As a school boy he had
drilled into him the habit of doing every thing well, and
the habit clung to him ever after.

In the year 1828, being fourteen years of age, he was
taken from school and placed in his father's dry-goods
store.   Though standing and serving behind the counter,
his mind, according to his own account, was with his
books.   Writing, when a young man, a little narrative of
his life for a friend, he says: " I left school for the purpose of obtaining a knowledge of mercantile pursuits,
into which I entered immediately, and in which I have
been occupied ever since.   Many a scolding have I suffered for sales made below cost, while my mind was wandering to the scenes I had so deeply studied in the
Songs of Anacreon or the Æneid of Virgil."

If he did not relish this life, it at least prepared him

for another which was more congenial. In 1830, being sixteen years of age, he obtained the position of book-keeper in the Methodist Book Concern, New York, then under the supervision of the Rev. Dr. John Emory and the Rev. Beverly Waugh. This now extensive publishing house had been founded in 1797 by the Rev. John Dickens, with a capital of $600, furnished by himself, and had grown, after not a few vicissitudes of fortune, to a solid prosperity. Its business was at this period rapidly increasing. Dr. Emory, a man of unusual sagacity, had essentially changed its methods, and his associate, Mr. Waugh, devoted himself with scrupulous care to its details. They were both attached friends of the M'Clintock family, and the senior agent, Dr. Emory, was, to the end of his life, Dr. M'Clintock's trusted counselor. What the young clerk owed to the almost paternal interest of his employers he could hardly estimate, but always freely acknowledged.

The salary would be considered a pittance in these days. It was six dollars per week; ultimately it became nine dollars; yet out of it the thrifty book-keeper accumulated, as we shall see, a little fund, which he appropriated to his education. Mr. Waugh had charge of the accounts, and M'Clintock came under his immediate superintendence. I am told by old friends that he made his first appearance in the counting-room in a "round-about," a blue-eyed, rosy-cheeked lad, full of spirit and activity, and settled down at once to his work. He boarded with the Rev. Samuel Merwin, whose wife watched over him with motherly care. Some of his

letters written during this period are preserved.   After
having been in New York a month he writes :—

NEW YORK, July 6, 1830.

MY DEAR PARENTS :—In answer to your inquiry whether I shall
have to go to Bennett, [a teacher of book-keeping,] I do not think
it will be necessary. Mr. Waugh continues sick, and during his
sickness I have kept the books almost altogether. I have very little
time to write this letter, so you must excuse it. I went yesterday
morning (5th July) to hear Mr. Merwin, (it cost me a shilling,) and in
the afternoon walked up Broadway. It is a very splendid street, indeed. I heard Mr. Luckey preach on Sunday, and like him very
well.

The meaning of ten dollars out of my wages is as follows : I get
paid monthly, (as I choose it,) and all I do not want for board I pass
to your credit and let you know it. . . .

Affectionately,   JOHN M'CLINTOCK, JUN.

A little later in July he writes : " Having had a good
deal of business to do down town, I know the town
pretty well.   The common writing to be done here is
not more than twice as much as our own at home ; but
about three times a month I have half as much to do as
the yearly balancing of the books at home."   He does
not forget his boyish enjoyments, but notes that he has
" a beautiful place to swim, on the East River—no danger, no cost, and can see the bottom."   In August he
writes to his father : " I have got pretty well used to my
business, and go on without instructions," and signs himself with evident pride, " First clerk Methodist Book
Concern."

In the early winter Mr. Waugh had made a favorable
report of his success in the performance of his duties.

He writes in relation to this to his mother: " I read the letter which Mr. Waugh sent to you last week, and I think it was very satisfactory. It would be the height of meanness for me, if I cannot do the balancing, to refuse to stay at six dollars per week, as Mr. Waugh has been so kind to me. He does not treat any clerk in the store as he does me."

This balancing of the books for the first time proved a sore trouble to the young accountant. He was but sixteen years of age, and the business of the house exceeded $250,000 yearly; and though bright, alert, and familiar with the theory of book-keeping, he was new to its practice. Toward the close of the year he says of one of his brothers: " He will probably have more skating than I will if I stay here, which depends altogether on my balancing. I would give it up, were it not for the disgrace inevitable upon such a step." He had already begun to form the habit of thoroughness, which was characteristic of him through life; it is not, therefore, surprising to find him writing early in January of the new year: " Two balancings must be finished by 15th of April, 1831. I have begun to go through my books again, to try and rectify them; if I do not find out the error, I shall not go through them again."

In March he mentioned again in his correspondence: " My balance book is exactly right on the debtor side, namely, $253,826 06, and on the Cr. side $9 91 cents too much. I shall close it, I think. You can have no idea of the labor and patience necessary to do it. If I had known it, I should never have undertaken it; but as I *have*, I intend to go through with it. I had rather make up your daily accounts six times than do it." Years after, when he had grown to fame, he turned, in my presence, to the bulky folios over which he had spent so many months, and referred, with a not unreasonable pride, to his youthful work. His neat, even handwriting was conspicuous on every page.

But though fully occupied with the duties of his clerkship, and as happy as a bright, growing youth could be, his heart was not in this work. To earn a support he had reluctantly laid aside his books, and looked forward to the time when he could return to them. His father, who in all this early correspondence displays a most affectionate solicitude for his son's welfare, writes to him near the close of the year 1830:—

PHILADELPHIA, *Dec.* 27, 1830.

MY DEAR JOHN :—If you cannot balance for want of knowledge, you had better go to Bennett; this (if you please) you may mention to Mr. Waugh. The following keep to yourself. There are three avocations, one of which I think you ought to follow for a living. 1. You might go to college, finish your education, and trust to it to furnish you the means of support. 2. Stay where you are until it might be thought proper time for you to begin a bookstore; or, 3. Return home and bend all your energies to become a first-rate dry-goods store-keeper. If your mind could be fully placed on the last, it would be more agreeable to your mother and me than either of the others: 1. Because we think you might do as well at that as any thing else; and, 2. Because we would then have the satisfaction of your being at home. I now leave it to yourself to determine, so that you shall neither murmur nor complain hereafter. I trust, my dear John, in whatever decision you may make, you will always reflect, How can I best serve God and prepare for heaven? This, you know, is our primary object respecting our dear children. You will please answer soon. My dear John, did you think of us on Christmas? You were much upon our minds and tongues.

I am, etc.,   JOHN M'CLINTOCK.

To this the son wrote the following reply :—

NEW YORK, *Dec.* 23, 1830.

MY DEAR PARENTS :—I received your letter of 27th inst. to-day. In answer to your inquiries respecting the balancing, I would say, that it is *not* for want of information or knowledge that I have not done it ; but there is a mistake somewhere which I cannot discover. I have considered the three propositions in your letter ; and, *first,* would say that I can give no decided answer at present, till Mr. Waugh says something to me cn the subject ; as, if he is pleased with my work, and will increase my salary as I should desire, I think it decidedly preferable that I should remain here : but *not otherwise!* As soon as there is the least whisper, on any hand, that I do not perfectly suit, so soon shall I leave the Concern. On the contrary, should Mr. Waugh or Dr. Emory incline to part with me, or be displeased with me, and not increase my salary at the end of *January,* when the next balancing will take place, which I shall try to do, I unqualifiedly accept of the first proposal, namely, to go to college and finish my education. My reasons for this course I shall give you in full, as follows, namely :—

1. I think it would be a *sin,* to say no worse of it, to waste all the education that I have had, and make nothing of it.

2. If I incline to study medicine, I shall have so good an opportunity with James, and at so little expense.

3. I have enough experience, and enough knowledge in the way of business, to obtain me a situation as clerk, whenever I please, should I not succeed in a profession. I can obtain five hundred dollars per annum—in this way.

4. My natural taste and inclination have always been for learning, and it always was a mortification of myself and my feelings to at-

tend dry-goods store. I believe this (dry goods) has injured my health, and would not agree with me, as a business to follow for a living. I am sorry that it appears to you preferable for me to be a dry-goods man; but I believe, if you consider all the circumstances of the case as above, you will think it best for me to go to college. Indeed, I always thought it your desire that I should do so. Middletown will be a very good opening. If I go in the course of a few months, I shall be prepared to join the college, which opens in October next, with credit and fair prospects. The opportunities for instruction at Middletown will be very good; very far superior to what can be in Philadelphia, and at about half the price. Mr. Burch will be able to give you all and any information on this subject. However, all this planning is mere *fudge* if Mr. Waugh increases my salary, as mentioned before. If he does, I have no doubt I shall be a bookseller. All turns upon this hinge. Now for something about myself. I have always tried, to the best of my ability, during my life, to conduct myself so as not to be a burden, a disgrace, or a grief to my parents, and never more so than during the past year.

Though I cannot dissemble, or picture things that I do not feel, and have a smooth tongue, and be disobedient at heart; though I say, I always show the worst side of my character *outside*, (which probably was the case when I was in Philadelphia last,) I always have, and always will, try to be a comfort to you in your old age. I leave all the above with yourselves, knowing that you will do for me whatever you think best. Give my love to all, etc.

Your dutiful son,   JOHN.

Early in 1831 the event occurred which determined his subsequent career. He had always been a pure, affectionate, dutiful youth, and had acted from conscientious impulses; but he now dedicated himself wholly to the Christian life. His own account of this important act is contained in the letters which he immediately after wrote to his parents:—

NEW YORK, *Feb.* 11, 1831.

MY DEAR PARENTS:—I cannot wait, I must tell you what great things the Lord has done for me. I have informed you that there is a great revival going on here. It has been progressing for eleven days. On the 3d inst. I resolved, in the strength of the Lord, that I would seek and serve him. And, glory to his name! in his infinite mercy, I believe that he last evening pardoned all my sins. I can do nothing but praise him. I went to the altar three times. Last night I stayed till I suppose about eleven o'clock, and Mr. Merwin came and knelt by me. He prayed to the Lord to bless John. He mentioned my pious parents, my father, my mother; how they had prayed, had agonized for me. Every word went to my heart, and during his prayer, I firmly believe, the Lord turned me from darkness to light, and from the power of Satan to the living God. Mrs. Merwin appeared as glad as if it were her own son, and Mr. Merwin too. Give my love to all.

The work is very great here among the young men. Ten, I think, were converted on Wednesday evening, and a number last night. We have meetings morning, afternoon, and night; prayer-meetings during the intervals all day, without cessation. Mr. Merwin and family send love to you.

Pray for your affectionate son,   JOHN M'CLINTOCK, JUN.

NEW YORK, *Feb.* 15, 1831.

MY DEAR PARENTS:—I suppose you received my last letter, wherein I gave you an account of what the Lord has done for me. To his name be the glory forever! I am resolved to press on to the mark for the prize of my high calling which is of God in Christ Jesus. You will read in the " Advocate " a short account of the great and wonderful revival among us, and also at Lansingburgh and White Plains. The north appears to be giving up: let the south keep no longer back. We have meetings in Allen-street Church from half past ten in the morning till, generally, eleven at night. I never saw such crowded congregations as we have now, and every soul appears to be as attentive as the preacher himself. The immense throng hangs over the gallery, breathless and silent, wondering at the work of the Almighty. The altars are crowded every time an opportunity offers. Eighty-two joined the Church on probation yesterday, and from appearances this is but the beginning of good days.

In haste, your affectionate son,   JOHN M'CLINTOCK, JUN.

The "Old Allen-street Church," as it is still affectionately called, was, in New York, very much such a one as the St. George's in Philadelphia, that is, it was noted for its vigor. After the lapse of more than forty years the revival of 1831 and 1832 is still mentioned as one of the notable events of its long history. It was strong in possessing such office-bearers as Schureman and Samuel Halsted, Henry Moore, Dr. Palmer, and others whose names and memories are still fragrant in the Churches. The accessions during this memorable year reached several hundred. Among the youths who then united with the Church was Robert Emory, the son of Dr. Emory, and in after life M'Clintock's close personal friend.

The young convert's time, when not occupied with business, was now wholly given to religious exercises. Meetings were held during the winter without cessation. He writes, "I attend regularly Saturday night prayer-meeting, class Friday night, and there is preaching every night." He remarks frequently on the great numbers who join the Church, and is all aflame with zeal. The powerful impulse of a new life was quickly felt in the re-awakening of his hunger for a thorough education. However faithfully he might perform his clerkly duties, he yet looked beyond them. The opening of the Wesleyan University at Middletown offered him, he thought, the long-desired opportunity. His correspondence with his parents in relation to this step was long and anxious. Considerations of means to meet the necessary expense, of filial obligation, were weighed carefully, and the decision was reached only after a minute discussion of every detail. With all his eagerness, however, he leaves the final decision to his father. July 9, 1831, he writes:—

After mature deliberation and a great deal of solicitude, with the advice—the considerate advice—of Father Merwin, I have concluded, if it is agreeable to you, to go to Middletown College. The college will commence on September 1. It would be necessary for me to leave the Book Room early in August, as there would be preparation necessary. Write immediately to Mr. Waugh; request him, if he can, to procure another clerk, etc.; though, if he will not, I shall have to remain here. If this attempt should fail I will give up going to college at all.

Read in the last " Advocate" the communication respecting the Wesleyan University. I could board for from fifty to seventy cents per week. You know that I always preferred a life of study, and that clerkship is not agreeable, though I have not said much about it. I think it a providential opening, and the best course I could pursue. After this, if I do not go *now*, it will be too late. I shall be on nettles till you write to Mr. Waugh.

He writes again that this would be the "pivot" on which his life would turn, and is confident that he can crowd the work of four years into two. His impatient eagerness brought a rebuke from home, and momentarily the scheme was abandoned, and under this impression he writes to his father:—

I see pretty clearly that the way is not, nor do I think it will *ever* be, open for me to go; and I shall give up all thoughts and intentions on that subject, I think, and turn myself, though it may be with violence, to business pursuits. The prosecution of my studies at Middletown would not cost at most over three hundred dollars. I have two hundred and fifty dollars now—but enough on that subject. It may be all for the best.

The tenacity in executing a cherished purpose, which always distinguished him, was conspicuous here. He sent home for his Cæsar, Sallust, Grammar, and Greek Testament, engaged a teacher to give him night lessons, and busied himself in getting ready for an opportunity which might never come. If the way does not open this year it may the next. His strong nature is a sufficient prompting, and so he writes to his sister :—

The subject that occupies all my spare time and fills all my leisure thoughts is that of going to college at Middletown. I have entered upon a course of study to enable me to prepare by next August to enter the University. Still, if it be thought best I should not go, and that I should turn my attention to being a merchant, I should like to know immediately, so that I may not be under the necessity of spending my nights this winter in study and my days in toil.

Still, I cannot see any particular use for my going to college ; but yet, on the other hand, there is something within that seems to tell me I must go. Should Providence continue to bless me with health and strength, I think that it will not be said that I have not improved my opportunities.

I should like very much, if I be enabled to pursue the college course, to obtain some foreign situation, as I am very desirous of visiting European countries, particularly Ireland, England, and France.

But this is all building castles in the air, which is not very profitable business for a clerk in the Book Room at nine dollars per week. However, I do not despair, if God be willing, that I shall yet be something more than that.

Early in 1832 he was able to give his employers, Messrs. Emory and Waugh, notice of his intention to leave on May 1. They were loth to part with their clerk, and wished him to remain till June 15. He is fearful of being detained still longer, and sends this message to his father: "Should Messrs. Emory and Waugh make any proposition to you relative to my remaining after June 15, I ask that you will not listen to them."

On the first of May of this year the General Conference assembled in the Union Church, Philadelphia, then commonly known as the "Academy." The Book Agents were these to render an account of their stewardship, and changes were expected. It was rumored that Dr. Emory, who, with his colleague, had laid solid foundations for the great house, and doubled its business, would be elected a bishop. This expectation was verified. Mr. Waugh was returned as senior Agent, and late in June young M'Clintock found himself free of the counting-room and at home.

He had developed rapidly in the two years; body and mind had grown; he had entered fully into an earnest Christian life, and had found his vocation. In the brief snatches of his correspondence which we have cited it has been impossible to reproduce its sweet affectionateness, and the deference this son paid to the wishes of his father and mother. A single word or hint from either restrained the eagerness of an impetuous temperament. In his intercourse with them there was no secrecy, no hidden purpose which he was ashamed to reveal; all was as open as day, and as loving as though he had been but a child. This combination of manliness and gentleness, of ardor and ready submission to recognized law, remained a life-long characteristic of Dr. M'Clintock.

He began this year a " Diary," which is the most valuable memorial now remaining of his busy life. According to the religious fashion of forty years ago, it is, in its earlier entries, mainly introspective—a register of aspirations, self-communion, and self-condemnation, such as is invariably to be found in personal records of this type. John Foster advises every man to write his own memoirs; a feat possible, perhaps, when life is closing, when one can dimly see its full meaning. Still, even the poorest diary is valuable as a history; and this one, which Dr. M'Clintock has left us, furnishes a very vivid picture of his daily activities. We shall use it freely in the course of our narrative.

Its first entry, dated July 29, 1832, is a devout dedication of himself to the service of God, a dedication never retracted. From 1832 to 1870, thirty-eight years, it remained the guiding principle of his conduct. It was the fruitful germ out of which all his subsequent life was developed :—

I, John M'Clintock, Jun., being seventeen years and eight months past of age, seeing the folly of all earthly things, and being determined to seek happiness in the religion of Jesus Christ, in which alone, I am convinced, it may be found ; do fully and willingly, yet firmly and steadfastly, "give myself up, through *Jesus'* power, his name to glorify." Resigning every earthly hope, every worldly enjoyment, (except in subordination to the great end of saving my soul,) I do, in the strength of the Lord God of Hosts, and trusting in the assistancc of his grace, dedicate my soul and my body, my time, my talents, and my all, to his service. May God help me!

Witness my hand,   JOHN M'CLINTOCK, JUN.

With the help of the Lord, without which I can do nothing, I will live by the following rules, until I shall find it expedient or profitable to alter or amend them :—

1. Rising as early as I awake. Prayer first. Reading the Scriptures by Stone's Guide—four chapters in the morning. Occupy one hour, if time will permit, before breakfast, in reading and prayer.

2. Uniformly pray at noon.

3. The hour before retiring to rest, (or at least part of it,) which I have fixed at half-past ten o'clock, must be devoted to religious reading and prayer, with the keeping of this diary.

4. Sabbath afternoons will be devoted to religious reading, prayer, self-examination, etc.

5. I will attend diligently (according to the rules which I have laid down) to the prosecution of my studies.

6. "Live, not to eat and drink, but eat and drink to live." May God assist me, that I may not trust in my own merits, or in the performance of duty, but in the blood of Jesus Christ his Son! Amen.

The attempt to make life purely mechanical, according to the scheme of these resolutions, was followed by the usual results. The ardent youth found himself continually failing. The very next entry is one of humiliation :—

"*July* 3, 1832. Truly I am fickle as the winds. This day I have made no progress in the life of godliness, but have sinned grievously against the Preserver of my existence. May he take away the pride of my heart!"

The next day he complains that he performs his religious duties in a dull and listless manner; soon after

3

that his faith is weak, that his mind wanders when it
ought to be fixed on serious subjects, that his prayers
are cold. The rigid subjection of his youthful nature
to the iron rule which he has prescribed for it creates a
perpetual conflict, in which he often suffers defeat. That
these resolute efforts to acquire self-discipline were not
ineffective one cannot doubt. His entries soon, however,
cease to be of the regulation pattern, and before the
month is out he sums up his wants in a single sentence,
which is wholly like himself: "These two things I desire
very much; 1. A clean heart; 2. A clear head." One
more entry, and we will dismiss the introspective phase
of the diary. It belongs to the latter end of July,
1832:—

All mankind are under sentence of death, certain to be executed,
and at an hour of which we know not. The short and uncertain
time allowed us between the sentence and execution will determine
our condition for eternity. Then thoughtless, unremitting pleasure,
is the greatest indecency; a fondness for the world, the greatest
folly; and self-indulgence, downright madness. On the contrary,
constant seriousness of temper, a universal care and exactness of
life, an indifference for the world, self-denial, sobriety, and watchful-
ness, must be our greatest wisdom.

(These are the words of Thomas Wilson, Bishop of Sodor and
Man.) Truly, then, I must lack wisdom, I must be a consummate
fool, and a "downright madman." Nor is this too harsh judgment;
for do I deny myself continually? On the contrary, are not my
thoughts too much taken up with supplying my wants and my appetites? Not, to be sure, the grosser appetites—eating, drinking, and
sensual indulgences. But when I fall upon an entertaining book,
how do I bury myself in it, forgetting all things else! and even, for
a time, forgetting God! This is not as it should be. Lord, help me

to keep *thee* always before my eyes! to have no other hope or trust but in the merits of thy Son, Jesus Christ!

And so this young man, searching himself after John Wesley's fashion, could find no greater charge to write down than this, that he loved his book too well! It was a failing he had all through life, but he soon learned that, if a failing, it leaned very much to virtue's side. The clean heart and the clear head came into harmony by and by.

Early in September of this year he left home for the Wesleyan University, Middletown. His boyish dreams were at last to have their fulfillment. But, as if to teach him patience, his pretty fabric of hope came down very quickly to the ground. In less than a week after his arrival at the University he was taken seriously ill. Days of pain and prostration followed, so that he was compelled to return home. "I intend, however," he records in his diary, "if my health will allow, to prosecute my studies privately this winter, and to go on again with a collegiate course, should my way be clear." Toward the end of October he entered the Freshman Class of the University of Pennsylvania, in his native city. It was in the middle of the term; his preparation was, no doubt, in some particulars defective. Hard work was requisite to bring him up, and the hard work was not wanting.

With a mind constituted and cultured as we have here seen, the predetermination of young M'Clintock to a ministerial life was almost assured. His Church had taught him the need of a divine call to this service, not certainly in any preternatural sense, but as made apparent

in a clear conviction of duty. This remains, according
to the teaching of Methodism, with the Christian minister, as the answer which he may give to his own conscience for assuming the sacred function. The call of
the Church has been deemed equally requisite as a direct
authorization, without which no one may assume to teach
the people. By this twofold vocation the Christian community is guarded, on the one side against the inroads
of fanaticism, and on the other against the degradation
of the ministry to the level of a merely secular pursuit.
"I have had," writes the subject of our memoir, "many
serious struggles as to whether I should determine to
prepare myself, if the Lord should call me, to the work
of the ministry. I have had much and very good advice, and after serious deliberation and prayer upon
the subject, have come to the conclusions: 1. To endeavor to live to the honor of God. 2. To bend all my
studies toward the ministry. 3. To wait the openings
of his Providence, and may he guide and direct me
through it all!"

He had not to wait long for "the openings of Providence." On the 24th of March, 1833, he makes the
entry: "I was informed yesterday that I am on trial as
an exhorter in the Methodist Episcopal Church. This
has been done without my knowledge, without my seek-
ing; if it be the will of God and he have opened the
way, I doubt not that all will be made clear." A month
after he received exhorter's license. He writes of himself:
"Though I feel my utter unworthiness, yet Christ is
worthy, and in him I trust for support and safety." In

November of this year he made his first essay at speaking in a church, was much embarrassed, but not discouraged by the result. His course of life is by this time clear to him, and he sums up his future career in these words:—

My mind is now pretty clearly made up that it is the will of God that I should be a Methodist preacher. Many causes have induced me to come to this conclusion, which I hope I have reached in the fear of the Lord, and with a single eye to his glory. I humbly believe that my heart is now firmly fixed to serve the Lord in any way that he may appoint, and though I am often, very often, drawn aside by temptation, I am still endeavoring to walk in the narrow way. I see, however, much sin, great depravity, existing in my heart; and my desire and prayer to God is, that I may be made pure and holy.

This final decision cost him no little effort. He was naturally, I may say instinctively, very ambitious, had a keen sense of the value of wealth, and the enjoyableness of a great fame. The Methodist ministry was to his mind a complete surrender of both. Its emoluments were then small, its opportunities of culture very slender, its incessant change disheartening to him as a student. He had learned by this time enough of his capabilities to be aware that he might expect to attain eminence in any profession; what opportunities he might have in an itinerant life for the gratification of his scholarly tastes he could not know. The prospect must have appeared to him dark enough. His dedication to this service was, therefore, a surrender of his preferences to his convictions of duty. True, he found, according to the divine order, that he who gives up all, finds all

again; but this was not so clear to him at the beginning.
Nor did he ever, in after years, look back with any lingering regrets upon the choice which he had made.   To
the end of his days the appellation which he most
prized was that of a " Methodist preacher;" whatever
else he was, he was a minister of Christ's Gospel, first,
last, and always.   His love went with his decision, and
he gloried in the vocation to which he had consecrated
his life.

The calls of the recognizing and approving Church
followed in quick succession.   In December of this same
year he was proposed as local preacher, on a month's
probation, as was then the cautious practice of Philadelphia Methodism.   " This proposal," he writes in his
diary, " was made without my knowledge, by one of the
old preachers; so that all my movements hitherto toward preaching the everlasting Gospel have been under
the direction of the Church.   I have not, therefore, to
all human appearance, ' run before I was sent;' and I
hope that so the case is in the eye of Heaven.   Were I
not convinced that it is my duty to preach the Gospel,
the whole world would not induce me to assume the
awful responsibility of the ministerial office; but, blessed
be God! I believe that his grace will be sufficient for
me in every form of trial."

About this time—the close of the year 1833—he witnessed and records an event which left a lasting impression on Philadelphia Methodism, the dedication of the
new Union Church.   The edifice which the new structure displaced was still known as the " Academy."   It

was begun in 1741, by Whitefield, whose design was
that it should furnish forever a preaching place for itinerant ministers. He left the property encumbered with
debt. In 1749 it was bought by Franklin, and converted into the first Academy of Philadelphia. Here,
in 1753, the college of the city, which subsequently
expanded into the University of Pennsylvania, was
placed. When, after the removal of the national capital to Washington, the president's house, on Ninth-
street, was vacated, the University was removed thither,
and the Methodists obtained possession of the south
part of the edifice. It was, as fitted up for their
worship, the embodiment of the simplicity so much
affected by the people of the Quaker city. The outer
doors opened directly upon the assembly room; the
sexes were separated in the arrangement of the seats by
a line distinctly marked. The solid benches, innocent
of all cushions, suggested massive strength. The white
pulpit, set well aloft, and reached by a winding stair,
looked to youthful eyes a place of awful sanctity. Here
assembled the *élite* of the Methodism of Philadelphia;
for the "Academy" was easily at the head of the
Churches. Its leaders, Dr. Sargent, Inglis, Benson,
Chubb, Wilmer, Yard, and others well known in their
day, were men of solid worth. James B. Longacre presided over the Sunday-school with a devotion that never
wearied. The society represented a type of Methodism
in which enthusiasm was moderated, but not quenched.
It was noted for its charities, among which its numerous mission-schools were not the least conspicuous.

The new church, which is still standing, was thought in that day a marvel of beauty. It is, however, no more than a plain brick building, with its gable facing the street, and wholly without architectural pretensions; but the luxuries of carpeted floors, and a pulpit of polished mahogany, and the harmonious blending of colors in the decoration of the interior, were then considered magnificent. "The collection," writes M'Clintock in his diary, "amounted to nearly one thousand dollars," a sum without precedent in those simple times. To some of us young folk the greatest charm of the church was the circulating library generously provided for its members; and what astonishment was created in the minds of its staid trustees when Dr. Sargent recommended the purchase of Walter Scott's romances, then greatly delighting the world, for its shelves!

Young M'Clintock's religious ardor was no drawback to his progress as a student. He was soon in the front rank of his class. The reports of Professor Reed, the Secretary of the Faculty, place him "number one on the merit roll." Heart and mind were both awakening to the highest activity. "We have recommenced," he says, "the University prayer-meetings on Friday afternoons. On last Friday I had some liberty in speaking and praying with a few fellow-students. O, that I were more faithful in relation to them!"

Having stood at the head of the Sophomore Class for several months he made a leap to the Junior, abridging his college term by one year. He thus speaks of this event :—

"By a strenuous effort I this day passed an examination for entrance into the Junior Class, University of Pennsylvania, thus abridging the collegiate term by one year. But though in literature my advancement has been gratifying to myself yet I fear that it has been at the expense of religion. O when shall I be entirely devoted to God! swallowed up in his will!"

This rapid ascent was the beginning of a series of strenuous exertions of all his mental and physical energy, which ended in impairing a fine constitution, and rendering Dr. M'Clintock a martyr to attacks of illness during the rest of his life. In one respect he could not help himself. His father's business was unprosperous, and not long after this date ended in disaster. But more than all else, it was then the practice of the Church to hurry young men of promise into the active ministry. There was a half-confessed fear that knowledge would spoil the nascent preacher and unfit him for his duties. Never was maxim more perverted than John Wesley's "Getting knowledge is good, but saving souls is better." It turned the scale against culture to the injury of many an ardent youth. No doubt the necessities of the Church were urgent. In the case of the subject of our memoir the conflict of feeling must have been severe. The pursuit of knowledge he could not give up, nor could he disregard the calls of the Church. He decided to do his full duty to both Church and University, and what he decided he executed with all the force of an iron will, but with such consequences to himself as this narrative will be much occupied in describing.

He entered the Junior Class of the University in March, 1834, ranking as number fourteen; by the end of July he is "number six, with distinction." This was nearly the last of his University residence; the rest of his college work he accomplished single-handed, while occupied with the active duties of the pastorate. His first summons was from the Rev. J. J. Matthias, to Flemington, New Jersey, where he spent the long college vacation of 1834 in preaching. Despite all his plans to the contrary, he found himself next autumn in charge of the Church at Elizabethtown, New Jersey. How this was brought about we will let him describe himself:—

ELIZABETHTOWN, N. J., *October* 17, 1834.

After much enjoyment of soul and body on the Flemington Circuit, I left it and returned to Philadelphia about September 1. The cause of my sudden departure was the failure of my father, who, by the accidents of business and other causes, was compelled to stop payment and close his concerns. The circumstances of his failure have been very trying and mortifying to himself and the family; but we have been kindly treated by all our true friends, though some who called themselves friends may have forgotten their friendship. I have enjoyed myself well in every respect since, and have enjoyed much of the favor of God. Yet how unworthy have I been, how vain, how trifling, how childish.

I entered anew, on September 15, upon my duties at the University, having formed the resolution to spend this winter closely in their performance. But call after call has been made upon me to fill vacancies in the ministerial ranks, and though convictions of my own weakness and incapacity, and desires for self-improvement, operated strongly, inducing me to remain at home, I began to think that duty called me to obey. Finally, my esteemed friend and brother William H. Gilder was compelled to leave his appointment at this place on account of ill health, and his powerful calls were added to the rest. After advice, thought, and prayer, I formed the resolution to set forward in the strength of grace; and in pursuance of this resolution left my home yesterday morning, and arrived in this place last night.

I have a fearful task before me. I must maintain the regular course of college study, and attend, at the same time, to the duties of the station. O God, my hope is in thee! Fearfully and tremblingly, yet with "a glad heart and free," do I enter upon this high and holy work. O Lord, be thou my strength and support, and I shall succeed.

It was, indeed, a fearful task he had before him, but he knew no such word as fail.

Nothing can exceed the affectionateness with which he writes and speaks of his parents. Though practically his own master and shaping his life for himself, he turns to them for counsel, or sends them words of good cheer. Every important step is freely discussed in his correspondence with them. He writes from home to his mother, who had left the city for a short time in poor health :—

PHILADELPHIA, *Tuesday, August* 26, 1834.

I arrived at home this afternoon in perfect health and spirits, and am glad to find that things are going on so well. I never enjoyed myself more in my life than since I have been gone : the kindest people, and some the most pious, that I have ever met with. I was up in Brother Force's district, at Asbury camp-meeting, among the mountains in Warren County, N. J., and was much persuaded to remain among them. I was also at Pennington camp-meeting, (Brother Gilder's,) where many kind friends inquired after you. Moreover, the presiding elder presses me hard to go to the Plainfield Station, until Conference, in the room of Brother Janes, who is ill; but I believe that my duty lies at home for the present, and, therefore, I shall stay there.

And now I wish to tell you that I am happy despite all circumstances outwardly, and pray sincerely that you may be so.

Do not let the matter which is now brought to a close distress you at all. Rest assured that our real friends will think none the worse of us; and we should not care for the opinions of others. I think all will go better; we shall have peace and quietness within, whatever may be without. You have children who will always labor to make you happy, blessed with health and strength; and " with the Lord on our side, we need not fear what man can do unto us."

P. S. Be assured that all is going on well at home. You need be under no uneasiness. Enjoy yourself now—do enjoy yourself.

The next, to his father, is in the same strain :—

ELIZABETHTOWN, N. J., *Monday, Jan.* 12, 1835.

I arrived safely, with all my. concerns, on the evening of the stormy Friday on which I left you, after a pleasantly cold ride of eight hours. My health has been very good since my return, so that, of myself, I have no news to communicate.

I have preached regularly three times each Sabbath. Yesterday we had the largest congregation, I think, that I have seen in the place, and very attentive, and I sincerely hope that good was done. Four joined at the love-feast : and we expect as many more to join at the next general class-meeting.

Our next, and last, Quarterly Conference for this station will be held on February 9. At the Quarterly Meeting, the presiding elder, Brother Matthias, in his conversation with me, thought it best that I should obtain recommendation from that conference to the Annual Conference, and told me that, should I be admitted, my stay in college from April until the time of graduation might be allowed without difficulty; and that, therefore, I could take a circuit at the ensuing Conference, a substitute being provided until I could join the station in June.

It has been my view of the subject to follow the plan laid down by the presiding elder; but, of course, I should not take so important a step without more particular advice than I have yet had from

you in the case. I, therefore, lay the subject before you for consideration, wishing an answer as soon as you may find time. I have had
no letter since my return, and am anxious to hear the state of
affairs.

I have not, as yet, attended Dr. Adrain, [his private instructor in
mathematics.] I shall study as much as possible before applying to
him, because the cost pulls pretty heavily on my slender purse, and
I wish to be as economical as I can. The books necessary for
this last collegiate term will be very costly.

I should like to know Dr. Wylie's opinion of my standing and
prospects in college, for I value his opinion at no small rate. My
friend ——, of Columbia College, lost the favor of his best friend
among the professors by crossing his will. However, I am not conscious of any such misdeeds on my part with regard to the professors in our University. I trust that I am on good terms with
them all.

It shall always be my endeavor to do all that I can, in any way,
for the happiness of my parents. And although I am unfortunately
deficient in the power of expressing outwardly, and at all times, my
good feelings, still I am unwilling to charge myself with wilful disregard of parental advice, or wilful injury of parental feeling.

Very decided objection was made by the new provost
of the University, the Rev. Dr. Ludlow, to M'Clintock's
long absence from college duty, necessitated by the taking of the pastoral charge at Elizabethtown. A part
of the winter was, therefore, spent in Philadelphia.
At the session of the Philadelphia Conference, April,
1835, he was received on trial as a travelling preacher,
and appointed to Jersey City. He removed immediately
to his new field of labor, and still continuing his studies,
graduated A.B. at the University, July 26, with distinguished honor.

He was now fairly entered upon his life-work, and saw his career plainly before him. His preparation for it had taxed all his energies, but his plan had been executed with entire success. Four years of university training had been crowded into three, and one of these had been spent in preaching. He was now in his twenty-first year. In person he was of medium height, florid in complexion, alert in movement, and winning in manner. His voice, though not of great compass, was melodious, and his bearing graceful. A stranger, seeing him for the first time, was struck at once with the large size of the head, and the almost spherical roundness of the forehead. His facility in the acquisition of knowledge, which he had by this time tested, gave him the assurance of rapid success. He had, however, paid too large a price for his victory. He was destined to find, very shortly, that the foundations of his strength had been undermined, and that much of his life was to be a long battle with disease.

LETTERS FROM JULY, 1832, TO JUNE, 1835.

I.

PHILADELPHIA, *July* 5, 1832.

MY DEAR SAMUEL:—Though but a short time has elapsed since my leaving you and your city, and though, during that time, I have been almost constantly engaged in a round of visiting and receiving visits, of outgoing and incoming, still I have found time often to think with regret on the numerous friends and enjoyments I left behind on quitting New York.

But, after all, home is still home. The heartfelt joy with which I know I am received in my own father's house, as well as the cordial and oft-repeated congratulations of my many friends, cannot but be grateful to a human heart, especially one of my peculiar temperament.

I entered upon my studies on Monday last with fixed resolutions, ardent feelings, and confident expectations of continuing the pursuit of them closely and successfully. I was in the full enjoyment of the rich blessing which Sterne has so beautifully and forcibly addressed :— "O blessed health! thou art above all gold and treasure : 'tis thou who enlargest the soul, and openest all its powers to receive instruction, and to relish virtue! He who hath thee, hath little more to wish for; and he who is so wretched as to want thee, wants every thing with thee!" I was soon taught, that in order to preserve this state of health I must be more regular in all things.

I have been highly gratified, and I think profited, too, by reading, during the past week, the "Life of Stoner." What humility, what judgment, decision, and true godliness were evinced in that man's life and conduct. And I think I have never read any religious experience that so fully coincides with my own as does his, laid down in his diary. His constant fear of the risings of pride, in particular, strikes me as exhibiting a peculiar feature of my own character. Does it not of yours? *Pride! pride! pride!*—"that secret bosom sin!" God help us to expel it!

I still find myself, notwithstanding my numerous resolutions, the same weak, sinful, erring mortal that I ever was. But God knows that my desire is to seek and to serve him ; to leave the world behind, with its allurements and its vanities, and strive to lay up my "treasure in heaven." Ah! I am but an earthen vessel! But, blessed be his name! "God has committed this treasure to earthen vessels, that the excellency of the power may be of God and not of us!"

Do you pray for me? Will you fix on a day in the week, and an hour, in which our prayers shall ascend before the throne for each other—when each shall know that, at the self-same hour, the other is supplicating the Father of both for him? Fix upon a time that will suit yourself, and notify me in your next—your first letter—which I shall look for daily, eagerly, and earnestly. My feeble prayers have been offered, and *shall* be offered up for you, that the Lord may guide you in the path of life by his unerring counsel—

> " A friend is worth all hazards we can run:
> Poor is the friendless master of a world ;
> A world in purchase for a friend is gain."

Truly the communion of friends is sweet. But if an earthly friendship is worth this sacrifice, of how much greater value is the friendship of Him " that sticketh closer than a brother? " Shall we, then, in consideration of almost nothing in comparison to the world, forego this friendship? God forbid it ! O, my brother, hold fast whereunto you have obtained ; and may your life indeed be with Christ in God.

Mr. Samuel A. Purdy.

II.

PHILADELPHIA, *Nov.* 17, 1832.

DEAR ANDRUS:—My quandaries have all been settled at last : law, physic, business, and every thing else have been given up, and I am now bending all my energies to the acquirement of knowledge— yes, college knowledge. I entered the University of Pennsylvania, as a Freshman, on 30th ultimo, and I have since been advancing in my studies with all desirable rapidity. My health is at present tolerable. Had I not been engaged in the University, I should have paid you a visit last week ; as some business in Massachusetts, together with my desire to see you all, would have warranted my taking the trip. But it is not so, and I shall now probably not see you until next year. At that time, *Deo volente,* I expect to enjoy that pleasure.

I intend to return to the Wesleyan University at the beginning of the Sophomore or Junior years, which will be either next year or the year following. With the institution to which I am now attached I am highly pleased. Professors, instruction, buildings, and all are first-rate, but then Dr. Fisk is not here, nor are the good religious brethren whom I was so highly delighted with at Middletown. The difference between the character of the students is truly surprising ; and in no particular is this difference more strikingly perceptible than in their conversation concerning their after life.

But though our students generally think nothing of religion or its Author, still they do not molest or interfere with those who follow Jesus of Nazareth. And I hope, by the grace of God aiding me, to be enabled to "hold on the even tenor of my way." I hope that the many temptations that surround me may all work together for my good, and that my soul and body, time and powers, may all be devoted to the service of Him who created and redeemed me. The follies of my fellow-students have thus far only served to disgust me with their trifling; and their ideas of pleasure and enjoyment have therefore only deepened the impressions made upon my mind, that "the ways of religion" alone "are ways of pleasantness," and that "her paths" alone "are the paths of peace."

Deeply sensible that I myself am *not* what I *must* be in religion, I feel at this time, more than ever, the need of God's assisting grace. And yet I am not near as earnest in prayer, as constant and uniform in devotion, as careful and watchful over my words and actions as I must be, in order to be able to testify by my life, and walk, and conversation, that I have been with Christ and learned of him. This testimony I must bear before my companions in the University, for I shall be a poor witness for my Master, indeed, if they do not find it out.

Dear Andrus, I wish you could take the wings of one of the steamboats and come to see me. It does delight me much to see any one from New York; how much would it, therefore, should you come? But I must close.

Mr. Timothy A. Howe.

III.

Philadelphia, *Jan.* 19, 1833.

I am now in possession of all that I can desire for the enjoyment of life: pursuing studies in which I delight without interruption, in the bosom of my own father's household; privileged with all means of temporal and spiritual improvement—what an account will I have to give for the use of all these blessings! May God help me to devote *all* to him and his service! I did anticipate on my entrance

4

into the University of Pennsylvania that my connexion with it would prove rather a clog to my religious enjoyments than an assistance on the road to heaven. But I now hope, through the blessing of our heavenly Father, that the latter will be the case in an eminent degree. There are among the students about fifteen professors of religion, belonging to different denominations. Among these are several of ardent, deep piety, and among them all there prevails a spirit of fellowship and unanimity, with a desire to promote the interests of religion among the students generally, that cannot fail, with the blessing of Heaven, of producing highly beneficial results both to themselves and to the institution. We hold a prayer-meeting every Wednesday afternoon after the college hours. I had attended but one of these previously to my illness, which was highly interesting. All appeared to be resolved to do their utmost as instruments in the hands of God in the promotion of a revival, and O! that God in his infinite mercy would abundantly prosper our humble, feeble efforts, warm our hearts, and strengthen our hands to labor in his cause.

I feel continually, my dear brother, the need of a closer walk with God. It is a great mercy, in my opinion, that God does at times show us our own depravity ; how far we are from coming up to the proper standard of Christian excellence, how exceedingly weak is our faith, and how unsteady our deportment. Then it is that the soul, fully impressed with its own utter weakness and inability, is induced to fly for refuge and strength to Him alone who can impart it, namely, Jesus Christ the righteous. O that you and I may live to grow in him continually, who is our living head ! May our life and walk and conversation show to the followers of the world, with whom we are surrounded, that the religion which we profess is not exhibited in word only, but in deed and in truth.

SAMUEL A. PURDY, BLACKWELL'S ISLAND

IV.

PHILADELPHIA, Jan. 17, 1833.

About first of November I entered the University of Pennsylvania under embarrassing circumstances, being far behind the class in point of acquirements, and entering at a time when they were reviewing what was all unbroken soil for me. I have, therefore, ever since my connexion with the University, been under the necessity of laboring closely and unremittingly at my studies in order to keep up with the class. At our late examination I was placed third upon the roll, which was far higher than I might have expected, but which, nevertheless, I may have deserved, as my application has been severe.

I am now just recovering from a severe attack of the disease which had nearly laid me low at Middletown, namely, inflammation of the bowels. From this, too, the providence of God has seen fit to deliver me, and I am now able to walk my room, and have been once down stairs. The disease has, doubtless, been owing to my imprudence in study, bad hours, late going to bed and late rising, with the improprieties in eating and feasting usually consequent upon the arrival of Christmas and New Year's holidays. Well, wisdom is learned by experience, and if I do not know how to eat, drink, and sleep hereafter my own be the blame.

I have made many valuable acquaintances in this city since my return, especially with a number of religious young men connected with the University. But, though they are polite, accomplished, literary, and pious, they do not, cannot, fill the place of my circle of friends in New York. There was an openness, a freedom, fellowship, if I may so speak, among the young men of our acquaintance, that put me immediately at my ease among them, and it is probably on this account that I place them, as it were, on a summit in my estimation which none have yet reached, and, it seems to me, never will. In some of my reveries (you know we are all inclined to such) I throw myself back to the fall of 1831, when the " Irving " was in its glory, (?) and when our weekly assemblages were held in the upper room of the pedagogue's temple in Broadway. I fancy our meeting, our mutual greeting, calling to order, and all the routine of our multiform business, and, in fine—I wish it were all to be " acted o'er again."

But this is all nonsense. You are in your goodly city of Gotham, busied in your lawful avocations, whatever they are, and I at pres-

ent an invalid student. Whether it be worth our while to trouble
our brains calculating upon futurity, and endeavoring to find out
what we shall be in this world, I think is a question. But, as to the
necessity of our knowledge of our standing in reference to religious
matters, what we shall be after we leave this world, I think there is
no question at all. If we believe the Christian religion, and do not so
live as to secure the benefits promised in it to the followers of Jesus
Christ, what are we?

From my knowledge of your principles, my dear James, I am encouraged to suppose that you have taken these things to heart, and
determined to devote the spring time of your days to the service of
your heavenly Father. I feel determined, let my worldly pursuits be
what they may, to follow God with full purpose of heart. And may
he aid me in the fulfillment of my resolutions!

Believe me your affectionate friend.

Mr. JAMES DAVIS, N. Y.

V.

PHILADELPHIA, *April* 5, 1838.

DEAR ANDRUS:—I am pretty well, and trying to do well. The
more I see of the world and the things of it, the more am I convinced
of the necessity of attending to the concerns of eternity, the more am
I "delighted in the ways of the Lord." Yet still, though I perceive
the vanity of all earthly things, their fleeting and unsatisfactory nature, the emptiness of the enjoyments which they can afford, still
these very "trifles, light as air," these gilded bubbles, often, too oft-
en, draw me aside from the straight path of duty, and occupy that
time and attention which should only be taken up in the pursuit of
less uncertain objects. That "as the sparks do fly upwards, so is the
heart of man to do evil," is a true saying, no man who has ever attempted to walk humbly before God will deny. For myself, in ten
thousand instances I have exemplified it by my wandering from God
and trangressions of his law. My hope, however, is still in "God,
and my trust in the rock of my salvation." To him I can come with
humble confidence, inspired by the free atonement of Christ, and say,

" Hide not thy face far from me, put not away thy servant in anger," and he " whose faithfulness reacheth unto the clouds," has provided that " if we ask any thing according to his will, he heareth us." Are not the promises of God exceeding great and precious ? How kind of our kind Parent to grant us such an assistance, such a guide as these abundantly furnish in our earthly pilgrimage ! O that God would enable us both to serve him with full purpose of heart !

I hear that James Floy preached in Forsyth-street not long since. If so I am almost certain it was good. He is a young man of prom-ise—talent. I have always thought he should be a preacher ; doubt-less he will before a great while. The Conference office appears to act something similarly to a mill, does it not ? Let me see ; Creagh, Davis, Floy ; who else ? More for aught I know.

'Mr. T A. Howe.

VI.

PHILADELPHIA, *Dec.* 5, 1833.

I made a bold attempt on last Sabbath week, but my trust was not in my own arm nor in my own ability. It was an attempt to preach on the Sabbath afternoon in one of our city churches. My reasons were the following. The preacher whose appointment it was had asked me to fill a small appointment on the preceding Sabbath, which I had declined ; and on the Thursday following he came to me and commanded me to fill the next afternoon appointment. I, of course, refused, but having conversed for some time, I finally stated to him that it was my desire to *avoid* every thing which I *ought* not to do, and to *perform* every thing which was my duty. I then left it with him to decide whether or not this was my duty. He promptly de-cided the question, and accordingly I made the attempt. I was not at all embarrassed, as I expected to be, in a first attempt of the kind, but still I found that what I had prepared to speak would not always be ready when it was needed. I spoke, however, with very little dif-ficulty, for about thirty-five minutes, and humbly pray that the bless-ing of Heaven may have accompanied my first pulpit labors.

Mr. S. A. Purdy.

VII.

PHILADELPHIA, *March* 28, 1834.

MY DEAR BROTHER:—On Friday and Saturday, 10th and 11th March, I was examined for *six hours* on the studies of the year in advance, and most happily succeeded, so far, that I had not a single "flunk;" and I was congratulated at the close of the examination as a member of the Junior Class. You know the feelings on such occasions—the joy, the lightheartedness—a feeling as if we were never to feel disappointment again. But ah! how soon do we lose these delightful feelings!

Well, think you that I shall study during vacation after all this? All that remains is to fix the time for your visit. How will the following do? Our Conference will hold from Wednesday, 10th April to 16th, perhaps, and my second examination will be held on Monday and Tuesday previous. The pleasure of your visit will be greatly heightened can you make it convenient to spend part of the time of Conference with us; which, you know, is a sort of Methodist festival. You will then see and hear many of our preachers, missionary addresses, etc., etc., which, no doubt, will prove some attraction to you.

Come, then, if possible, between 10th and 13th April, and thus part of the time of your stay will be Conference time; and my vacation will last from 10th April to 1st May. I hope that you and I will both be in good health and spirits. By the way, I have suffered severely from a pain in the back, which, at present, troubles me much; but I hope to be delivered from this shortly.

It appears, then, that I shall leave college in July, 1835, and, *Deo volente*, in April, 1836, I shall join the Methodist traveling connexion. You ask for my experience in relation to this all-important concern. If I begin this, my letter will be filled with myself; but it may interest you somewhat.

One thing I may mention, that from the earliest hour in which I thought of eternal things, the impression has rested upon my mind that I should one day be called to the work of the ministry. This

of course, was but an impression, and would never have weighed
with me unsupported by other considerations. The course of life
pointed out for me by my father was the practice of the law, and
with this end in view he commenced my classical education in the
year 1822. In 1826, from various circumstances, I determined to
leave school for a time, in order to acquire a knowledge of mercantile
affairs; having in ultimate view, all the time, the study of the law.
In 1830 I left my father's store, and, by appointment of the Book
Agents, entered their office as book-keeper. At this time I was very
unsettled in religion, and my course of life was altogether unthought
of. You may remember the great revival of 1831, in Allen-street,
in which it pleased the Lord to bring me to myself, the circumstances
of which time will never, never be effaced from my mind. I bowed
at the altar several times, and but little light was afforded me, until
the call of the Lord sounded in my ears, the vineyard of the Lord
opened before me, and it was clearly impressed upon my mind that
until an entire devotion of my all to God was made, and that without
reservation, there was no blessing for me. I pledged my soul to the
work; I obtained the light of his countenance; my soul felt the joys
of his salvation.

Notwithstanding this I have often vacillated, and in October of
1832 I was on the point of commencing the study of law in this city.
The day was fixed on which I was to confer with one of our lawyers
on the subject, my father having already arranged the preliminaries;
but again the call of the Lord was not forgotten, and on the very day
appointed as above, instead of waiting on the lawyer, I called on
Rev. Professor Wylie, of the University of Pennsylvania.

Yet I was undecided; lofty prospects were unfolded in the world;
my ambition, which has almost proved my ruin, prompted me; and
I had no obstacles. But, to my surprise, I received notice from the
preacher in charge (1833) that I was called to the office of an exhorter
in the Church. Here, then, my way first opened in the Church.

In January, 1834, I was (unexpectedly again) called by the Quarterly Conference to the office of local preacher; and the Lord blesses
me in my feeble efforts. Here, then, dear brother, you have the out-

lines. A volume would not contain a record of the struggles and vicissitudes on this subject; these you must imagine.

Mr. James Davis.

VIII.

New Germantown, Hunterdon Co., N. J., *Aug.* 4, 1884.

You will perceive by the date that I am in a new location. I am here, as a minister of the Methodist Episcopal Church, at the call of Rev. J. J. Matthias, presiding elder of East New Jersey District; and really, I am as happy as the day is long. I arrived on Friday, made myself welcome at the house of the Hon. Judge Kennedy—from which hospitable mansion the present epistle issues, to bear to you the story of my hopes and fears, my joys and sorrows. The life of a Methodist preacher has many of both—truly a checkered career of hopes and disappointments. It startled my bashfulness, at first, to know that I must go, uninvited and unexpected, to the houses of individuals of whom I had never heard before, and make myself welcome, whether in reality so or not. It frightened me to learn that I must introduce myself to all, good or bad, religious or irreligious; that I must go to their houses, talk with them, pray with them, without knowing whether or not it were agreeable to themselves. And, to tell the truth, I felt rather queer in approaching the first house which I entered in my new character. I had seen the owner in Philadelphia once, but the good lady was altogether new to me, and you know that she is the most important half in such a case. But my queer feelings vanished when I found myself received as cordially as if I had been the king himself, and every effort exerted by the whole family to make me happy and contented. And so it is every-where. I go in, tell them who I am; that I am come to see them, to talk with them, to lodge with them; then all is kindness, and friendship, and love. The whitest table-cloth is spread, the corn is plucked for the first time this year, the pantry and the milk-house are put in requisition to supply the wants of the preacher, who, poor fellow, must take of every thing on the table a superabundant quantity or they are not pleased.

Many, many are my joys and comforts. It is a delightful thing to feel that the affection of the poor and the rich alike are open to me; that the houses of the poor and the rich alike are my home; that they follow me with blessings, receive me with welcome, and bear me up with prayers. It is delightful to be permitted to speak with them of the goodness of God, to direct their hearts to him, and to offer up, on each family altar, the tribute of praise and the earnest petition. It is delightful to behold them on the Sabbath tripping in youthful buoyancy across the field, or walking in the solemnity of age upon the beaten pathway, toward the house of God. And it is a delightful thing to be permitted to lead their hearts in the worship of the divine Being, to elevate their thoughts for a season, at least, from earth to heaven, and to fix their minds upon the pure and holy principles of our religion. Would to God that I were better prepared for the high and holy office; that I had more of the spirit of holiness; that I were more deeply devoted to the work unto which, I believe, he has called me. I desire to have no other name on earth but the name of a devoted and laborious preacher of the cross; to have no other glory but the glory of "saving souls from death and turning sinners from the error of their way;" to have no other honor but that honor which descends from God.

Mr. James Davis.

IX.

Philadelphia, *Feb.* 10, 1834.

I am, and have been for several days, very unwell indeed, and am now in rather a light-headed and heavy-limbed condition, though, I trust, in a state of convalescence. I commenced my studies in the University on the Tuesday after I left you with great glee and great enthusiasm, went on in the course successfully until five days ago, when *that* was all brought to nought by the hand of sickness. With the details of a disease or its remedies I need not trouble you, inasmuch as you are especially conversant with such matters; nor need I describe pathetically the distressful feelings with which I reflect upon college and its operations, inasmuch as all this has been done for you by our friend, C. H. L., with whom I can now sympathize more fully and abundantly than ever. I may say, however, that before many days I hope to be delivered from all these sorrows, and to enter again upon collegiate duty.

Have you read the two concluding pieces of President Olin in the "Advocate?" If you have not I pray you do so at once, and let them have all their weight. It appears to me that they are true, and if so, then certainly alarming. "Two thousand new ministers needed *at once* in the Methodist Episcopal Church!"—is not this enough to cause every young man in that Church who has had any opportunities of intellectual improvement to look in upon his heart, and to see whether there are not *some* impressions there of the Holy Spirit's influence? The views of President Olin upon this point, namely, the call of the Holy Spirit to the work of the ministry, coincide with what my own have been upon the subject for some time past. I trust that the Lord will manifest his Spirit fully unto you, that you may be called into his vineyard, and that right speedily.

Our Illinois scheme advances but slowly. The calls, however, from the West country are still loud and pressing, and I am by no means satisfied but that many of our young men will be called for to go and fight for the truth in those lands of beauty. I learn that one at least of our most influential preachers will be transferred from the Philadelphia to the Illinois Conference in the course of the next year, and I know not how many of the smaller fry have been spoken of for the Western Conference. Well, if the cause of God demand it I have no doubt they will be ready, and I trust I shall, if the duty be clearly laid open before me. Of two things, however, I must be *ascertained* (to use an antiquated term) before I shall take my determination : 1. That I can be more useful ; 2. That I will not be doomed (as the Catholics) to *perpetual celibacy*, which is no part of my creed whatever.

Dr. Samuel A. Purdy.

X.

Philadelphia, *June* 18, 1835.

My Dear Friend :—Our examination commences on Wednesday, 24th instant, and will occupy four days, after which, *Deo volente*, I shall

take up the line of march for the region round about New York, when
I hope to meet you, and all my good friends, in peace and pleasure.
I have been thinking to-day of the "living" and its affairs—wondering
whether it is prosperous or defunct, whether the flame of genius is
there glowing, expanding, or dying—extinguished. O, I trust not!
for I hope better things from all its members. Perseverance must be
your motto in this as in every thing else. By the way, writing the
word "*perseverance*" made *phrenology* to rise up before me in all its
length and breadth and majesty. I have been studying the sublime
science somewhat, and have (by way of experiment, *à la Bacon*) had
my own cranium examined. Well, phrenology *must* be true, *for the
man gave me a fine head*—causality, comparison, ideality, etc., in
abundance. Are you not convinced?

I must say, in justice to the man of phrenology, that he pointed out
not a few of my foibles and weaknesses in investigating the detri-
mental part of my character, or, rather, my *caput*, and I am by no
means prepared to say that phrenology is a humbug, and its professors fools or impostors. Combe reasons very prettily, and somewhat
manfully, too, and I know not but that he may be in the right. Have
you read the little book in the Alexandrian? It is full of beauties.

Not the least of my perplexities and troubles at this present time is
my station in Jersey City. Sabbath after Sabbath rolls away and I
am not there, and my solicitude becomes very strong at times, I can
assure you. I have written to Brother T. A. Howe to have the ap-
pointments of June 21 and 28 filled for me. Will you do me the favor to see him, and enforce the matter if he has not received my letter? I feel very anxious that all should go right, as far as possible,
during my absence.

I am looking forward as usual to a year of enjoyment. Though
I must be in labors abundant, I hope to be in joys much more
abundant. Thrown once more into the midst of New York friends
and New York associations, I shall almost retread those delightful
years which did

> "So wing their way with pleasure,
> As bees fly home with loads of treasure."

Is it not best always to look on the bright side? Surely it is, in view of enjoyment, at least, in this changeful scene of strange vicissitudes, the better course to think all its changes improvements, all its vicissitudes varieties of pleasure. But there is a better philosophy to be brought to bear upon the question, which tells us that though " sorrow endures for a night—joy cometh in the morning; " which tells us to " rejoice alway and be glad in the Lord." Thanking the Lord for all his benefits and all his blessings, let us trust him for all that is to come and all will be well.

Have you ever read Coleridge's " Friend ? " It is a remarkable book, indeed. If you have time get it and peruse for yourself. A mighty mind, filled with all human knowledge, and offering itself and all its cultivation upon the shrine of religion, is no common sight.

Remember me affectionately to all.

Dr. S. A. Purdy.

CHAPTER II.

1835-1839.

Life as Pastor in Jersey City—Letters to his Mother—Compelled by Ill Health to Quit the Pulpit—Appointed Assistant and then full Professor of Mathematics in Dickinson College—History of the College—The Members of the First Faculty—Intimacy with Robert Emory—Dr. Durbin's Fame as an Orator—Daily Life of Professor M'Clintock in his New Position—Great Variety of his Studies—Educational Leaders of American Methodism—Second Failure of Professor M'Clintock's Health—Passages from his Diary—His Extensive Reading while an Invalid—Anxiety to be Able to Preach Again—His Method as a Student—Letters.

THE young minister being now relieved of his burden of double duty, applied himself with zeal to pastoral work. Jersey City had then a population of scarce five thousand; the Methodist Society, now known as the Trinity in York-street, worshipped in a frame building set up on the meadow. Mr. M'Clintock made his home with Jabez Wakeman. Esq., one of the leaders of Methodism in the city. His compensation was one hundred dollars a year, which sum was technically known as "a single man's allowance," and board. He preached, visited, studied with enthusiasm, and was, to use his own language, as happy as the day was long. He gives a very pretty picture of this life in two letters to his mother :—

JERSEY CITY, *October* 13, 1835.

At half-past eleven, on this Tuesday evening, I sit down to write you a letter. And if I tell you, first, how much I am engaged, how much I am trying to do, and what efforts I make to accomplish all my plans, I think, at least, that you will not suppose me idle. In the first place, the basement of our church takes all my time, much of

my anxiety, and a great deal of my labors ; as money *must* be raised,
and there is no one to raise it but myself. I do not despair, however,
of getting it entirely finished and ready for our purposes by the first
of December.   In the next place, there are sermons to be preached,
class-meetings to be attended, prayer-meetings to be kept up, sick
and poor to be visited, and books to be read and studied ; and all
this, without fee or reward, except the poor hundred dollars that is
obtained for me with difficulty from those who attend on my ministry ! Well, well, no one *can* say aught against the motives (at least
in the money point of view) of him who enters upon the duties of a
Methodist traveling preacher. Sometimes, when I think that I might
be making money—much money—perhaps helping you all instead of
being burdensome, I think of giving up all and embarking in the
world of adventure to seek my fortune. But when I remember " the
kingdom that is not of this world "—when I remember, that in a very
few years we shall all be in the grave, and that it will matter little
then *how* our lives have been spent, if they have only been spent in
the service of God ; when I remember your own advice, instruction,
and counsel in religion, knowing that yourself and father would
rather see me a preacher of Christ, though poor and unable to help
you, than to see me rich in this world's goods and regardless of God,
I determine to continue in the path in which I have started, and,
by the help of God, to be a faithful minister of the Lord Jesus to my
life's end.

I find greater pleasure in the performance of my religious and
pastoral duties *now* than ever I did before, greater comfort in studying the Scriptures, and greater light in understanding them ; and it is
my chief desire, as it is my principal effort, to be thoroughly furnished
from the Scriptures for my Christian and professional life. Give love
to all.   Your affectionate son,   JOHN M'CLINTOCK, JUN.

In 1836 he was re-appointed to the station, and thus
describes to his mother his entrance on the second year
of his pastorate :—

JERSEY CITY, *Saturday Evening, April* 23, 1836.

I have now been with the people of my parish some ten days since my return, and have met with the greatest kindness and affection in every quarter. I am very comfortably and pleasantly situated here; much more so than I deserve, seeing that I have as yet done so little good in the world. Our prospects here for the coming year are quite flattering, our church will be neatly and pleasantly finished, and the congregations, I have reason to think, will be better than in the past. My greatest desire is that some may be converted, so that our little society in this place may be strengthened by an accession of members, and the hands of our men of Israel sustained.

To-morrow I expect to preach in the morning in Jersey City, afternoon at Bergen, and night again at Jersey City; on Monday night is class-meeting; Tuesday, trustees' meeting; Wednesday, Sunday-school meeting; Thursday, prayer-meeting; Friday and Saturday, vacant. So you see my evenings are pretty well taken up. Well, the mornings I devote to study, the afternoons to visiting the flock; thus my time is all apportioned to respective duties, and, indeed, I find but little of it to spare for other pleasures than those which result from the duties of my office as a preacher of the Gospel. O, before I forget it, let me tell you that I practice your precepts: I eat no pie, no cake, have given up the habit of smoking, chewing, and snuffing.

And now I must prepare my sermons for to-morrow, so good night, mother mine; and may the Lord bless thee, and preserve thee long in life to bring up the remainder of your family (as you did faithfully those that have gone from you) in the "nurture and admonition of the Lord," that they may be prepared to live and prepared to die. And although I have as yet done little or nothing to repay you for all your kindness and affection, I hope that, in the good providence of God, I may yet be able to do something for your comfort. And my parents, I trust, need never be ashamed to own as their son,

JOHN M'CLINTOCK, JUN.

Soon after his re-appointment his health failed, and he was compelled to resign. This is his account of it:—

64 LIFE AND LETTERS OF

Sunday, Sept. 26, 1836.

For eighteen months I have been preaching the Gospel, in a weak
way indeed, but yet honestly, in the Methodist Episcopal Church in
Jersey City, New Jersey. Since the Conference in April last I have
done but little, as my health was severely tried by the excessive
labors of the last winter. *I preached generally three times on every
Sabbath, and had a meeting of some sort on almost every night in
the week. In April I commenced spitting blood, which continued
for some weeks, and was finally thrown off.* But from that time to
this I have hardly been without pain in the breast, and uneasiness in
the throat. My physicians tell me to quit the post or die. It is hard
work, but after many weeks of effort, this day I resigned the pastoral
charge of my little flock in Jersey City. To-night the church was
filled to overflowing, and hardly a dry eye in the house! God help
them and keep them! Amen! Amen!

A visit to Saratoga brought no relief. He was compelled, therefore, to look elsewhere than to the pulpit
for occupation, and especially such occupation as would,
at the same time, retain him in the service of the Church.
He did not need to look very far. He was, during the
summer of this year, unanimously elected to the Professorship of Mathematics and Natural Philosophy in
La Grange College, North Alabama, of which institution
the Rev. Robert Paine (now bishop in the Southern
Methodist Episcopal Church) was president. While considering the question of accepting the offer he was nominated Assistant Professor of Mathematics in Dickinson
College, Carlisle, Pennsylvania. This venerable school
of learning had suffered greatly from the fluctuations of
fortune. Founded in 1783, through the active exertions
of Dr. Benjamin Rush and other eminent citizens of

Pennsylvania, it aspired for a time to be a rival of Princeton. For a Presbyterian school it was fortunately placed. The Cumberland Valley had been originally settled by the Scotch-Irish, who were sturdy Calvinists, and altogether a strong-willed, indomitable race. They had been in the country districts supplanted by the pains-taking Germans who followed after them, but retained their ascendency in the large towns. Carlisle was an important centre of Presbyterianism. Here Duffield, one of the leaders of the New School organization, was pastor for many years. Dr. Nisbet, the first president of the college, was a splendid example of the Scotch Presbyterian learning, shrewdness, and wit. Among his successors was Dr. John M. Mason, who was, in his day, easily the chief of the Presbyterian pulpit in the United States. Among the Professors was M'Clelland, the marvellous rhetorician, the tradition of whose power in speech lingered in the Cumberland Valley long after his time. Among its graduates were Bethune, Krebs, and Chambers, who have adorned their profession in the city of New York. It was a college in a border town, that is, it was near the slave State line. It is not, therefore, surprising that it gave to the country the honest, but narrow, Roger B. Taney, and the equally honest, but vacillating, James Buchanan.

Despite its advantages, Dickinson College, as a Presbyterian school, never attained a stable prosperity. With entire good-will on the part of its original proprietors, it was conveyed to the Methodist Episcopal Church, the members of the old board of trustees resigning, one

5

by one, and assisting cordially in electing the required
number of successors. The transfer was honorable to
all parties. Either from the force of habit or from the
confidence in the liberality of the newly elected trustees,
Presbyterian as well as Methodist, students flocked to
the institution after its re-opening. Then, and ever after,
Church distinctions were obliterated in every part and
parcel of their college life—a rebuke of the folly which
separates the young men of the country, during the process of their education, into petty groups, as though the
members of one Christian community would be certain
to contaminate the members of another.

The first Faculty of the re-organized Dickinson was
well chosen. At its head was the Rev. John P. Durbin,
then in the fullness of his power as an orator. He suffers the rare disadvantage of having lived two lives, and
of having been so eminent in each, that the fame of the
one has obscured the fame of the other. To the present
generation of Methodists Dr. Durbin is known as a great
administrator; thirty years ago he was known as one of
the most extraordinary, in the production of popular
effects, of public speakers. With him were associated in
the Faculty, Merritt Caldwell, Robert Emory, and William H. Allen. They were men who proved their quality in subsequent life. Dr. Allen, who filled the chair of
the Natural Sciences, has long been President of Girard
College, Philadelphia, and has taken rank as one of the
leading educators of the country. Caldwell and Emory
both died in 1848, after having attained distinction, and
given promise of a future which was, alas! too soon

clouded. Emory had shortly before his election carried off the honors of Columbia College, in the city of New York; Caldwell and Allen were graduates of Bowdoin.

President Paine had offered to Mr. M'Clintock the choice of the Professorship of Mathematics, or that of Languages, in La Grange College. The latter was in doubt which line to take, but the Faculty of the University of Pennsylvania urged him to devote his life to mathematical studies. Of this judgment he gives some account in his correspondence with President Paine :—

JERSEY CITY, *August* 2, 1836.

I have had several communications with the Faculty of my *Alma Mater*, the University of Pennsylvania, since the receipt of your letter, on the subject of my future course in literary life. The strong recommendation of the Faculty (with the exception of the Professor of Languages) was to devote my whole efforts to mathematical pursuits, it having been their opinion throughout the course of my studies that I should succeed best in that department. The Professor of Mathematics, E. H. Courtenay, (whose name, of course, is known to you,) was particularly urgent in this case, and seemed to think that I should deeply regret any other course hereafter. In reviewing my studies, and endeavoring to determine in regard to the burden of my future efforts, I have hesitated here, and finally, feel satisfied that my course in the matter shall be regulated by circumstances. Should your institution, or any other, offer me the mathematics, or the languages, or the department of English literature, I should accept either, and make it the business of my life. You are aware that I am yet but a youth, and that, although I have tasted of the spring of science, I have many a deep and delicious draught before me yet—in prospect, at least.

The offer of the Assistant Professorship of Mathematics in Dickinson College was finally accepted, with the assurance of the nomination to the full professorship in case satisfaction was given. It is needless to say that satisfaction was given, and in July, 1837, he was elected full professor. Shortly after removing to Carlisle he was married to Caroline Augusta Wakeman, daughter of Jabez Wakeman, Esq., of Jersey City. "She was born," he records in his diary, "the same day, in the same year, with myself. God bless the bonds!" The bonds were blessed. The estimable lady whom he had chosen was in full sympathy with him as a student and scholar, and animated and cheered him in the prosecution of his multifarious tasks. She made his home a rest to which he ever turned with joy.

He was now in a position, of all others, most congenial to his growing mind. His ambition was healthfully aroused, if that were at all needed, for he was on trial for a permanent appointment. His associations satisfied both his scholarly and Christian tastes. He lived with his colaborers of the college Faculty on terms of closest friendship. Dr. Durbin, being some years his senior, and having had large experience of public life, was a valuable counsellor. With Robert Emory, the Professor of Ancient Languages, he formed a life-long intimacy. Each was the other's *alter ego*. They were alike and yet unlike. Both were affectionate, buoyant, and full of the inspirations of hope. In Emory the logical faculty predominated over all others, and gave to his mind a judicial exactness; M'Clintock's equally great logical force was swayed by a mercurial temperament and a lively fancy. In the acquisition of knowledge the

latter was ardent, and swift as the wind, but in the eagerness of the pursuit oblivious of a prudent self-care; his
associate, though equally ardent, moved with a more deliberate step. Of the two, Robert Emory was, however,
the first to wear himself out; he died, as we shall hereafter see, before the promise of his earlier years was
more than partly fulfilled. Professor Allen created perpetual surprises by his great versatility. He passed
from department to department with a facility that
made one doubt which was the one he most preferred.
Professor Caldwell's high moral character impressed every
one who came near him. New England ruggedness was
in him tempered by a tender moral sensibility. He became in time the trusted adviser of the thoughtful young
men of the institution.

Of these professors, who made up the first Faculty of
the College under its Methodist organization, Dr. Durbin
stood most conspicuously before the country. He had
already achieved a national reputation. The announcement that he would address an audience would, anywhere
in the United States, crowd the most available place of
assembly. Critics were sometimes puzzled to define the
secret of his power, but when he had once been heard,
conceded his power without question. His opening of
a sermon was always disappointing; indeed, it might be
said that he had in the pulpit a twofold manner, a twofold voice, and a double personality. Beginning with
composure, his first purpose, as far as he might admit
a personal purpose, seemed to be to subdue expectation. In distinct but quiet tones he would proceed

with the exposition of his theme. His mode of treatment was ingenious, sometimes subtile, always striking.
Before the hearer was aware new thoughts were suggested, or old thoughts had been placed in fresh lights.
Apparently the orator was holding an animated conversation with his hearers, (for the tone was wholly col-
loquial,) but, in reality, he was weaving a spell which by
and by he would use with electric suddenness. All
the time the fact most obvious was his impassiveness.
There he stood, calm as a statue, using only explanatory
gesture; but for the large, lustrous eye, one might doubt
if he were capable of strong emotion. Unexpectedly a
statement would kindle into an animated description,
and description passed into glowing declamation. The
long-repressed torrent of sensibility once let loose, the
orator was transformed. Voice became deep and full,
the gesture broad and sweeping, the eye flashed; the
audience, startled by this assertion of power, yielded at
once. Strong men would lean forward and half rise
to their feet; others would sit entranced, wholly oblivious of place and time. When caught up to the loftiest
height of feeling and thought, the voice would cease,
and the orator slowly resume his seat.

In all this there was genius guided by consummate art,
but the art was well applied. It was conditioned, moreover, by the necessities of the speaker himself, whose
slender frame would bear only a certain degree of strain.
Yet in the very tempest of impassioned address, President Durbin was a marvel of grace. Not a movement
offended the eye, not a tone was overdone. The self-

possession so conspicuous in the earlier passages of the discourse never deserted him; to the last sentence he was master of his powers; he had, it would appear, placed limits for himself that he would never transcend.

Unfortunately for the tradition of Dr. Durbin's eloquence, the days of the fullest exercise of his oratorical force were not the days of reporters. Passages from his sermons which might serve as life-like descriptions have wholly perished. It was a time, too, in the history of our country, when oratory was rated higher than it is now. Without doubt a reading people grows insensibly more critical, less susceptible to the onsets of emotional excitement, and more suspicious of those arts which make oral address effective. If eloquence is a joint result to which speaker and hearer both contribute, we can plainly see that the hearer of to-day does not contribute as much as the hearer of thirty years ago. The change is as perceptible in the British Parliament as in the United States Congress. Plain, business-like statement has superseded rhetoric, and close attention to statistics, emotional appeal. Durbin, Bascom, and Maffitt formed, in the period between 1826 and 1840, a trio of Christian orators who were the wonder and admiration of the masses throughout the length and breadth of the country. Maffitt's preaching was so extraordinary, that in some towns of the South-west business would be almost wholly suspended during the period of his stay. Of the three, Dr. Durbin's method will alone, I think, bear the scrutiny of exact criticism. Simple, lucid English, a voice pitched in the conversational key, and emotion which, if strong,

was always just, were the constituents of his eloquence,
and with these the sternest criticism can find no fault.

These persuasive orators had one advantage, which has
unfortunately been, in our time, almost wholly surrendered. They proclaimed the divine justice as well as the
divine compassion. No timidity, no sentimentalism, with-
held them from depicting the terrors of the final judgment of the human race. They dealt with the future
accountability of men as a reality, and brought it home
to the consciousness of every hearer. The habit, common in our day, of avoiding whatever goes beyond the
faintest reference to these themes, was unknown to the
great preachers of that generation. They did not hesitate to treat them dramatically, and in such treatment
to use all the resources of their art. Nor was this a
peculiarity of the Methodist pulpit only; in the explica-
tion of the judgment and the separation of the just from
the unjust, Lyman Beecher was as energetic as John P.
Durbin, and both could appeal, for authority, to the example of the old English divines.

With such happy surroundings, Professor M'Clintock
entered on his new life most cheerfully, as will be seen
from his letters to his sister :—

Dickinson College, Carlisle, October 15, 1836.

I have enough to write about to fill this sheet and more, but there
is not time enough in the world to do every thing. Still, I am glad
to have the opportunity, on this Saturday evening, to spend a portion of my time in writing to my dear sister. You know from my
letter to father that I arrived here safely, and was in good health ; I
am glad to add, that since I wrote my health has been much better

than usual; that my duties, though sufficiently laborious, have not been too much for me; and that I get through them all with comfort to myself, and satisfaction, I hope at least, to those around me. The regularity of our college life will be very serviceable to my health; at least, I think so. The order is as follows:—First bell, half past five A. M.; prayers, six A. M.—breakfast immediately after prayers; recitations, nine, ten, eleven, or nine, ten A. M. and four P. M., or ten, eleven A. M., and four P. M., never exceeding three recitations a day. The students generally are moral, studious, and well-behaved, and many of them are pious. Evening prayers at five P. M.—tea immediately after prayer. Last bell, nine P. M. Thus the bells are:—First, half past five A. M.; second, six A. M.; third, eight A. M.; fourth, nine A. M.; fifth, ten A. M.; sixth, eleven A. M.; seventh, twelve M. (dinner); eighth, two P. M.; ninth, three P. M.; tenth, four P. M.; and five, seven, eight, and nine P. M.

On Sabbath, after breakfast, two classes meet at eight o'clock; preaching, eleven; dinner, half past twelve; Bible class, (which I shall visit,) three; preaching, half past six, as usual. On Tuesday evening we have a social meeting for literary conversation, etc. On Wednesday, Faculty meeting; Thursday, preaching; Friday, prayer-meeting; Saturday, debate; so that days and evenings are pretty well filled up. I had written as far as the last sentence last evening, when I was called to the society for debate, so that I must either finish this on Sunday morning, or suffer it to go unfinished for a time. Surely there can be no harm in my writing a letter to you, even though it be on the Sabbath day.

Of his election to the permanent occupancy of the chair which he was filling provisionally none who knew him had any doubt. Quick in perception, clear in statement, and broad in his generalizations, he was the ideal of a brilliant professor. Being absent from college for a year, I did not meet with Professor M'Clintock until the fall of 1837. He had then established for himself a fine reputation, and his manner had all the confidence of success. The dullest student felt the contagion of his enthusiasm. The apter young men were encouraged to make explorations in mathematical science beyond the limits of their text-books. Lectures on the history of mathematics exhibited its growth and connexions. Every day's contact with our fresh and radiant professor gave us a new impulse.

If any of the young men who came before him were indulging in dreams of what they could accomplish by the force of genius, a few days of contact with him effectually knocked the nonsense out of them. The gospel which he incessantly proclaimed was the gospel of labor. Nothing to be won without honest work was the one maxim which he would not suffer to be forgotten for a moment. As he taught he practiced. The one fact most visible in his life was its strenuous devotion to culture. The lamp in his study was, of the many lighted in the evening, the last to be put out. Away into the small hours it still burned. It burned too long for his own good, but he came before us each morning fresh and elastic, till the prostration, which before long overtook him, suspended the performance of his duties.

This union of brilliance with laboriousness made Professor M'Clintock the most wholesome of teachers. He was not a plodder, yet no plodder could be more painstaking. It mattered little what was in hand, if done at all it was to be done well. Whatever was to be known must be known to the bottom. A sound discretion, how-

ever, insured him against being lost in details. His logical habit of mind brought all particulars into close
subordination. His ambition was as large as his powers.
He could say without presumption that he had "taken
all knowledge for his portion," and he needed only nerves
of steel and a frame incapable of exhaustion to secure full
possession. While teaching college students mathematics his own studies spread out in all directions. Though .
with a good appetite for all learning, he had a choice.
To physics he seemed somewhat indifferent; but languages, logic, metaphysics, and theology, with history,
poetry, and belles-lettres, had for him charms which he
never wished to resist. The old problems of the validity
and the limitations of human knowledge were an endless
fascination to him. From the beginning he had had no
intention of being a mere mathematician. Indeed, he
expressed repeatedly to his friends his dread of the
narrowing effect of exclusive devotion to mathematical
study. He planned early a broad range of intellectual
pursuits, and adhered to his plan with fidelity.

The opportunity enjoyed by himself and his associates was very fortunate, but they proved equal to it.
Methodism originated in a university; its leaders were
scholarly clergymen of the Church of England; but the
necessities of his position compelled John Wesley to
commit it, after his death, to the care of imperfectly
educated successors. The scholars who should have
aided him held aloof. They were scandalized by lay
preachers and field preaching; they forgot that Wesley
set laymen to work because he could find few clerical

helpers, and that he betook himself to the fields only when he was driven from the churches. In the American colonies the clergymen of the Established Church had little or no connexion with Methodism, and on the breaking out of the War of Independence numbers of them returned to England. Plain, self-educated men, with a few exceptions, laid the foundations of the Methodist Episcopal Church. They were vigorous and forceful preachers, thoroughly understood the doctrines which they handled, and led by one of the greatest of ecclesiastical generals, Bishop Asbury, had penetrated all accessible parts of the States and Canada. Thrown into antagonism with the theological culture of their time, they fought a hard, and, in the end, victorious battle. If their opposers were better versed in books, they were more skilled in human nature, and had, by a species of intuition, grasped the art of preaching. From the habit of opposing educated men, many came to oppose education itself. The failure of the first attempts to found institutions of learning, was, for a time, interpreted as a providential interposition, forbidding further experiments. The splendid examples of self-education in English Methodism—Walsh, Clarke, and Watson—were held up for imitation, and, no doubt, inspired the most prodigious exertions. As a matter of course, this abnegation of the helps which the experience of ages has provided for the training of the human mind could only last for a time. The necessities of a growing Church compelled the provision of a suitable educational apparatus. It is curious to observe with what caution the

first measures were taken; what care was used to speci-
fy that learning must be duly "sanctified," what misgivings were felt lest the educated men should disdain the
humble labors of the itinerant service. It was considered
an important point of administration that they should
be "well broken in," if needful, by sending them to hard
work on scant fare in wild regions. The schools had
fought the Methodist ministry so long, that these same
ministers had no little dread of the schools, even when
founded and fashioned by themselves.

Leaders were, however, not wanting at this critical
juncture, and among them Drs. Wilbur Fisk, John
Emory, and John P. Durbin, must always be conspicuous. They, with a few others, may be said to have begun the second, or educational, era of the development
of American Methodism. Dr. Fisk's name will be forever
identified with the founding of the Wesleyan University
at Middletown; Bishop Emory was the first President of
the Board of Trustees of Dickinson, and negotiated its
transfer from the Presbyterians; Dr. Durbin had been
a professor in Augusta College, Kentucky, and was one
of the earliest advocates of thorough theological culture.
Their authority gave weight, their eloquence persuaded,
and the Church, with such guides, entered courageously
on its new path.

The members of the first Faculty of Dickinson College had, therefore, all the advantages of a fine position.
They did not need to build on other men's foundations,
but could lay their own. No great reputations over-
shadowed them. They could create according to their

own ideal, and had room and verge enough to work
freely. Looking back, I can see more plainly than was
possible then, that the opportunity was to them all a
powerful inspiration. Young, eager, and in every sense
strong, they wrought in harmony, side by side, and with
a sense of ever-increasing power. They did not perceive
that the goal which they sought was farther off than
they believed. They were not conscious how much in advance they were of the great body of practical men from
whom, in the last resort, the nourishment of all important American institutions must be derived. What they
built, however, stands and will stand; and not the least,
they built themselves up to a power which American
society has felt beneficially in every direction.

The young men trained by this first Faculty of Dickinson and their immediate successors have given a
good account of themselves. In the State, Creswell and
Marshall; in science, Baird; in Church administration,
Bishop Bowman, of our own, and Bishop Cummins, of
the Reformed Episcopal Church; in the pulpit, Thomas
Verner Moore, Deems, Ridgaway, and Tiffany; in literature, Conway (who has left his early faith, but retains
all his early love for the men under whom he was
trained) and Hurst; in foreign missions, Maclay; are
examples of the fruitfulness of their educational work.

The following letters reveal the joyousness of Professor M'Clintock's life during this period. The first is
to his wife's father:—

I have no complaints to make. Our life goes on at present in a
smooth, contented round of healthful occupations and rational enjoy-

ments. These are the bright days for us ; how long they may continue I cannot say. But we try to lay up our treasure " where moth and rust cannot corrupt." Perhaps there is not much self-denial in this, for we have very little chance of laying up treasures anywhere else. But we are well off, as we calculate to come out clear of all encumbrances at the end of this year, if Providence favors our little enterprises. College is prosperous, at least as far as its internal movements and management are concerned. Many matters without look rather squally, but we hope for the best.

In a letter to his wife's brother, Mr. E. B. Wakeman, he expresses an intention which he never carried out :—

I am pretty well occupied, but think, sometimes, of commencing law this fall. I could connect it advantageously with my other studies, and be ready for the bar in two years—of course, not with any view to practice, but merely to know a little of every thing that goes on in this wicked world.

He had scarce completed his second year as professor when his health gave way. This was the first of a series of distressing bodily affections which troubled him, and at times wholly disabled him. Uniform good health he never enjoyed. Periods of prodigious activity would be followed by periods of enforced abstinence from all serious work. This first attack was a constriction and inflammation of the œsophagus, which made it impossible for him to swallow solid food. It was treated with caustic, and the treatment subjected him almost to the tortures of a long martyrdom. Ten years after this, Dr. M'Clintock supposed himself to be subject to heart disease, and lived under a constant apprehension of sudden death. Frequent attacks of swooning gave plausi-

bility to his fears. He was, to use a common phrase,
"easily upset;" some part of the bodily machinery was
ready to give way, compelling him to lie by for repairs.
I mention these facts because they help to explain his
life. The suspension of exertion which sometimes puzzled those who knew him but slightly, the unrest which
showed itself in a desire of frequent change, were but
symptoms of unsatisfactory health. That he held himself so firmly to his work as he did, is the best evidence
we have of the tenacity of his determination to do the utmost possible with himself as long as his strength lasted.

His diary furnishes the best picture extant of his life
at this period. It is a narrative of his reading, studies,
hopes, and fears, enlivened by acutest criticisms of books
and men. He was now but twenty-four years of age,
yet looked with clear eyes upon the world before him.
He would not suffer his understanding to be imposed
upon, but saw and judged for himself. Most noticeable,
too, is the ardor of his pursuit of knowledge while prostrated by disease. He would read in every direction, no
matter what the penalty. The unconscious self-revela-
tion which appears in the passages here appended will
be, I trust, a sufficient justification of the freedom with
which the diary is quoted :—

Oct. 13, 1838. For two months past I have labored under a distressing affection of the throat. My professorship at Carlisle is neglected, and I am now in Philadelphia, under medical treatment. For
weeks I have been unable to swallow any thing thicker than milk,
and even that sometimes with difficulty. I know also what *nervous*
disorders are, for the first time in my life.

Tues., Dec. 18, 1838. My throat is somewhat better: can swallow milk or soup thickened with a little flour. For four months now have I been comparatively idle, and useless either to myself or others ; and have found it hard to discipline my mind to submission to divine Providence. But I begin to feel resigned, to acknowledge His hand, and to hope that even this sore affliction will work out good for me both in this life and in that which is to come. I have spent the time in Philadelphia for the sake of medical advice, and have found every comfort in my father's house—cheered also by the presence of my dear wife and little one. My child, Sarah Augusta, was born Monday, September 10, and is now a sweet babe. God preserve her!

Wed., Jan. 2, 1839. Have entered upon a new year. God has lengthened my life, though I feel that I hold it by a very feeble tenure. My mind is quite unsettled. I cannot meditate closely upon religious themes ; but my confidence in God's love, through Jesus Christ, is unshaken, nay, increasing. My nerves are in a wretched condition—all unstrung, so that thought, to any great extent, is impossible. If it be thy will, O Lord, grant me relief!

Read part of the Life of Girard, the rich banker of Philadelphia. A great mind—devoted to wealth—forgetful of eternity!

Jan. 3, 1839. Read the Epistle to the Philippians—always a faithful people. Paul had no censures for them. Read Byron's Journals and part of Don Juan. A wicked man, yet with some good features. His works cannot live—no elements of durability, of immortality, about them. He and Moore have much to answer for, in the corruption of morals which they have poured like a flood upon young minds. How different from Wordsworth and Coleridge, diffusing streams of pure, beautiful morality and deep thought upon the world.

Sun., Jan. 6. Read First Epistle to Timothy, and perplexed myself for some time with chapter v, 24. The only meaning which I can attach to the passage is this: Paul contrasts *open, daring* sinners with hypocrites ; some men are so desperately wicked that the odor, as it were, of their iniquities precedes them. How fertile of precept and wisdom for the Christian preacher are these epistles to Timothy—sound, practical wisdom too—such as will carry a man

6

safely through all difficulties, in the Church and out of it, if faithfully followed. Paul was not *imprudent*, and he deprecates rashness and imprudence in others. Would that some of our hasty spirits, that embroil Church and State with their crude notions and ill-digested theories, would imbibe somewhat more of his practical good sense—his careful, religious *prudence*. Read a project in the "Christian Advocate" for a celebration of the Centenary of Methodism—which had its birth in 1739—funds to be collected and applied to building Mission Houses in New York. I don't like the plan—there is not enough economy in the management of our religious funds. Read Second Timothy, Titus, and Philemon; the same spirit and meaning in all Paul's writings—authority mingled with love. I have not heard a sermon since last September.

Mon., Jan. 14. Read in Coleridge's "Friend" his essay on *Method*, the object of which is to prove the superiority of *law* to *theory*, as a basis for method. A very profound yet luminous essay. Read part of the Appendix to Cousin's "Psychology." Low-spirited and nervous to-day. I suppose I may be truly called a hypochondriac—a name and condition that I have feared almost as much as that of maniac. Read the last chapter in Taylor's "Physical Theory"—a very attractive book. The germ of it may be found, I think, in Coleridge's "Letters and Recollections." Poor nerves of mine, what could have shattered them so!

Tues., Jan. 15. Read in Walter Scott's Life the account of his misfortunes and his fortitude under them all. Walter Scott was not a religious man—little thought of a future life, I should judge from his writings and his biography. Read Second Epistle of Peter; mind not sufficiently concentrated to understand it completely. Went on with Walter Scott; he was weak enough in some points. What a contrast—Scott and Wordsworth! Scott would have fought with Gourgaud; he was superstitious, vain, mind full of world and world's thoughts; selfish, I think, to an extreme; but, strangely enough, generous withal. I would not do him injustice; he has beguiled many a weary hour. But why should there be *any* weary hours? Surely there are sources enough of enjoyment, without such floods of paltry fiction as have been thrown upon the world since Scott began to write novels. Read in Grecian history the rise of Thebes; battles of Leuctra and Mantinea; up to the deaths of Pelopidas and Epaminondas. *N. B.* I don't believe the stories of Spartans rejoicing that their friends were slain in battle, and mourning over those that returned as disgraced. Spartans were men—their nature was *human* nature.

Thurs., Jan. 17. Rose at eight; delightful sleep last night; feel pretty bright this morning. Read Cooper's Review of "Lockhart's Life of Scott." Poor enough, in all conscience; though not quite so unjust as some affect to think it. Read also a "Reply" to the same in the "Knickerbocker," and if the article itself was vapor, the reply is double distilled gas—it is just *naething* at all. I said, a few days ago, that Scott was destitute of religion. I recall it; for first, I should not say such a thing of any man; and second, I have since read Lockhart's account of his decline and death, and it has changed my views of the man considerably. At all events, it brought tears to my eyes, opening a fresh well-spring of love in my heart. But, after all, how far are such men, nay, how far are any men, from the scriptural standard of a religious life! I know my own deficiencies, others know some of them, but I know myself better than any man can, and I know that I am very far from being the pure, devoted Christian of the New Testament.

I am not bigot enough to suppose that there are no good men out of the Methodist Church, but I think her the best of modern Churches, both as to her ecclesiastical polity, her usefulness to the world, and the general purity of her clergy and laity. I know, too, that the Methodist ministry affords few inducements to worldly, ambitious spirits; but, with all this, I have found the same petty jealousies, the same pursuit of individual aims, the same lust of power, the same envy of superior talents, among Methodist preachers, that I should have expected to find among "the potsherds of the earth." Where then, alas! shall I look for purity? Into my own heart? Eheu! what a den of thieves has that heart been! . . . There is too much *prescription* in the Methodist Church, and there is too much *proscription* for individual opinions. A man can hardly be independent with any hope of rising in the Church. This state of things causes a mean, truckling spirit to grow up among the young men, which, in a great degree, renders them intellectual slaves to a few not very intellectual masters. This has always been the fault of the Church—I mean of the universal Church—it is not as it should be, it is not in accordance with the laws of Christianity. "The spirit of power, and of love, and of a sound mind," is incompatible with this sort of mental bondage; and, sooner or later, the Methodist Episcopal Church will pay the penalty of her encroachments upon the absolute freedom of the individual mind, by storms and contentions, if not by her entire disorganization and dissolution, unless a wiser policy shall be struck out by her leaders and pursued in her government.

This criticism of the Methodist Episcopal Church is very plain and pointed, but is descriptive of all human organizations, secular or ecclesiastical. The problem of the harmony of authority and liberty is as old as human nature, and has never been perfectly solved. A system so centralized as that of Episcopal Methodism tends to a severe restriction of the play of individualism. By a spontaneous instinct it seeks to form instruments, and is fearful of deviations from its one method. The history of the organization shows, however, that it came most naturally by this spirit. Given an ecclesiastical scheme created by scholars, and handed over to men not trained scholars, though able and practical, the latter will find their only safety in adhering rigidly to its prescriptions. They know this one thing; they have not the wide and various reading which will place at their disposal the rich fruits of universal experience. Their conservatism is their best protection.

Yet the disaster predicted by this young and thoughtful critic as certain to follow from the overmastering force of the connexional element in Methodism has been happily averted. American Methodism proves every year more tolerant of individualism, and is solving, we may hope with entire success, the problem of a strong yet free government.

Some additional extracts from Professor M'Clintock's Diary will show how he improved his time during this period of enforced absence from college duty :—

Sun., Jan. 20. Read part of the Apocalypse ; find it is as dark as ever—a sealed book to me, with the exception of the introductory chapters. Read in the " London and Westminster Review " an article on Protestant and Catholic popery, in which the writer attempts to fix the boundary between reason and faith in regard to religious truth, or rather, to settle the relative rights of reason and Scripture. He charges Christianity, falsely, with requiring a belief of that which contradicts reason ; which is not true in any proper sense of the word contradictory. Read on this subject Coleridge's " Aids to Reflection," pp. 120, 209, etc., wherein is to be found a far more philosophical and satisfactory view of the subject. I have regretted that Richard Watson permitted himself ever to use the language, above denied, as the language of Christians, though he very clearly explained himself in the same connexion. (*Vide* " Watson's Life," by Jackson, *ad fin.*)

Tues., Jan. 22. Rose at half past eight ; good sleep last night ; feel better this morning. Continued reading the Revelation. Who can understand it ? To whom has it yet been a revelation ? Read the History of Philip of Macedon, and an outline of the conquests of Alexander the Great in Asia.. The accounts are, to say the least, all exaggerated, while that of Quintus Curtius is, in many particulars, absolute invention.

Wed., Jan. 23. Rose at nine. Read Revelation, chapter xviii, *ad fin.* Read also part of the history of David's reign, from Second Samuel. How honest is the record! all crimes and follies narrated, without attempt at palliation or excuse. Read part of the history of Alexander's Successors. Only twenty-eight years from the death of Alexander, and not one of his blood remained on earth! Breathing easier to-day. Great storm of snow and wind; afterward very cold.

Thur., *Jan.* 29. Rose at nine; poor sleep till the small hours last night; pain in the breast this morning, with glandular swellings; hope they wont be troublesome.

Read First Kings—history of Solomon's reign—badly begun with the murder of his brother Adonijah. Read in Hoffman's "Thoughts of a Grumbler;" rather a superficial affair. Obtained Life of Episcopius; can't read it for a day or two, they growl at me (*scil.* wife, doctor, etc.) about reading so much; and lo! I read next to nothing. Read part of Pope's Life; what a vain creature he was!

Letter from C. Gill, editor of "Mathematical Miscellany," asking me to contribute some articles for that valuable periodical! Poor me! can't even bend my mind to *read* a book of mathematics, without thinking of writing.

Thurs., *Jan.* 31. Continued reading Johnson's "Life of Pope"—finished it. It was not written with Johnson's usual care. The parallel between Pope and Dryden I have had occasion to notice before. I like not these constrained parallels, either in history or in criticism. Plutarch's inaccuracies and exaggerations are mostly to be found in his parallels, which might be omitted from the "Lives" without great loss to any body.

Sun., *Feb.* 3. Rose at half past nine; had good sleep last night; head a little better this morning. Read Solomon's beautiful and comprehensive prayer at the dedication of his temple. How strange, that with such a strong mind, such high privileges, and such great religious attainments, he should have fallen! Perseverance of the saints, indeed!

Tues., *Feb.* 5. O! when shall I be able to keep this record without giving it so much the aspect of a medical diary? When shall I be free from an invalid's anxious cares, matutinal self-examination, even ing potions, midnight blisters, and the countless *nugæ* that make up my useless life at present? Yet, perhaps, not altogether useless! Perhaps I may he again restored to health and strength, again able to tread with a buoyant, joyous step, as once I was wont, the glad earth which I now hardly dare to tread ; again able to snuff the sweet summer breezes from our own hills in Cumberland ; to gaze upon those splendid sunsettings, the farewells of the dying day, which we know only in our own valley; and O! most blessed thought of all, again able to stand up in the sacred place and preach the Gospel of Jesus Christ to men! It seems to me that I could preach as I never thought of preaching before ; that I *know* that of the vanity of life and the power of religion that I never dreamed of before ; and, perhaps, God has intended this affliction for a severe but precious discipline to my unworthy mind and heart! Could the blessed anticipation ever be realized, how joyfully would I exchange my professor's chair for the humblest circuit in Methodism, so that I could only preach, with all the energies of a sound mind in a sound body, the glorious Gospel of Christ Jesus! And my dear wife is of the same mind ; ready for circuit or any thing else, to be in the line of duty.

Thurs., Feb. 7. Rose at half past eight. Read newspapers and *dawdled* until ten, then read three chapters in First Kings—the history of Jeroboam and Rehoboam. Drs. George and Samuel M'Clellan called, examined throat, etc., prescribed caustic! caustic! caustic! Something was said about a seton in the chest, but I don't want it ; I have tortures enough without artificial ones.

Sun., Feb. 17. Rose at eight; delightful night's rest, God be thanked! Dear little babe, how full of life and vigor she is this morning; every muscle in vigorous exercise, kicking and romping and screaming like a little witch. She is five months and one week old, and measured this morning two feet three inches and a half. The blessing of Heaven rest upon the child! Continued the history of kings of Israel and Judah; what a record of follies and crimes it is! Read a little in Prideaux's Connexion.

Mon., Feb. 18. Made analysis of part of chapter xxii, part ii, of Watson's Institutes: hard work trying to educe order from chaos.

Read part of Reuben Apsley, by Horace Smith; a good story, told plainly and well, especially the middle portions, but bad at both ends, or rather at both beginning and end.

Tues., Feb. 19. Spent an hour in conversation with W. H. Gilder. Talked of attempting a weekly religious paper in this city in the Methodist Episcopal Church, designed to advocate the real interests of Methodism, "without partiality and without hypocrisy." Wish sincerely that such a paper could be established, though I do not feel much like taking the responsibility on my own shoulders, especially in money matters; but, perhaps, if my health be not sufficiently restored to allow of my attending to my duties at Carlisle in April, it might be well for me to attempt it.

Sun., Feb. 24. Rose at nine. Good sound sleep last night, and feel pretty well this morning. All go to church; but we must stay at home. Well, the Lord is not confined to the mountain or to Jerusalem, and we may enjoy his presence and smiles in our little chamber. Read in First Chronicles; how beautiful and comprehensive is the *prayer of Jabez*, in chapter iv ! I thought of passing by the first nine chapters entirely, as containing nothing but dry genealogies; but, then, I should have missed that sweet prayer, lying like a well in a desert.

Had wife read to me in the evening from Wordsworth's "Excursion," and sister Jane, an article on "Rituals," from the "New York Review;" which article, by the way, is a beautiful specimen both of reasoning and eloquence. My own mind has been made up for some time upon the question of forms of prayer. I believe that our fathers erred, in this country, in yielding to the wishes of the people, and abolishing the use of forms of prayer in the Methodist Church. Could it be done safely, I would be glad to see them introduced.

Thurs., Feb. 28. Finished the "Life of Drew." He certainly accomplished great things with small means; but, as he himself admits, it is the *contrast* between his opportunities and his performances which entitles him to eminence. His works are great, not absolutely, but relatively to his circumstances.

Read most of the "Life of Joshua Marsden." Rather a feeble

mind, I judge; but a man of good feelings and virtuous principles. After all, *these* are infinitely more valuable than *those*.

Thurs., March 7. Raked up from the dust of father's book-shelves the old numbers of Stockton's "Wesleyan Repository," and was much interested in running over them. I *suppose*, though I am not sure of it, that the publication was very unpopular with the Methodist preachers at the time. It was too bold entirely; attributed too little infallibility to our system. The same spirit exists at this day to a considerable extent.

Fri., March 15, Baltimore. Rode up to the Conference Room, in Sharp-street, (Wesley Chapel,) and found the Conference in session; Bishop Andrew in the chair. The case on hand was that of Brother Asbury Roszel, who was to be continued on trial. J. A. Collins objected, on the ground of his having been retained at Carlisle during the year, and that he would probably be retained hereafter. There was a pretty full discussion of the principle on which Methodist preachers are put into colleges. Dr. Bangs spoke very well on the case, and the Bishop laid down the law very clearly; though I differ, *toto cœlo*, from his sentiments in regard to our college work, as expressed in his speech. His doctrine was, that the college situations were subordinate to the general itinerant work, and that it is wrong to keep men in them who might be useful in the ranks of the ministry; on which account laymen are to be preferred for professors, etc., when they can be had. Now, I do not believe that our educational system ought to be regarded as subordinate to but co-ordinate with the general religious system; and I cannot see on what other ground the Bishop is at all justifiable in appointing preachers to colleges and schools. And, moreover, if I believed the sentiment of Bishop Andrew *just*, I could not continue my connexion with College another hour, consistently with my views of a Methodist preacher's duty. Besides, it is my deliberate opinion, and one not formed from theory, or *à priori*, but from actual experience in colleges, that *all* the professors should be ministers of the Gospel if possible. The interdependence of sound learning and sound theology is too close, the bearing of scientific doctrines upon religion is too intimate, to allow

all these interests to lie in the hands of men who have never made
theology a peculiar study.   And in our Methodist Colleges there are
additional reasons for filling all the professorships with ministers ; in
that case only are they directly responsible to the Conferences which
sustain the Colleges.

Thurs. morning, March 21. Dr. Buckler, the celebrated physician
of this city, called on me yesterday and examined my throat.   He
assured me that this indolent inflammation must have been of long
standing, and originated in a morbid condition of the stomach.
Advised me not to use the simple *bougie*, nor any mercurials, but
simply to travel, use a mild aperient every morning, and keep cool.
He also ordered a revulsive of caustic potash upon the back of the
neck, and advised a trip to the Red Sulphur Springs of Virginia during the summer if possible.   I was considerably pleased with his
opinions.

Sun., March 24, *Philadelphia.* How kindly does Providence adapt
our desires to our circumstances ! One year ago, I was choice in my
food, and required a great deal of it to satisfy my appetite and support nature. *Now* I live upon my fluid diet, with hardly a thought
or wish with regard to any other food ; my appetite is good, but is
stayed by a few tumblers of milk, and I find it sufficiently nutritious.
Thank God for all his mercies !

Fri., March 29. Thirty-four leeches applied to the back of my
neck this morning.   They may, perhaps, prevent a recurrence of last
night's disagreeables. Day spent at home. Read Job ; read in Taylor's "Home Education ;" also Scott's "Count Robert of Paris."

Wed., April 3. Left Philadelphia at five P. M. yesterday in the
cars, and after a less fatiguing and troublesome ride than I had anticipated, reached my father-in-law's house, in Jersey City, at about
half past eleven P. M.   Found wife up with the dear little one in her
arms ; but O, how changed from the fair creature that I left but a
few weeks ago ! The rich glow of her sunny cheek was gone, the
sparkle of her eye had vanished, and she lay there, little more than a
lump of clay. Still she lives, and there is hope. The doctor gives
us some encouragement. God save the child !

Sat., April 6. Nine A. M. Babe is dying; the sweet spirit will soon be a cherub! She is dead! O God, thou art trying me in the fire!

Sun., April 7. Buried our little love, at least her mortal part, in the vault at Bergen Hill. So vanish earthly joys! Another tie to the skies! Poor wife, it is indeed a blow to her.

Mon., April 22. Left Philadelphia at six A. M. in the railroad cars; reached Carlisle at five P. M., one hundred and twenty-eight miles in eleven hours, including about two and a half hours' stoppages at different points on the road. The day was delightful, and I found the journey not near so fatiguing and oppressive as I had anticipated.

Thurs., April 25, *Carlisle.* Have been reading, for a day or two, Sampson Reid's "Growth of the Mind;" a most beautiful production, abounding in elevated truths, imbued with a pure and spiritual philosophy, and written in a most chaste and elegant style. Strange that so clear a mind should submit to the delusion and folly of Swedenborgianism!

Sun., May 19. The past week has been one of great blessings and much enjoyment. The exquisite sweetness and purity of the atmosphere, the opening of fresh flowers daily, the songs of innumerable birds, all have contributed to keep me much in the open air, and my health has improved accordingly. I have been under the homœopathic treatment all the time, but am really at a loss to know whether I derive any benefit from it, or whether all my improvement may not be attributed to the delightful circumstances with which I am surrounded.

Fri., May 24. Heard recitations on Tuesday and Wednesday in Paley's "Evidences." Dined Wednesday on thickened milk, of better consistency than any thing I had taken before since last September. Have great pleasure in the kindness of friends here; truly they abound in their love to us, and I know not wherefore.

Wed., May 29. Have read a good deal in Swedenborg, and really am at a loss to imagine how any man in his wits can find any thing here to attract him. There are, it is true, many pretty visions, many strange fantasies, many brilliant pictures, and many profound truths;

but these are so buried up in masses of the veriest nonsense, so obscured by absolute ravings, that the man must have little to do who
can afford to spend time in searching for them. Gutted, to-day, T.
Jackson's "Centenary of Methodism." Commenced on Monday
Prescott's "Ferdinand and Isabella," and Philip's "Life of Bunyan."

Mon., June 17. Mrs. Allen died at half past nine A. M., on Saturday, after a week of almost unintermitting agony. She died in peace,
aged twenty years. God grant that I may be ready for his call if I
should be the next summoned away! It is somewhat strange, that
within the last few years every member of the Faculty of Dickinson
College has received some cup of bitterness from the hand of Providence : President D. lost his wife ; Professor E., his father ; Professor
R., his brother ; I lost my sweet babe, and the use of my throat ; and
Professor A. has this day buried his wife. Perhaps God has a controversy with us. O that we were more devoted to his cause and to
his glory !

Tues., June 25. Finished, to-day, reading Prescott's "Ferdinand
and Isabella ;" a clear, perspicuous history, in the very best style of
historical writing. It hardly pretends to be a philosophical history.
Am much pleased with Townsend's "Notes on New Testament,"
except his notions on High Church. Derive great benefit and improvement from Campbell's "Dissertations and Notes." Watson's
"Exposition" is not what I hoped to find it. His style is destitute
of simplicity, which is the first requisite in the style of an expositor.

Sun., July 7. The worst feature of my present affliction is, and has
been, that I cannot preach the Gospel. I sometimes think that the
rod has thus been laid upon me in order to prevent my preaching ;
that one so worldly, so sensual, so trifling, so led away by frivolous
aims, so desirous of worldly honors, so careless in regard to divine
things, and so ignorant of them, should not occupy the sacred desk
as an ambassador for Christ ! If it be so, O Lord, purge me still
more thoroughly, that, in the end, if it be consistent with thy holy
will, I may be permitted again to lift up my voice in calling sinners
to repentance. But I have little zeal for God. If I had a proper
zeal, I could do much for his cause, even though I do not preach ;

on the contrary, however, I fear that I have made my feeble health a plea for the neglect of many duties! God forgive and cleanse me!

Tues., July 9. Commencement week—hurry, hurry, bustle, flurry, all the time—no opportunity for reading, writing, thought, or any thing else. Examinations have closed; went off very well. Emory *will* leave; sorry, indeed, I am. While I do full justice to the purity of his motives, and the uprightness of his intentions, I am well convinced that he has erred in his judgment in regard to this matter. Perhaps, however, Providence will overrule it all for good.

I have been requested by a correspondent to describe Professor M'Clintock's method as a student. I hesitate somewhat to comply. It is not easy for the artist to disclose the secret of his power, much less easy is it for one who has no more than the opportunities of an observer. As this memoir, however, will be read by Methodist ministers, such account as I can give of Dr. M'Clintock's student life may be helpful in the way of suggestion. The methods of scholars are probably very much alike. Given an insatiable hunger for knowledge, with opportunity for its satisfaction, and knowledge will be gathered. I should put this unappeasable hunger for truth as the first fact; Dr. M'Clintock *would* know whatever was to be known. He would open ways for himself into every field of knowledge, and would survey it, if he could do no more. His mental independence was the next striking feature of his method. He did his own thinking. He was not content to be any man's echo. The passages from his diary already quoted prove with what vigor he used his critical faculty. It was not common, at that day, for young men to speak so freely of the worthies of Meth-

odism; but he always insisted that the one lesson to be
learned from the life of John Wesley was the lesson of
intellectual self-reliance. In exploring a subject a certain tact made him quickly familiar with its literature.
What others had thought and said upon it came readily
to his hand. He thus gathered about him speedily the
materials for complete investigation, would instinctively
find the right clew, and would then push forward till he
saw what he wished to know with the utmost vividness.
His mind never leaped to conclusions; he might anticipate them, but would march up to them, keeping on solid
ground. His multifarious reading was carefully indexed,
so as to be always within reach. Important passages
were copied at length. On every leading topic he had
a large body of notes drawn from the best authorities.

In using this abundant material his first aim was to
attain a perfect insight, and then to exercise an independent judgment. He was not overmastered by his acquisitions, but kept them under due control. He effected this by his organizing power, which was the
dominant faculty of his mind. To reduce knowledge to
its all comprehending principles was no less a pleasure
than a necessity for him. His habits of composition were
most laborious. Nothing slovenly from his pen was
ever allowed to see the light. His critical judgment
held watch and ward over every paragraph. He was
most solicitous of criticism, and scarcely ever produced
an important review or essay that he did not ask his
most intimate friends to point out defects in either matter or form. Through this process of discipline his style

became clear, crisp, and faultless in form, though it was perhaps lacking in warmth. In preparation for public addresses there was a like carefulness observed, but with it there was a large trust to his spontaneous power. His sensibilities were quick, and kindled readily in the presence of an expectant audience. He was equal to extraordinary occasions, could interpret the inarticulate emotion of his hearers, and give it voice and expression with a power of eloquence which left little to be desired. I shall speak, however, of his oratorical gifts more at length in subsequent chapters.

LETTERS FROM MAY, 1836, TO MARCH, 1839.

I.

JERSEY CITY, BERGEN CO., N. J., *May* 27, 1836.

For one whole year have I been preaching Christianity under the direction of the Philadelphia Conference, and in that year I have learned that to be a faithful preacher, something more is requisite than sound moral feelings, or strong religious excitement. A man must have some intellect, and some lungs, too, in order to perform all the duties of a Methodist preacher successfully. During the year I have had considerable opportunity for study, and have partially improved it, both in following up my collegiate studies, and in penetrating the mysteries of the theologians: though in these latter I have certainly made as yet but little progress. In fact, unless my views of these subjects change much in the lapse of years, I shall never be a theologian, in the common sense of the term, though I should live and preach for half a century. My chief studies at present are, " Longinus on the Sublime," of which I am attempting a translation, (just commenced, however,) and the writers on " Moral Philosophy ; " with which matter I intend to make myself as well acquainted as the nature of it will admit. In the mean time, I purpose to prepare myself for a future professorship in either Language or Ethics, so that should I be called upon from any quarter, I may be ready to answer.

During the present spring my health has been very poor—the result of laborious preaching. I find that continued preaching will soon destroy me—the excitement is too great for my very excitable temperament. My health, comfort, happiness, and usefulness, I am well convinced, would all be better were I in a situation more congenial to my feelings, and more suitable to my weak capacities, than that of a stated preacher. It requires qualities that I do not possess. Thus far, however, I have gone, I think, under the direction of a kind and gracious Providence, for whose guidance I still look, and whose openings I shall implicitly follow.

PROFESSOR EMORY.

II.

JERSEY CITY, Sept. 2, 1886.

DEAR FATHER:—I received a letter yesterday from Mr. Paine, President of La Grange College, informing me of my election to the professorship of Mathematics and Natural Philosophy—salary, $900 per annum. A new session opened August first, and will terminate in January. The present incumbent will retain his office until my arrival, should I accept and reach La Grange before first of October, beyond which date he cannot remain, so that I am urged to hasten my departure. The college is located in Franklin County, Alabama, ten miles from Tuscumbia, on the summit of a mountain, with one of the finest and most extensive landscapes in the United States. The pecuniary condition of the establishment is good—and prospects still brightening. There are two large three-story brick buildings—one having one hundred feet, the other seventy-two feet front, with a laboratory and chapel. The place is proverbial for health. The number of students varies from one hundred to one hundred and forty; their character for scholarship and morals inferior to none in the western colleges. The Faculty are: President, Professor of Mathematics, Adjunct Professor of Languages, Professor of Chemistry, Professor of Languages—with a tutor. Faculty harmonious—for some years united.

The reasons for my accepting this professorship are various ; some are—first, the healthfulness of the situation, and its southern climate, which my constitution needs. Second, the excellence of the offer, which indeed somewhat surprises me. Third, its being for the Mathematics, to which our Professors so strongly urged me. Fourth, the providential circumstances which seem to direct me strongly to the acceptance of the offer. I shall not be able to tarry *here* long —I cannot subsist without employment, nor can I live without study. For this, the opportunity and the necessity will both arise from the office in Alabama.

There are reasons against my acceptance, the chief of which is, the distance from home. This, however, is not, and will not be insuperable. Could I obtain a suitable situation in Carlisle or Randolph— Macon, I should prefer it, but there is no opening that I know of. In reference to Carlisle I am yet in the dark, having heard nothing from Mr. Durbin, and not knowing for what situation he would wish my services. If you know, I should be glad to learn, in your answer to this, whether I am wanted at Carlisle (if now wanted at all) as a teacher in the Grammar School, or as an assistant in the College. A knowledge of this would be a great kindness to me. You will find inclosed a letter to Mr. Durbin ; after you read it, please seal it up and send it to him if in Philadelphia, or if not, send it immediately to Carlisle.

III.

CARLISLE, *March* 20, 1837.

DEAR FATHER :—From Mr. Durbin's communication, I have very little doubt in regard to the result of the election, and suppose, therefore, that my labors here have been satisfactory. At all events, I am conscious of having well discharged every duty devolving upon me in the office. I have been somewhat perplexed in regard to the propriety of my being ordained, and I have not pursued the Conference studies so as to pass an examination. I shall abide by the decision of the bishop—or rather, his advice in reference to the ordination. I have always had a very salutary dread of taking strong

7

vows of any kind : and especially religious vows in awkward circumstances. The ordination of local men and professors I can hardly
understand. Still I may be ignorant, and merely mention the thing
to let you know what my thoughts have been.

IV.

PHILADELPHIA, *February* 15, 1830.

The feelings evinced by your remarks upon the itinerancy, and especially upon the prospect of your own connexion with it, are such
as I cannot but approve : indeed, I sympathize in these from the bottom of my heart, for they have been all my own, both before and
(but in a far greater degree) *since* I have been laid upon the shelf as an
invalid. As to one of your principles, I have been, and still remain,
somewhat doubtful. I refer to the doctrine that it is improper for an
annual Conference to admit into the ministry any individual whose
relations to society would not be changed by the said admission.
Certainly it seems to me, that if our educational system is to he viewed
as a co-ordinate—or even subordinate—branch of our religious system, whose design is to prepare men for the reception of Gospel
truth, and to carry that truth home to their hearts—if, I say, our
educational plans are to he regarded, I can see no more difficulty in
admitting a man and permitting him to remain in college, than in
sending him to the roughest circuit in Methodism. The mere fact
of our connexion being called a *travelling* ministry does not impose
the necessity upon every one who may be admitted into it of pulling
up stakes and setting off at once, in the letter of the system, to travel.
Nor can the mere formal difference between receiving a man as a
professor, and appointing him as a professor immediately after he is
received, be of any avail. It strikes me the whole difficulty lies in the
supposition, that if a man is received into the ministry hampered by
"any such connexion," there is a contract implied, if not expressed,
that he shall always remain in such situation, and that his relation to
the Conference must never subject him to the performance of any
other duties. But certainly there is no such implication ; or if it be

supposed that there is, it can easily be guarded against by a distinct statement at the time of admission.

As for my own health, I sometimes indulge the hope that I may be again able to perform my duties at Carlisle—nay, that I may again be permitted to preach the Gospel of Jesus Christ to men. Should this be the case, I feel persuaded (though I may deceive myself, as many have done before) that the affliction which I have endured will have been a precious discipline to me, and that I shall never again be able to look with indifference upon the great work of human salvation, never again be able to preach, without an earnest previous preparation of prayer, as well as of thought. O how differently do we estimate worldly things when they appear to be receding from us; when that reality to which we must all come at last, though so few are able to appropriate it to themselves in health—the reality, namely, that we must die—is pressed upon us with all the force of immediate nearness! Such thoughts have been my almost constant companions—not, indeed, because I have been in any danger of immediate death, but because (perhaps) I have been shut out from the world and its employments, and have had leisure for that self-reflection which can be so seldom enjoyed amid the bustling labors of active life. I hope to be with you in April, *Deo volente.*

PROFESSOR EMORY.

V.

BALTIMORE, *March* 19, 1839.

DEAR ROBERT :—Let me say that your determination [to leave the college and enter the travelling ministry] creates general regret both among preachers and people, and your best friends are sorry that you should have found such a course necessary to your peace, and especially at this time. I have not heard a preacher speak upon the subject who has not thus expressed himself, and many have fears for the effect. Permit me to say, too, that your modesty alone (which I must admire, while I regret its results) could lead you to suppose your connexion with the college of small importance. I *know* that the prosperity of the school has been considerably identified with your name, and that your disconnexion from it will be of serious, though I hope only temporary, injury. I have now spoken my mind freely. In all probability the close relation that we have sustained to each other, by our connexion with the school, is now sundered for ever. I had, indeed, expected its severance ere this, but by another agency—the hand of death, whose presence I felt in my own bedchamber. But that hand seems to be lifted, and I may yet live to enter upon my duties again in September. If I shall be so permitted, it will be the only bitterness in the cup of pleasure which I shall take up when I enter upon my work, that I shall see you no more in our college halls, and commune with you no more in our college sociality. God bless you, my brother, wherever you are, and however you may be employed! If you go out, God grant you great success in the work of the ministry—and under all circumstances, though you may have many more valuable, you shall find no more sincere friend than   JOHN M'CLINTOCK, JUN.

PROFESSOR EMORY.

CHAPTER III.

1839–1847.

An Ideal Life—Carlisle and the Cumberland Valley—Rapid Progress in Study—Social Habits—Improvement of Health—Centenary of Methodism, October, 1839—Reading on Christian Perfection and the Human Will—Grief at Parting with Robert Emory—Transfer from the Chair of Mathematics to that of Ancient Classic Languages—Ordained Elder by Bishop Hedding—Illness and Death of his Mother—Recovery of his Voice and Return to the Pulpit—Characteristics and Power as a Preacher—Estimates of Carlyle and Goethe—Stability in his Opinions and Steadfast Adherence to Evangelical Doctrine—Profound Interest in the Slavery Controversy—Active Opposition to the Annexation of Texas—Letters in the *Christian Advocate* on the Duty of the Church—Publication of Greek and Latin Text-Books, and Neander's " Life of Christ"—Letters.

IT was very much an ideal life that Dr. M'Clintock led while a professor in Dickinson College. The valley in the midst of which Carlisle stands has often been compared by the imaginative to the happy vale of Rasselas. Encircled lovingly on either side by the Blue Mountain ridge, and enveloped in an atmosphere of crystal clearness, on which the play of light and shade produced every hour some new and striking effect, it was, in a measure, withdrawn from the tumult of the world. The tumult might be heard in the distance, but did not come near enough to disturb the calm of studious pursuits. The town preserved the tradition of the learned culture which has distinguished it from the beginning of the present century. Its population was not enterprising; manufacturing was but little, if at all, known to it. The rich soil of the valley poured out every year abundant harvests, and the borough was no more than the centre of exchanges, or the market for supplies. The steady pace and even pulse of agricultural life seemed here to tone down the fevered excitement which is the usual condition under which American society exists.

Helped by these favoring circumstances, the years from 1839 to 1847 were most fruitful to Professor M'Clintock as a student. The change in the former year from the chair of mathematics to that of ancient languages led him into new and congenial occupations. The pleasure of acquiring knowledge was always perhaps greater to him than the pleasure of imparting it. He used to say, jocularly, that a college would be delightful if only there were no students. He was, nevertheless, a most faithful and laborious teacher; in point of fact, his classes stimulated him and gave zest to his exertions. He had the art of connecting the work of the students with his own culture, and, if on a higher plane, was moving in the same lines with them. What he was investigating he would often give them to investigate, and so kept himself in the class-room fresh and full of vitality. During the most of this period he was free from anxious cares, and could surrender himself without interruption to his cherished studies. That was, indeed, an ideal life in which the long hours could be devoted to the exploration of the philosophy of Greek accents, the mysterious force of the particle ἄν, and all the fascinating subtleties of linguistic pursuits.

He was greatly aided by his social advantages, and made them helpful to his more serious occupations. It was not often that he could be induced to spend a whole evening in society. Time was too precious, he said, and he begrudged the surrender of so many hours. Every day he would take pains to see some friend, would beguile a half hour with pleasant chat, and then be off again to work. In such pauses from labor he would be as playful as if his life were a long holiday. Brief snatches of social enjoyment suited him better than ceremonious observances, though to these latter he gave, when required, due attention. He had the magnetism which made him a charming companion, and if he drew much from society, he also gave much to it. From the many bitter things against himself which he wrote down in his diary, he always made one reservation—that he had the capacity of loving. Wherever he might be, he would gather friends about him, and gain through them a fresh relish of existence. His sympathies were catholic, and enabled him, whenever he willed it, to touch the world at many points. He could enter quickly into the life of others, come to an understanding of it, and establish agreeable relations with them, without an unnecessary expenditure of time. His social power supplemented his talents, and contributed largely to his success.

By the opening of the college year, in September, 1839, his health was fully restored, and he entered upon his work with enthusiasm. His diary here presents the best picture of him and of his multifarious studies:—

Tues., Sept. 17. *Carlisle.* Busy day again—examining students for admission into college—all is hurly-burly, tumult and labor—but to-day will be the last of it, I hope, as recitations are assigned for to-morrow.

Fri., Sept. 27. How delightfully time glides away! My throat improves: I have constantly the gay and buoyant feeling of convalescence; can attend to all my business; study with greater ease than ever. Thank the Lord for all his mercies! Perhaps I shall yet be able to preach again; if so, Lord, prepare me for the work!

Fri., Oct. 4. Commenced Hebrew with Dr. H., yesterday, don't like him much; do not suppose him, from what I have yet seen, to understand the language philosophically.

Thurs., Oct. 24. Usual duties at college attended to. Have read lately much in Mahan's "Christian Perfection," a most excellent exposition of that Christian doctrine by a Presbyterian clergyman. My religious experience is getting deeper and wider. I have a constant sense of dependence, and gratitude such as I have seldom known. And yet I have little or no religion. God help me!

Fri., Oct. 25. The centenary of Methodism! This day a million of hearts will keep as the Sabbath! This day a million of voices will unite in singing the high praises of God in Methodist chapels! What a stupendous exhibition of moral power does the Methodism of this day exhibit!

Heard R. Emory in the morning, from "They that sow in tears shall reap in joy. He that goeth . . . sheaves with him." It was a neat, clear, and perspicuous exhibition of the rise, progress, and doctrines of Methodism. I closed the meeting after Mr. Emory with singing and prayer, being my first public church exercise! God be praised for all his goodness! J. P. Durbin preached a centenary sermon in the evening which was highly spoken of, but I did not hear him.

Sun., Oct. 27. Finished to-day reading Mahan on "Christian Perfection." Find in it much to approve, and but one or two points to condemn. The man evidently feels what he writes; there is life and energy in it; it comes warm from the heart. Certainly it has stirred me up more than any practical treatise that I have ever read, and my mind has, for some days past, been dwelling strongly on the subject on which he writes. Read also part of Fletcher's last Check which treats of this subject, and gleaned the views of Campbell and Macknight from their commentaries. How strangely meagre are Mr. Watson's remarks on this subject, both in his "Institutes" and "Dictionary"—nay, in his Exposition also. This is our twenty-fifth birthday—mine and my wife's! One quarter of a century of life gone! How little of it has been improved and fully devoted to the glory of God!

Sun., Nov. 3. A fine, beautiful Sabbath morning! Read in "Townsend" before church. At eleven heard a most clear and beautiful discourse on Psalm i from Alfred Griffith, our presiding elder, and closed the meeting after him with prayer. What occasion of thankfulness have I for the almost miraculous recovery of my throat! Blessed be the name of the Lord! In the afternoon we had a delightful season at the sacrament of the Lord's Supper, in the administration of which I assisted. Of course I could not literally "eat" the Bread; but I trust that the ordinance was blessed to my advantage notwithstanding. Would hear Mr. Durbin this evening if possible: perhaps the time will yet come when I shall not only be able to attend all the services of the sanctuary, but assist in the performance of them.

Sat., Nov. 9. Heard Junior Class in analytical geometry this morning. How beautiful is that great work, the offspring of the teeming mind of Descartes! I often think that injustice is done to Descartes in common fame. I know that all men of real knowledge and discernment allow him to have possessed mighty intellectual powers and pure moral purposes; but, mainly on account of his unfortunate speculations, distinguished although his *vortices* were as a theory which none but a mind of the most wonderful acuteness could have conceived, his name has come to be associated, in the public or vulgar estimation, with Atheists and Alchemists!

Mon., Nov. 18. Read in "Upham on the Will" and Tappan's review of "Edwards on the Will;" also an excellent article in the "American Biblical Repository" for October, on Cause and Effect, considered in Connexion with Fatalism and Free Agency, in which Edwards' doctrine of the Will is fairly and completely overthrown.

Fri., Nov. 22. Another clear, cold, windy day. Recitation in geometry unusually pleasant and interesting. I never have had more success in teaching than during the present session, thank Providence for all his goodness! My health seems steadily improving; and I am, perhaps, approaching the time when I shall rejoice in the possession of a *mens sana in corpore sano:* certainly my mind acts with more rapidity, vigor, and certainty, than it has done for years. Read the evangelist's account of Christ's triumphant entry into Jerusalem. What a close fulfilment of Zechariah's prophecy! Read in the evening the introduction to Edwards and Park's "Selections from German Literature," which is a fine production indeed; its spirit and tendency are just what they should be; too latitudinarian for a strict orthodoxy—such an orthodoxy as claims entire infallibility for human interpretations—but not too liberal for the spirit of the Gospel. Studied a good deal in Greek syntax, Æschylus, and mechanics—the doctrine of parallel forces.

Sat., Nov. 23. Heard Junior Class in analytical geometry; gave them a lecture upon the advantage of such studies in forming habits of attention, recollection, and quickness of apprehension. Took occasion, also, to enforce upon them the necessity of acquiring the power and fixing the habit of solitary thought—meditation, reflection; without which, I informed them that they could never be strong men. Read the "Prometheus Vinctus" for an hour with R. E. A sweet and noble spirit he is! I love him more and more, day after day. Afternoon, read a couple of chapters in "Cicero de Amicitia." What a spirit of beauty lives in the writings of that man!

Wed., Nov. 27. Letter from Dr. L. The Book Committee at New York decided against the expediency of publishing my "Analysis of Watson's Institutes." The blockheads doubt whether it would be useful for the young men! Wrote to Dr. L. to send it back in a package of books which I have just ordered.

Sat., Nov. 30. Read and studied a good deal to-day. Evening, Messrs. Durbin, Emory, Caldwell, Allen, and myself, met for the purpose of commencing a critical investigation of that great *crux philosophorum*—the human will. We take Upham's book on the Will for the basis—and a wretchedly written affair it is. Our meeting was interesting and profitable. I shall observe the mental characteristics of my associates as closely as possible in the course of these meetings, as I shall have an opportunity to do so.

Tues., Dec. 10. Usual duties performed. Very busy also in writing Lectures on " Differential and Integral Calculus " for my Senior Class in college. I am decidedly of the opinion that the method of infinitesimals ought to be introduced to the minds of students earlier in the mathematical course, and their minds habituated to it, so that when they come to study the very abstruse principles on which any theory of the calculus must rest, they will not have the additional disadvantage—additional, I mean, to their entering upon a very difficult path of being entirely in a new world.

Wed., Dec. 11. Pretty good health — excellent spirits. Read a good deal on the will; and after Faculty meeting in the evening the subject was discussed, in connexion with our text-book, (Upham's,) by Durbin, Caldwell, Emory, and self.

Thurs., Dec. 26. A bitter day. Parted with Robert Emory, whose connexion with Dickinson College is severed. I knew not how my heart was bound up in him. It is full now, almost to breaking; the world seems desolate. I must endeavor to turn back the tide of my love upon my own poor heart again. Rather, must I fix my affections more steadily upon "things above," not on things "on the earth." The blessing of God go with thee, my brother! my friend!

This parting from his colleague he frequently mentions as a very sore trial. They had known each other from youth. The two young men were nearly of the same age. Robert Emory had been so much associated with his father in counsel that he had attained what might be termed a precocious maturity. In the chair which he occupied in Dickinson College he had won for himself a reputation for broad and accurate scholarship, and skill as an instructor, of which any one might be proud. His mind inclined, however, to administration more than to literature. He had inherited his father's sound judgment, strong will, and great executive power, and was considered by all who knew him to be predestined to the episcopal office, which his father had adorned. A conviction that it was his duty to enter upon the active work of the ministry had decided him to relinquish his professorship. He would begin, too, at the beginning, and accepted, therefore, with all cheerfulness, though he had been offered one of the highest offices in the church, the position of a junior preacher on an old-fashioned circuit. To his chivalrous spirit the evasion of his full share of the privations and exposures of a Methodist preacher's life would have presented itself as a crime. Polished, gifted, and finely cultured as he was, the humblest details of ministerial duty had for him, through their connexion with their higher ends, a dignity which glorified them, and made their performance, in his estimation, an unceasing pleasure.

The lives of these two men were so knit together in the bonds of friendship that it is difficult to convey an adequate impression of the character of the one without some description of the character of the other. They were, after this separation, unexpectedly associated again in college life. In the year 1842, when President Durbin went abroad, Professor Emory acted as *pro-tempore* president; and in 1845, upon Dr. Durbin's resignation, he was unanimously chosen his successor. In person he was tall, and of commanding presence. His manner was instantly suggestive of large converse with the world, and familiarity with every nicety of usage. Of scholarly

shyness no trace was observable in him. Under this grace
and suavity of the man of the world there lay such a
spirit of self-abnegation as made him an example of the
highest form of Christian excellence. To lose himself continually in some object out of, and greater than, himself,
was the one law of his conduct. It was impossible to
spend an hour in his society without receiving a strong
impression of his disinterestedness. He would preach
with as much painstaking care to a handful of hearers in
a roadside school-house, as to a cultivated city congregation ; would sit down by the side of a child to teach it
a lesson in the rudiments of Christianity, or, after holding
nightly service with his people, would ride away for miles
to watch by the bedside of a sick preacher. It was in
rendering this last-named attention that he laid the
foundation of the disease which carried him prematurely
to the grave. The readiness with which he threw aside
worldly advantage for the sake of higher objects would
have seemed stoical, had it not been obvious that his
nature was pervaded by Christian sensibility.

I know that this language will be called extravagant, but
it will not appear so to the living who remember Robert ˙
Emory, and to whom I can appeal for attestation of the
accuracy of this description. Professor M'Clintock wrote
thus of him after his death : " Of all the men whom I
have yet known upon earth, he was the purest and best.
During nearly half of his earthly life I knew him, for the
last twelve years I have been in almost daily intercourse
with him ; and I never saw in him one act of guile,
never heard from him an unworthy sentence, never per-

ceived in him an unchristian temper. To be with him daily was to enjoy the most blessed of opportunities 'to mark the perfect man and to behold the upright.' "

At the opening of the year 1840 Professor M'Clintock completed the exchange, which he had for several months contemplated, of the chair of mathematics for that of the ancient classic languages. He had, as he said, some misgivings, but they did not extend beyond himself. This was soon followed by his return to the pulpit, which, with other events of this period, we will let him describe :—

Fri., *Jan.* 3, 1840. Heard first recitation in classics to-day ; Junior in "*Cicero de Officiis.*" Succeeded better than I had anticipated. Throat suffers a little ; I have some misgivings ; but, on the whole, hope predominates.

Sun., *Jan.* 5. Fine day; weather a little warmer, though still severely cold. Read "Watson," etc., preparing for recitation this afternoon. Went to church, and participated in the holy sacrament of the Lord's Supper, with some profit, I trust. Heard recitation of class in theology, and discoursed with them a little on the grounds of the argument for the Divine existence.

Sun., *Jan.* 19. Afternoon ; the subject in the theology class was the attributes of God—Unity and Spirituality. The immateriality of mind was brought in, with various kindred subjects, on which I enlarged with freedom, and, I hope, with profit, for about an hour and a half ; but my throat suffers somewhat from the effort.

Sun., *April* 19, *Burlington, N. J.* This must be a memorable day ! I was this morning ordained elder in the Methodist Episcopal Church, at Burlington, New Jersey, by that reverend and holy man of God, Bishop Hedding. The sermon was a fine specimen of a pure, excellent style of preaching ; more like Mr. Wesley's preaching than any other man's, that I can remember, in the Church. The text was, " For thus it behooved Christ," etc. The sermon was, 1. The sufferings and resurrection of Christ: (1,) their causes; (2,) their effects. 2. The duties and privileges resulting: (1,) duties, to *preach* repentance and remission of sin; and, (2,) privileges to *hear* these glorious doctrines. It was a delightful, profitable sermon—plain, practical, pointed. The solemn services affected my heart. God make me faithful, and, if it be thy will, restore me to health, that I may be enabled again to preach the unsearchable riches of Christ !

Mon., April 27, Carlisle. Left Philadelphia at six in the morning in the cars for home, with wife, sister Margaret, and my dear mother, who is remarkably emaciated and feeble. I feared the effects of the journey upon her wasted frame. We provided a mattress for her to lie upon, and spread it for her in the cars, so that she was very comfortable until we reached Lancaster, where we changed cars. However, she sat up very comfortably until the end of the journey, and seemed very little fatigued when we reached home at five P.M.

Fri., May 29. Since the last entry in this book I have seen, heard, and learned a great deal. My enjoyment of four or five days has never been so great before. On Friday, 22d, left home for Baltimore, at one o'clock P. M., in company with Professor Caldwell and his wife, in our carriage. On Sunday morning heard a very excellent discourse from Rev. W. B. Christie, on "Enter ye in at the strait gate." His voice is very poor, his enunciation indistinct, but the sermon was good, and calculated to be useful. In the evening, at Rev. Mr. Duncan's church, heard a discourse of the very first order of excellence, from Rev. Robert Newton, of England, on "Pray without ceasing." I was pleased, nay, delighted, and abundantly edified. It was, in my judgment, a perfect sermon : clear, perspicuous, simple, forcible—full of the spirit of religion—the love of Christ. His voice has greater richness and compass than any that I ever listened to; it is, indeed, almost superhuman. Although he is no orator, in the proper sense of the word, he is yet a most admirable preacher.

Sun., May 31. A day of great mercies and great enjoyment. Heard President D., in the morning, on " None of these things move me," etc. A very fine sermon. I closed the meeting with much enlargement. At night T. Bowman preached, and I ventured to exhort after sermon. Talked nearly fifteen minutes, and then read hymn, and prayed with very little difficulty. God be praised! Perhaps I shall yet preach again.

Sun., June 21. A great day! For the first time since August, 1838, I tried to preach to-day in the Methodist Episcopal Church. Preached an hour and ten minutes on Prov. xx, 6, and found myself little or no worse after the effort. *Laus Deo!* Afternoon I heard a stirring sermon, and one very appropriate to the circumstances, from H. Slicer, in the Market House.

Fri., June 26. Mother's health continuing to fail, it was thought ·best, both by herself and father, for her to be removed to the family home. It was sad, indeed, to make arrangements for my revered and beloved mother to leave my home to die! Cousin B. came up from Philadelphia on Wednesday, as father could not leave his office, and it was decided that we should leave on Thursday morning. Accordingly, at half past ten o'clock we conveyed mother, then very weak, in the carriage to the hotel, where she remained until the cars came at eleven, when we all started for Lancaster. Mother endured the fatigue of travel much better than I expected. We made her comfortable by spreading a bed for her in the cars, on which she reposed until we reached Lancaster, at half past four P. M. She seemed better in the evening than when we left home in the morning. I remained at Lancaster with them all night, and then left my dear mother, much affected at parting with me, at half past four o'clock this morning, and reached home at noon. I am all anxiety to hear how she fared during the rest of the journey to Philadelphia.

Sat., July 4. Left home in the cars at half past four A. M., and after a very tedious, uneasy, nervous kind of ride, reached Philadelphia at three P. M., and my mother's bedside at half past three. Found her still alive and sensible. She attempted to kiss me and to press my hand—said that she knew me, and, in answer to a question, feebly pronounced my name, "John." It was the last word she uttered. She lay in a quiet slumber; her respiration became more and more feeble, until finally, at seven P. M., her gentle spirit took its flight.

There was no pain, no struggle, no uneasiness; but peacefully and quietly she left the world. Her mind was as calm and tranquil during her death-scene as it had been during her whole sickness. No shadow of apprehension ever crossed her mind; no uneasiness in regard to the future; the fear of death was entirely removed. My noble mother! my blessed mother! I can hardly realize that thou art gone—that I shall never again hear thy voice of love, or behold thy face of beauty!

Sun., July 12. On Wednesday I left Philadelphia at six A. M., and reached Carlisle at five P. M. Heard Professor Allen deliver his most excellent Baccalaureate address in the evening. Thursday, Commencement, the best we ever had. Yesterday, went with Bishop Waugh and others to the mountain. To-day, heard the bishop preach two excellent sermons—morning and evening—and Brother J. A. Massey at the Court House in the afternoon.

Tues., Sept. 8. Have not written for a month in my Journal. Busily engaged in arranging garden, grounds, etc., in moving books to College, and have spent many days in active exercise; consequently am rapidly gaining health and strength.

Tues., Oct. 27. Twenty-sixth birthday of wife and self. Health good; worldly affairs prosperous; doing something, I trust, for posterity. What vicissitudes! Two years ago this day I thought my work was done!

Thurs., Dec. 31. The last day of the year! I have been reviewing its course—it has been a wonderful year indeed to me! My health has been restored beyond my hopes, and I am now able to work for my Master. I have committed my blessed mother to the grave—her image has been with me much of late. She was indeed a noble woman! And now she is in heaven!

Sun., Jan. 3, 1841. Preached this morning on John xii, 25, for an hour and twenty minutes, with great good feeling and manifest impression on the congregation. I have preached now six times within a month; besides very frequent attendance at night meetings. Hardly a sermon that I have preached of late but has been blessed to the building up of the Church, or to the conviction and conversion

8

of souls.   The Lord be praised !   The Lord prepare and fit me for more abundant usefulness, and place me wherever, in his divine providence, I can be most useful !

Very noticeable is the joy which the recovery of the use of his voice and his return to the pulpit gave to Professor M'Clintock.   His experience of suffering, and his abundant reading during his illness, had added greatly to his resources as a preacher.   His sermons from this period on were both richer in their substance, and more highly charged with feeling.   He had at all times been perspicuous and scriptural, but his pulpit discourses were now full of impassioned eloquence.   In his preparation he aimed, first, at a sound exposition of the passage in hand.   Nothing loose or uncertain here would satisfy him.   What in the Old or New Testament was not clear to his mind he laid aside.   It was his habit to present the lesson he would enforce in the fewest and simplest words.   The results of his wide and various reading appeared in statements of such lucidity that any one of ordinary intelligence could comprehend them.   The parade of erudition he heartily despised, and for stilted rhetoric he had a supreme contempt.   He had an equal dislike of startling propositions which would prove, on examination, to be but half true, and never indulged in them.   Yet, on the other hand, he did not commit the error of throwing down before his hearers masses of truth in an awkward and helpless fashion.   Grace controlled his manner and shaped his matter.   He had the true artistic sense, and was studious of perfection in form.   As the discussion proceeded from point to point, his voice developed its richness, his feelings kindled, and communicated their excitement to his audience.   Passages of highly-wrought but chastened rhetoric would awaken momentary attention, but would soon be lost in the flow of his rapid utterance.   His congregation followed his discourse with the keen satisfaction which comes of the gaining of a clearer knowledge of truth, and a healthful quickening of their best impulses.   Throughout all, the one chief object of preaching—the winning of men to Christ—was never for a moment left out of sight.   He considered no sermon worth attention of which Christ was not the Alpha and the Omega—the beginning and the end.

On the platform Professor M'Clintock was as effective as in the pulpit ; and he was always in demand for important occasions, when the claims of the great charities of the Church were to be advocated.   His preparation for these addresses was just as careful as for his sermons. As a result, they were remarkable for their freshness and power.   I remember when, on one occasion, he had so trite a theme as " Home Missions," he invested it with a new interest by an elaborate description of the breadth and magnificence of the land which we Americans call our home.   He saw facts and events in their large relations, and interpreted their meaning with unusual sagacity, so that when he stood upon the platform he was able to lift his hearers up to broader views than it was their habit to take, and to kindle in them an enthusiasm for great Christian enterprises.

His growing popularity as a preacher brought him

numerous invitations for special services. During two of his long vacations he made, in company with his friends, S. S. and S. A. Roszell, extensive tours in the valley of Virginia, where he addressed the people at their camp-meetings, and made friends, of whose unbounded hospitality he speaks with the greatest admiration. His appearances in the Methodist pulpits of Baltimore, Philadelphia, and New York were frequent, and extended his reputation as an orator. He was in demand, also, as a lecturer; but the lecture system was not then organized, and lecturing, therefore, received but a small share of his attention. Through all these various activities he was continually becoming better and better known as a growing man, and was making himself a centre of interest and hope.

His Diary is here again the best record of his studies and his inner life :—

Thurs., July 29. My mind has been calm, easy, and happy for some days. Clouds that have surrounded it have broken away, and I look into the future with brighter anticipations than I have indulged for a long time. My faith is strong. I am determined, by God's help, that it shall never be weakened. To do nothing wrong is my settled maxim. May I only fulfil it as earnestly as I resolve it, and then I can look up to my heavenly Father without fear, trusting in his mercy through Christ Jesus !—Letter from R. E. His mind is yet unsettled about coming here. He does not see the line of duty distinctly. God strengthen his vision ! I wish he had my eyes for a little while as spectacles.

Fri., Dec. 3. Read Carlyle's "Review of Taylor's Historic Survey of German Poetry," in the third volume of his "Miscellanies." Continued reading Carlyle's "Miscellanies." A few great thoughts are continually struggling for expression in all his writings ; he sees them through all mediums. Whatever he begins with, these always come up—*toujours perdrix*—so it ought to be: at last they will come out and make themselves heard among men.

Sun., Feb. 13, 1842. Read "Garrettson's Life" and Carlyle's "Characteristics"—the latter through. A powerful but perplexing essay—troubles me a good deal.

Wed., March 29. R. Emory will be with us next week, and will remain a year as acting president of college. *Laus Deo!*

Wed., Nov. 16. Pursuing study of German, Hebrew, etc., which, with college duties, keep me occupied about thirteen hours out of the twenty-four, so that I have little time to give to friends, etc. My health is tolerably good, but yet I find that my close confinement operates injuriously. Glanced hastily over Dickens's "Notes on America." He is in the wrong box this time. Strange that a man should risk so much for the sake of making a little money. To run over a great continent in six months, and then write and publish a book upon its people and institutions in three more—what greater folly could he be guilty of?

Dec. 25. Another Christmas day! Each year is shorter than the last! Preached this morning from Matt. ii, 2, with brief and imperfect preparation; of course it was not a very successful sermon. I am more than ever convinced of the necessity of careful preparation for the pulpit. Since the last entry I have been more or less unwell, and for an entire week unable to do duty in college. Am now better, and hope to improve greatly during the short vacation. Studied hard and well during the session in Greek, Latin, German, and Hebrew. Read most of Lord Bacon's Works; Carlyle's "Sartor Resartus;" Wigger's "History of Pelagianism and Augustinism;" Goethe's "Wilhelm Meister;" Whately's "Kingdom of Christ;" many of Carlyle's "Essays" again; Macaulay's "Miscellanies," do.; with all the reviews, etc. My moral being is in a strange way. Some points of good are very strongly developed in my character, and some weaknesses seem invincible. The best thing about me is, the capacity of loving. I *love*, and I am happy in loving. No man has more to be thankful for—friends and friendship—than I.

Dec. 31. Last day of the week, month, year. Gone, gone—forever gone! What a host of sins of mine have gone with those hours! Am I wiser than I was a year ago? More learned I certainly am—but am I any *wiser* for the learning? I fear not.

Though his review of the year is so critical and self-depreciating, his life at this time was really full of joy. To the satisfaction of increasing his scholarly acquisitions was added a boundless domestic contentment. His letters to his intimate friends overflow with high spirits; this one, for example, written near the end of December to his wife's parents, has nothing sombre in it :—

CARLISLE, Dec. 21, 1841.

The few remarks that I have to offer on this occasion may be presented under four heads :—1. My head; 2. Caroline's; 3. Emory's; 4. Margaret's. (By the way, Emory's ought only to have been an *inference*, and not a separate head.) As to the first head, my friends, it is as large as ever and better filled—adding to its furniture every day. Externally it has not as large a covering of hair as it once had, but it still has a sufficiency. As to the second head, which is closely connected with the first, and derives most of its importance therefrom—but if you should therefore suppose, my friends, that the second head is in any wise unimportant, you would err most grievously, from it emanate all orders for the refection of our inward man; it, and it alone, can declare whether the morrow's breakfast will, or will not, be enlivened with coffee and buckwheat cakes. The head is a good one, and works harmoniously and happily with the first. It has a good share of energy and activity—fruitful in expedients, firm in recollection, keen in judgment. But, my friends, I fear I am becoming tedious. Let us pass now to the third and most interesting head, perhaps, to be treated of this evening. Outwardly, at least, it is much more seemly than either of the others : adorned with two brilliant, sparkling eyes of jet, with two rows of shining teeth, cheeks like the south side of a peach, and other ornaments to match.

Inwardly, we can hardly say yet, my friends, what it is.' But, judging of it as an *inference* from the first and second heads, which we are fairly entitled to do, we can fearlessly predict that it will, hereafter, be a wonder to country bumpkins why it don't burst—so full of learning. *On the great whole*, this head gives some surprising demonstrations. Therefore, leaving this head upon its crib pillow, let us pass to the fourth, which is also at this juncture lying in the "arms of Murphy!" On this head, my dear friends, it is not necessary to dilate at length—it is getting to be quite *domestic* since Mr. Taylor, the school lecturer, called heads *domes* of thought. This head had like to have got broken by a tumble on the ice to-day, but fortunately escaped, and is now presented for your edification. By way of application, friends, and not as a distinct head, Maria may be mentioned. We say, not as a distinct head, for there is no distinctness about her to-day, *consekens* of having a big tooth pulled out, and she is *applying* herself diligently to all curative measures.

And now, friends, take heed to your ways—ours here are very slippery since last night's sleet, so we walk in the street, to keep us from falling, upon the ice sprawling. And therefore we go, all gently and slow, from home to the college, to distribute knowledge; and backward with speed, to get our own feed. So we live daily, sprightly and gayly, merry and free. Fare ye well. J. M'C.

Professor M'Clintock began the year 1843 with the same energy as marked the close of 1842. He entered fully into the meaning of Goethe's aphorism, that "the day is long to him who knows how to use it." Some illustrations which I place here will show the manner in which every hour was utilized; they are not by any means exceptional, but represent his habit of working:—

Wed., Jan. 4, 1843. Rose at quarter before seven: seven to eight, recited in Sallust; eight to nine, breakfast, etc.; nine to ten, Prom. Vinc. Read Mackenzie's account of the mutiny on board his ship, the "Somers," which resulted in the hanging of Spencer, son of the Secretary of War, and his two associates ; think he acted like a true man : ten to eleven, "Medea ; " eleven to twelve, *Cic. de Oratore* ; half past twelve, studied Greek, etc. Dinner, etc., until quarter before two; talked over Wordsworth until half past two : half past two to five, read " Review of Watson's Institutes," in *Christian Spectator*, and various articles in the " Foreign Quarterly Review." Am studying the character of Goethe—a strange mystery—but begin to have a clew that may lead me out of the labyrinth. Night, read an article on Merck's correspondence in " Foreign Quarterly" for July, 1836. Poor Merck ! Goethe is there presented in some rather unlovely aspects. But what a soul was Herder's ! and what a heart was Wieland's !

Thurs., Jan. 5. Rose quarter before seven : seven to eight, Sallust ; eight to nine, breakfast, etc.; nine to ten, read, studied Greek, etc.; ten to eleven, recited " Medea ; " eleven to twelve, read articles on Greek history, etc., in Blackwood, volume forty-nine ; twelve to half past one, dinner, etc.; half past one to half past two, P. O. A——'s Lat. Recit., etc. Continued reading of " The Excursion." What power ! What purity ! What simplicity ! What elevation ! What a contrast to Goethe — cold, selfish, immovable statue that he was. Each had equanimity, but how different : the one, the equanimity of Apollo ; the other, of Apollo Belvidere !

Fri., Jan. 6. Finished Austin's " Recollections of Goethe." More and more astonishment ; hardly less mystery than ever. Evidently there was great susceptibility of all feelings about him, and he de- termined to control it—succeeding by the force of an irresistible and overpowering will. Finished Prophet Hosea—can make nothing satisfactory out of him. Great vision before me, caused by filling my mind up with Goethe ! Let me imitate him in steady persever- ance, devotion to culture, and independence, and I shall do well— *nach meinen art.*

The references in the Diary to Carlyle show how deeply he was stirred by that eccentric, but most stimu- lating thinker. The cool estimate of Goethe, just cited,

was made soon after he came under the spell of the
mighty magician.   It will naturally be asked whether
there was, in the history of Professor M'Clintock's mind,
as the result of his contact with views of life, the
world and God so unlike his own, a period of unsettled
opinion.   Did he pass through a crisis of doubt, of distrust of all he had once viewed as spiritually true, and
end by framing for himself a new system of faith?   If
he experienced such a crisis he never spoke of it; he
never surrendered his hearty trust in the evangelical
creed to which he had committed himself in early life.
He had no occasion to take down his theological opinions
once a month and label them with fresh valuations.   His
brain was strong and steady; if he read in all directions,
and gave hospitable reception to the thoughts of all thinking men, he stood firmly on his own ground.   His analytical faculty was here of great service to him; he was
quick to detect a fallacy, and was not easily misled by a
specious proposition.   That he meditated much on the
problems which vex the human soul, his reading shows
plainly enough.   He was one of the first of Americans
to furnish our country a full exposition of the Positive
Philosophy, was a correspondent of Auguste Comte, its
founder, but was never so dazzled by any philosophical
scheme as to lose the vision of "the master light of all
our seeing," Jesus Christ.

He was fortunate in having come early under the influence of Coleridge, and had learned from him the recon-
ciliation of spiritual life and philosophy.   He loved to
quote to the young men who were interested in theol-

ogy the sentence with which Coleridge completes his literary biography, "that the scheme of Christianity, though not discernible by human reason, is yet in accordance with it; that link follows link by necessary consequence; that religion passes out of the ken of reason, only where the eye of reason has reached its own horizon, and that faith is then but its continuation." He always insisted that a simple, childlike faith is compatible with the largest knowledge, and that the Christian consciousness is frequently the best solvent of doubt. I find neither in his diary nor in his letters any such record of mental anguish as gives a melancholy interest to the life of Frederick W. Robertson. No great convulsion wrenched him from his old foundations; he remained securely in them, and built upon them to the end of his days.

From the time of his contact with Neander, however, there was noticeable a quickening of his confidence in those spiritual truths to which he always firmly held. In connexion with Professor Charles E. Blumenthal, he presented "Neander's Life of Christ" in English dress to the American public. The translation led to a correspondence, and finally to a personal intercourse with the great Church historian in the city of Berlin, where Professor M'Clintock was met with a cordiality and tenderness which touched him very sensibly. He found in Neander German learning, coming, after traveling a wide circuit, to the position taken by Wesley, that Christianity is more than all else a life—that it is "a power which, as it is exalted above all that human nature can create out of its own resources, must change it from its inmost centre."* Neander was the pupil of Schleiermacher, who had in early life been educated among the Moravians. What the Wesleys, and through them the English-speaking races, owed to Moravianism, is well understood: may we not trace to the same fountain the stream of Christian teaching which has done so much to quicken spiritual life on the continent of Europe?

The subject of our memoir watched the antislavery controversy with deep solicitude, and interpreted with clearest insight all its meaning. The slave system excited in him intense abhorrence; yet he discriminated between the system itself and the many who were, without fault of their own, helplessly involved in it. He saw the full import of the annexation of Texas as a slave State, and excited himself to the utmost to resist its admission to the Union. He dreaded the consequences which were certain to follow the consummation of such an unrighteous measure. For this reason he scanned with anxiety the prospects of the presidential election of 1844, which followed so soon after our stormy General Conference of that year. To his brother-in-law, Mr. E. B. Wakeman, of Jersey City, he writes: "I shall strain every nerve to rebuke this abominable Texas iniquity with pen and tongue. The days of the Republic are numbered, and of right ought to be, if by its means slavery is extended one inch, or prolonged in its wretched existence one hour." He is so full of this subject that he recurs to it repeatedly: "I am no aspirant," he writes to the same correspondent, "for the honors of the Republic, and may,

* Introduction to "Neander's General Church History.'

therefore, do what my conscience bids, without any care for the smiles or the frowns of the sovereign people. I am resolved that, hereafter, as far as my influence extends, people shall not be left in the dark on this system of slavery. No fear of running heads against the wall either. There are walls in the way of those who abstain from doing right, as well as of those who lead mankind into good paths." He writes again: "After all, I feel it in my bones that I shall devote a good part of my life to this great evil."

By arrangement with Dr. Bond, he prepared, early in 1847, a series of articles for the "Christian Advocate," in which he sought to animate the Church to a more positive exercise of its power for the extirpation of slavery. In opening the discussion he modestly confesses that he had before refrained from it because of a distrust of his capacity to meddle with so grave and difficult a question, and his lack of the advantages of experience and age. "I am now inclined," he adds, "to doubt the validity of these reasons. I begin to feel, as a good man in another hemisphere once expressed himself, that 'it is certain I shall die, and I *may* die to-day; but it is not certain that I shall ever be old.' My testimony may be of little worth to others, but it is essential to my own peace of mind that it should be delivered." He acknowledges that the great increase of antislavery feeling in the free States had been effected by the abolitionists, and while passing criticism upon their work, as it then appeared to him, pays a hearty tribute to "the energy, the almost reckless daring, the unflagging perseverance," they had shown. Yet he does not rank himself among them, for he adds, "I never could be an abolitionist proper, for I never could believe (and never shall, so long as facts that now exist remain) that *all* slaveholders are sinners, and should be cut off from the fellowship of Christianity." These were not extreme positions, but they represented the convictions of a mind that honestly sought the truth, and aimed to be just to all men. His sincerity was, soon after the publication of these essays, demonstrated by his incurring the risk of fine and imprisonment through his strenuous exertions to help the slave. If on so grave a theme he formed his opinions cautiously, he was ready when the time came to jeopard all he held dear for their sake.

But this is anticipating the narrative somewhat. In the year 1845 Professor M'Clintock and the writer united in the preparation of a series of Latin and Greek elementary books on the method of "Imitation and Repetition." These joint labors gave me the opportunity of a close intercourse with my associate, for it was our habit for months to spend the evenings together from an early hour often till midnight. The old method of teaching a language by filling the memory first with all its forms had been discarded in the case of the modern tongues, and a combination of analysis with synthesis substituted. Under the new system, practice in the use of each form went along with its presentation. It had at that time been already applied in England to the Latin and Greek; the series which was published under our joint names was, if I mistake not, the first of the kind in the United

States. The books found a ready acceptance; their plan has since become universal; and, though thirty years have elapsed since the appearance of the first volume, they still retain an honorable position in the schools.

While this undertaking was in progress, Professor M'Clintock, in connexion with Professor Blumenthal, prepared for the press, as already stated, during the years 1846 and 1847, a translation of Neander's "Life of Christ." The well-executed English edition of Strauss's "Life of Jesus" had already appeared in London and was finding readers on this side of the Atlantic. Neander's work, which, though not in form, was, in fact, a reply, had the merit of breadth of view, and an extraordinary sagacity in the interpretation of the Gospel record. He differed from Strauss, as a great lawyer who rests his case upon universal principles differs from a pettifogging attorney. The appearance of this "Life" in English dress took Neander by surprise, and he almost deprecated the transfer to America of the strifes of German theology. In an address to his Christian brethren of the United States he expresses, with a simplicity and sweetness which are very beautiful, the fear that his book may lead some who read it into trials of their faith which they are not able to bear, and may awaken questionings which it will fail to answer. A condensed history of the rationalistic and mythical schools of Scripture interpretation was prefixed by Dr. M'Clintock, which placed the reader in a position to understand the exact state of the whole controversy.

LETTERS FROM JUNE, 1840, TO MARCH, 1847.

I.

CARLISLE, *June* 23, 1840.

DEAR ROBERT:—Your whole establishment is now broken up here, root and branch, and the name of Emory is no longer among the names of Carlisle. The example is a bad one—at least the disease is catching, for Mrs. M'C. and myself are both getting full of the notion of trying the itinerancy again, especially since my effort of last Sunday, which went far beyond my own expectations. I preached for an hour and ten minutes, with but little inconvenience at the time, and no ill effect since, except a trifling dryness of the throat. The mercy of God is indeed greater to me than I had hoped ; and I begin now to cherish a pretty sanguine expectation that I shall yet again be able to preach regularly, as of old. My sensations on commencing to preach were not a little strange. I had laid aside my commission, closed my accounts, and thought my work was done ; it was like beginning a new life. God be praised for all his goodness !

Professor EMORY.

II.

MONDAY, *January* 24, 1841.

DEAR ROBERT:—I do not believe a word of Macaulay's doctrine that the times make the man. Did they make Shakspeare, or Milton, or Goethe ? His whole doctrine of poetry being only an imitative art, and therefore finding its most congenial soil in an uncultivated age, seems to me to be contradicted by all experience. The reasoning that is brought to sustain it is *à priori*, and one chapter of facts destroys it. Man talks figuratively, it is true, in early periods, but that is a very different thing from making poetry. To say that striking, physical images make more impression upon a rude people than upon a cultivated race is one thing ; to say that true poetry is, therefore, more likely to exist among the former is quite another. There is no logical connexion in the argument, and, as I have said, it seems to me that the facts are all the other way. I cannot believe that a man must be half a savage or a maniac before he can be all a poet. Macaulay talks of poetry in that essay and elsewhere as if its very trade were deception—that it has no business with reality, and that to enjoy its delights one must surrender his mind to the delusions of fiction ; whereas its object—more decidedly, perhaps, than we can say of any other branch of literature—is to preserve and teach the highest truth. But I must not run on with this trash. I have got into the strain of my recent lecture on " Love of Truth," and shall expend a good deal of it on you if I do not haul off.

I see that I have run against a snag in the last part of your Christmas letter : " Is it desirable to have the feelings of a child with the body and the mind of a man ? " Do you recollect the opening lines of Wordsworth's poem, which contain the germ of his whole doctrine of human life—" My heart leaps up when I behold ? " etc. Just look at them. Then read his magnificent ode on " Intimations of Immortality from the Recollections of Childhood "—" Shades of the prison-house close about " us all only too soon. Says Coleridge, " To carry on the feelings of childhood into the power of manhood ; to combine the child's sense of wonder and novelty with the appearances which every day, for perhaps forty years, had rendered familiar—

" ' With sun and moon and stars throughout the year,
And man and woman '—

this is the character and privilege of genius." Is it not desirable, then, if Coleridge be right ?

The " Quarterly "—I am happy to find that my share in it meets with considerable approbation. The article has had an unusual share even of Methodist laudation. Was I just in criticising your style ? Was it too harsh to say that it is not *elegant ?* Sometimes I think it was not best for me to have said so ; but I think it true on the whole. What think you ? It seems to me you do not write enough, and do not labor sufficiently to polish what you do write. Is it true ? If not, correct me ; if it is, *mend.* Dear Robert, it seems to me that the Church can do only one thing in regard to so heinous a crime as slavery, namely, to bear her testimony against it, and use all her influence for its extirpation. Is it not so? And will not God's curse come upon us if, either directly or indirectly, we sanction slavery? A little more folly on the part of the South, such as the unlawful, abominable treatment of Mr. Torrey at Annapolis, will make the North abolitionist throughout. We have tampered with the evil too long already. Our Church has been quoted in favor of slavery, I fear with too much truth. The first thing to be done is to be honest and God will take care of us. The expediency will follow. Give me your views of the doings of the convention and of Torrey's arrest.

My health is improving, but I am absolutely overpowered with work. I trust you will be with us in April. My heart yearns for your coming. I pray that Providence may open the way fully, and that you may come. I long to be comforted by your presence and strengthened by your faith. I long for the face of a friend into whose eyes I can look and see no darkness. I think I have told you before that your only fault is, in my mind, that you have not affection enough; but I trust, if you come here, to make you love me to my heart's content, even on the principle of gratitude. God grant that you may come!

Professor EMORY.

III.

A CONFESSION OF FAITH.

CARLISLE, *February*, 1841.

I believe and therefore speak. So said St. Paul, and so say I. Don't ask me what I know, for I know nothing that is not grounded at bottom upon a simple act of belief. The man who talks about understanding his nature or his destiny may be very wise, but either he or I must be a madman. Your letter shows no feelings or thoughts, I believe, that have not formed part of my own experience. You need not think you are alone in such things. They form no part of my present existence. Why? Because I have reasoned myself out of them? Nay, I should have reasoned myself into Bedlam first, but because I have rested myself in simple trust—so simple that any child might exercise it, yet so profound that all philosophy cannot fathom

9

it—upon the Great Divine Man, the pattern of purity and sorrow, Jesus Christ, the only perfect being of whom I have heard in the whole history of the world. I have no other secret to impart. I believe in Jesus Christ. Am I tempted? so was he; I resist, and there is no sin. I have I suffered? so has he, who glorified sorrow in his life and death. Pain is not evil, pleasure is not good; faith alone is good, and sin, or unbelief, alone is evil. Such is my simple creed; all the universe could not drive me from it. All bastard philosophy (and God knows I have pestered my brains with it as much as most men) cannot shake it. No temptation can overturn it, or overcome me so long as I abide in it. Do you ask whether this belief has saved me? It has. How? All I know about it is expressed in these words: it is the power of God unto salvation for all them that believe. That is all I know about it. How do I know that I am saved, then? Why, thus: If I relax this faith an hour, the universe becomes a shoreless, crazy whirlpool, and my brain runs giddy as I·look into it. Look into it I must, for I am in the midst of it. But with this faith that universe is for me a firm, rock-built city—a dwelling for my soul. All the discords, dissonances, the mad storm of human voices, the angry curses of guilty men, the inarticulate wail of wide-spread anguish, the noise of wars and murders; think you that I have no ear to hear these things? I do hear them, and I feel that they would drive me mad almost if I did not believe. The image of Christ rises up before me, pure, perfect, mild, serene, sorrowful, yet with power beyond all else that I can conceive. It is the image of God. My salvation beams from those gentle eyes; it is spoken from every lineament of that placid countenance. Look upon him, my brother, and see how mildly and kindly, with sweet tones, sad yet earnest, he asks you to give over your vain strivings and rest in him. Look upon him and you are saved.

Some people think religion is a kind of bargain-and-sale business, a barter of so much happiness in this life for so much in the next; a mere working for wages, not deep, inward, heart-subduing reverence, but a low, sordid hope of advantage or fear of pain. And yet they recognise Christ as the model of religion. Just think for a moment how widely different all this is from his character, and you will see how deeply they have sunk below the purity of his faith. What advantage did Christ look for? What could he look for? What pain had he not to fear? I tell you honestly that I see but little of the faith of which I speak among men. Many substitute the vulgar motives to which I have just alluded in its stead. Many have their paltry souls crammed full of cant and hypocrisy. What of all this? I know that I believe; I know that my religion is not cant. I am determined to be honest for myself; I believe and therefore speak. So much I had written when I received yours of yesterday. I have not time to add more without losing the mail. Read that beautiful parting address of Christ contained in the fourteenth, fifteenth, and sixteenth chapters of John. Recollect his words recorded in Matt. xi, 28: "Come unto me, all ye that labor and are heavy laden, and I will give you rest." Nowhere else can rest be obtained. Take those sweet words to your heart in simple confidence and all will be well. I shall write again to-night or in the morning. My mind is cleared, my heart is freed, not because I am free from care—I am full of it—but because I believe. God bless you! and may your mind be set free when you read these lines. Believe and it shall be done to you. You will find in the end, as I have found, in the language of the French philosopher, Cousin, that Christianity is the perfection of reason.

Mr. R. B. M'CLINTOCK.

IV.

"Faculty meeting, Wednesday night, March 2, 1842: Resolved, that Rev. Robert Emory be requested to deliver the Baccalaureate Address to the graduating class at the ensuing Commencement."

CARLISLE, *March* 5, 1842.

DEAR ROBERT :—The prime object of this letter is to request your compliance with the above resolution. Professor Caldwell is unable to perform the duty, and the faculty unanimously and earnestly desire you to do it. Please signify your assent at your earliest convenience. You have not yet answered my last letter. I

see that some of the obnoxious slavery laws have passed your House
of Delegates, but have not learned yet whether they have gone through
the Senate.   In the order of Providence all this will doubtless issue
in good.   One good thing it will do ; bring out the real proslavery
men of Maryland so that the world can see their position.   And the
world will drive them from it.   It seems to me that the doom of
slavery is sealed.   A great apostle of liberty ought to rise up, doubtless will rise up, in the country, and immortalize himself as the leader
of this great work.   Who shall he be ?   Is there danger of much excitement in your city or State on the subject ?   If any proceedings of
interest occur, please send me the newspapers that may publish them,
as I get none from Baltimore.

I was preparing an article on Prometheus for the April number of
the " Quarterly," but have given it up, finding that I cannot make it
suitable for the journal without detracting from its literary character
to too great an extent.   I purpose now preparing one on the " Methodist Itinerancy," to show what it is, and what conservative, evil, and
destructive elements enter into its composition.   Do not all machiner-
ies contain within themselves the seeds of dissolution ?   Or, to make
the figure better, will not all machines wear out in time ?   Have not
all such worn out in the history of the race ?   What one has been permanent ?   Is our itinerancy mechanical, and therefore self-destructive ?
Or is it a providential institution—spiritual—and therefore endowed
with life ?   I now incline rather to the former opinion, but know not
what issue my study of the subject may lead to.   How does your life
of Asbury get on ?   I suppose this slavery affair is occupying attention.   If you can come at Carlyle's " Essays," read, in volume four,
the review of " Walter Scott's Life," and of Varnhagen von Ense's
" Memories," for some strange views on the subject of biography ;
also volume three, the essays on " Biography " and on Boswell's
" Johnson."   If you have not read them, do so before you write more
of your biography.   The man is a wonderful thinker, honest withal,
as few review writers are ; indeed, any other writers in these times.
You will find more gold in him than in Macaulay.   This last seems
to me always to write as a partisan—no matter what the subject may

be—his erudition is greater than his judgment or taste. But he is unquestionably one of the strongest writers of the age—not, however, a philosopher.

Professor EMORY.

V.

JERSEY CITY, *August* 18, 1843.

Now for letter. They were much disappointed in not seeing you at Middletown. Professor Lane and his wife entertained us during our stay there. We had invitations to dinner and tea more than we could dispose of during our stay. Indeed, the hospitality of the friends at M. was unbounded. Our visit was as pleasant as we ever had anywhere. Dr. Bond's speech came off on Tuesday night to a fine audience. Emory's oration was the best thing I have ever heard from him, and gave universal satisfaction. Everybody was delighted. Olin came with us to New York, and he, Dr. Peck, and I, went in company to Wilkesbarre. I do not think I was ever so much taken with a man as with Dr. O. His mind is of a high order, well cultivated, and furnished with various knowledge. His extensive travels have freed him from local prejudices and narrow views. He is deeply pious, but entirely destitute of cant. His manner is free and his affections ardent, and he makes no kind of attempt to conceal them. Playful to a remarkable extent, and fond of fun and pleasantry as even I myself, he never violates propriety or loses real dignity. Of what is commonly considered dignity he is utterly destitute. I was with him day and night for better than· a week, and found him all that I have stated above, and more too. We reached Wilkesbarre on Thursday night, and found Conference in full tide. The time was so taken up that I can hardly give you any account of it. Our old friends there all treated me with the greatest kindness, and asked a great deal about you. Dr. Olin preached on Sunday morning to an immense audience, and with great effect. I never knew any man combine such powerful feelings with clear judgment and sound sense. He becomes intensely excited, and his physical frame, from the top of his head to his toes, sympathizes with the excitement. He is no orator, but remarkably eloquent. We left

Wilkesbarre on Tuesday, went through the most romantic regions I ever saw to Mauch Chunk, Tamaqua, and Reading, and reached Philadelphia on Wednesday at one o'clock.

When will you return? We expect to leave here next Thursday or Friday for Philadelphia, stay there a week, and then back to Carlisle again. Indeed, we are getting anxious to see the valley and our old friends again once more. And then we shall have Dr. Durbin along with us too, full of information, talk, and pleasant incident. I hope you have enjoyed yourselves highly, and that your health is very much improved by your trip.

Professor M. CALDWELL.

VI.

CARLISLE, *October* 31, 1844.

DEAR DR.:—Yours of the 28th was brought to me last night as I lay in bed, and although I was in much pain of body, it really made me forget my ailments, for awhile at least. I feel better to-day, and have got out of bed mainly to write this letter. Your severe introduction is meant as a facetious way of excusing yourself, I suppose, for not answering my last epistle. Perhaps, however, you never received it. Of one thing you may be assured, that I wrote you a long letter in reply to your last, and have since heard nothing from you until last night. I have been working pretty hard, but not at any thing which will bring me either honor or reputation, at least for awhile. My time is principally taken up with a species of literary labor which I don't fancy much, but which brings me in money, a thing that I am now very much in need of. Misfortunes of friends have stripped me pretty bare, and I must, at least for a time, work for money only. I trust the degrading necessity will soon be removed. You see that we all have our embarrassments. You, it appears, must drudge for money to put the University on its legs; and I, to pay other people's debts. After all, if good is done, it is, perhaps, as well. I trust your plans will all be successfully accomplished.

The University must be sustained! But it is a great pity that it was not originally placed on the North River, and our establishment never started at all. At present, I believe, we are on a better footing than you in money matters, and in all other respects at least equal; but then neither of us is any thing. As for Church matters, we don't all think alike here. I deprecated the publication of ——'s article. It smacks too much of policy for my taste: the same shallow expediency which (*pace* your vote) displayed itself so painfully in the action of the late General Conference. People can see through all this. The South will accept no such compromise, and it is only treasuring up for ourselves, as you say, trouble for the future to agitate such projects. I have restrained myself from writing on the subject with much difficulty; but it is best. We do not believe here that any compromise will be effected. The South will go off. If I see any danger of a compromise, I must write and speak against it. I shall burst if I don't, as Dr. Arnold used to say. It would be far better to let Maryland and Virginia go, and to keep the whole North united on an antislavery basis—the true basis for northern people. I am more and more disposed to believe, that if the curse of slavery is ever removed from us it must be by other people than slaveholders, and I do not intend to be backward hereafter in enlightening the people of these parts on the subject. That two hundred and fifty thousand slaveholders should rule this great empire is a thing not to be endured—and it can't be endured much longer.

The Rev. Dr. Olin.

VII.

PHILADELPHIA, *July* 27. 1846.

MY DEAR FRIEND:—Instead of meeting you in London, as I kept hoping and expecting until the steamer of the 15th started, I am here in Yankeedom still. I had made up my mind again to go, on the very last night, and had the money in my pocket—my wife, too, was packing up my trunk—but, after all, my sense of duty prevailed over my selfish desires to gratify myself, and I determined to remain at home. The reason that has prevailed upon me all along is such as you would approve, and my own conscience is easier here than it could have been if I had crossed the water.

You cannot imagine how glad I was in reading, by chance, the other day, a letter from Mr. Richardson, in Paris, to Professor Allen, to find mention of you and Mrs. Olin. It set me off to Versailles with you at once, and I traveled round with you on all the trip which the letter referred to quite joyously. Indeed, I had a very cheerful dream of it for awhile, and think there must be something in animal magnetism, especially if I could learn that you had thought of me at all that day. You may rest assured of one thing, that nobody in America has thought more, and more affectionately, about you since you left our shores. · I left home on Saturday, 25th inst., my wife not very well, and children all well. Preached here twice yesterday, and feel very well and very happy this morning—quite as happy, at least, as can be, seeing that I am *here* and not *there*. Don't suppose that I am discontented about it, however, for I am not. You recollect stopping with me here at my sister's on the day that we arrived in the cars from Pottsville, after that momentous journey to the Oneida Conference. Well, I am sitting again in the same long parlor, with the same good sisters about me, who beg me to give their love to Dr. Olin.

Professor Johnston is about to go West, and promises to call on us at Carlisle on his way. I shall spend the vacation (after next week) at home, pruning my trees and flowers, playing with my children, listening to my wife talk, and working in my study. Don't you envy me? All the pleasure wont be yours, after all. I pray God that you may be very happy, however, and that your health may be great-ly built up by your voyage. And now good-bye, and graciously per-mit me to write a line to Mrs. Olin, who bore so kindly with my stupidity in those sleepy days when I was with you in Middletown.

May God have you in his holy keeping, and return you to us with renewed health and vigor!

Rev. Dr. OLIN.

VIII.

ON THE FORMATION OF AN AMERICAN BRANCH OF THE EVAN-GELICAL ALLIANCE.

PHILADELPHIA, *December* 81, 1846.

MY DEAR FRIEND:—Your letter of 23d ult. has remained un-answered much longer than my feelings or wishes themselves would have dictated. But I have good reasons. I needed long and anxious meditation upon the subject of your letter, and upon the views which you entertain in regard to it, before I could answer you; and besides, I have been for the last six weeks or more in a state of mental torpor, the like of which I have never felt before. In your varied experience you may have known the same—an utter distaste for thought or labor, constituting, indeed, an absolute incapacity for either; a disposition to sit listless and brooding through the livelong day, and to lie wake-ful, yet useless, almost through the night. Within a day or two I feel some return of the powers of life, and almost the first real thing I do is to answer your letter. Not that it is any labor to write to you. Indeed, had not the subject of your letter been so grand and absorbing I should doubtless have found some comfort, or at least got rid of some of my discomfort, in writing. But the question of the Alliance, and the dark one that lies beyond it, is enough to give pause to the strongest mind, in the exercise of its fullest powers; and you cannot wonder that I have staggered under it, with the pressure of sorrowful and morbid feelings upon me. Before I say more, let me assure you—though, indeed, I think the assurance can hardly be neces-sary—that there is no man living whose friendship I value more, and whose opinions I would more gladly take upon trust, than your own. So cordial is my regard for you, and, at the same time, so thorough my respect for your intellect and judgment, that I can, with reluct-ance, bring myself to differ from you at all. I am not sure that in the present instance I differ from you so very widely; but you will pardon me, I know, for freely expressing my real sentiments.

The object of the "Alliance" is to secure, as you state, a larger

Christian union than now exists. The Conference was held in London (not in New York or Charleston) for this purpose, and delegates were there from all Christendom. If we form an organization next spring, it must be for the same purpose as that which was aimed at in London, viz., not mere affiliations of Christians in separate countries into separate connexions, but a general union of Christians in all lands. Now, in one word, can that object be accomplished by forming an Alliance for this country, freely admitting slaveholders? Could such an organization hold any connexion with the European branches? Nay, would it not cut off effectually, for many years, if not forever, the possibility of the general Christian union to which we all look, and for the promotion of which the Conference met in London? If the object, then, as you say, be to promote general Christian union, should not those who wish to retain slaveholders indiscriminately hesitate a little? All that you say goes to show, (and, perhaps, in that you are correct,) that so far as the American branch goes, it would be larger for the admission of slaveholders. But would not the General Alliance be effectually killed? If it would not, I am in error.

I must say, I go rather for the general alliance of Christendom than for the special union of American Christians. And I am inclined to hope that even this last would follow, in the course of years, a union founded on an antislavery basis rather than the opposite. All this time I have not alluded to the moral aspect of the question—the right or wrong of the admission of slaveholders—because your letter puts the main stress upon the practicability of the alliance. May it not all be summed up in the question, Is a general alliance of Christians practicable if the American branch admits slaveholders indiscriminately? I have totally misunderstood the English feeling if it is. All the papers that I have received from England confirm me more and more in the opinion that if we receive slaveholders on the same footing as others we shall stand alone, and that they expect antislavery action from the American branch next spring. Were not inducements to this expectation held out by some of the Americans in London? Was not a good deal said, and more implied, as to the possibility of meeting this question better in New York than in London, and of meeting it better, too, without the trammels of English dictation than with them?

Perhaps in all this I am influenced by my feelings. To tell the truth, my abhorrence of slavery grows apace. Year after year I feel more and more that something should be done by every good man in this land to deliver it. It may be that the dark subject dims my vision. I hope not. One needs all his eyesight to deal with overgrown evils. But I cannot stifle my convictions ; I cannot down with them, even at my own bidding. Yet I am no abolitionist in one sense of the word. I do not believe that all slaveholders are sinners; I know that some of them are pious men, so far as human judgment can go, and I would not harm them, even in my thoughts, for the world. I pity them. But their hapless condition must not entrap our judgment by attracting our sympathies. If they must suffer I can pray for them, but cannot stop the progress of the ark of God to still their groans. But O! what a sad subject it is. Even writing to you in quietness, I find my heart beating violently with agitation. To-night, at least, I can dwell on it no more. God have mercy upon us, and upon our favored but guilty country! I trust him still, but I could not trust him if I did not follow my honest convictions. Wrong they *may* be ; but wrong I *must* be if I do not act upon them, or, at least, if I act against them. God have you in his holy keeping, my cherished and valued friend! Good-night.

Rev. Dr. OLIN.

IX.

CARLISLE, *March* 21, 1847.

DEAR MRS. OLIN:—An apology for not writing to you, on my part, would be out of place, for more reasons than one. You cannot, in the nature of the case, care enough about it to require one, and I cannot presume enough upon my relation to you to conceive even that it is necessary. But I am simply about to say that I have a sort of nervous timidity about it—partly bashfulness, and partly vanity, doubtless; so that the less I say about it the better. I wrote some time since to Dr. Olin, but have received no answer ; and I have had so many proofs of his kindness that I cannot attribute his silence to any other cause than illness, though I have heard nothing directly to that effect. I now feel that I cannot rest quietly any longer, and I must beg of you to let me know about him and yourself.

A few nights ago I sat, in a moment of rest from writing, thinking of many things, but *most*, of my friends. One of those overmaster-ing impulses that come upon us sometimes so irresistibly (at least it is so with me—is it not so with you?) seized and carried me off to Middletown. I turned around and told Mrs. M'C. that I thought I *must* spend our week of vacation in a trip to visit you, and she echoed the *must* very energetically. So you see that I secured at once, not only the *royal* permission, but command, to do what I most longed to do. And why not? Alas! that we are of the earth, earthly! Alas! that our purest wishes and best affections should be at the mercy of so paltry and so base a thing—but the truth must be told; the *res angusta domi* has nipped many a fine project in the bud, and it cut off this one of mine even before the first sprout be-gan to appear. I *must* go to New York, I suppose, in May, at the time of the Alliance Convention, and my purse is not deep enough to hold money for the two journeys—or, if it is, I have not got it to put in. So I must put up with a disappointment—self-made, to be sure, but none the less poignant and painful on that account.

I have often wondered what temptation would be strong enough to bring Dr. and Mrs. Olin out to the "*crassa Bœotia* of Pennsyl-vania Dutchmen," as the gentle Professor ——, in one of his merry moods, called this sweet old town of Carlisle. Why should it be an impracticable thing? Is not traveling good for Dr. Olin? Has he not done up all the traveling there is in that eastern region between Passamaquoddy and Fort Moultrie? Would not a new route be a blessing and a comfort to his eyes, if not to his bones? (Part of our railway is a *little* rough!) And have we not a comfortable little house—not grand nor gay, but one of those humble cubbies that lightning never strikes, and the fell winds pass over, in pity for its feebleness? Now, he fairly promised me once to come, and the promise yet remains in full force and virtue. Why, I ask again, should it be a thing impracticable? Think it over, please, and call to your aid one of those invisible but potent spirits that carried me off bodily to your pretty city the other night—and then, when he gives the impulse, don't let so vulgar a thing arrest it as, to my sorrow and poverty I confess it, keeps me from going next week to Middletown.

I have done two wrong things in this letter; namely, quote Latin and talk of money. But the little Latin can't do much harm, as it is very poverty-stricken, and is going direct to the University besides. And, after all, I have not talked so much about money as the want of it, so that I may be acquitted of that indictment too.

How often I wish I was a professor at Middletown! (Don't tell any of the Faculty, lest they think I am plotting to eject them.) Not that I think yoûrs a better town, or a better college than our own, or rather, putting both together, not that I think Middletown *and* the University better than Carlisle *and* Dickinson. But I should love exceedingly to spend part of my life with Dr. Olin—and I suppose he will stay, for some years at least, in Middletown. Not, too, that I don't love my friends here, for I do dearly, (you see this is the sober second thought,) but I should like to go *there* for all, so long as your husband is there. I am sorry that I cannot insinuate that your presence would be the attraction, for I told him the same thing four years ago, on board of a canal-boat in the Lehigh River, under ground some fifty feet or less, and yet some eight hundred or a thousand feet above the level of the sea. I don't know that he will remember what I said; but I am sure he'll remember the canal, and the strange experiments we made in the art of sinking, going down the mountain by water. It was a strange, wild scene; and I remember trying to make him say it was grand, or sublime, or rugged, or any thing out of the traveler's vocabulary of adjectives; but he put me off very decidedly, for "he had seen the Drachenfels," or some other very stony place—no, it was a great rocky region somewhere near *Pesth*, I think, on the Danube. I felt inclined to brag of the superiority of Pennsylvania; but as he had seen *both*, he had a decided advantage of me, and was cruel enough to make use of it. However, if I live, and am miserly enough to avoid all expensive journeys merely to see my friends, I shall see *Pesth* and that black mountain one of these days myself, and then we can argue the point on equal terms.

I have written just as I felt, and hope my letter will find you in a happy mood. That you will be so I am sure, if Dr. O. is well; and so, in wishing that, I have wished what most concerns both of us. Tell him how much I love him; and believe me to be your sincere and obliged, but most unworthy friend.

CHAPTER IV.

1847.

The Cumberland Valley a Highway of Migration—The Negroes of Carlisle—The Pursuit by Messrs. Kennady and Hollingsworth of Three Slaves—Symptoms of Riot at the Office of a Justice of the Peace—Collision of Negroes with the Sheriff's Officer—All Parties brought before Judge Hepburn on a Writ of *Habeas Corpus*—The Judge's Decision—Attempt Made in the Court-room to Rescue the Slaves—The Blacks Baffled and Overawed—The Attitude of Pennsylvania in Relation to Slavery—The Prigg Case before the Supreme Court of the United States—The Pennsylvania Law of 1847—Arrival of Professor M'Clintock at the Court-h use—Co-operates in Procuring a Second Writ of *Habeas Corpus*—Interposition in Behalf of a Negro—Attempt to Carry the Slaves Away—Resistance by Negroes of the Town—A *Melée* in which Mr. Kennady is Struck Down—Great Excitement in the Country —Professor M'Clintock Charged with Instigating a Riot and Arrested—Trial of Professor M'Clintock and Twenty-eight Negroes—The Testimony for the Prosecution—Scenes in the Court- Defense and Acquittal—Protest of the Judge—Conviction of Thirteen Negroes and Sentence of Ten to the Penitentiary—Their Release by the Supreme Court—Letters.

WHOEVER has studied the topography of Pennsylvania has observed the numerous ranges of hills which, running parallel with the Alleghanies from northeast to south-west, form the outlying walls of the inner and loftier mountain system. Some of their intervening valleys are so narrow that even in the longest and brightest days they lie much of the time in deep shadow ; others again are of such capacious breadth that they sustain an ever-growing population, distributed over ample farming spaces, or concentrated in villages and towns. Of these, the valley known as the Cumberland, after reaching the southern line of the State, sweeps on through Western Maryland, Central Virginia, and East Tennessee, till it is lost in the plains of the far South. It has always been a highway over which a migratory people have travelled. The Scotch-Irish and Germans who settled Central Pennsylvania had, long before the late civil war, followed the course of the valley into Maryland and Virginia. Concurrently, however, with this flow from the North, there had been a flow upwards from the South. The comparatively mild form of slavery which prevailed in the border Southern States offered many facilities for emancipation. Educated under the teaching of Methodism, some conscientious masters had manumitted their bondmen ; other slaves had bought their freedom. Once free according to the forms of law, a strong impulse led not a few of these blacks to seek a fuller enjoyment of their newly-acquired rights than was possible in their old southern homes. Slaves who helped themselves to their liberty knew perfectly well that it was not safe to linger near the border line, and rested not till they had found their way to New England or Canada.

The borough of Carlisle had received its full share of these immigrants from the neighboring Southern States. Taken together, they were a quiet and orderly element of the population. Some of them were freeholders, and had comfortable homes of their own ; others, if less thrifty, were above want. A number of the men were employed in the service of the college, and were liked as civil and obliging persons. The blacks of Carlisle were neither beggars nor vagabonds. Among them was to be found the inevitable gray-haired patriarch, whose age was anywhere in the neighborhood of a hundred years that one might choose to guess. He was an old rapscallion, who

had his own story to tell of the way he had bought himself out of slavery. A few of us built for him a house of
about twelve by fourteen feet, where he lived in the perfect enjoyment of his independence, and carried himself
with all the air and state of a lord of the manor.

Early in June, 1847, two slaveowners from Maryland,
James H. Kennady and Howard Hollingsworth, came to
Carlisle in pursuit of three runaway servants. One of
the runaways was a man of fifty years, and known as
Lloyd Brown ; another was a girl of ten, and a third a
woman of fifty, called Hester. The owners were from
Hagerstown, where they lived in good repute among
their neighbors. They had an unquestioning conviction
of their right to their human property, and expected
with entire confidence that the authorities in Pennsylvania would make their title good.

A colored man in the borough claimed the woman,
Hester, as his wife ; and, whether from this cause or some
other not known, the blacks were excited to the point
of offering a determined resistance to the arrest of the
fugitives. Excited they had every reason to be ; but a
union to fight the battle out with the captors was for
them an unheard-of exhibition of courage. On the morning of the second of June the owners appeared with the
captured fugitives before a justice of the peace, made the
usual claim, with proofs that were considered sufficient,
and received a certificate delivering the negroes into
their custody. They then asked for a commitment to
jail, where the three slaves might remain in the keeping
of the sheriff until it was convenient to remove them to

10

Maryland.   The request, though wholly illegal, was granted, and the officers proceeded to make the removal. At this point a negro named Norman, the reputed husband of Hester, seized her by the waist and tried to carry her off.   The deputy sheriff, a strong, muscular person, struck him a heavy blow which knocked him against the wall of a house, at the same time declaring that another attempt at a rescue would be met with a pistol shot.   The blacks were for the time intimidated, and the fugitives were carried off to the jail, which stood, and still stands, on the main street of the town.   The sheriff and his prisoners were followed by an agitated crowd, largely made up of women, many of them armed with sticks and such missiles as they could hastily pick up.

Early in the afternoon a writ of *habeas corpus* was obtained by Mr. Adair, one of the lawyers of the borough, bringing all parties before the presiding judge, Hepburn, at the court-house.   By this time the symptoms of a violent outbreak were so threatening, that a posse of officers was summoned to the aid of the sheriff.   The crowd of blacks hung about the jail till its doors were opened again, and then they followed the sheriff and the slaves, but by no means in silence, to the court.   The illegality of the imprisonment was decided very quickly, and the slaves were taken out of the hands of the sheriff and handed over to the keeping of their owners.   Messrs. Kennady and Hollingsworth had, however, been arrested on a warrant from a justice of the peace for forcibly entering the house in which the slaves were found.   They had gone from the court-room to give the necessary bail, and had requested the sheriff and his deputy to take charge of the fugitives until their return. The willing officers undertook this service, illegal as it was, and stationed themselves close to the prisoners' box. The blacks of the town, who by this time were maddened to fury, rushed to the box, lifted the woman, Hester, out of it, and made way with her towards the door; the deputy, who had beaten off the woman's husband earlier in the day, drew his pistol and swore he would shoot any one who attempted a rescue. The doors of the court-room were hastily closed, and escape rendered impossible. The judge, seeing a riot imminent before his eyes as he sat on the bench, ordered the room to be cleared. The crowd, white and black, were forced out, and the captors and their prey remained within, sheltered by the Constitution of the United States, as it then was, with the reluctant assent of the Commonwealth of Pennsylvania.

The good old Commonwealth was most reluctant to stain her hands by giving aid to such work. By the act of March 1, 1780, passed nine years before the adoption of the National Constitution, slavery was abolished in all her borders. All persons thereafter born in the State were to be free. Her love of liberty had been expressed in the act of 1788, which declared that every slave brought within her domain "by persons inhabiting or residing therein, or intending to inhabit or reside therein," should be immediately deemed and taken to be free to all intents and purposes. By the same act the separation of husband and wife beyond a distance of ten miles was forbidden. Her law of 1826, framed for the twofold purpose of preventing kidnapping and carrying out the obligation to return fugitives from labor imposed by the Federal Constitution, had been declared to be null and void by the Supreme Court of the United States. Edward Prigg had been indicted under this law in the Court of the County of York—which adjoins Cumberland —for illegally carrying off a slave woman to Maryland, and had been convicted. By consent of the two States the case had been appealed to the Supreme Court of the United States, in order to determine where the power of legislation in regard to fugitive slaves resided. Justice Story read the opinion of the Court, which was summed up in this sentence : " We hold the power of legislation on this subject to be exclusive in Congress." Chief-Justice Taney read an opinion, which was still more emphatic: " Every State law," it said, " which requires the master against his consent to go before any State tribunal or officer before he can take possession of his property, or which authorizes a State officer to interfere with him, is unconstitutional and· void. But, as I understand the opinion of the Court, it goes further, and decides that all laws upon the subject passed by a State, since the adoption of the Constitution of the United States, are null and void, even although they were intended in good faith to protect the owner in the exercise of his rights of property, and do not conflict in any degree with the act of Congress."

This decision was a heavy blow to Pennsylvania, which had always been distinguished for a scrupulous observance of inter-State obligations, and as much for tenderness towards all who sought the privilege of an asylum upon her soil. It left her a helpless looker-on while the slave-hunter tracked and pursued his prey. Time was chosen for a deliberate answer, and in the winter of 1847 the answer was given. Taking the Supreme Court at its word, and following the principle laid down in the Prigg case to its logical conclusion, the State, through its legislature, enacted a law forbidding its judicial and executive officers to bear any part whatever in the recapture of fugitive slaves. By this act every judge, alderman, or justice of the peace in the Commonwealth was forbidden, under penalty of a heavy fine, to take cognizance of the case of any fugitives from labor, from any of the United States or Territories, arising under the law of Congress of 1793, or to grant any certificate or warrant of removal of any such fugitive. Any person claiming a negro as a fugitive from labor who should, under any pretence or authority, seize, or attempt to seize, and carry away in a violent and tumultuous manner such negro or mulatto, was held to be guilty of misdemeanor and liable to a heavy fine. It was declared also to be unlawful to use any jail or prison of the Commonwealth for the detention of any person claimed as a fugitive from labor. This law was passed, as we have stated, early in 1847, and was approved by that most democratic of governors, Francis R. Shunk. It meant to say plainly, "If the jurisdiction over the recovery of fugitive slaves is exclusively in the United States, then the government of the United States must provide the means for such recovery. The Com-

monwealth of Pennsylvania washes her hands of all this
business. She submits to the humiliation of having her
soil made a slave captor's hunting ground, but warns
the hunters of what they may expect." It was grandly
spoken, and to no citizen did the passage of the law of
1847 give a more heartfelt satisfaction than to Professor
M'Clintock.

Of the earlier proceedings in the case of the fugitives
whom we left shut up in the court-room, Professor
M'Clintock knew nothing. It was his habit, towards five
o'clock in the afternoon, to go to the post-office, then on
the same street with the court-house, but not quite opposite, for his letters. Calling as usual this afternoon, he
was informed by the postmaster of the progress of the
investigation, and went over to see and hear for himself.
He arrived at the moment the judge had pronounced
that the slaves were improperly in the hands of the sheriff.
As he entered the room he met an Episcopal minister,
who expressed a doubt of the testimony which had been
offered to prove that the woman and the child were
slaves. He had a rude greeting from some of the excited whites who made up a large part of the crowd in
the court. "There," shouted some one, "goes a d—d
abolitionist." "Look at M'Clintock," shouted another
voice, "the d—d abolitionist." Taking his seat inside
the bar with the counsel for the negroes, he asked them
if they had seen the new law of 1847; they had not even
heard of it. It was then mentioned by counsel to the
judge, but the judge was not advised of its existence. As
far as could be ascertained a certified copy was not to be

found in the borough, and the only newspaper copy was in the possession of Professor M'Clintock himself. The capitol of the State in which the law was enacted was within twenty miles of Carlisle.

Passing on to the door of the court-room, in obedience to the judge's order to clear it, Professor M'Clintock saw a white man raise a stick threateningly over the head of a negro, saying at the same moment, "You ought to have your skull broke." The negro protested that he had done nothing. "Then," said the professor, "if any one strikes you apply to me, and I will see that justice is done to you." Filled with the idea that all the proceedings were illegal, he discussed with two of the lawyers of the borough the bearings of the new law upon the case as they went together down stairs. It was determined by Mr. Adair, the counsel for the negroes, to get out a second writ of *habeas corpus*, and to try before the judge the question of the ownership of the woman and the girl. While the papers were preparing, Professor M'Clintock hastened to the college for his copy of the Act of 1847. He returned as quickly as possible and rejoined Mr. Adair, who by this time had his petition ready. As they came from the rear of the court-house, and stood a moment upon the front steps, the slave owners, with their slaves, came down the stairs from the room above. A carriage had been driven up to the edge of the sidewalk for the reception of the whole party. Mr. Kennady followed close after his servants, and with a billet of wood beat off the negroes, who, in a high state of excitement, crowded in upon him. The man Lloyd Brown was forced into the carriage, when a desperate rush was made for the woman and the girl. Norman seized his wife, Hester, and bore her off; some one else, not known, clutched the child. The crowd dashed across the street, and down an alley-way adjacent to the market-house, with Mr. Kennady in full pursuit. He was well able to pursue, for he was six feet in height, stoutly built, and in the prime of life. A storm of missiles followed the negroes as they fled, and fell upon both pursuers and pursued. Just as Mr. Kennady had crossed the street, in his tussle with the rescuers, he was tripped by some boards lying upon the sidewalk and fell heavily. Before he could rise he was struck repeatedly by the negroes as they rushed past him in their flight, severely hurt, and rendered helpless.

It was all done, as one might say, in the twinkling of an eye. The amazed lawyers stood upon the court-house steps, Professor M'Clintock among them, but without the slightest power to check or prevent the outbreak. A doctor who was opportunely near came to Mr. Kennady's assistance, and procured a settee, on which the wounded man was carried to his hotel. His left arm, right hip, and abdomen were badly bruised, one knee-cap was torn from its integuments, and blood was flowing freely from a wound on the back of the head. The physician, who had reached the ground in time to see a part of the disturbance, testified that he saw Mr. Kennady " endeavoring to hold on to his slaves with one hand, while he was beating off the negroes with the other, and at the same time receiving blows from sticks and stones." He had underrated the determination of the negroes to resist him, and had paid for his mistake a fearful penalty.

As the news of the rescue, and the hurt done to the slaveowner, spread through the borough, the population—especially its less intelligent portion—was ablaze with excitement. It was M'Clintock, was the outcry, who had instigated and led the riot ; it was M'Clintock who had cheered the negroes on to the commission of violence, assuring them that he would take the risk of all consequences. He had expressed, as every man of right feeling would, sincere sorrow for the harm done to the slaveowner ; but no account was made of that ; he was "a d—d abolitionist," and the unreasoning anger of the moment fell heavily upon him. He was immediately arrested, as also were the negroes, as far as they could be identified. No distinction was made between the Christian scholar and the poor creatures in whose behalf he had vainly interfered ; the popular feeling linked him and them together as alike guilty of a breach of the peace. It was rumored that he was to be arrested at an hour of the night too late to admit of his procuring bail, but he was fortunately spared that indignity.

When the news spread through the country the excitement became more intense. As usual, the distorted story was the first to reach the press, and elicited the severest comments. The " New York Herald " was furious against Professor M'Clintock. The Philadelphia " Ledger " quickly corrected its error, while the " Bulletin " and the " Spirit of the Times " steadily held the attention of the community to the real facts of the case. A meeting of the southern students of the college, who numbered nearly one hundred, was called, in which resolutions of confidence in their professor were adopted, and embodied in a card to the public. The excitement was rapidly subsiding when the death of Mr. Kennady cast a deep shadow upon the events of the second of June. For three weeks he had progressed rapidly toward recovery, was in good spirits, and looked forward to a speedy release from his confinement, when suddenly, and without warning, he passed away. Nothing appeared to connect his death directly with the contusions received during the struggle with the negroes, but the fact of his decease gave to the riot a gravity which otherwise it could not have assumed.

The friends of Professor M'Clintock did not desert him in this important crisis of his life. They gathered about him and gave him assurance of their support. Joshua M. Giddings sent him words of good cheer. Thaddeus Stevens was ready, even solicitous, to take part in his defence. For years a leading member of the bar in Adams County, which directly adjoins Maryland, Mr. Stevens was known throughout the State as an aggressive abolitionist; his courage and force of character compelled men to respect him, no matter what they might think of his opinions. On the 3d of June Professor M'Clintock wrote an account of his part in the events of the day preceding to his brother-in-law, Mr. E. B. Wakeman, and on the 10th a still fuller statement. The two letters disclose the composure with which he contemplated the contingencies before him, and as well the anxiety which underlay it all the time:—

CARLISLE, *June* 8, 1847.

DEAR EDGAR: We had quite a *case* here yesterday. A gentleman called me into the court-house as I was passing, about five P.M., to see a *habeas corpus* tried for those fugitives who had been arrested and committed to jail. The judge pronounced them illegally in custody, and discharged them from the sheriff's hands; but they were still kept in the court-house. After awhile they were taken out to be put into a carriage that was drawn up in front of the court-house, and a rush was made, two slave women carried off, the other, a man, retained. In the riot the owner was severely wounded, and a boy in the crowd mortally. With all this I had nothing to do. But in the court-room, before the parties came out, I told the judge of the law of last session on the reclamation of fugitives, which made all the proceedings illegal from the beginning. A negro of the town was threatened with having his skull broke. He said he had done nothing, and I told him if that was so I would see justice done him. And after all was over an old negro woman called to me to save her from jail, as she had done nothing but try to keep her old man from getting into the riot. I told the officer that if he carried her off illegally I should see her righted; and he let her go.

All that I did was to try to do my duty to the laws of the land. But the slavecatchers have spread abroad the report that I incited the riot, and have sworn to it, and I am under bail to appear at August court. They will find that the saddle is on the wrong horse.

I believe you now understand the whole case, and perhaps you will think I have done no wrong. I am glad that my noble wife has spunk enough neither to be afraid of mobs nor ashamed of her husband.

Mr. E. B. WAKEMAN.

CARLISLE, *June* 10, 1847.

Your letter and David's were duly received. I answer you both in one, as my hands are pretty full of business. For all your expressions of sympathy and kindness I heartily thank you; in a time of trial all such words are worth their weight in gold. And I know, too, that the deeds will not be wanting to back the words, if there is any need of them. You are perfectly right in supposing that I have done nothing illegal or wrong. If to sympathize with the oppressed be a sin, I plead guilty; if to aid them, without violating the law, be a sin, then I am a transgressor; but not otherwise. I do not know that I can add any thing to my own statement of facts made in the last letter. But the charges, the rumors, and, I am told, the affidavits, go far beyond that. Luckily, so far as I can learn, there is no man of the slightest character who can or will venture to swear against me; while there are scores who will testify on my side, that I did nothing tending to incite to riot. The papers here are so miserably cowardly and sycophantic that they have not even given any statement of the palpable infractions of the law of Pennsylvania that were perpetrated on the occasion. They have all abstained, however, from connecting my name with the accounts of the riot. The court does not sit until August 25, at which time I shall have to be here. A most violent article has appeared in the "Hagerstown Torchlight," full of abominable lies, with my name and supposed deeds filling two columns.

The southern students of the college have signed a document stating that they are satisfied, after the fullest examination, of the falsity of the charges brought against me, and declaring that my separation from the college would be an irreparable loss both to themselves and the institution. On that point, however, my mind is made up; just as soon as things are cleared up a little I shall cut loose from this concern; not that they have not treated me well, but that I cannot bear its multiform restraints. Dr. Emory has behaved nobly through all this business; neither of you could have done more or better. I only fear that his health may be affected by the pain and anxiety it has caused him.

That good will come out of it in the end I am sure. As for the personal ill repute that will be brought upon myself, it cannot last long, and will probably do me good in the issue. I have had my mind in peace and comfort through the whole affair, and do not wonder at the tranquillity of other men in worse contingencies. I suppose the nerves string up of their own accord in such emergencies.

They talk of bringing civil suits against me in the Circuit Court of the United States for the value of the slaves, and the personal injury sustained by the claimant; if they do it will be rich and useful. Philadelphia will be worth a visit then. It is now late and I am tired, so good-bye.

Mr. E. B. WAKEMAN.

The entry in his diary on the evening of June 2, written while his mind was all aglow, makes some repetition of the story, but is of too much interest to be omitted:—

June 2, 1847. This day at five P.M., as I was passing the court-house, Mr. Sanderson (postmaster) called me and asked if I wasn't going into the court-house. "Why?" "There is a case of fugitive slaves," etc. I went in. Mr. Thorne told me at the door that there was doubt about the woman and child being slaves, but not about the man, (there were three in all.) The case was over in about five minutes after I entered. The judge decided on the *habeas corpus* that the sheriff had no right to imprison the blacks, and dismissed them from his custody, saying at the same time that the masters had certificates from the justice of the peace on which they could remove them. This I knew to be contrary to the late law of Pennsylvania, and I went up to Judge Hepburn (after the court had adjourned) and asked him about it. Found that neither he nor the lawyers *knew any thing about the law*. There was no proof that the woman and child were slaves; the man admitted it. Adair told me he would get out another writ to try the question of property, which had not been gone into. At his request I went home and got the law. After my return I stood on the porch talking with several young lawyers, who exhibited the most miserable ignorance of the Constitution of the United States. During the conversation the slaves were brought out, and *before* the writ of *habeas corpus* had been returned by the judge. The free blacks, seeing their fellows about to be carried away into interminable bondage, made a rush and carried off the woman and child. In the *melée* one of the slaveowners, named Kennady, was badly hurt.

As I was coming home the last time I heard, near the court-house corner, several persons saying, "Let her go, she has done nothing," and turning I found a man hauling off an aged colored woman. She said she had only tried to get "her old man out," and I told the officer that if "she had done nothing, and he arrested her illegally, I would see justice done her." I then came home.

After tea I heard that I was charged with inciting the riot, and that a writ was out against me. All sorts of stories were told, and many of the students were very much excited. They held a meeting on the chapel steps at seven P.M. Emory went there and said a few words; when I heard of it I went out, and gave them the true account; told them to go down and ask any decent person they chose and they would find it confirmed. They behaved very well. It was stated in the evening that our house would be mobbed. The town was in great excitement, and it was thought best for my family to sleep at Dr. Emory's.

The truth of the case was, that my human and Christian sympathies were openly exhibited on the side of the poor blacks, and this gave mortal offence to the slaveholders and their *confrères* in the town.

Thurs., June 3. At eight this morning I went down to Esquire Holsapple's and gave Emory as bail for my appearance at court on August 25. The students are all right.

By the time the day of the trial arrived (August 25th) the case had expanded beyond its personal relations, and had become a "cause," on the opposite sides of which eager contestants were enlisted. No money, it was said, would be spared to insure the conviction of the professor. There was a full array of counsel. The prosecuting attorney, J. Ellis Bonham, was assisted by three of the leading lawyers of the county. For Professor M'Clintock his friend, Wm. M. Biddle, appeared, and also Mr. Adair, who had been so active in procuring the *habeas corpus*, Mr. Graham, and Wm. M. Meredith, one of the famous leaders of the Philadelphia bar. The defendants, twenty-nine men and women, were all indicted in one batch together, the gentleman and scholar leading the list. A separate trial was asked for him, but was refused. It was well. He had taken his place by the side of God's poor, to give them the benefit of his larger intelligence and to shield them from wrong; it was not unbecoming for him to share their lot. There could be no better position for a follower of Christ and a minister of his truth.

An excellent jury was impanneled. Among them was a stanch Calvinist, one of that rugged race who had originally settled the Cumberland Valley, and who were as immovable as their own Blue Mountains in the maintenance of their convictions of right. Mr. Bonham, the prosecuting attorney, was a gentleman of refined feeling as well as an able lawyer. He wove together from the testimony which he expected to produce a combination of charges against the subject of our memoir, which, if the Commonwealth's witnesses had only been trustworthy, would have overwhelmed any man that ever lived. In the mad excitement of the hour witnesses imagined that they had heard him use vulgarisms of language with which he was incapable of soiling his tongue. One was ready to swear, and did swear, that he had cried out to the blacks, "You ones, go ahead; I'll see you through." Another, that, standing on the court-house steps, he had shouted, "Now, boys, is your time; go ahead; I'll see you through, or be responsible for damages." Another, that in the court-room, when the rescue was attempted from the prisoners' box, he had called out, "Go ahead, boys, and stand your ground." These, and others who testified for the State, had transformed the scholar, who for gentleness was known of all men, into a vulgar rough, busying himself in rushing from group to group, and rallying them in uncouth terms to their bloody work. The intrinsic improbability of these stories should have been their refutation, but the atmosphere of passion in which so many of the parties to the prosecution were involved distorted their vision, and rendered them incapable of seeing or describing with correctness.

Leaving for a time the immediate facts of the case, the prosecution took a wider range, and demanded a conviction as a means of appeasing the South and making slave property secure. "Your verdict," said the State's counsel to the jury, "either one way or the other, so far as these defendants are concerned, is but a drop in the bucket, compared with the other momentous issues which hang upon the result. The rescue of these slaves has had a most pernicious tendency in the South, and rendered the property of every slaveholder insecure. The slaves now think that they can get protection and aid from the whites, and their conduct has become marked by

insubordination and violence. . . . Whether these defendants committed this outrage, or whether they did not, is
a matter of trivial importance to your southern brethren,
compared with the consequences which may flow from
your verdict to the social and political organization of
whole communities. If you decide that these outrages
can be committed with impunity, the foundations of the
Government will be broken, this union of States will be
rent in twain, the fagot will be the arbiter of right and
wrong, and the glare of a civil and, perhaps, of a servile war
will light up the land. Your southern brethren look to
you, gentlemen of the jury, for protection, and that by
your verdict you will stay the lawlessness which threat-
ens to overwhelm them." A most pathetic picture of the
wailing of the widow over the dead body of her husband
closed the able presentation of the Commonwealth's case.

The appeal to render such a verdict as would soothe
the exasperated sensibilities of the people of the South
was preposterous, but it illustrates the temper of the
times. When the witnesses for the prosecution were
brought on, it was found that they had seen and heard
entirely too much. One who was certain that, at the
moment of the outbreak, the professor was in the act of
talking to three negroes, was confuted by proof that the
three were white men, two of them respectable lawyers
of Carlisle. The man who had heard him say, "You
ones, go ahead, I'll see you through," stuck to his story
under cross-examination. He was certain of it. Another witness swore that the professor's face was, during
the riot, "swollen to an unnatural size." By what pro-

11

cess of nature the swelling was produced the witness did
not explain, but evidently considered it an effect of great
excitement.   On the other hand, Mr. Adair, the lawyer
who had humanely interested himself in procuring the
habeas corpus, accounted for Professor M'Clintock during
all the time from his first appearance in the proceedings,
with the exception of four or five minutes.   They were
both, he said, working together to procure relief for the
slaves according to the forms of law.   A Presbyterian minister testified that he and the professor had walked down
stairs from the court-room to the front door arm in arm,
and that the latter was calm and perfectly master of himself.   Another witness had heard him say to an excited
negro, " There must be no fighting; you must not strike
any body, but if any one strikes you, come to me and I'll
protect you."   And these words were the key to all his
conduct on that memorable afternoon.   He would, as a
good citizen, obey the law, but would, at the same time,
do all that was in his power to defend the weak.   Finally,
the most cruel charge of all, that he had expressed pleasure when told that Mr. Kennady was hurt, was disposed
of, the witness to that point failing to stand by his assertion ; and another, a most respectable business man,
testifying that Professor M'Clintock had expressed profound regret when informed of the catastrophe with
which the riot had closed.   There remained the im-
pregnable fact that the blacks had shown a disposition
to unite for a rescue all through the day, and that they
were in no need of instigation from Professor M'Clintock or any one else.

The court-room presented during the trial a spectacle such as has rarely been seen in Cumberland County. The case, from its nature, touched the extreme points of society, and the extremes were represented in the crowd that filled seats and aisles, and watched, with breathless interest, the fluctuations of the legal conflict. The passions certain to be awakened by an outbreak of the endless slavery controversy were there concentrated, and were exerting their utmost force. No prisoners' box could hold the many defendants; they were massed on one side of the room, under guard of officers of the court. They were a motley group of black, brown, and yellow, and as they gazed on the proceedings in which they were interested parties, with the helpless air so peculiar to their race, they excited in the spectator a deep feeling of pity. They had not, however, been left to take care of themselves; competent counsel appeared in their behalf. Their codefendant, who had tried ineffectually on the second of June to aid them, sat beside his lawyers, and took an active and intelligent interest in the conduct of the case. Personal friends were there to give him the support of their presence. The venerable Alfred Griffith, whose homely face, halting gait, deafness, and sterling sense withal, would have made him a much-noticed man in any gathering, sat close to the witness stand, and with strained attention drank in every word of the testimony and pleadings. He had come to hear and judge for himself, and, when the trial was over, published a well-reasoned vindication of his old friend, Professor M'Clintock. More than all, there rested upon the par-

ties to the case an indefinable sense of its meaning
which could not be expressed in words, an apprehension
that it pointed to woes to come, a dread that this collision of two systems of life and civilization at a single
point was but a foretokening of what might be, should
the collision occur at ten thousand points, and involve
all the communities living on either side of the slave
line.   Here were consequences sad enough attending the
effort to secure right and justice for three slaves; what
would they be when it was attempted to secure right and
justice for three millions?

Small attention, as may well be supposed, was paid by
the prosecutors to the negroes. Their theory of the events
bound them to employ their utmost resources to procure
the conviction of Professor M'Clintock, and they spared
no effort to that end.   The attack upon him in some passages of the trial was very bitter.   The death of Mr. Kennady had intensified feeling. The prejudices of a large
portion of the community were with the prosecution.
At the beginning the prospects of the defence were far
from assuring, but as it progressed the integrity, the humanity, the courage of Professor M'Clintock became so
conspicuously clear as to sweep away all hesitation.   Mr.
Meredith closed for the defense in a polished address;
Mr. Watts (now United States Commissioner of Agricul-
ture) summed up for the prosecution, and struck heavy
blows; but, fortunately, their object was invulnerable.
The judge charged the jury fairly enough, and on Saturday evening gave them the case. By Sunday noon it
was rumored that Professor M'Clintock was acquitted,

and on Monday morning the jury so declared in their verdict. Over half the negroes were cleared, and thirteen convicted.

To the surprise of all persons who were present, Judge Hepburn protested against the verdict, and especially the acquittal of Professor M'Clintock. He informed the jury that if the case had been one involving only dollars and cents he would have set their decision aside. He insisted that when he ordered the court-room to be cleared, the line was drawn between the peaceable and the disorderly, and that when Professor M'Clintock told the negroes " to stand their ground " (which he never did tell them) he became at that instant a rioter, and as guilty of all the acts of violence as though he had taken part in their commission. The bar and citizens were astounded by this breach of judicial decorum. The truth was, that the sheriff's officers had undertaken an illegal service in assuming to guard the prisoners' box, and to convert the court-room into a prison, after the slaves had been taken out of their hands, and remitted to the keeping of their owners. They had provoked a breach of the peace by going outside of their duty. If, however, the judge's opinion was against the verdict, far different was that of the community. The trial had revolutionized popular feeling; the decision of the jury on the facts was received with acclamation. Congratulations from all quarters poured in upon the much-tried professor. His friend, Emory, who, prostrated by sickness, had been unable to attend the proceedings, but had in the preparations for them been a confidential

adviser, received him after his acquittal with the warmest
demonstrations of affection.   The sharp agony over, Professor M'Clintock went out of the court with a stronger
hold upon the community in which he lived and the
country at large than he had ever had before.   Some
ill-disposed newspapers persisting in using the protest
against the verdict to his prejudice, he issued a card to
the public in which he conclusively reviewed all the facts
of the case.   Following his usual practice of taking the
straightforward way to an object, he had, in October, a
long interview with the judge, at the close of which the
latter professed that his opinions had undergone a material change.   After this the subject was dropped by
them both.   It was not in Professor M'Clintock's nature
to cherish ill-will against any one.   He was ready to believe that the judge had taken an honest, if prejudiced,
view of the facts, and in that belief he rested.

Of the thirteen negroes found guilty, ten were condemned to three years' imprisonment in the Eastern Penitentiary of Pennsylvania, at labor, and to pay one dollar
fine to the Commonwealth, with the costs of the prosecution.   This was a terrible and unprecedented penalty
for a breach of the peace.   Believing it to be illegal,
Professor M'Clintock took steps to have the sentence reviewed by the Supreme Court of the State.   He con-
sulted with Charles Gibbons, Esq., of the Philadelphia
bar, and the result was a writ of error which brought the
case before all the Supreme judges in May, 1848.   The
errors assigned were (1) the imposition of imprisonment
in the penitentiary instead of the county jail, and (2) the

imposition of imprisonment "at labor." Judge Burnside, in delivering the unanimous opinion of the court, used this emphatic language: "When I came to the bar there were old and experienced judges on the bench and aged lawyers in practice, but I never heard of (or witnessed) any person convicted of a riot being sent to the penitentiary. Our laws do not authorize the sentence inflicted in the case before us, and the sentence is reversed. As the prisoners have been confined in the Eastern Penitentiary about three fourths of a year, we deem this as severe a punishment as if they had been confined in the county jail, where they legitimately should have been sent, for two years. They are discharged." *

The triumph of the good citizen could go no farther. He had been taunted with knowing more law than was for his good, and he had proved that his understanding of his obligations to his native State was correct beyond impeachment. He had been arrested for leading a riot, and he had demonstrated that his only offence had been a fearless discharge of the duties of humanity. Acquitted himself, he had followed, with compassionate interest, the poor creatures whom he had on the second of June generously tried to help, and had set in motion the measures which secured their restoration to their homes. The alacrity with which Mr. Gibbons performed his service as counsel entitled him to all honor. It was a triumph for him, too; but it was especially a triumph of justice, the more conspicuous, because it relieved those whose ignorance and lowliness unfitted them to protect themselves.

* See Penn. State Reports, vol. viii, p. 223.

LETTERS FROM JANUARY, 1847, TO JANUARY, 1848.

I. LETTERS TO DR. M'CLINTOCK.

I.

HOT SPRINGS, *July* 20, 1847.

DEAR SIR:—I had written to Mr. Adair that I could not be at your court. He had written me on behalf of other parties. I then thought that your court was on the 2d and 3d Mondays of August. Learning from you that it is on the 25th, I will make every effort to be there. As soon as I get home (first week in August) I shall be able to give you a definite answer. I desire to aid in the defence, if possible, although you have able counsel.

With great respect, your obedient servant,

THADDEUS STEVENS.

Prof. JOHN M'CLINTOCK.

II.

LANCASTER, *Aug.* 2, 1847.

DEAR SIR:—On my return home I find so large a number of suits in which I am concerned on the trial list for the fourth Monday of August, that I fear it will be out of my power to be at your court that week. I felt a great desire to aid in that trial because of certain principles which I thought ought to be maintained before the juries of this country in all similar cases. But I confess I feel the wish to be engaged in your defence somewhat abated since I have seen the declaration of your principles and views as promulgated by the trustees and president of your college, as I fear the stand which I should take (on inalienable rights and the Declaration of Independence) would conflict with those views, and the views of other counsel, and might injure your institution. I fear I could not repress my feelings within what your trustees would deem prudence, although I doubt not with a fair jury such a bold and *true* course would insure your acquittal. But your case is in able hands, and will not suffer by my absence. With great respect,

THADDEUS STEVENS.

Prof. M'CLINTOCK.

III.

Lancaster, *Aug.* 9, 1847.

DEAR SIR:—I do not find it in my power to make my arrangements so as to attend your court. I have too many causes on the list for that week to be able to arrange with all. I doubt not of your acquittal, but I fear for the colored defendants. Their *skin* testifies against them in this Christian community.

With great respect, your obedient servant,

THADDEUS STEVENS.

Rev. J. M'Clintock.

IV.

Hookstown, Baltimore Co., Md., *June* 21, 1847.

REVEREND SIR AND BROTHER:—I cannot refrain from expressing my indignation at the vile attempts that have been recently made to impeach your character. How much easier it is to slander and persecute an opponent who is in the right than to neutralize the force of his arguments. You need not marvel, therefore, at the treatment you have experienced. You recollect De Foe's "Hymn to the Pillory." Your persecution reminds me of those famous lines which have been so often quoted:—

> "Tell them the men that placed him there
> Are scandals to the times;
> Are at a loss to find his guilt,
> *And can't commit his crimes.*"

O if you knew how many prayers have gone up to God since your first article was published in the *Advocate*, that your strength might not fail, you could not be disheartened! There are thousands whose hearts beat in unison with yours, and yet, alas! how few, like Luther, are willing to brave a threatening world, and give utterance to the truths in words like these: "It is neither safe nor prudent to do aught against conscience. Here stand I. I cannot otherwise. God assist me. Amen."

That the Lord Jehovah may bless and comfort you is the prayer of your unworthy brother in Christ. JOHN M. JONES.

V.

ANTISLAVERY OFFICE, PHILADELPHIA, *June* 10, 1847.

PROFESSOR M'CLINTOCK :—

MY DEAR SIR :—I take the liberty of inclosing you an authenticated copy of the late Act of Assembly of this State in relation to fugitive slaves. You may possibly have occasion to refer to it and may not be in possession of one duly authenticated.

Allow me at the same time to avail myself of the opportunity of expressing to you the interest and gratification with which I have watched your progress for some time on the great question of slavery. I have rejoiced to see your eyes opened to so good a degree to the enormities of this system, to the guilt of the Church in relation to it, and the duty of energetic action for its overthrow. The late occurrence in Carlisle, in which I perceive you took a prominent, and, from the malevolence with which you are assailed for it I should infer an honorable part, has much increased my interest in your behalf. Unless Carlisle has greatly changed for the better since I was one of its residents, your liberal views of truth and duty find but little sympathy from those around you. "Open thy mouth for the dumb ; plead the cause of the poor and needy," does very well to fill up the rhetoric of a studied sermon ; but when reduced to every-day practice, and especially when applied to the degraded slave and his despised brethren here at the North, it is quite another thing. Woe to the man that is guilty of such extravagance ! His name is cast out as evil ; he is branded as a disorganizer in the Church and a disturber of the peace of society. Possibly you may not have yet gone far enough to incur all this odium. The regularity and conformity to prevailing usage of your previous ways may have acquired for you a stock of character sufficient to save your reputation from the hostility which your late course was calculated to awaken. But if you persist, my dear sir, be assured that all this odium, and more, will come upon you.

Such views of Christian truth and duty as you have avowed the Church will not tolerate, nor the world away with—at least not in any other form than *the abstract.* I trust you have duly considered this; that you have counted the cost. Excuse me if I confess that in this regard I feel much solicitude for you. Not that I have any fears of your deliberately going back from any clear convictions of duty; but lest, in the clamor your Christian-like course will raise, you should allow the remonstrances and expostulations of those whom you may regard as fathers and brethren, wiser and better than yourself, to shake you in your conclusions, and persuade you to substitute their views of duty for your own. Many have been led away from the truth, under circumstances like these, by an improper confidence in others. I trust you will be enabled to resist all such influences. May God strengthen you, and enable you to set your face like a flint; confer not with flesh and blood! You have a work to do; take counsel only of Him who sends you. Remember that " if any man—*any man*—will live godly in Christ Jesus, he *shall* suffer persecution." But, then, " *blessed* are ye when men shall revile you and persecute you, and say all manner of evil against you falsely for my sake. Rejoice and be exceeding glad, for great is your reward; for *so* persecuted they the prophets which were before you." But why need I quote this? It is all familiar to you, and perhaps more so than to me. Such passages, however, come to one's mind on occasions like the present. If not too much trouble, please drop me a line saying how much, if any, truth there is in the statement copied into the " Ledger " of Tuesday from the " Hagerstown News," that you urged on the colored people to rescue those slaves in the riot case. It is not a matter of much importance, but I feel some curiosity to know.

Yours, in much sympathy,   J. M. M'KIM.

VI.

JEFFERSON, OHIO, *July* 18, 1847.

MY DEAR SIR: We have seen notices in the newspapers of a riot at Carlisle in consequence of attempts to retake fugitive slaves. We now see it announced that a Mr. Kennady lately died of wounds received in such riot. It is also stated that the friends of Mr. Kennady charge you with his murder, and are about to institute proceedings at law to punish you for the aid you lent the fugitives. Censure is also thrown out against the court, which seems to have in some way been called to decide some questions ; but we have as yet no distinct statement of the facts connected with the transaction. Indeed, we are entirely ignorant of the circumstances attending it. For the purpose of information I now respectfully ask a statement of the material facts for my own satisfaction, and, if agreeable to you, for publication, as all matters relating to our connexion with southern slavery are interesting to our people.

That fugitive slaves have the clearest moral and legal right to defend themselves against their masters, or their masters' agents, when on the soil of Pennsylvania or Ohio, I think no reputable lawyer will deny, even though in such defence they should slay their masters and all who assist their masters to arrest them. It is equally clear that every man possesses the right to inform such slaves of their privileges while in our territory. We may instruct them fully, we may furnish them arms for the purpose of defending themselves, without incurring any liability. Indeed, I should regard such an act as a high moral duty. The slaveholder of Virginia is guilty of as great an outrage upon the laws of God and the rights of man, when he comes upon Ohio soil to arrest his fellow-man and force him into servitude, as he is when he goes to Africa for the purpose of kidnapping the unoffending people of that country to bring them into slavery.

But we permit slaveholders to come upon our own soil and seize our fellow-men and drag them into interminable bondage, under our constitutional compact. That compact must be observed. According to the decisions of the United States Supreme Court, we are not permitted to defend the slave against his master. Second, we may not secrete the slave from his master : and, third, we must not rescue the slave from his master's custody. Here our duties under the Constitution cease. Beyond them we may act according to the dictates of humanity and justice. The slave has made no stipulations, nor has the Constitution nor the law of Congress prohibited him from the exercise of his natural right of self-defence. That great first law of nature remains in full force in Pennsylvania and Ohio, although the slave States have declared it obsolete within their territory, and have affixed the penalty of death to its exercise by any slave within their bounds.   They have given to the master or his agent the right to shoot a slave who runs from him when ordered to stop ; they have given to the white man the privilege of killing any slave who raises his hand against such white man, even in self-defence; but, thank God ! those laws are confined to such States ; they have no existence in Pennsylvania and Ohio.   And when the slave crosses the State line ˙ and enters either Ohio or Pennsylvania, he instantly regains the right to defend himself, the same as every other American being within our States possesses.   Did I say he regained the right ?   I will add, he reassumes the duty of self-defence.   To defend his right to the enjoy-ment of life and liberty with which God has endowed him, becomes in him a paramount duty.   He does not possess the moral right tamely to surrender up his own liberty, or that of his offspring in coming time, to the will of a barbarous master.   Cowardice in such case becomes criminal; and although we have stipulated that we will not protect him, we leave him in the full enjoyment of his own right of self-protection.   I am myself no advocate of non-resistance in such cases.   On the contrary, for many years I have, when called on for professional advice, directed such fugitive slaves to arm them-selves, and in case their masters should press them and they should have no other mode of escape, to kill such master or their agents, whether few or many.

It occurs to me that possibly a new question may arise at Carlisle ; one that has never been discussed to my knowledge.   I under-stand that some people of your place aided the fugitives in defending themselves ; perhaps it was colored people, but that does not alter the case.   Such persons would undoubtedly be liable civilly for the pen-alty provided by act of Congress of 1793, as it would be a violation of our compact; but would such persons be liable to a criminal prosecution for such act, even if they killed the master or his as-sistants while actually defending the fugitive slaves ?   May they not defend the fugitive as they may a citizen of Pennsylvania, so far as the laws of Pennsylvania are concerned ?   Is there any act of your legislature declaring such defence punishable? There is no such law of the United States, and if your citizens can be punished criminally for such act, it must be under your own laws.

I trust that should legal prosecutions be instituted in regard to those fugitives, or the death of Mr. Kennady, that the attention of legal gentlemen will be turned to this subject, and that the people of our free States will claim, that in assisting to arrest fugitive slaves, they incur the danger of being slain with impunity by such slaves or their friends. I commenced with the intention of soliciting facts, but have been led into a legal essay. Please excuse my truant pen.

Very respectfully,   J. M. GIDDINGS.

Professor M'CLINTOCK.

P.S. I would not say that Congress has not the power to declare it criminal for a slave to defend himself, or for any other person to defend him; but I only say it has not done so as yet.

11. LETTERS FROM DR. M'CLINTOCK, AND HIS CARD TO THE PUBLIC.

I.

CARLISLE, June 10, 1847.

Your letter was duly received, and thank you for it, too. There is no ground for uneasiness at all on my account, as you will see from the papers in which the students' statement is given. All is quiet here. I have done nothing, you may be assured, in the slightest degree wrong, and even Dr. Emory says that I was not *imprudent;* so you may rest assured that all will go well. I simply obeyed the dictates of justice and humanity—that's all.

We are all very well; all this disturbance has not lost us a night's rest or the enjoyment of a meal's victuals. To be persecuted by the vile and wicked is surely no ground for unhappiness, and I do not intend to be unhappy or even uneasy. The judge is doubtless mortified because it has leaked out all over the country that he did not know the law, but I have no doubt he will do me justice when the case comes up for decision in court. As for my leaving the college I have been ready to do it at any time for years past, and am even anxious to do it now, so nobody need be troubled on that score. The southern students are unanimous in declaring that I shall not leave the institution.

The children are fat and hearty. Caroline has not given way in the least amid all this tumult. She has too much pluck for that.

I have written so much to-day that really I can write no more.

Miss JANE M'CLINTOCK.

II.

CARLISLE, *June* 10, 1817.

DEAR FATHER: You will have seen, before this reaches you, the statements in the papers in regard to my sharing in the riot here and their contradictions. It is only another instance of the persecuting spirit of slavery and its abettors that this base attempt to injure me should thus foully be carried on.

I did nothing that was not perfectly legal—nothing that would not have been done by any man of common humanity under like circumstances. My presence at the court-house was purely accidental. It happened that I knew the law, which the judge and justice did not; but that is no crime.

It is needless for me to write you details of the riot, and besides, I am too busy to write much at length. Be assured that all will come right. The lawsuits may be expensive, but my friends will doubtless help me. We are all very well. The students are perfectly satisfied that all these charges are false.

Mr. JOHN M'CLINTOCK.

III.

CARLISLE, *June* 10, 1817.

I don't know how you got the notion that Caroline took sick about this riot business; but you were never more mistaken. It did not trouble her in that way at all. She has entirely too much substance to give up in that fashion.

I think you are pretty well aware of the state of facts here. All the faculty and all the students, northern and southern, are with me. The substantial middle class of the town are with me. The upper crust and the rabble are with the slaveholders. The former have

too much fellowship with the aristocracy of slavemasters not to be
on their side : the latter, as usual, try to keep up a depth lower than
their own, and the blacks serve that end.   The indictment will run
against me along with twenty or twenty-five *other* negroes, and will
go so before the grand jury, who may ignore the bill in my case if
they choose.   But that is not likely, as some of the fellows will swear
awfully—so that I shall have to meet the matter in court, August 25.
Then I shall be tried with all the blacks—though it seems strange
law to me if I cannot have a separate trial.   But of all that in its
time.

The slaveowners have gathered up all the evidence they could here
in the shape of depositions, and published it with variations and
ornaments in " The Hagerstown Torchlight."   I have since received
Maryland and Virginia papers which refuse to copy from " The
Torchlight," stating their disbelief of the yarn.   But if they swear
to all that is in that paper they will commit fearful perjury, and will
probably convict your humble servant, and give him some thousand
dollars fine and costs, with a year in the penitentiary.   Moreover, the
slavemen are gathering their witnesses with a view to suit in the Circuit Court of the United States, and if I am cast here, they will push
it there.   But I don't think they will attempt it if the grand jury ignore
the bill, or I am acquitted.   So now, I reckon, you know as much as
I do.

Let the thing go as it may, I have nothing wherewith to accuse
myself.   In any issue it cannot but do good ; and so I thank God
and take courage.   It may embarrass my purse for some years, but,
if my health and strength continue, I have no fears on that score.
And my friends have stood by me like wax—all that I have deemed
to be my friends.

The southern trustees will probably come up boiling with wrath, to
have me expelled.   Bless their dear hearts ! they need not trouble
themselves.   I am ready enough to go any minute of the year ; nay,
I shall clap my hands with joy to get rid of all these petty vexa-
tions and annoyances.   In case I leave this fall, I shall ask you to
rent a small house for us in Jersey City, or to hire us half yours, or to

board us until spring, whichever you may find most agreeable—always provided I am not in limbo.

Mr. E. B. WAKEMAN.

IV.

CARLISLE, *July* 1, 1847.

Emory thinks that I should institute a libel suit against " The Herald " before the trial comes off here ; or, at least, take the preliminary proceedings thereto. All this slander and abuse will work good in the end, not only to the antislavery cause, but to myself personally. Of that I am well assured. But the parties who have got up the prosecution, backed by the gold of the slaveholders, will strain every nerve to convict me. Perjury by wholesale will not be spared.

Nothing could be more absurd than the attempt to connect Mr. Kennady's death with his wounds. He was rapidly recovering from the latter, was very well on Thursday night, ate freely of sponge cake, against the prohibition of his physician, and died at four o'clock in the morning.

There is little or no excitement here. The examinations are now going on prosperously. The trustees meet on Wednesday next. Of course they will sustain me—or the college will be broken up at once.

Mr. E. B. WAKEMAN.

V.

CARLISLE, *Aug.* 15, 1847.

I thank you for your assurance of presence and countenance next week. It is just what I expected of you. Why can't you make your fixings so as to be here on Saturday night? Then you can spend Sunday with us quietly and comfortably. As for court week, you know, I shall not have much time or opportunity to talk with you. Pack up, then, and be here on Saturday night. One day cannot make much difference, as we shall expect you on Monday night at any rate. But I shall look for you in the cars on Saturday.

Meredith is coming from Philadelphia in my behalf. He stands at the head of the bar, but what kind of criminal lawyer he is I don't know. I don't apprehend any thing awful. It would have been a

12

great comfort to have had Stevens here to score the southerners, but he could not come.

Bonham tells me I can take the "Herald" to our grand jury, find a bill, and have a requisition on the governor of New York for Bennett's body, bring him and try him. What would you think of that? May be I shall do it with the Maryland fellows.

Good-bye, I have various epistles to write, and it is very hot.

Mr. E. B. WAKEMAN.

VI.

CARLISLE, *Oct.* 6, 1847.

DEAR ROBERT:—We all concur in opinion that you have done wisely in not returning here, although it would be pleasanter to see you again before you sail. The arrangements for your departure are now finally made, I see, as father informs me in a letter to-day that he has taken passage for you and Mrs. E. in the "Emily." I wish I could go to Philadelphia to see you off. Nothing, you may be sure, but college prevents me from going. I have lost so many days already that I must not absent myself further. But I can pray for you, and do, that you may have a prosperous voyage, and a restoration to health and strength as its consequence.

I wanted to have a long talk with you while here, but it could not be. It is not necessary for me to speak in *gratitude* to you for all your kind friendship to me, and especially for its manifestation in the recent trial case. You know, as well as I can tell you, that I value you more than any living man, next only to those of my own blood, and hardly next even to them. It pains me deeply to think that anxiety in regard to my case may have contributed to aggravate your disease last month. I feel so deeply, too, my unworthiness of your regard that I sometimes blame myself for allowing you to be here at all, while at the same time your sympathy and approval were worth as much to me as all the world's besides.

All these trials that you and I pass through must be designed for some good end. In my own case I can see their necessity, in yours I cannot. But He knows who inflicts them. What troubles me most is, that I cannot see any improvement in my moral character from them ; I cannot feel that I am more humble, more holy, than I was years ago, before the heavy course of afflictions began to which I and my family have been subjected. It ought not to be so; it must not be so. Thoughts like these have occupied my mind a great deal during the last week, confined as I have been ; I trust that good will come of them. Sometimes I think that this listless, lifeless, loveless life would be changed if I were preaching at an appointment; and then again I know that intercourse with God does not depend on time or place, and think that I am trying to throw the blame upon *negotia* that ought to lie at my own door. Again, I think of falling back upon the old-fashioned Methodist life, even here at home, prayers with preachers, and such like; and then the fear of cant and pretence comes over me like a shower bath. But I did not intend to go on in this strain when I commenced. Still I feel better for it, and if you don't, you have excused me so often that you are used to it.

I wish you to send me the best directions you can about letters to you before you leave, and to communicate promptly afterward where and how we shall direct to you. If you wish newspapers sent, say so, and what ; and any thing else that I can do, only let me know and it shall be done, if I have health and strength. With the letter to the " Public " I have thrown off that riot business forever, I trust, and shall now devote myself entirely to college work and writing. My health is unpromising, however ; this bronchial attack still hangs on, and such a thing at the beginning of autumn portends badly. But I hope it will soon be over.

The college is doing admirably well, classes very full, and of very good material, too. I do not think any thing can break us down except our own negligence or ill-health. During the present year I hope to exert myself more successfully than ever, and then to wind up my work here next spring. But of that I do not talk at present. And now I stop ; will write to you again at Philadelphia. Do not reply except to answer the business questions I have put to you ; I know that writing is not good for you.

Rev. President Emory.

VII.

TO THE PUBLIC.

Although my name has been connected with the Carlisle riot of the second of June by the public prints in nearly all parts of the country, I have thus far made no statement of the case in my own behalf. Notwithstanding the exaggerated, and even absurd, reports which gained currency before the trial, I did not deem it proper to make any such statement until the trial itself should have been held ; nor had I supposed it would be necessary even then, as, from my knowledge of the facts, I could not rationally look for any thing else but an acquittal, which heretofore (at least, in other than political trials) has been generally deemed among civilized men satisfactory proof of innocence. But as I find that attempts are still made in certain newspapers, especially in Maryland and Virginia, to blacken my character upon the ground that the presiding judge protested against the verdict, leaving it to be inferred that the twelve gentlemen of Cumberland County who formed the jury did not render a true one according to the evidence, although bound by their oaths to do so, I deem it due to myself to offer a few words for the consideration of all honorable (not to say Christian) men, whether north or south of Mason and Dixon's line.

Without entering into any minute details, I now simply state, upon my own personal veracity, that my first knowledge of the case was obtained while accidentally passing the court-house at about 5 P. M., although the slaves were arrested as early as nine or ten o'clock in the morning ; that I entered the court-house under the impression, derived from a clergyman at the door, that there was no sufficient proof that the woman and child were slaves ; that I knew nothing of the persons or character of the gentlemen claiming the slaves ; that my efforts in the case were directed to legal proceedings and none other ; that no word or act of mine was uttered or done with reference to forcible or riotous resistance ; that the riot was a source of the profoundest pain to me ; and that no man regretted its unhappy consequences more deeply than myself.

This statement, I say, is made upon my own personal veracity, which will, I know, be a sufficient guarantee for its truthfulness with my *friends* in the Southern as well as in the Northern States. The substance of it was amply proved upon the trial, and on that proof the jury acquitted me, as no intelligent jury could have failed to do. I think that any right-minded man who will examine the testimony on both sides, even as given in the imperfect newspaper reports, (that of the "Carlisle Democrat" being the most complete, though even that is imperfect,) will be able to explain it in accordance with the above statement. I have no disposition to complain of the witnesses for the prosecution; least of all to charge any of them with perjury. My acts and words were misunderstood by them at the time; and under a wrong view of my objects, they involuntarily gave the coloring of their own feelings to what they saw and heard. All men are liable to do this, especially in cases suggestive of prejudice or passion; and every one knows that questions involving the interests of the colored race are of this sort. In the recent trial, acts, and even words, testified to by witnesses for the prosecution, bore a very different aspect when stated by those for the defence; thus verifying at least one sense of the maxim, *cum duo dicunt idem, non est idem.* Many of the witnesses for the Commonwealth are personally unknown to me; but I do not think that any of them would charge me with *intending* to excite a riot.

It is very true, that so far as the judge's opinion, publicly announced after the verdict and since widely circulated in the newspapers can go, I stand before the American public branded as a rioter. But I have the satisfaction to know that men learned in the law, older and wiser than he, and more experienced in sifting testimony, who carefully attended to the trial throughout, with no interest in my conviction or acquittal beyond the interest of truth and justice, were satisfied that my conduct was vindicated by the evidence, and that the verdict of the jury was a most true and righteous one. That some mistakes were committed by the jury in regard to the colored defendants is not to be wondered at. There were, I think, thirty-six persons embraced in the indictment, of whom twenty-nine were put upon their trial; and although the counsel for the defence asked that my trial should be separated from that of the colored defendants, on the ground that the minds of the jury must necessarily be confused by the amount of testimony that would be offered, the Court refused to separate. A Mansfield could not have kept the multitudinous evidence in regard to all the defendants clearly before his mind without careful notes; and even then he might have been puzzled, as the bar certainly were in one or two instances on the recent trial. Moreover, the grand jury returned a wrong name in finding a bill against *Rachel* Johnson, instead of *Richard*. The traverse jury were sworn upon the indictment thus found; and when (after the trial had gone on for some time) the mistake was detected, the bill, without the consent of the traverse jury or the counsel for the defendants, was sent back to the grand jury, kept by them during the adjournment of the court, and returned with the name corrected. The prosecuting attorney, with the consent of the court, but without that of the defendants, then entered a *nolle prosequi* against Richard Johnson, and the trial proceeded without the traverse jury being again sworn. With what reason the jury can be blamed, therefore, for accidental error in their verdict, I leave for all impartial men to decide; especially, when it is added that their attention was withdrawn from the colored defendants to a great extent, and concentrated upon myself, throughout the trial, by the course of the pleadings. The result of this concentrated attention was a verdict of acquittal in my behalf.

My cordial thanks are due to the citizens of Carlisle, who have shown me so much kindness during the progress of this trial, and also to the editors of various newspapers in Maryland and Virginia, as well as in Pennsylvania, who have taken the pains to give both sides of the story. I trust that not only they, but all who have published accounts of the trial, will copy this statement.

JOHN M'CLINTOCK.

CARLISLE, *September 25, 1847.*

CHAPTER V.

1847, 1848.

Calm after the Storm—Increase in the Number of College Students—Generosity of Dr. M'Clintock's Friends—Illness of President Emory, and his Departure for the West Indies —Illness of Professor Caldwell—Correspondence of Dr. M'Clintock with his two Sick Associates—Letter from one Dying Man to Another—Death of President Emory and of Professor Caldwell—Professor M'Clintock's Resignation of his Professorship—His Growth during the Twelve Years—His Life in Carlisle considered as a Preparation for his Subsequent Career.

THE alternations of trial in this period of Professor M'Clintock's life followed each other in quick succession, and from the character of his temperament affected him very deeply. His sensibility to all impressions gave keenness both to his sorrow and his joy. His elastic spirit, however, carried him onward victoriously, and enabled him (the causes of disturbance once past) to resume with vigor the many undertakings with which his hands were filled. The college opened for the fall term of 1847 the next month after the riot trial, and to his great delight students flocked to it in larger numbers than ever before. Some of its friends had expressed gloomy forebodings of the future ; but the event proved that there was no occasion for fear. In November he writes to his associate, President Emory, who had gone to the West Indies for the restoration of his shattered health :—

I am able to attend to all my college duties, and to get on a little with the " First Book in Greek." If the college did not require one to spend time in hearing recitations, or attending to students, I should think a professor's place one of the pleasantest in the world ;

as it is, I feel myself happy at my work, but more happy in the prospect of being in freer circumstances next year. "Neander" is
printed, preface and all, but the Messrs. Harper do not think it best
to publish until February, so as to have the book fresh for the spring
trade, and I suppose they are right. And as you take almost as
much interest in my affairs as in your own, it may gratify you to
learn that several friends, as large-handed as yourself, have sent me
aid toward the expense of the riot case—the whole amounting to
about five hundred dollars. Did ever any body have such friends?
But do you know (I shall feel better to let it out) that I have had
more strange and bad feelings about the kindness of my friends, than
about all the malice of foes. The weight of obligation crushes me,
and I feel as if I must rid myself of it somehow. This is pride,
doubtless, but I hope something better is mixed up with it.

If I have traced successfully the outlines of this life, so
as to make of it a well-defined picture, I have shown in
what close bonds of friendship the members of the Faculty of Dickinson College lived together. They were
large-minded men, who fully trusted one another, and
never found their trust betrayed. Dr. Durbin, the first
president, who left in 1845 to enter upon the pastorate,
and then upon his great work as missionary secretary,
wrote, in 1850, to one of his old associates: " My visit to
Carlisle awoke in me the beautiful and anxious memories
of the days that may never return. I remember them
with pleasure and pain. They were the days of my manly
friendships — peace — peace! Ah well, they may be renewed hereafter." The little circle was now about to be
broken, and its members scattered. President Emory
had, while travelling, in 1847, been taken with bleeding
of the lungs, and had been ordered to a warmer climate.

Professor Caldwell, the senior of the Faculty, whose health had been precarious for several years, had gone to his home in Portland, Maine, to end his days. The prospect of losing these friends made the continuance in his post painful for Professor M'Clintock to contemplate. He believed, too, that his office imposed restraints upon the full expression of his opinions which he was not willing to bear. He had been admirably sustained by the college authorities and the southern students, but he knew perfectly well how incurable were the prejudices created by the angry debate between the North and the South. Invitations came to him to take the presidency of Genesee Seminary, of Alleghany College, a professorship in the Wesleyan University, and from some of his friends, the editorship of the Methodist Quarterly Review. The college proposals he declined, and with regard to the last he determined to wait the course of events.

The entries in his diary from this date are few and very brief. As his cares multiplied, and his correspondence grew in volume, there was little time or strength left for an exact summary of each day's proceedings. Such passages as the following tell their own story :—

Sunday, Nov. 21. Class-meeting at half-past eight. Took bad cold at ——'s funeral on Friday, and suffer much from it to-day. Got letter from —— last night, which afflicted me deeply. The iron is beginning to enter my heart. One wave of sorrow after another has rolled over me for the last ten years. My head is becoming gray. Yet I have many blessings, *Laus Deo!* Did not go to church to-day, feeling too unwell.

Tuesday, Nov. 29. Sat up last night till two o'clock studying and comparing Greek and Latin accents. Read "Dion., Sext. Empir.," "Herodotus," etc. Got clearer views than usual. Letter to Nadal from J. P. D. with one hundred and twenty-six dollars, on account of riot! Really my friends overpower me.

If, however, his diary is meagre, his correspondence with his two sick associates and other friends contains a full history of this last and eventful year of his college life:—

To President Emory.

November 26, 1847.

I have to-day received a letter, asking me if I were willing to take the presidency of Alleghany College. Aint I rising? Lima, Newark, Alleghany, all in a row! I think you will agree with me in saying that no man who wants to study hard should undertake the presidency of a college. I continue to receive kind offers from Middletown, on condition that I leave here next year; but, of course, I have no views in that quarter.

The signs of the times indicate that the Church property will not be divided. The plan most in favor now is to give the Church South, *in perpetuo*, the right to purchase books at cost—not cost of stereotype plates, buildings, etc., included, for these were laid in part with their own money — but simple cost of work, wages, etc. On the whole, I don't know but this plan would give them their own pretty effectually; and if it would, it would save great difficulty in division, and great waste, too. I am glad to say that Griffith is coming round to our view of giving the South its share—indeed, he expressed himself the other day pretty effectually about it. If he had done this sooner, and had pledged Bond to it, the whole Church would have been ready for it by this time.

January 1, 1848.

Abel Stevens's plan to give the Methodist Episcopal Church, South, books at *cost* price, (not including the cost of stereotype plates, etc.,) seems to be becoming more popular than any other at the North. But at the South it is utterly distasteful. I can hardly see how a lawsuit can be avoided about this wretched property, and am often tempted to wish it all burned up. The Church controversy makes less stir than it did ; but that is because men's minds are made up to break the plan of separation to pieces next May, and begin our missionary work South as well as North. No other proposition to pay the money but Stevens's will be likely to carry at the next General Conference.

January 28, 1848.

Your letters are provokingly abstemious of all statements in regard to your health. We gather partly that you are improving, and partly that you are not. Do be more explicit—especially if you have *good* news to communicate. I told you in my last—and will now repeat again for fear you should not get it—that Mr. Griffith and others of the Board think that the way will be clear for me to take the presidency of the college next July. But I feel an almost invincible repugnance to undertaking the responsibility—especially under the unfavorable auspices under which I must necessarily do it. It has been suggested that Dr. Olin should take the missionary secretaryship, and I take his place at Middletown ; that would be (for *me*) out of the frying-pan into the fire.

January 31, 1848.

I have no idea that my friends in New Jersey will send me to Pittsburgh. All that I can do will doubtless have to be done by lobbying and by stuffing some of the real live delegates. There are a few points on which I feel great interest, and on those I have already succeeded in indoctrinating certain strong men. Old friend Griffith will go to the death, I think, for an equitable division of the Church property. He says it's a great piece of business for the blubbering brethren who voted the plan of division with tears in their eyes to come out now to undo their own act by repudiation. So far as he can, he will hold them to their bargain—a bargain which he had no hand in making, and always thought wrong and foolish, but which cannot be broken *salva fide.* I trust the northern brethren will yet see this question in the same light as we do here, and let us rid ourselves of this miserable money fight in a way worthy of honorable and Christian men.

April 21, 1848

I received eighteen votes in Jersey for General Conference. Don't you think I ought to go and take a seat on the strength of it? My future movements are quite uncertain. There is little probability of the General Conference electing me to the *Quarterly Review*—indeed, I don't see the slightest chance of it. They still propose the presidency of the college to me, but I have little idea of being Jack-at-a-pinch in that way.

To Professor Caldwell.

May 8, 1849.

It may be that you take too strong a view of your case; but if you do not, and the end of your labors is really at hand, I do not know that any consolation to us could be so great as the calm and steady confidence which your letter evinces. You may leave a little sooner than the rest of us; it wont be long. Life is precious for its uses—when these are gained, the change of one mode of existence for another, and a better, is not a thing to be deplored. Such, I think, were my own feelings during my severe illness, when, doubtless, I was much better prepared for such a change than I now am. With calm reliance upon the great Author of life through our Redeemer, such as you enjoy, death will have no sharp sting; the grave will have no victory to boast of. So, my brother, if you must go before us, we shall not grieve for *you*, but for ourselves—and that, too, but briefly, for our little history here will also soon be wound up. May we all meet in a better land!

We have letters from Emory, from Charleston. There is no improvement in his health, and he does not look for any improvement hereafter. His health is failing regularly, and he will probably come up to Baltimore in a few weeks, though his movements in that respect are not fully decided upon. He writes in great peace of mind and religious confidence, with no idea of prolonged life in this world.

May 19, 1848.

I returned on Tuesday from Baltimore, where I had been to see Emory. I conversed with him in regard to his religious prospects as fully as his feeble condition would allow, and found his mind calmly and firmly stayed on Christ his Redeemer. His peace of soul, he told me, surprised even himself. No fear, no uncertainty, no hesitation even; but a fixed and steadfast confidence of acceptance in Christ Jesus. Of course I expected nothing else, but yet it was gratifying to receive such comforting testimonies from his own lips.

In spite of the contents of your letter, I cannot but cherish a hope that your disease may not have gone so far as you suspect. And yet I am not sure that it is right to cherish such hopes. For our friends, as well as for ourselves, it is doubtless better for us to say, "Thy will, O Lord, be done." He knows what is best for us, far better than we can. With Christ, "who is our life," within our hearts, it cannot be hard to die. Death is not death for such. I preached on Sunday week from the words, "Because I live, ye shall live also"—the Redeemer's life the pledge and surety of his children's. In the spirit of that text there is no death. All is life in Christ. "The first Adam," says Paul, "was made a *vital* being, the second Adam is a *life-creating* spirit." As sons of the life-giver, our lives cannot fail. A change, to be sure, there is in our mode of existence; and what we call death is the transition-point of that change; but it is no dissolution, thank God!

It is blessed, indeed, for us to learn from your letters how perfect your confidence is. May your peace abound yet more and more, and the very God of peace sanctify you wholly in soul, body, and spirit!

May 27, 1848.

I have been occupied day and night in preparing Emory's funeral sermon, which I preached this morning in the church. I trust that the Holy Spirit was with us, and that the contemplation of our dear departed friend's lofty character may have stimulated many to strive to follow him as he followed Christ. The text was 2 Tim. i, 7: subject, the *Spirit of Christianity* a spirit of—I. *Energy*, not "fear," but *power ;* II. Softened and animated by *love ;* III. Guided by *en-lightened intellect*—"a sound mind." These heads afforded tolerable means of unfolding the life and character of our beloved president, who, I think, lived a breathing commentary upon the passage, and a constant illustration of the spirit of Christianity.

That our hearts are subdued within us under the dealings of God you may well imagine. Emory's death, and your illness, no favorable termination of which can be hoped for, according to your statements, must, indeed, weigh heavily upon us. It is hard for us even to conceive why our Father should take away those who seem fitted to be his best and most available instruments in the very bloom of their usefulness, and when their labors seem to be most of all needed. Yet he is our Father still. What better can we do than to say, "It is the Lord; let him do as seemeth him good." As he told his weeping disciples shortly before his own death, "What I do ye know not now, but ye shall know hereafter," so let us hope that in that better world we shall see *light in his light*, even upon these, the very darkest of his dealings with us.

The feeling of the students is most profound, and the results of Emory's death to them, as of his life, cannot but be salutary. The town, too, has shown much more sympathy and feeling than I had deemed it capable of.

It may be thought that it was a melancholy task to carry on a correspondence with two dying men—one of them in the extreme north of the United States, and the other in the West Indies. But to these three friends the Christian religion was the most real of all realities. They had staked their lives upon its promises, had shaped their conduct by its precepts, and had drawn largely from its consolations. Wholly free from cant, or pretence of any kind, they contemplated the separation which was clearly inevitable with an affectionate interest in each other, but with, at the same time, a perfect trust in God. Professor Caldwell, in whom quiet heroism was a conspicuous trait of character, a few days before his own decease dictated the following letter to President Emory:—

PORTLAND, *May* —, 1848.

From the last I heard from you I suppose we may be about equally near the boundary that separates the two worlds; and being able (though barely able) to write a line, I avail myself of the Providence which it thus grants of giving you one more expression of my affection, and of testifying the unspeakable goodness of God in sustaining me thus far through a sickness of great suffering and physical depression. So marked has been God's favor to me through Jesus Christ, that I have been enabled from the first to feel that all is for the best; and now, that I draw near to the final issue, that even death is gain.

I doubt not God is equally present with you. May he sustain us to the end! Give my love to your family friends, who I am happy to learn are with you. So soon to meet, I will not say farewell. God be with us both till we reach our better home in heaven.

A letter from one dying man to another is something unusual, but one such as this is rare indeed in literature. The tolling bell which summoned the students and people of the borough to pay their last tribute of respect to the memory of the deceased president, sounded soon again to announce the death of the senior professor. Professor M'Clintock felt from this time that his life in Carlisle, which had been so congenial in its companionships, so rich in the fruits of his own growth, and so abounding in happiness, was torn up by the roots. It was impossible for him to remain where the painful memory of so many broken ties pressed upon him. He

needed relief, and sought it in a new sphere, new activities, and new relations with his fellow-men.

To Dr. Olin.

May 27, 1849.

Let me say how deeply penetrated we all are with the spontaneous offering of your Faculty in the resolutions sent to us, and read
in faculty-meeting on Friday. As no usage demanded such an utterance, it is the more grateful to us all. The resolutions have been
communicated to the family, to whom also I took the liberty of reading your letter. It soothed and softened their hearts.

Your estimate of my dear friend is a very just one indeed. On one
point you need correction : he not only found you " congenial," but
admired and loved you fervently ; indeed, I am sure that I have
never known him speak in terms of higher esteem or warmer affection for *any* man than for yourself. Count him, then, among the
loving friends that you are to meet in heaven. *O præclarum diem,
quum ad illud divinum animorum concilium cætumque proficis-
camur !*

You will hardly think that I exaggerate when I assure you that
Robert was the best and purest man that I have ever known. His
aim was so entirely single that his whole life was clarified by it. His
religious experience, since the memorable manifestation of the Spirit
which he received, in 1835, after days of solitary wrestling with God,
has been always of the most satisfactory tenor. On the question of
his acceptance with Christ, there has never been any doubt or darkness, and so it continued to the very last. I reached Baltimore on
the day of his arrival there, (Thursday, May 11,) but he was so weak
that I could not see him until Friday morning. On that day and the
two following I had various conversations with him, but all very
brief, as he was utterly prostrated. " My peace is abounding," said
he ; " it has been great during all my sickness, and is still *so* great
and *so* unbroken that I wonder at it myself." There was no false
confidence, no want of self-scrutiny, but he had Christ in his heart ;
his life had been hid with Christ in God, and Christ was with him in

his dying hours. On Wednesday he made his will, and afterward, as if loth that his last strength should be devoted to worldly matters, he bore testimony to all that were present of the love of God, and of his sure hope in Christ. On Thursday he was still more feeble, and on Thursday night, at half-past eight, he quietly went to sleep in Jesus. So may we rest in Christ!

My feelings have been, I fear, almost morbid; but I am more than ever determined to try to do the duties which God may lay upon me faithfully. If I can be convinced, or can convince myself, that it is my duty to remain here, I shall most assuredly do so. Whatever others may think, I am sure that I am not the right man for the office of president. I write to you, as I believe you will know and admit, without any cant. I assure you that I am not disposed to think too humbly of myself. I do not doubt my intellectual capacity to fill the post creditably, as such posts are commonly filled in this country, but I have not the moral fitness. I am too impulsive, too unsteady, to be taken as a model for young men; and the young men of a college will make its president their model, if he is a man of any mark at all. For mere position of any sort I have no kind of ambition; and my happiness will be secured by the humble relations of a station in New York more effectually than by any office in the Church.

Again, my convictions on the slavery question unfit me especially for this place. I could not take it under any gag, and I might become an incendiary before any body would know it. You see I can make out a pretty strong case.

One of Emory's last anxieties was in regard to the division of the Church property. I told him that I thought some equitable plan would certainly be adopted, and he thanked God most fervently for the prospect. It looks ill now for the realization of his hopes and mine; but I hope still for the best.

In the warm midsummer, when the reapers were gathering in the rich harvests of the valley, Commencement came, with its pleasurable excitements and troops of

13

friends. There were long and anxious consultations, for the old was to pass away and the new to begin. The gaps left in the Faculty of instruction by death and contemplated removal were to be filled, and these were so many as to mark the close of one period of college history and the opening of another. Universal regret was created by Professor M'Clintock's resignation, and every honor that his friends could think of, as appropriate, was paid him. It was for him, too, the closing of a distinct period of his life. He could look back over the twelve years spent in Carlisle with unalloyed satisfaction. He had come thither a young man, but little known, and with powers but little tried. He had grown as few men can or do grow in the same length of time, and had prepared himself for the larger activities of succeeding years. He had secured from the Church and the world the recognition, which is the strongest incentive to continuous exertion. Hitherto he had been wholly a student; henceforth he is to be both a student and a man of affairs, and to attempt the difficult problem of harmonizing two opposite modes of life. Here, in the quiet of this old borough, he had set up his first home, had tasted the first sweetness of domestic joy, and had felt the first sharp strokes of sorrow in the death of children, kindred, and friends. His various experience had enriched him both in what it brought and in what it took away.

His subsequent career was prosperous, but no such light rested upon it as glorified these twelve eventful years. Perhaps it must be so. In the long day which we call human life the sun can rise but once; the freshness of the early morning can be but once; the exhilarating sense of power, not yet wearied, can be ours but for a brief space; the splendor with which we ourselves clothe all things visible,

"The light that never was on sea or land,"

we pour forth over the world, and it soon fades, to remain with us after only as a precious memory. The transition in Professor M'Clintock from the exuberance of his earlier manhood to the sedateness of middle age was very clear to his own mind, and very distinctly noticed by his friends.

But the death of Robert Emory was for him a loss never repaired. He had counselled with him, had leaned on him for support, and had found in him one to whom he could impart "griefs, joys, fears, hopes, suspicions, and whatsoever lay upon the heart to oppress it." Their correspondence, of which I have given, in proportion to its bulk, only few illustrations, is beautiful in its unreserve. "I have thought," writes Professor M'Clintock, when they were separated in 1840, "since your departure, that I was almost too hasty in undertaking to teach the classics. I fear my knowledge will fail me when I come to sit in the chair which you have filled; I fear that the contrast will be too great, and that I shall lose the respect of the students. Deeply do I lament the irregularity of my mental action, the want of stedfastness in my moral progress, the lack of fervor and zeal in my moral character. I would follow after you, my brother, my friend, though I shall do it *haud passibus æquis.*" And in the same year again: " My reproof (of neglect of correspondence) was a very gentle one; at all events, I meant it to be such, for I felt gentle enough, as I always do when writing to you or thinking of you. You are right in saying that no experience will ever make me prudent. I am satisfied that my nature, almost, must be altered before I can be, either in word or deed. I say and do things, every day of my life, for which I am sorry when I lie down at night and think over the events of the day; not that I do bad things, but simply because I do imprudent things. Is there any remedy for this evil? I wish I could travel a circuit with you for a year or two. You did me great good when you were here, but, now that you are gone, I fear I shall relapse again."

The travelling together longer was not to be. They had come to the parting of the ways, and while one faded into the infinite distance, the other remained to cherish the recollection of a sweetness and purity which had blessed so many years of his life.

CHAPTER VI.

1848-1852.

THE General Conference, which met in 1848 in the city of Pittsburgh, elected Professor M'Clintock to the editorship of the "Methodist Quarterly Review." His predecessor, Rev. Dr. George Peck, was made editor of the "Christian Advocate." The new position was in every way agreeable to the subject of our memoir; its duties accorded well with his scholarly tastes. No time was lost in completing the necessary arrangements for settling his household, and by midsummer his home was re-established among his wife's kindred in Jersey City. He found, however, that in this change he had left blessings as well as ills behind him. He missed the associations which had made his Carlisle life so delightful. The dropping in for a half-hour's chat, the "lingering over the dying embers of the fire" before saying good-night to some wholly trusted friend, were impossible in the great and bustling city. Living, as he did, so entirely in his affections, he felt that something was lost which could not be at once replaced. In his correspondence he dwells much on the "old times" which were never to return. Nothing pleased him better than to gather at his house, in Jersey City, as many as he could of his former associates and their families. Then there would be days of merriment and fun, of joke and gleeful reminiscence, which carried him back to the years when they were all young together.

The precarious condition of his health helped, perhaps, to make his return to New York less enjoyable than he had hoped. Shortly before leaving Carlisle he was seized with a spasm of pain which disturbed the action of the heart, deprived him for a time of consciousness, and left him greatly prostrated. It was, no doubt, brought on by overwork. He was for two years after subject to like attacks, which came upon him without warning, and kept him in constant apprehension of sudden death. The trouble proved to be only functional, and was removed by judicious treatment, rest, and travel. While it lasted, he was incapable of laborious exertion. Long sitting at his desk brought on a recurrence of the distressing symptoms, and compelled him to lay aside book and pen. Vigorous preaching was, under these circumstances, out of the question. Uncertain whether he might not suddenly lose his consciousness while in the street, he frequently used the precaution of taking a companion with him when going to his office in New York and returning home again.

But somehow, whether sick or well, he was certain to
have a good time. If he could not do all the work he
wished, he did what he could, and trusted to the favor
of Providence for the rest. He accepted sickness as a
discipline, and always said that he needed it for his
good. It depressed him, as it depresses every vigorous
man, but he had been so long schooled to pain that he
yielded to its visitations with something of a child's sub-
missiveness. It was his portion, and what sweetness
could be extracted from it he would find. His letters,
however, will tell all this better than I can:—

NEW YORK, *July* 26, 1848.

If you could look in upon us to-day, either at 200 Mulberry-street
or at Jersey City, you would find busy folks. At No. 200 I am striving to get my drawers, shelves, tables, papers, etc., arranged to suit me,
so that my work may go on smoothly hereafter; and in Jersey City,
Mrs. M'C., Mrs. Wakeman, and the children are up to their eyes and
ears in straw and dirt, unpacking beds, kettles, pots, and pans, from the
various boxes in which we stowed them away in Carlisle. Think of
such feeble folks as we are, with broken hearts and weak chests, doing
so much packing and unpacking. If my circulation was impeded at
Carlisle, it has had a pretty good flow since I left, as not a single
dollar was in my purse when I reached New York.

Of course we are among the best of friends here—and at home—
but it does not seem like home. It will be a long, long time before
our Carlisle friends and Carlisle life will lose their hold upon our
affections or our memory. The associations formed there, so close
and intimate, we cannot have the like of again—the circumstances
that allowed us to form them cannot come again. So much of our
life has gone—may we renew those happy affections in a better
world!

We are glad to hear that you have gone into your house—you will surely be more comfortable in every respect. How pleasantly we could spend our vacation with you, if we were there. But I talk of vacations as if I had any part in them--but that is all gone. You must not think us dissatisfied in any sense with our new position ; but we cannot easily forget the old one, and the old friends that ever clustered around us there. And we are glad that it is so. Long as we live, will we love our Carlisle home and friends, and you especial- ly, whom for so many years we have had in such close intimacy. If it were possible, how glad we should be to have you near us, and enjoy your fellowship again.

August 10, 1848.

I go over to the Book Room every day, and do up all the business that is to be done. I have not attempted to write much—that is, any thing that requires labor and thought; nor shall I for several weeks to come. The business of the office, with the arrangement of the library, directing carpenters, workmen, etc., is about all I do, and it is just the kind of work for me now. The children are hearty, but, like their parents, they miss Carlisle, and would like to go back.

To Doctor Olin.

NEW YORK, *October*, 1848.

Whether I have actual organic disease of the heart I know not. The first attack was on Commencement Day, July 13, and if it were purely nervous I should think it ought to have vanished by this time : but instead of that, I have more or less of it every day. When I re- frain absolutely from study and writing, I get on quite well ; but after hard reading, thinking, talking, or writing a few pages, all is undone again. I aim to do as little as I possibly can, but even that effort tries me, where so much work is staring me in the face. I don't know that I can give any more information about my ailments, and will therefore drop 'em—at least from my letter.

I take to the full all your exhortation : and have my head and heart full of things to say to the preachers and the Church on the subject of culture. But in my present health (there it is again !) I dare not write. Cannot you give me something on the subject? Even a few pages at a time? You can rouse thousands with your trumpet tones. Will you do it? My "abjuration of conservatism" is precisely expressed in one sentence of your own letter—"*the error of such conservatives consists in their attempts to stay and reverse, instead of accelerating, progress.*" I mean, and hope, to be a conservative of the forward kind; not falling into any extravagance, or ism, if I can keep out, by the grace of God, but striving to get the Church at its work of growth within and without. The "naughtiness of slaveholders" I shall not meddle with until I see good reason to; much rather the naughtiness of impoverishing our itinerancy by admitting boys who can hardly read and making preachers of them; the naughtiness of baptizing infants and then treating them as if they were heathen, until the breath of a revival comes over to convert them, instead of holding them as initiated into the Church, as our standards do, and training them up for her service and God's. Only help me in all this and I will mend your quotation: "*Olin meminisse juvabit.*"

On the matter of the relation of baptized infants to the Church, my mind and heart are constantly at work. I think I have written or spoken to you before about it, and that you agree with me in whole or in part; but I should like to hear from you more definitely. I have just received Bushnell's "Christian Nurture," and really I must go great part of the way with him. Have you read the book?

To his Carlisle Friends.

October, 1848.

I have just read a new book, with a taking title, "The Conquerors of the New World and their Bondsmen," which would interest you I think. It treats of the discovery and first settlement of the West Indies, and tells how the white people abused the brown people, who faded away before them like a mist, and how the black people were brought in to fill the gap and toil in chains and bondage. The romance of that strange history is ever new, told by whom it may be— Irving, Prescott, or a nameless nobody, it is still the most attractive of all histories, unless, indeed, perhaps the more wondrous romance of Napoleon and *his* bondsmen, which Mrs. M'Clintock finds ever new and ever delightful. She is even now reading a most charming little book, the "Autobiography of Heinrich Steffens," a professor in the University of Halle, a most genial man of letters and philosophy, who was driven from his books by the thunder of Bonaparte's cannon after the battles of Jena and Auerstadt ; and who afterward followed the Prussian army in its pursuit of the retreating French in 1814 even up to the walls of Paris. It is a most graphic set of pictures—and I wish you could see them ; but the book is not published in this country and I only stole this copy from Harpers'. It has to be returned. *My*, but isn't my letter getting *bookish !* If I were to tell you all the books I have gutted (excuse the word, but there is no other in the language for it) this week, I should have to take two or three sheets instead of one. I wish, most heartily, that I could run in and have a talk, but those pleasant days are over. Let us strive to do the duties of life as well as to enjoy its fleet pleasures ; that so, through Christ, our merciful Redeemer, we may enter the world of perpetual pleasure hereafter.

December 9, 1848.

My health is better this week than for several weeks past. The pain in my heart returns more seldom, and is less violent when it does come, and altogether I feel more confidence in my chest than I have lately done. But the buoyant, youthful—even extravagant— spirit of life which I used to enjoy, seems gone forever. Life appears sombre to me, even in my most cheerful hours. Not that I am gloomy or lowspirited at all—I don't think that feeling has had possession of me for many hours in years past—but the bright light that used to stream over every object seems fading more and more. My heart clings to my friends (those who are left) more closely than ever, and it seems almost a sin not to be seeing them, or thinking about them, or writing to them, all the time. Did you ever have such a feeling as that ? Sometimes I think I am unlike every body else.— and a great "fool for my pains." But after all it is best so.

To Doctor Olin.

December 3, 1848.

Your coming here will be a wonderful blessing to me—unless you make a very short visit, or I am hindered from enjoying your society. At such times, and at such only, do I regret that I live in New Jersey, and not in the city. But it must be managed somehow—for I have not seen the face of a friend since I left Carlisle—except Floy's for a few minutes. It's a very barren soil about here. There is no one at all that I can take to, male or female—and it is not a happy way to live. My health, too, is so uncertain, that it seems folly to keep away from one's friends. Whether I am to be a grumbling, nervous invalid for the rest of my days or not, is a very grave question, and from present appearances I fear it must be answered in the affirmative. I tried to preach a Sunday or two ago and had to sit down before I had much more than begun, leaving Bishop Janes to take up the dropped thread, which he did, I am told, very successfully—better, doubtless, than if it had not been dropped. But I won't inflict my heart-beatings on you, as they are all physical, and, therefore, should be borne as silently and patiently as possible.

Who *can* write me such an article as ought to be made on the duty of the Church toward her baptized children? Do help me out with this—it makes the blood run quick in my veins to write the sentence, I feel so strongly on the subject. And so I have felt for long—a sense of almost personal guilt about the children, as about missions—the two great elements of the kingdom of Christ on earth, both of which we Methodists are leaving almost untouched. But I must not dwell on these matters, or I shall be excited and hurt.

Your sermon is selling widely and will do great good. I shall help to spread it, and thus try to do something indirectly. I fear that my preaching days are over—indeed, they never were to any great extent.

To his Carlisle Friends.

July 3, 1849.

How uncertain every thing in this life appears to me of late. Even the very houses and trees appear unsubstantial and treacherous to

me--stars, sun, moon, sky—all appear so transitory. What a contrast between these feelings and those of earlier life, when I had confidence in every thing—a buoyant spirit within, and all things bright
without ! The " buoyant spirit within," I suppose, makes the chief
difference—and that, I fear, is gone from me forever—at least for
this life. But if we ever reach heaven, I judge there will be nothing
to repress or chill the heart—nothing to give this dreary sense of uncertainty—to overspread the fairest scenery with darkness as here.
But I did not dream of writing in this strain when I began.

February, 1849.

Well, there's a wonderful difference between visiting at Carlisle,
and working in New York. There it was nothing but pleasure from
morning till night—seeing friends whose faces brightened at one's approach and whose hearts were rejoiced by one's presence—while here,
no one cares who you are, morning, noon, or night. But how foolish
it is to be drawing these contrasts ; I'll just stop it and tell you some
news. We are just about to purchase a house here that will cost us
$4,500. I keep up as happy and cheerful a spirit as possible, and at
home, with my family and books, I am happy indeed. But so far as
the happiness of enjoying the society of congenial friends goes, I have
none of it, and that far, suffer a sad drawback upon life.

March, 1849.

It is Sunday night. You are sitting in the parlor, I suppose, (unless attending to hospital duties up stairs—I hope not,) reading, your
mother on one side and —— on the other ; the children near by, if
they have not gone to bed. I am sitting at the table, the grate burning brightly at my left hand, and sperm candle before me, in that
very candlestick which you, doubtless, remember, and Mrs. M'C. in
the arm-chair, near the fire, reading the " Wesleyan Missionary
Notices," with strange accounts of the cannibals of the foreign
islands eating people up, fighting with sharks, and such like entertaining amusements. The children are in the front room (my study
is the back room, up stairs) fast asleep. Now there is a description

from which you can readily figure out a picture, if you love us enough
to take the trouble, and I am sure you do. Give me as close a detail when you write, and I will work up the painting exactly before
my mind's eye. I have thought a great deal about you to-day, and
about old times, and I cannot go to bed without writing you a letter.
O how I wish I could "drop in" and have a talk about the "old
times," instead of merely mentioning them on paper. But it cannot
be, and this is the nearest approach to it that can be. If you think
as much of getting one of my letters as I do of yours, this poor substitute for talk will please you. I preached last Sunday in this town
for thirty-five minutes, without injury, and have passed the week in
such comparative comfort and health that I tried the experiment
again to-day in Thirtieth-street, New York. Mrs. M'C. says I am
getting so well as to forget all my prudence, sit up till midnight, etc. ;
but I don't do it often, and don't work *very* hard.

March 15, 1849.

That visit to Carlisle was of inestimable service to me ; won't you
prescribe a dose of the same remedy again ? I would consent almost to be sick once a quarter for the pleasure of taking the medicine. And you, too—*you* have a long letter promised, of which I
have as yet seen nothing. Hard work has not kept you from it—I
hope sickness has not. You will be bound, as soon as you receive
this, to dispatch the epistle at once, and I shall watch the mails for
a proof of your punctuality and promptitude.

Poor Mrs. M'C. has a headache to-night, and sits by my table trying
to read it off in Chateaubriand's life. An eventful life, indeed, it
was, from his boyhood in the forests of Brittany, his youth in the
salons of Paris and amid the terrors of the Revolution, his manhood
in America—Baltimore, Philadelphia, Pittsburgh, Niagara, Mississippi—his prime again amid the wars of Europe, as author, diplo-
matist, poet, novelist, expounder of Christianity ; take it altogether,
his was a rare life. Begun before the death of Louis XV., he lived
through the reign of Louis XVI., the Revolution, the Republic, the
Consulate, the Empire ; again Louis XVIII., Charles X., the Rev-

olution again, Louis Philippe, and then died in the opening of the Republic of 1848.   You may imagine what a flood of memories the old man must have had to pour forth in writing his autobiography at seventy !

I wish I could be with you (now nine P. M.) and chat over all these matters, instead of scribbling them with bad ink, (as you will perceive ;) but *this* is infinitely better than *nothing*, is it not ?   I will think so when your answer comes.

To Doctor Olin.
                                                  March, 1849.

Professor Holdich called on Saturday, but, much to my regret, I was absent at the time.   In regard to his successor I really feel unprepared to advise.   —— is impulsive, I know, but I really believe that such men, if under the control of the grace of God, make the best instructors of youth.   A genial, open nature, is of all others most necessary for a teacher.   A slow mind or a cold heart is an insuperable objection.

The summer of 1849 was spent with his family in Lycoming County, Pennsylvania.   A secluded valley, at the base of the Alleghany Mountains, offered a quiet retreat, and here, with fishing and other forms of out-door life, he spent a delightful season, much to the benefit of his broken health.

To Doctor Olin.
                                                  November 27, 1849.

I am quite as tired of all *laudation*, in all places, as you can be. Sometimes I feel tempted to do nothing but abuse people.   I wonder if that would mend the matter?   Praise is losing all its value, if it ever had any.

I am pestered to death with volunteer contributions for the " Review."   Men who have just learned the Greek alphabet send me critical and exegetical remarks on passages of Scripture.   Others give original sketches in Church history, made out of Mosheim and

Dr. Ruter. Others discuss final perseverance in series of elegant extracts from " Watson's Institutes " and " Fletcher's Checks." Others give me copious analyses of good Bishop Asbury's journal. Others send in Dr. Clarke's ideas on disputed Scriptures—whereof Dr. Clarke knew nothing. Is it not delightful ? Such zealous, painstaking, thorough, scholarly work, going on in so many different quarters at once ! Hope for the world.

To his Carlisle Friends.

February 11, 1850.

Your letters were such little *scrimpy* things to what they *used to was*, that I thought they were only a kind of prefaces to letters to follow by the next mail or so, like the little balloons that aeronauts send up before the big one is inflated fully, and let off to be gazed at. But, as it seems yours were the real balloons after all, I suppose I was all wrong in not gazing at them, and writing at once, just as if they had been ever so big. But you don't dream of any want of *love*, whatever want of *letters* there may be in me. The truth is I am sadly overworked. For weeks I have not got to bed till twelve or one o'clock at night, and at hard work all day besides. It is now approaching eleven as I begin this letter, and divers others are waiting their turn before I go to bed. It seems to me I must be one of those wicked ones for whom there is no rest ; and yet I try to be busy only at good things all the time.

The " Methodist Quarterly Review " is the oldest of the periodicals of the Church whose name it bears which have had a permanent life. Originally established in 1818 as a monthly magazine, it was, like its model, Mr. Wesley's " Arminian Magazine," devoted largely to topics which are now usually treated in the weekly religious newspaper. It was to some extent superseded by the appearance of " The Christian Advocate " in 1826. In 1829 it was suspended, but in 1830 was reissued in Quarterly form by Dr. John Emory, then senior Book Agent. Dr. Emory also edited the " Review " until his election to the Episcopate in 1832, and contributed, with his own pen, the principal original articles. Professor M'Clintock aimed to enrich the " Quarterly" by enlisting in its service the very best writers of the time, as well without as within the ranks of American Methodism. He sought out the men whom he wanted, and urged them to their best exertions. As a result he was able to spread before the readers of the " Quarterly," during his administration, Dr. Stevens's brilliant essays on Channing and Lamartine, Dr. Olin's exposition of the Religious Training of the Young, and his eloquent appeal to the Young Men of the Church. The elder Dr. Bond contributed an article on the Methodist Church, South, the closing passage of which is, perhaps, the most powerful arraignment of Methodist complicity with slavery ever written. Dr. Schaff furnished essays on early Christianity, afterward incorporated into his Church History; Dr. Jacobi, of Berlin, an Analysis of the newly-discovered Writings of Hippolytus, and the editor himself, appreciative estimates of Neander and Olin. Drs. Floy, Curry, T. V. Moore, (of the Presbyterian Church,) and Mr. H. T. Tuckerman enriched its pages with articles of the finest quality on topics which, at that time, were uppermost in the minds of cultivated men.

It was the purpose of Dr. M'Clintock to keep the " Review " fully abreast of the age, and it fell in with that purpose to give to its readers a searching analysis of Comte's Positive Philosophy, in a series of papers by

Professor Holmes, of Virginia. Comte's system of Positivism was then rising into notice as a fearful portent, the last and strongest expression of the atheistic view of the world. Its denial of a place for theology and metaphysics in the realm of knowledge ; its theory of the successive stages of intellectual progress, by means of which these two were ruled out ; its endeavor to organize sciences, new in name, if not in substance ; its hierarchy of all the sciences—made its exposition and the statement of its defects, in the opinion of Dr. M'Clintock, of supreme importance to all educated men. Laying down the broad proposition, that what cannot be scientifically known is not knowable—that inquiries into the origin and destiny of the universe are fruitless, because beyond the capacity of our intelligence—Comte opened again the question of the certainty and limitations of human knowledge, or, as it is now phrased, of science and faith, which at present fills the world. Dr. M'Clintock had the sagacity to perceive that the advent of Positivism was the beginning of a long discussion, and entered upon it with all his characteristic energy and enthusiasm. The contributor to whom this task was allotted performed it with such candor as to elicit expressions of gratification from Comte himself.

This was a bold line of policy for Dr. M'Clintock to pursue. At the outset of his editorial life he was met with the suggestion that a "Methodist Quarterly Review" was an entire mistake, that it was beyond the needs and the appreciation of the body of ministers for whom it was designed. His friend, Dr. Olin, was of this

14

opinion. " I should say," he writes, "make it less a
'Review;' a little more a magazine. The 'Quarterly'
is about as well adapted to our literature as the arch-
episcopal palace of his grace of Canterbury to one of
our bishops. The idea of keeping up a *dignified* periodical for the credit of the Church is preposterous. There
is no true dignity where there is no adaptation."

After giving this advice of one of his trusted friends all
its due weight, Dr. M'Clintock decided to adhere to his
original purpose, and to make the " Review" the organ
of the very best Christian thought. He believed that his
Church had something to say on the life questions of
the age, and ought to say it. Its literary resources
might be scant at the moment, but they would increase if encouragement were given for their growth.
He cherished the hope that the "Quarterly" might
both give tone to the Church's thinking and encour-
age literary production. Just criticism would help
the preachers to discriminate the bad from the good,
and would keep before their eyes the highest ideals of
literary excellence. In a word, he held firmly to the
conviction that there was a place for the " Review " as a
stimulant and guide of the literary activity of the Church.

Before the editor entered upon his work the General
Conference had directed him to make the " Quarterly "
" more practical." " But how?" he asks in his first address to his readers. Not, surely, by lowering its tone
in point of literature and scholarship; that could never
have been meant." He will, therefore, obey his official
superiors, and at the same time adhere to his own sense

of what is fitting. He aimed at the practical in articles on Biblical exegesis, the faith, discipline, and polity of the Church, and the social and political questions of the age.

As to the first he insisted that the interpretation of the Scriptures being the chief business of ministers, it was the duty of the " Review " to give them help in that department. In the treatment of Methodist questions he demanded freedom. " Nothing is gained," he writes in his announcement, " to religion or the Church by attempts to cut off investigation or to stifle honest opinions. Time was when this was thought to be a Christian duty. There are, doubtless, some who think it such still, who would shut up men's minds forever in their own narrow inclosure, putting a barrier to inquiry at the precise point which they have reached, as if wisdom must die with them. To these men every new view of the wants or duties of the Church is heresy, and all scrutiny of an old one presumption. With such we have no sympathy. We are set for the defence of the Church, whose servants we are ; her best and surest defence is to be found in calling out her energies for the great work of advancing the kingdom of Christ, and in showing that she is not, as her enemies say, a bulwark behind which all forms of social wrong and crime can intrench themselves securely."

These are the words of a brave and fearless spirit, and to the line here laid down Dr. M'Clintock adhered faithfully for the eight years of his official term. In treating public questions he rejected, as he heartily despised, the " false conservatism, at once domineering and timid, despotic and servile, which would stand as still as possible when all the world is in motion;" but no less did he disdain the "morbid appetite for new measures which forms some men's substitute for virtue." He had the conservative instincts which come of large scholarship; but loved progress, too, as every one will who has a hopeful and "forward-looking mind." To raise the literary character of the "Review" he added departments of Theological and Literary Intelligence, and extended the Critical Notices so as to include the best English and foreign books which it might interest his readers to be acquainted with. He set his face as flint against the indiscriminate puffing of Methodist publications. "It seems to have grown," he writes, "into a sort of common law among our periodicals that all books from our own presses, or from those of our friends, should be lauded, of course. It is high time for us to be just to ourselves. And we give our brethren of the newspaper press notice that they may begin with us, if they please; if our journal is liable to censure in any particular, we hope they will bestow it." Added to all these, essays on Biblical and philological criticism and the high themes of philosophy rounded out his editorial scheme.

He knew that in working out this conception of a "Review" the difficulties to be met were formidable. At the time of his entrance upon his office the Church had not done much more than lay the foundations of its first Biblical school; its authors of acknowledged reputation were very few. He understood, too, perfectly well, that the practical religious interest had dominated hitherto in American Methodism, but he saw clearly that this interest would be safe only in so far as it was illustrated, defended, and protected by a corresponding literature. As all life which is destined permanently to affect the world finds for itself fitting literary expression, so, he was confident, the great vital force of Methodism would, in time, issue in appropriate literary creation. To stimulate other minds to the exercise of their best activity was, therefore, the one duty which he laid upon himself during these years. As was said, during the war, of General Sheridan, that he carried an atmosphere about him that invigorated the courage of every soldier, so it may be said of Dr. M'Clintock during this part of his life, that his mental energy was felt by all men with whom he came in contact. His growing acquisitions made him always fresh; his geniality disposed him to communicate freely what he knew; his imagination colored and magnified the objects of his interest, and his warm feeling gave them life. It was during these years that he projected the "Cyclopædia of Biblical, Theological, and Ecclesiastical Literature," which was subsequently undertaken by him and Dr. James Strong. Originally it was proposed that four scholars of the Church should prepare the work under his supervision as official editor of books. The men were named, and a meeting was had with the Book Agents, who, after much deliberation, decided that the undertaking was beyond their means. Another of his cherished ideas was a series of theological text-books for Methodist ministers. He urged his friend, Dr. Olin, to write a volume on moral philosophy. Nothing could have been better, but Dr. Olin's precarious health forbade the attempt. He also urged the appointment by the General Conference of committees to revise the standard catechisms and the liturgy of the Church. Of both these committees he was an important member.

He had not been long established in his new home before it was darkened by the loss of its brightest light— his devoted wife. Her health had been feeble for months, but no fatal result was anticipated either by herself or her husband. In the winter of 1849–50 alarming symptoms appeared, and by early spring she passed away. Mrs. M'Clintock combined sweet affectionateness with a calm temper and extraordinary capacity of endurance. In times of trial her firmness was invincible. She entered fully into her husband's pursuits, and, by cheering, lightened his labors. Their home was sunny and happy, a centre of attraction to the many friends who came within the circle of its beautiful life.

March 17, 1850.

Two weeks ago yesterday my dear Augusta died. I cannot yet realize it. Every thing wears a strange aspect. I don't know whether you will understand me ; but perhaps you will when I tell you that a sort of mist seems to hang over every thing. Even streets, houses, and all familiar objects appear thus. I work, work hard, but it appears mechanical, and even unreal. Is it not well that this earth is thus shown to be not our home ? By and by we shall be strangers in it, as our fathers were, and shall feel that our kindred and our home are in heaven above. So one can become a stranger, even in the home of his youth and love, as all that made it home for him vanish into darkness and silence. One after another they are going. For some years I have felt no confidence in human life. I feel less than ever now. All my arrangements seem to me provisional and temporary; a few years ago I talked of them as permanent. There is no permanence here; God does not mean that there should be. There, and there only, where Christ is and where our loved ones are, is our continuing city.

I did not think she would die soon until a day or two before her end. Nay, on the Thursday I thought she had turned a crisis, and would rally. Not supposing her end near, I did not talk with her about it. From a number of expressions of hers that her mother and my sister have since mentioned to me, I infer that she thought of it. But her fortitude and firmness were so indomitable that never a fear, a complaint, or an anxiety escaped her lips. In respect to that quality of endurance, I never saw man or woman that approached her. To the last she was far more careful of others than of herself.

May 15, 1850,

My own thoughts and affections are far more taken off the world than they have ever been before, and perhaps it is for this result that afflictions have rained upon me so heavily and incessantly. It needed great affliction to remove the film from my eyes, and to let me see the world as it is. How worthless, how trifling do all purely earthly enterprises and affairs seem when the shadow of death hangs over us, as it now perpetually hangs over me! Don't think that I am gloomy, or that I wish to infect your own thoughts with gloom; far from it; but such appear to me to be the realities of life, and I don't know why. I have just put down what I feel.

To recruit his health, Dr. M'Clintock determined on a trip to Europe in the summer of 1850, in company with his friends Mr. James Bishop, of New Jersey, Mr. J. W. Harper, Jun., and his cousin, Mr. William Divine, of Philadelphia. Mr. Divine's daughter was also one of the party. During all this long journey Mr. Bishop watched over the invalid editor with brotherly care.

STEAMER WASHINGTON, FRIDAY, *May* 24, 1850.

How often since Monday have we wished that you could peep in
to see how delightfully we get along! I do not wonder now that
people who have been at sea want to go again—such a perfect *abandon* of feeling, casting away of all care, thought, and anxiety I had
not conceived possible. We left you at twelve; at two we dismissed
our pilot. A poor fellow had smuggled himself on board in hope of
getting a free passage; but unfortunately he had made himself
drunk, and couldn't hide. He was a Scotch tailor, of very good
appearance. He begged hard: "O, captain dear, give me a steer-
age passage. I'll be of great service on board. I'll mend all your
clothes." No use; go he must, and when the little cock-boat came
alongside for the pilot, the mate tied a rope round the tailor's waist
and let him down, saying, with much more wit than reverence, "The
Lord gave, the Lord hath taken away, blessed be the name of the
Lord." At half past three we sat down to dinner with good appetites. In about three minutes Miss D. got up, looking very white,
and hurried to her room. In five minutes more William had to run.
The next to go was Bishop. I stood it out till the dessert came,
and then thought it prudent to get below. For about an hour we sat
there, D., B., and I, who occupy one state-room, casting up in turn,
beating each other's backs, and laughing till we almost burst.
Badly as we felt, each saw the other's movements in so ineffably
ludicrous a light that we could not keep still.

The ship is very steady and comfortable. The attention is beyond
any thing I had supposed. We have plenty of water, abundance of
ice-water in our state-room all the time, a lamp burning all night, and
any thing we choose to call for. The table is superabundant and
superexcellent.

We have Forti on board, the opera singer, and he sang the "Marseilles" for us yesterday (Maretzek accompanying him on the piano)
in his very best style. It was really magnificent. His state-room
is next ours, and he lets his lungs out every morning just about as
we are getting up, and of all lungs I have seen or heard of, his beat.
Since the first day my heart has not troubled me.

Saturday Morning.—Our run thus far has averaged over two hundred miles a day. Yesterday it was two hundred and thirteen. It will get faster every day, as we burn about thirty tons daily, and the ship sails better as she is lightened. Before we get across we expect to run two hundred and fifty and two hundred and eighty miles a day. The sea is very rough now, and many passengers are sick ; but I have stood in the bows for hours, rocking as if in a swing, and enjoying it more than I ever did a swing. How I have wished the children along ! There are about twenty children aboard, and they are as happy as crickets.

TUESDAY, *May 23.*

We have made much more than half our passage. On Sunday morning I preached a short sermon of about thirty minutes from 1 John iv, 19 ; most of the passengers were present, and they were very attentive. It did not hurt me at all. I have not been a particle seasick, though Sunday night and all day Monday we had a severe gale from the north-west. The sea ran, as they say, "mountains high," a thing of which I had no just conception before. I kept the deck nearly all the time to see and enjoy it, in spite of wind, rain, and spray. The funniest sight of all was the dinner-table, at which as much crockery has been broken within the last few days as would keep you in store for a twelvemonth. The dishes are all secured to the tables with racks, but when the tables tilt up suddenly at an angle of forty-five degrees no racks will keep soup from flying. We have made some very pleasant acquaintances among the passengers, and some of them (Germans) will be of use to us after we get on shore.

My health has improved very much, as proof of which I may tell you that I walked the decks for three hours yesterday in a storm of wind and rain, which kept all the passengers below but two or three.

I will now close up. It has been storming, and raining, and blowing all day, but we are fast nearing the English coast. If nothing happens we shall see it on Sunday, and land at Cowes on Monday. Thence to Bremen is forty-eight hours. I shall probably write a short letter from Bremen.

" The first-class cars are occupied," the Germans say, "only by princes and fools," as the fare is too high for sensible people ; but we took them twice, by way of experiment, and the way hats were doffed and bows made was a caution.

Of the splendor of Berlin I need not stop to speak. I had no conception of the old world until I came here, and I could not transfer my present conceptions to you if I were to write for a week. I have been received with the utmost kindness by Professor Jacobi, and all the rest of the professors I have seen. I took tea on Wednesday with Mr. Fay, our *chargé;* last night with Dr. Twesten, of the university, who has a very pretty daughter that speaks English ; to-morrow night, I am engaged to Professor Jacobi, and have two invitations for Sunday, one to Nitzsch and one to Becker. I should have enough to do receiving civilities if I were to stay here a month. They don't ask blessing here at table, as we do, at preachers' houses or any others ; they don't make much of Sunday, either. Last Sunday, in Magdeburgh, our *valet de place* wished to get us tickets for the opera ; and so it is every-where. However, there is less business done on Sunday than I had supposed.

It seems selfish, I was beginning to say, for me to enjoy any thing here, when my loved wife is lying in the cold ground. Often and often this feeling comes upon me overwhelmingly. But a year ago we were travelling—she and I and the two children—in a pleasant carriage among the mountains of Northern Pennsylvania. I was sick, and she tended me by day and watched me by night ; and O how happy we were, in spite of sickness and care ! And now every thing is changed. They say that Time heals all wounds, and I have lived long enough to know that he does heal some ; but ah, they ache sadly in the healing and leave deep scars behind.

I have just returned from a walk around the old walls and fortifications of the town. The roar of the Rhine was in our ears nearly all the way, even amid the noise of the streets. I stepped on the plat-form behind the old cathedral—a building, by the way, some eight hundred years old, at least part of it—and looked around on the city and the river, and gazed on its beauty as it were on the beauty of a dream. We have no Alps, no Rhine, in America. And so I might say of a thousand other things. Here, too, in Switzerland, there is no royalty; one is not annoyed every hour, as in Germany, with the sound of drums, or with the sight of troops marching and counter-marching. Nor have any passports been demanded of us, or any examination of baggage, from the time we entered Switzerland until now that we are leaving it.

To Doctor Olin.

July 21, 1850.

You know so little about this European world that I suppose I ought to fill up several sheets with minute accounts of cathedrals, palaces, museums, picture galleries, and the like, for your edification and instruction. But I cannot take the time to enlighten you in this way. Take a voyage across the Atlantic once, or buy Murray's Hand-books, and get Mrs. Olin to read them for you quietly at home, and you may get some glimmering notion of what we travellers have seen. Nevertheless, I do think that I have seen some things that you have not. You never landed at Bremerhaven, did you? You never went, uninvited, to a German country-seat to tea, and found yourself amid ten or a dozen sprightly German women spending an afternoon in a peasant's cottage, fitted up for a lady's abode, and wandered about 'mid parks and pleasure grounds talking broken German to a very accomplished lady, whom you had never seen before in your life? But Bishop and I did all that. Indeed, throughout Germany, I have found it the easiest and pleasantest thing in the world to get into good society; and one learns in that way more of the life of the people in a week than he could otherwise in a year.

Our route was from Bremen to Hanover, Hamburgh, Brunswick, Magdeburgh, Berlin, Halle, Leipsic, Dresden, Nüremberg, Augsburg, Munich, Lake Constance, Zurich, Mount Rhigi, Thun, Berne, Basel, Strasburg, Heidelberg, and finally to Frankfort. Our longest delays were in Berlin, Dresden, and Munich, where there was most

to see. In Berlin I found the professors at the university all politeness and attention. I could have spent months pleasantly with
them. I took tea with Dr. Twesten, rector of the university, and
the leading dogmatic theologian of Europe, and found him a genial, cordial old man enough. He was inclined to be a little severe about black slavery, but I told him that our slaves were all
black, which, unhappily, was not the case in Berlin. He seemed
much interested in Methodism, and very ignorant, indeed, about it.

At Professor Jacobi's, however, I enjoyed an evening with six or
eight of the professors and of the city preachers, brought together
for our gratification. Of course, Bremen Methodism was a topic of
discussion ; they all thought it an unnecessary movement, except an
old gentleman who had been a missionary in Bombay, and had there
become familiar with Methodist missions, and he told me to send
as many good men as we could, not merely to Bremen, but to any
point in Germany. We had to explain the whole polity of Methodism, of any knowledge of which they were all—except Jacobi and
the old Bombayan—perfectly innocent. Strauss, for instance, had
never seen a prayer-meeting, nor, indeed, had any of the others ;
and I had to go through the whole ceremony of one from beginning
to end. The acme of their wonder and bewilderment was reached
when they were told how the preachers were supported ; they all admitted that they would have a poor allowance if they had to depend
upon the voluntary contributions of the people. I charitably told
them that in less than ten years they would find a large church
edifice, probably with a nice steeple, in Bremen, and that the
preachers would be well supported by the voluntary contributions
of Germans, whereat they not only opened their eyes, but pretty
plainly gave me to understand that they thought me a very decided,
though perhaps amiable, enthusiast.

To his Daughter.

MUNICH, *July 6, 1850.*

One day I looked out of my window in the *Hotel de Saxe* at Dresden, and saw in a large bay-window of the opposite house a little

girl, about as big as you, playing with a lady. The lady wanted to sew, or pretended to ; but the little girl would just let her begin, and would then throw both arms around her neck and kiss her—or kiss her eyes or her forehead—and so she kept on. The little girl's back was toward me, and the back of her head and her hair were so much like yours, that, if it had been near home, I should have thought it was you. You may imagine that it made me a little homesick. Indeed, I would gladly go home for a night, if possible, and have a chat all together, and tell stories in the twilight before prayers ; but that pleasure I must postpone for some months. In the mean time I pray that God's blessing may rest upon you, my dear child, and that you may be good and obedient to your aunts, so as to be a comfort to them, and to me when I hear from you.

MUNICH, *July* 7, 1850.

It is a queer country, this. I think you would enjoy a visit to it amazingly. The people seem determined to enjoy this life, at least, though, from all outward appearance, they do not think much about preparation for the next world. The streets have been full to-day (Sunday) of gay groups of promenaders ; battalion after battalion of troops has passed my window, and military music has been playing near for the comfort of the townspeople. At noon the stores are all opened, and the Sunday, for any religious purpose, is held to be over. I just looked out of my window, and saw a lady in the house opposite sitting with her work-table before her, sewing away on a frock for dear life. All the theaters, operas, concerts, etc., are open to-night. In fact Sunday is generally their most profitable day for business. I dined to-day in the restaurant attached to the hotel, and in the same room several gentlemen were playing billiards while we were eating our dinner. Recollect, too, that this is Sunday. You may ask why I write on Sunday ; but if I don't, the letter won't reach Liverpool in time for next Saturday's steamer, and so will lose a week.

PARIS, *July* 28, 1850.

You can hardly imagine the pleasure with which I received two budgets of letters yesterday on our arrival in this great city. For two hours Paris and all its attractions were forgotten; even the breakfast went away almost untasted.

I have decided to settle at *Bonn*, on the Rhine, above Cologne, as I think it will make a better and pleasanter winter residence than Heidelberg, though not quite as cheap. It is more central and accessible, being only thirty-six hours from London, thirty-six from Paris, and twenty-four from Berlin. I can get news from home there very promptly, and shall also, I think, find pleasant acquaintances. One of the professors, a very eminent man, (Professor Dorner,) who treated me with the greatest kindness and attention while there, has engaged to secure me lodgings as soon as I write from London that I am sure of going to Bonn. So that matter is all settled.

Paris, after all, caps the climax. It is the showiest, the absurdest, the most attractive, the most wicked, the most contradictory of all places on the face of the earth. In spite of revolutions, perils, and broils, if *this* world only were to be considered, Paris would be the most desirable spot in the world to live in. At the Hotel Maurice, where we stopped the first night, there are no less than sixty Americans now, and there are multitudes more scattered in different parts of the city. We shall stay here a week, and then get on to London, where the Conference commences July 31.

PARIS, *July* 80, 1850.

After a long round in Europe we are.arrived, at last, at its capital, for such is Paris. Our route has been, I think, an excellent one, and it has allowed us to see a great deal in a comparatively short time. From Munich we went into Switzerland, visiting the Lakes of Constance, Lucerne, Zurich, and Thun, and ascending to the top of Mount Righi, which affords a view of three hundred miles reach, bounded by the Jura Mountains on the east, the Tyrol on the west, and the chain of snow-clad Alps on the south. I suppose the world does not furnish another such a view. From Switzerland, by

Basel and Strasburg, to Heidelberg, where I stopped to look about a little, thinking that I might perhaps stay a year there. Thence to Frankfurt-am-Main, where we spent a very pleasant Sunday, and then down the Rhine to Bonn. The beauties of the Rhine have not been exaggerated; indeed, they cannot be. In one or two spots the Hudson gives some idea of the natural beauties of the Rhine; but it can convey none of that which art and ages of history have done for the Rhine. At Bonn, on the Rhine, I was so well pleased with the situation of the place, with the university, and the professors, that I determined, if the boys come over, to settle there for the winter. The kindness of the Germans is proverbial, and I found all accounts of it fully verified in my own case.

You would have been amused if you could have seen us the other day at the National Assembly. We had procured tickets, with great trouble and expense, as they are very hard to get. The galleries of the House of Representatives are arranged one above the other, like boxes in a theater, and our tickets took us up into the third loft, where we could neither see nor hear very well. I told the sergeant who showed us our seat that we did not like the place, and wanted to go lower down. " I can't help it, sir," said he, " your tickets are for this tribune." " But," said I, " we are Americans, and one of us is a member of one of the legislative assemblies in America." As soon as he heard we were Americans he redoubled his politeness, and finally told me to send a note down to the *quæstor*, who could, perhaps, give us better seats. He sent down Bishop's, and Divine's, and my own. Directly he returned with orders to take us into the " tribune of the diplomatic corps !" So we went, and found there Josiah Randall, who had got in by our embassador's ticket, and wondered how on earth we had found our way there.

I preached this morning in the Wesleyan Chapel at twelve o'clock. Before preaching they read the prayers of the Episcopal form, and, in spite of all my wishes to the contrary, I was tired of them before they got through. The forms may be good, but they would certainly be the better of considerable abridgment.

To Doctor Olin.

NEW YORK, *Sept.* 26, 1850.

You have heard rightly that I have gained strength and fatness by my four months of idleness ; and the experiment satisfies me pretty well that with an out-of-door life and a quiet mind I may yet be restored to sound health. But I cannot deceive you or myself so far as to say that I have yet reached that point. The trouble of my heart has mainly disappeared as my general health has improved ; but it is there yet, and gives me warning ever and anon against any excess. I have had to work for nine days pretty steadily, and I feel the effects of it. I have, therefore, no hope of doing fully the duties of my station here. Any possible performance, in the present state of things, is so far below my ideal of what the office and the times demand, that I fear my spirits will soon fail again, and I shall feel inclined—perhaps from a sense of duty, perhaps from a craving for repose—to give place to some stronger man, who can do what I cannot. A few months, however, will probably decide this question.

One of my first efforts, after visiting my family friends in Pennsylvania, will be to get up to Middletown. I intend to take as many trips as the state of my purse will allow, as it will not do for me to change suddenly from so very active a life to sedentary habits. Like the swallow, I must settle down to my nest in gradually narrowing circles. And if it were not so, I have love enough for you to go much farther for the opportunity of seeing you in health and of hearing you talk, to say nothing of my regard for Mrs. Olin, which I could not exaggerate in words.

My own opinion is, as it has been, that I ought to have remained abroad until next spring, but, as circumstances almost compelled my return, I feel satisfied with the result, and rejoice in being again within reach of my friends. O that more of them lived in or about New York !

To the Rev. T. V. Moore.

Nov. 18, 1850.

Could I get to Richmond without being lynched ? Wouldn't they take me up on suspicion of enticing away slaves ? Seriously, I have fears that I could not venture even that far into the region of slavery without the risk of insult at least.   No papers abused me more violently in 1847 than the "Richmond Enquirer" and "Richmond Whig;" but perhaps all that, too, has gone into the omnivorous "tomb of the Capulets."   Well, I feel strongly inclined to run the risk when I go to Washington, which will be some time in January or early in February, (D. V.)

To Mrs. J. W. Marshall.
Jan. 24, 1851.

Well, you have had your Virginia trip, and must now subside into Bœotian, Pennsylvania, dullness again.   Tell your stronger half (the Professor of Languages) that I have not been able to go over to the office since sending his package, but that I shall go in a few days, and then I will send off the rest of his books.   You must not suppose my inability springs from ill-health ; it is a job of heavy work that has been impending for a long time, and which I am staying at home to accomplish.   A few days will clear it off.   I only work hard from nine to four, so you see there is no danger of my getting into the old Carlisle habit of digging and delving all day and all night.

I am not unhappy, writing to my dear friend ; but it would be far happier if I could just drop in upon you all for a couple of hours' chat.   I wish you could find a nice house near you for fifty dollars a year rent, where we could live for two hundred and fifty dollars more, and then I will come, live as a gentleman of leisure, and *drop in* every day !   Have I not an enlarged ambition ?

I am inclined to think I shall be in Carlisle some time next month or early in March—but don't tell any body.   I mean to take it for a real luxury of a visit—all visit and nothing else.   And, besides, I intend to get a new coat, if I can raise the *chink*, as —— says.   Don't tell this, either.

Ah, what a foolish letter ! but it must go, just as it is.   God bless you !

To the Rev. T. V. Moore.
May 7, 1851.

You have seen Whately's "Historic Doubts," I suppose.   A new pamphlet has been put out treating the modern history of France
15

and Napoleon after the mythic method of Strauss, and showing it up very well. You will find it noticed in the "Athenæum," No. 1214. Have you read Newman's "Phases of Faith," "The Soul," "The Hebrew Monarchy?" These are the books that are likely soonest to corrupt the youth of this country. Already I have received sad letters from divinity candidates about them.

This is a very fragmentary and worthless letter, but I can make it no better. I should be quite at sea in advising you as to the mode of taking up your subject. The root of the modern scepticism lies in the proposition that *religion is independent of history;* and hence that it matters not whether documents of religion are really historical or not. To take the negative of this position, or to assume the positive ground that the *true* religion has not merely had a development in time but that we have a veracious and final record of that development, would cover the whole ground—answering Voltaire, Lessing, Strauss, Newman, Emerson, Parker, and all the rest in one. But *to do it—hic labor, hoc opus!*

If you will write to me on any precise points, as they may come up in your thinking, I will write as freely as I can. Nevertheless, as you may see, my own thoughts are undigested. Much and long have I thought and read of these things—oftentimes with pain and anguish of mind. But I have clear daylight of heart now, if not of head.

June 12, 1851.

I may, during my travels, see some rural nook that will tempt me to set up a more permanent tabernacle than any I have yet tried to establish. I long for the country and for rest; and if I find a pleasant, retired, shaded place within my means, I shall, without doubt, purchase it, with a view to looking for such rest next spring. In quiet I might do something, I hope, that would serve the Church and the world in the way of writing—free from the wear and tear of office, and from the constant calls that beset one so importunately in a New York residence. These may be dreams, but they attend me by day as well as by night. There is, at all events, a rest reserved for the people of God. May we be so happy as finally to enter into it!

April 4, 1851.

Next spring, if I be not re-elected to the editorship, I hope to retire into some quiet country retreat, and devote myself to the care of my children and of my health. Indeed I have many doubts whether I ought not to do it even if the General Conference does conclude to keep me in the editorship. The *basis* of my constitution is, I think, not shaken; but I require more rest and exercise than I can command in this or any other church post. I have some inclination toward New Brunswick, where my friend Bishop is building a house for himself; but it is not quite rural enough for my ideal. How positively charming even the very notion of such a rest is! Do you never find such feelings come over you? a sort of anxiety to be out of tumult and bustle, at liberty to think or not to think, to walk, or ride, or talk, or pray, or sleep, just as you please? I trust there is no wrong in indulging such dreams—for *invalids*, of course, only, are they justifiable.

In the summer of 1851 Dr. M'Clintock was called to mourn the loss of Dr. Olin. Like himself, Dr. Olin was full of warm sympathies and those tender solicitudes which make close friendship both possible and enjoyable. They met for the first time in 1843, and at the close of that year Dr. Olin wrote : " I congratulate myself upon having formed your acquaintance, on having become, in no common sense, your friend, and on having secured your correspondence. This interest will, if it please God, and you are minded favorably, have a future to it, and I shall often enjoy the happiness of an interchange of sentiments and counsels with an intelligent, warm-hearted Christian man, in whom I fully confide." A few years later he asks, playfully, " When does friendship become old? And may we not now call ourselves *old* friends?" In this spirit their association with each other was maintained until it was broken by Dr. Olin's death. Unfortunately for Dr. M'Clintock, the message sent to inform him of his friend's peril failed to reach its destination, so that he was not made aware of Dr. Olin's illness until after it had ended fatally.

August 22, 1851.

We are saddened by the death of Dr. Olin. That good, grand man has passed away from the earth. I regret most bitterly that I was not able to be with him in his illness. He telegraphed for me to New York, but they did not know where to send after me, and so I heard nothing until the Monday after his death. So Carlisle and Middletown are both without presidents. I think it most likely that Collins will go to Carlisle, but who will go to Middletown? The trustees (or some of them) wish me to give my name, but I cannot consent to it. My health is now regularly improving, I think, and I feel it my duty to remain in my present post.

In October, 1851, Dr. M'Clintock was united in marriage with Mrs. Catharine W. Emory, the widow of Robert Emory, who still survives him. In the same month he was elected to fill the place of Dr. Olin, as president of Wesleyan University. The invitation was accompanied by every evidence of cordiality that could be desired, but in view of uncertain health was declined. The winter was spent in writing and preaching, of which latter he did, for a sick man, an enormous amount. He made during these years specialties of the Sunday-school system and missions, and had many calls to present his well-considered views on both topics.

The new Catechism, on which he and Dr. D. P. Kidder wrought together, was much in his thoughts. " My ideal," he writes, " is to have such a Catechism as can be learned by any child and retained, and to have laws passed making it the duty of every minister to catechise the children in addition to Sunday-school instruction." There were times during his editorship when he felt that he was not doing the best work of which he was capable. "Am I never," he asks in his diary, "to do any thing better than translation and criticism?" Much that he did, as an editor, was necessarily buried out of sight. It was all under ground, as he sometimes complained, and this fact inclined him to look for a retired spot where he could gather together his best thoughts, and embody them in some literary product of permanent value to the world. He planned in this regard more than he executed; but so will every man who has a love of labor and an active brain.

To the Rev. T. V. Moore.

January 18, 1852.

If I had the physical health, I should greatly desiderate a pastoral appointment, with two sermons to preach on Sunday, and time for work during the week. Your position now is, I should fancy, just one of the happiest a man could have, so far as outward things go to make up human happiness; and I trust you wont abandon it soon, unless for a better post, say in New York, where you ought to be, and where I hope you will be before I leave these parts. Look out for a call on the first important vacancy that occurs.

I do not see much hope of getting to Richmond this winter; I wish I could. Shall you be on this way? Our household is now very small, compact, and agreeable, (at least I think so,) and we shall stay at home until the middle of April, with the exception of two or three days in February, that I must spend at the meeting of the Board of Trustees in Carlisle. So come, and I assure you I

wont run away. We expect to break up our housekeeping here by
about April 15, and shall then be unsettled until after the session of
our General Conference in May. If they re-elect me to the " Quarterly," I shall take a house in Newark, Elizabethtown, or New
Brunswick, so as to get further away from the tumult of the great
Babel. If they don't re-elect me, I shall probably settle at Germantown, or some other village adjacent to Philadelphia, and live in
quiet as long as God spares me, writing what he may help me to
write. Either prospect is agreeable.

The review of Positivism in the pages of the " Quarterly " led to a correspondence with M. Comte, and a call
for contributions to his support, which was cheerfully
responded to by Dr. M'Clintock. Two of the philosopher's letters are appended to this chapter. The first
was published by M. Comte himself; whether the second
has been before in print I am not aware. It is interesting as presenting his own account of his philosophic
education.

LETTERS FROM JANUARY, 1847, TO APRIL, 1852.

I. LETTERS TO DR. M'CLINTOCK.

I.

PARIS, 7 *Homer* 64, *Wednesday, February* 4, 1852.

To DR. J. M'CLINTOCK, EDITOR OF THE METHODIST REVIEW, NEW YORK.

SIR : In the number of your " Methodist Quarterly " for January,
1852, which I received last Thursday, I have just read a conscientious
review of my principal work, written by an eminent adversary, containing, indeed, numerous involuntary mistakes, which are, however,
but trifling, and may therefore be spontaneously corrected hereafter.
This generous proceeding, to which I have been but little accustomed from the French press, induces me to extend, even to such
adversaries, my personal appeal to the western public, which indeed

merely supplements that of 1848, so generously referred to in this
memorable article. If I knew the anonymous writer, I would be
happy to address him personally, and to express to him my sincere
gratitude. But I trust, sir, that you will kindly be my interpreter,
and accept for yourself also one of the inclosed copies of my circular
letter. I cannot but congratulate myself upon this momentary in-
fraction of the happy rule of mental hygiene which for many years
has closed to me, systematically, all papers or reviews, even scientific
ones, and has permitted me no other habitual reading than that, ever
new, of the true masterpieces of western poetry, both ancient and
modern.

Public morality requires now that this desperate call of undeserved
distress should receive a fitting response from the other side of the
Atlantic, the better to stigmatize both the persistent lukewarmness
of most of my friends and followers, and the ignoble zeal of my aca-
demic persecutors. Besides our common occidental origin, I cannot
look upon myself as an absolute stranger to a republic to which I ·
came near transferring my then opening philosophical career in 1816,
under the friendly patronage of the worthy General Bernard, and
even, indirectly, of the noble President Monroe. However that may ·
be, my present communication will clearly demonstrate the deplora-
ble extremity to which is reduced, in the very midst of his long self-
sacrifice, one who, after having founded the Positive Philosophy, is
now erecting upon that solid basis, and in greater perfection even
than he promised, as stated by his loyal adversary, the religion of
humanity.

In order to convince you, sir, concerning the full continuity of a
peaceful activity, which must appear endangered by such a position
as the present, I would wish to send you at once, as also to my honorable anonymous opponent, the first volume of my second large
work, published in July, 1851 ; a work which I promised to write
when, ten years ago, I completed my first. This " Système de
Politique Positive," as stated in that well-kept promise, will consist
of four volumes, the second of which I am now engaged in writing.
It will probably be published next July, and the other two succes-

sively at the same time in the two years following. Should you kindly assist my unparalleled inexperience of all questions of detail by informing me as to the best means of forwarding these things to you, you would soon receive the two copies above mentioned of the first volume, which is already known to some Americans.

This little philosophical gift you may accept without scruple as a feeble testimony of my respect, as I am my own publisher, and can therefore dispose of copies as I choose. In the mean time, I enclose herewith, together with my circular letter, a copy of the "Tableau Cérébral," which sums up my positivist theory of human nature, and is a most handy synopsis of this new volume, as well as a philosophical programme of the systematic course of lectures which I have for the last three years delivered before a private society, including both sexes, with the generous sanction of the only government which has heretofore respected fully the intellectual independence which I have at last earned by ceaseless sacrifices. From this circumstance, as a philosopher, you will be able to understand and appreciate the comforting fact that modern civilization can radically transform even the spirit of persecution, which is now limited to the destruction of fortune only, being unable to reach life or even freedom.

After a long and honorable career, more consistent, perhaps, than any ever before, I have contracted the habit of living altogether openly, according to true republican principles. If, therefore, you see fit to disseminate the enclosed circular, or even this letter, I leave the matter entirely to your kindly judgment, whatever publicity you may choose to give it, asking only that it be literal and full. I would, however, desire that you should first consult in the matter that eminent citizen of Philadelphia who, without ceasing to be my worthy intellectual disciple, is at the same time my chief temporal patron, Mr. Horace Binney Wallace, who is too well known to need any further indication.

Salut et Fraternité,   AUGUSTE COMTE,
                        10 *Rue Monsieur le Prince.*

II.

Dr. J. M'Clintock, New York.

PARIS, 24 *Dante* 64, *Saturday, Aug.* 7, 1852.

SIR : I have been deeply touched by the worthy enclosure in your letter of June 29, received July 15. This noble participation of two eminent philosophical opponents tends to characterize more fully the true nature of the free subsidy which is to shield from undeserved poverty the conscientious thinker whom they are unwilling to combat otherwise than by fair arguments, free from all material pressure either active or passive. However, from the true religious standpoint, where love is higher than faith, we feel that a certain brotherhood unites all those who, at this time, are sincerely striving to overcome intellectual and moral anarchy, whatever may be the opposition otherwise existing between the doctrines they hold with this great common aim.

Apart from the conflict of our doctrines, I have really no important correction to ask of him, except in regard to the influence he assigns to my early relations with M. de Saint Simon, who was in no respect either my teacher or my precursor. Mr. Lewes has all too carelessly repeated the absurd supposition, put forth by both my declared and secret enemies, concerning this assumed filiation. It is natural that Mr. Holmes should accept without inquiry a supposition thus adopted by one of my principal followers. I will therefore avail myself of the present opportunity to elucidate this point of my history.

Simple comparison between our doctrines would suffice at once to demonstrate the fallacy of such a theory. Had Mr. Lewes made such a comparison, instead of allowing himself to echo a malignant falsehood, he would have discovered that Positivism could not, even vaguely, have been derived from Saint Simon's system. Mr. Mill, who had compared them, never fell into this superficial error, so far as I know.

In the place of this absurd origin, which I have steadily disowned, I trust that impartial judges will henceforth deem it their duty to declare my true philosophical filiation, as it appears both from the whole of my works and from my own statements. I have always acknowledged Condorcet as my chief direct forerunner, and I accept no other. Scientifically, I proceed from Bichat and from Gall, the last scientific thinkers who have preceded me and prepared the way. Philosophically, I proceed indirectly from Hume, and incidentally from Kant, to go no further. But, in reality, the great Condorcet is the thinker I have most properly succeeded. I regret having placed him, in my " Positive Philosophy," below Montesquieu, to whom he was much superior. In my public lectures I have already rectified this mistake, which my present work will finally correct. In that philosopher we find the true connecting link between the eighteenth and nineteenth centuries. He was, like me, thoroughly prepared by scientific study, although the sciences, at that time, were not sufficiently developed to regenerate the mind. In the midst of the most anti-historical crisis that ever can exist, he attempted to base politics on history. I early felt the value and the defects of that effort, the carrying out of which I considered, at eighteen, as the chief object of my life.

Such, then, is my real philosophical descent : through Condorcet I belong to the great school of the eighteenth century—that of Diderot. The little schools of Voltaire and Rousseau, essentially inconsistent and therefore purely negative, are now absolutely extinct, although their remains are still agitating the undisciplined mind of the West. But the complete and organic school, the school of Diderot, Hume, and Condorcet, survives in me. What it then vaguely aimed at by means of the " Encyclopédie," is systematically realized by Positivism. The aim—absolute regeneration—has remained the same ; the means only have developed. None of my contemporaries has been of any real assistance to me in that task. The nineteenth century offers to my mind truly but one eminent thinker—Joseph de Maistre—and to him I always did full justice ; but from the first I spontaneously absorbed all that his works, retrogressive though they be, evolved that was deep and lasting, whether against the dogmas of the Revolution, or for the historical appreciation of the Middle Ages. If his work had not preceded mine, I could readily have dispensed with it, since, before I saw it, I had in my own way produced essentially an equivalent to it from the progressive standpoint. Still; after Condorcet and Gall, he is really the only thinker to whom I am at all seriously indebted.

Before I received your letter I had already found means to forward to you, at last, the two first volumes of my "Politique Positive." I delivered them, for you and Mr. Holmes, to a young Frenchman who is going to settle in New York. But I shall soon avail myself of the usual means to transmit to you the important essay entitled "Catéchisme Positiviste," which I am now writing before I commence, next November, on the third volume of my "Politique Positive," to be published in May or June, 1853.

Salut et Fraternité,   AUGUSTE COMTE,

                                  10 *Rue de Seine.*

II.—LETTERS FROM DR. M'CLINTOCK TO HIS FRIENDS.

I.

JERSEY CITY, *June 9,* 1848.

On my way from Carlisle yesterday, (Thursday,) I received the despatch containing the mournful news of your and our loss. Much as I had expected and looked for it, it still came with a shock upon me from which it was hard to recover. Yet my own grief, profound as it is, at thus losing my long-tried associate and friend, sinks into nothing in view of yours. But even yours, deep and poignant as it is and must be, is full of rich consolations, toward which, I trust and hope, you are able to turn your heart. He died, as you would have wished him to die, with so sweet and delightful a sense of his Saviour's presence that it was merely a translation for him from one degree of communion with Christ to another. How truly and faithfully he lived, and how Christ honored him in his death!

How strange it is that we feel, on the death of our friends, almost as if *we* were not to die, as if *we* had a lease of life. Yet how soon will we follow them! Even now Emory has saluted Caldwell, and soon both of them will salute *us*, if we are faithful to our calling as they were. The world seems worthless indeed, in view of these verities; what it offers seems all shadow and uncertainty, in comparison with the *certainty* of death, and of the life beyond. So, when my last reached you your dear husband was gone!

But I hardly know what I am writing, or whether what I write will do you any good. Yet I know it will. I would that I could see you in this hour of sadness and darkness. Your Saviour, however, is with you. He will one day clear up all this darkness, and banish all this sadness. Within that blessed home of the just all is light, and peace, and joy for evermore.

I shall leave here on Monday or Tuesday for home. Until I get there, I fear, I shall not hear all the particulars which I am so anxious to learn. God will bless and care for you, I am sure; his tender mercies will abundantly abound to you in your day of bereavement. *He* can comfort you, and he alone can. Return soon to your Carlisle home; it will be better for you and for Rosa. God bless you, my dear friend, and be assured of my deepest sympathy and affection.

Mrs. R. C. Caldwell.

II.

April 80, 1849.

Are you at work yet? Would it not do you good to run away for a little while? I have bought a house in Jersey City, and shall move into it in a day or two. There will always be a room for you. Come and stay with me days or weeks. It will do you good—I know it will me.

Our April "Review" has received great commendation — your articles especially. I think the number throughout a very good one. I could make a more learned journal much more readily with the contributors I have engaged—but that is not what is wanted.

Rev. T. V. Moore, Richmond, Va.

III.

New York, September 9, 1851.

Few things in the course of my life have so much affected me as the death of your husband and my friend. If any thing could add poignancy to such a grief, it is that I was far away, and not even cognizant of his danger, until the terrible news came that he was dead. How quickly would I have obeyed his summons, had it only reached me!

I should have written to you sooner, but I could never bring my-self to do it, though I have often sat down for the purpose. What words to use I could not find—words that should express my own feelings, and that should be fitting words to say to you at such a time—and I cannot find them now. I cannot yet realize his loss. I cannot but think that I shall look again into those benignant eyes, and hear again that voice which I never heard save in tones of tenderness and kindness.

If I have had any thing to be proud of in late years, it was in that I had a place in your husband's list of friends. If I had any thing to joy in, it was in loving discourse with him. Ah! if I had only known how soon this pride and joy should end—end, I mean, for this earthly life—how I would have grasped eagerly at every oppor-tunity of seeing and hearing him.

May God bless you and your boy with all temporal and spiritual blessings in Christ Jesus!

Most sincerely, your faithful friend.

Mrs. JULIA M. OLIN.

IV.

JERSEY CITY, *December* 20, 1851.

It would have been, indeed, a great inducement to go to Middle-town—the thought that we might have you again for a neighbor. But there were other reasons why I should have been glad to go: college life suits my tastes and habits better than any other; the work is just the kind of work I like; the post is one of high honor and usefulness; and we should have had a pleasant and fixed home in that most beautiful city, with good society all about us. But in spite of all these attractions, I was forced at last to come to the con-clusion that my health would not endure the work, its confinement, its responsibilities, etc., and on this account I gave it up. I had a letter from Professor Allen yesterday, asking me if I would not con-sent to take the presidency at Dickinson, but I wrote him at once that I could not think of it. Indeed, I should greatly prefer a quiet home in some country village, with my books around me, to any public employment; but the Church seems to want me in my present post, and I can do the work, I find, without injury to my health. So that. as long as the Church wishes to keep me here, I shall remain.

We shall remain in our present abode till about April 15, when we must break up here. We expect to get a house in New Brunswick, but it will not be ready for us until August or September, and we shall therefore have to board in New Brunswick during the summer. Can't you come to see us before we break up? You do not know how much pleasure it would give us to see you.

Mrs. R. C. Caldwell.

V.

Jersey City, *April* 18, 1852.

Will you come to see us? We have taken a snug little domicile at New Brunswick. just opposite the college building, which you may have noticed in passing to New York—just three hours ride from Philadelphia, and one from New York—the most convenient stopping-place in the world, where I shall be delighted to see *you*, and Kate will be delighted to see *her*, and we shall *both* be delighted to see you *both*. So, when will it be? and when shall we expect you? Our own movements are planned as follows: we remove from here to New Brunswick the week before the first of May, but shall not commence housekeeping at that time, as I have to spend the month of May at our General Conference in Boston, and we shall go there, bag and baggage, to board during that time. Early in June (D. V.) we shall settle ourselves at home in New Brunswick, and be ready and glad to welcome you and yours. I say (D. V.) with regard to our plans, and may use the formula with special propriety just now, for my little darling Augusta lies ill of a fever, and her continued illness may disturb all our arrangements.

How I should love to see and know your noble-minded friends! These things give us some conception of what human nature might be—nay, I suppose in God's mercy these higher spirits are intended to keep our hearts from sinking utterly as we see more and more of the baseness and depravity of the race in general. Robert Emory gave me a higher idea of the capabilities of humanity than I should ever have reached without some such visible embodiment of the marvelous power of goodness, inwrought by the Divine Spirit, in this wretched nature of ours. You *are* a happy man, with such friends and such prospects. Forgive me for saying that I think you deserve them, so far as I might say such a thing truthfully of any man. That you could not leave Richmond under present circumstances I can readily imagine—that you *ought* not, I am about as well satisfied. The lines have indeed " fallen unto you in pleasant places ; " but with love, and prayer, and faith, that need not be a snare. Sometimes I wonder whether it is right for us to enjoy ourselves so much in this world, so full of woe and wickedness as it is, and feel as if Christ needs us to disburden ourselves, and gird ourselves like Xavier, to work intensely for him, and then die. But, after all, Christianity is needed for salt and leaven to the every-day life of man, and unless our whole modern system of society is false and rotten, we are bound to take our places in it, and help, so far as HE may give us power, to purify it. My own physical incapacity is often a sore trial to me when I see so much to be done, and feel so anxious to take an active part in the fray—but then again He can do without me, or can use me, weak and worthless as I am, and I am content. His blessed will be done.

Rev. T. V. MOORE.

CHAPTER VII.

1852–1857.

THE longing for rest, so often repeated in Dr. M'Clintock's correspondence, appears, at first sight, inconsistent with his eagerness for work. His character had, in this respect, two sides, as is perhaps true of every man of energetic temper. To have a hand in every movement and a word in every debate was as natural to him as to breathe. His clear insight of the merits of public questions, and his warm interest in them, gave him both reason and motive for the expression of his opinions. Yet he relished equally well the quiet of student life. As much as he enjoyed the advantages which official position brought him, he chafed under its burdens, its wear of nerve and patience, its many, and to him profitless, details. Then, again, his method of work necessitated a frequent abstinence from labor. He plunged into his literary and other undertakings with an eagerness which before long exhausted his vital force, and compelled him

to desist. His friends repeatedly urged him to spare
himself, and to moderate his excessive industry. "You
ought," wrote Dr. Olin to him, "in all good conscience,
to be in bed before eleven o'clock, and to get up not
later than six. You would then, I think, soon be well.
Don't work too hard. Study not more than six hours.
It will make you wiser than your generation, which you
may thus live to serve. Why shouldest thou destroy
thyself?"

And so it came, from the frequent reactions which set
in after strenuous exertion, and from his strong love of
home and its comforts, that during all his years there
was ever before his imagination the vision of a restful
life, free from all public responsibility and care. Time
and again he tried to realize his ideal; succeeded for a
short period, and then broke up his quarters to accept
official position again. The modest home which he occupied during his first residence in Carlisle he improved
and adorned to the extent of his means. "We intend,"
he wrote to his wife's brother, in 1843, "to make divers
improvements and alterations for the increase of our
comfort. We cut a door through the parlor into the
garden, and put a little porch and arbor there for summer evenings; we put a paling fence in front of the side
lot, where the ugly board fence now is; and, finally, we
erect a pretty portico at the front door." A porch, if he
could so have it, broad and long enough for exercise, and
an arbor for summer evenings, were always elements of
his pictures of home.

After his re-election to the editorship of the "Quar-

16

terly Review," in 1852, he removed to New Brunswick,
N. J., in order to escape the bustle and excitement of
the city. His own health and that of his wife being
wretched there, he removed once more, in the spring of
1853, to Carlisle. Here he purchased, for a moderate
price, a beautiful house on the edge of the town, with
ample spaces in front and rear. A wing was added for a
library, and before many months he had all the appoint-
ments of the place suitably adjusted for the life of an
editor, student, and amateur cultivator of the soil. He
did not need " ten acres " to make him enough ; a little
more than one amply sufficed.

Having now the opportunity, he soon gathered about
him, and at no excessive cost, the elements of a delightful home. In his student habits here, as every-where,
there was nothing of monastic seclusion. It would have
been impossible for him to shut himself up in his library,
and, turning the key, surrender himself in solitude to his
books and manuscripts. The library was the centre of
the house, from which light and cheerfulness radiated in
every direction. On the front it looked out through the
trees upon the South Mountain, and afforded the eye in
summer a soft and pleasing landscape. In the winter an
open fire burned in the grate, a perpetual invitation to
all comers to gather about the hearth-stone. The books
filled the shelves and overflowed upon tables and chance
resting-places. They were well arranged, however, yet
not set up in stiff, stately rows, as if forever on a dress
parade. The instinct of their owner brought those most
required well about him, and so disposed them that they

were suggestive of free and loving companionship. The fresh, new books—those one most wanted to see—the magazines in their earliest fragrance, and, with the dew of the press still upon them, were always there. Work was with Dr. M'Clintock eminently social. He preferred to have some one of the family sitting by the fire and reading while he wrote at his desk. If that could not be, he would, when wearied, take a few minutes for a chat and a laugh, and then return to his tasks again.

In this new home he could indulge to the full his personal tastes. He was the soul of hospitality, and, except when sickness forbade, was rarely without invited guests. He was continually planning to have the friends whose companionship he enjoyed to visit him, and in his frequent excursions would take them in his way, and renew his personal intercourse with them at their homes. His house was one in which something was always going on, and the going on very enjoyable. He made it a point of principle to shun a stupid, humdrum way of living, and would quote Goethe's counsel, not to let a day pass without refreshing one's self with a little bit of poetry or a simple song. Wherever he might be he attracted society to him. Young and old, the well read and the scantily read, alike felt the power of his geniality. To young persons especially he was very delightful, opening in their minds a new sense of the charm of learning, and giving them, in the most unaffected manner, valuable hints for the carrying forward of their culture. He corresponded much with younger men, and would take the utmost pains to help them when troubled with the hard questions of metaphysics or theology. Correspondence is with some scholars a laborious duty, at best an interruption of their cherished occupations ; with Dr. M'Clintock it was one of the chief pleasures of life, and was so managed by him as greatly to extend his influence and power as a public man.

In the by-play which he provided for himself in this Carlisle home, he was as enthusiastic as in his more serious pursuits. His chickens, if not the finest the sun ever shone upon, were at least extraordinary chickens ; his horses had most, if not all, the virtues that could be engrafted upon horse character. His delight in nature, and in the creatures that serve human wants, was very beautiful. It was a thousand pities that he had not during all his working years, like Arnold of Rugby, a quiet retreat where he could at times have relieved himself of the strain of labor, and found rest in a change of interests and cares.

Left to himself, and without out-door occupations to tempt him to active exercise, Dr. M'Clintock was too much inclined to sedentary habits. He took little pleasure in bodily activity for its own sake. A tramp in the nipping, frosty air—a wrestle with the driving north-west wind, or a mountain climb—had no attractions for him. He could speak very prettily of "the soughing" of the winds of the valley as they whirled about the house, but preferred to listen to it from the inside, with his feet well up to the fire. In the earlier years of his Carlisle life he did something at gunning, and was quite proud of his practice as a marksman; but gave it up in later years. Of fishing he was never very fond. He was, however, a capital sailor, and on the sea was supremely happy. The ocean air was for him the best of tonics, and relieved him at once of his bodily ills. But he could not always be on the sea; there remained for him, therefore, only such activities as grew out of the half-rural life which he established for himself during his second residence in Carlisle, and elsewhere.

July 10, 1852.

My New Brunswick home, simple as it is, seems very pleasant to me on my first return to it. It is very warm out of doors, but the air comes cool through the trees into the windows of my study. Kate sits near me on one side, sewing away for dear life, and Augusta on the other reading Tom Hood. Am I not happily surrounded? I wish most heartily that you were here to make up the quartette. But we cannot have all our wishes gratified in this life; and so many of mine are filled to my heart's content, that I should be base indeed were I not happy and at ease. And so I thank God continually for

> "Hope and health,
> For peace within and calm around,
> And the content, surpassing wealth,"

which can only spring, even amid the most propitious worldly circumstances, from right relations to God and an humble trust in Christ, the only source of certain happiness. I trust that you are continually drawing fresh supplies of joy and peace and comfort from this perennial fountain; that your Christian life is growing continually, and that your hold upon Christ is becoming stronger and stronger all the time. You can find joy, as I have said, nowhere else; but when you have this, all the joys and pleasures of life are transfigured by it — made sweeter, purer, more elevated, and permanent.

NEW BRUNSWICK, *Nov.* 22, 1852.

I didn't go to the Boston wedding because I could not get away. Certainly I shall not go to Boston without running out to Andover. if it be only for an hour, unless I can't help myself. I have not left home since you were here, except spending one Sunday in New York, where I had to preach, and one night in Newark, where I gave my old lecture on " Truth."

There are many books you ought to read with Edwards, Tappan, and Bledsoe. My health since you left has been about as usual—admitting of about half work, and that not the hardest kind of work. I don't know that I shall ever be good for much again; but I am not at all disposed to repine. I am thankful for a multitude of blessings. We have nearly decided to remove to Bergen in the spring, where we are building two cottages together, which, if I go there, will be thrown into one, making a very commodious abode. But we don't drive the pegs very deep in fixing our plans, for they are liable to be unsettled at any moment. Indeed, with such a state of health as mine, one does not feel much inclined to lay plans for the future, anyhow.

I get more and more out of patience with Calvinism every day. Paul's doctrine of grace and election extends the sphere of Christ's love as much as possible; Calvin limits it as much as possible. But I don't want to write or think about this matter. Study it just as much as you please, but hold fast your sound faith, and never become a necessitarian.

NEW BRUNSWICK, *Dec.* 8, 1852.

"Literary men rarely gladden the hearth-stone!" My doom is settled then, and I am not among the class of "better brothers," for a gladder hearth circle than that which gathers nightly around our *coal-stove* (!) in the front parlor it would be hard to find. There is, first, myself, (I put the *aged* in front,) of whom I will say nothing, for you will have it, let me say what I will, that I am sulky and crabbed, like all mere book-worms. Next comes Kate, who asserts roundly that you're a slanderer, and that "literary men" *can* gladden the hearth-stone. Next appears Maggie, my youngest sister, whom you would like exceedingly, I am sure, and who is prepared to like you wonderfully. My boy comes next on the stage—a noble little fellow of twelve ; but the charm of the house is my daughter Augusta, of eight, a veritable little angel. Then Kate had two little ones before I caught her. And we get on as happily as the day all the time.

To Moncure D. Conway, at Cambridge.

New Brunswick, *March* 11, 1858.

I had heard of your going to Cambridge, and was gladdened by the receipt of your note yesterday. Believe me that I shall always take a deep interest in your progress, and that I have the utmost confidence in your integrity.

You *cannot* "be secure from the influences of men in pressing toward a firm faith." God does not mean that we *should* be thus independent of each other. The longer you live, the truer you will find this. If you will let me know the special line of study on which you propose to enter, I can speak more confidently about books, and will gladly say any thing I know to you.

Carlisle, *June* 22, 1858.

There has been, and is yet, a vast deal of out-door work to do in getting the place in order. I am up before six, and do as much out-door work as possible before the heats come on. Then I retire into my library, which is entirely sheltered from the morning sun, and if I have any *vim* left, spend it at work. My health is vastly better than it was ; indeed, I begun to think my head very nearly well ; but in setting up my books, though the most of the work was done by Mr. Stayman, I hurt myself, and it has taken me ten days to get over it.

To the Rev. W. H. Milburn.

August 9, 1858.

In May we moved bag and baggage to Carlisle, where we purchased the house formerly occupied by Professor Allen, at the ex-

treme west end. We have a very commodious home, an acre of
ground finely planted with shrubs and fruit-trees, a good horse and
carriage, a very milky cow, a lot of immense Bramah fowls, and, to
crown all, a big black-haired baby girl. This last feature is about
five weeks old, and does credit to her breeding, as all young babies
in some strange way do. I spend about three hours a day in my
library, the rest of the time in walking, chatting, riding, working in
the garden, superintending chickens, etc.—all which avocations are
very agreeable, at least as long as the novelty of the thing lasts. So
you see we are almost as rural as you are yourselves. Tell your
wife that chickens worth only five dollars a piece are no fowls at all.
I have a rooster and four hens worth one hundred and twenty dollars. Poor ——! How unhappy she must be with such little bits
of fowls !

To Mrs. R. C. Caldwell.

May 14, 1858.

The bell is just ringing for afternoon worship. I attended this
morning ; once a day is as often as I can go to church with
safety. Yet my health is very much better than it has been ; indeed,
better, I think, than it has been for five years. The out-door life is
every thing for me ; and I have far greater inducements to go out
now than I have ever had before. I am becoming quite a gardener,
spending two hours often at a time at work among the flowers and
vegetables. Early in the spring I could only stoop a little at a time,
and then it caused dizziness ; now I spend any length of time at
light work with pleasure and profit. Our garden is in good trim—
cherries are pretty large, strawberries getting form, trees all clad in
the fullest leaf, and the promise of a rich result in all things. Yet
it has been with us, as with you, a very backward spring. The bell
has ceased, and they have gone into chapel. We have preaching
there twice a day. I wish you could worship with us. The chapel
is newly painted, and is very clean and sweet. We have an excellent choir, and a very fine toned melodeon ; and we sing with the
spirit and the understanding also.

To a Divinity Student at Andover.

January 22, 1854.

Congregationalism offers you an appearance of freedom and settled pastorate, and a comfortable support. These points are all in
its favor. But it has so many disadvantages that I think nothing
could bring me to throw in my fortunes with it but a necessity of
making myself comfortable before all things. Its lack of organization, its oyster-like isolation, its incapacity for aggressive movements,
except at the expense of its fundamental principle—all these are
against it. It is at best a provisional and transition system, fitted
only to anarchical times and ungovernable men. Utterly unscien-
tific in its form, it has no bottom on which to rest, but the very rest-
lessness of men's minds. Any Church which has even an attempt
at organization is for me to be preferred to this. On the other
hand, it is a great attraction to Methodism that she is so highly organized, and therefore so vital. Whether her organization is to be
permanent is a question ; but even if provisional, it is a step toward
the Church of the future. A Congregationalist has an influence, but
a *personal* one ; a Methodist minister has the weight of the whole
body to sustain him. That the latter is a more Christian idea than
the former, it seems to me no one can read the New Testament and
doubt. But to particulars as touched on in your letter : I think it
certain that Methodism will adapt herself to the wants of the times
in her itinerancy, etc. Regarding her organism as a living one
I cannot doubt this. But it is clear that the time has not yet
come.

There is so vast a field for itinerant labors in the territories opening
upon us in the West, that no scheme can be broached yet which would
even tend to withdraw us from the gigantic work to which the age
calls us, and which we are striving with no small success to perform.
But this is a fast age. I should not wonder to see our itinerancy
modified in ten years. In the mean time we are doing an immense
work in educating our people. I suppose there are more boys and
girls in Methodist schools in America than in those of any other de-

nomination. We want, and shall want, capable teachers and professors, editors, etc.

To J. O'C. Paris.

June 28, 1854.

We are to be drenched with Comte here, by the circulation of
Lewes's Abstract and Miss Martineau's Version of the *Phil. Positive.*
You will smile and sneer when I tell you that I expect to see you
live long enough to recognize a world of philosophy and religion beyond Positivism. It is too intensely subjective a system (an odd and
absurd criticism you may *now* say) to hold a mind like yours. And
worse, it is an arbitrary subjectivism, voluntarily restricting human
thought to the little world of man, and the globe he inhabits. Already you combine with it, as Comte did before you, a metaphysical
entity, which you call humanity; by and by you will get back to a
theological view of some kind. Endless vibration—the course of the
individual mind, as of humanity. It was Leibnitz who said that nature is but the horologe of God.

To the Rev. Dr. T. O. Summers.

March 10, 1854.

It will give me very great pleasure, indeed, to receive your volumes; indeed, I think you to blame for not sending them sooner.
There is no reason in the world why the books issued from your end
of our camp should be kept from our people. But we seldom see
them unless we send an order and buy them, which is, you know,
the last of editorial movements.

Your report in the "Southern Christian Advocate" gave me infinite gratification. We must take on the character of a Church, or
we shall inevitably go to pieces in a generation or two. No church
life can be kept up without baptism and its necessary results.

In the summer of 1854 our friend made a second
voyage to Europe in search of health. His wife, sister,
and brother-in-law were of the party. The trip took
in England, France, Germany, and Switzerland; by

September the travellers returned mended up and in high spirits.

To his Son, Emory M'Clintock.

STEAMER ASIA, *June* 22, 1854.

By looking at the map you will see exactly where we are just now; but as I have not any child at hand to take this letter to the post-office to-day, it will have to wait until we get to Liverpool to be put into the mail. We have had thus far a very pleasant passage, too pleasant, indeed, at first, as it did not make any of our party sea-sick; and when it did get rough we were all too good sailors to be affected by it. Mother and Atta were a little bit qualmish, but that was all. To-day the swell is very great, and the ship rocks to and fro like a drunken man; but the ladies are on deck walking about and enjoying the fine breeze and the beautiful sight of the ocean. It is not easy to write in such a commotion as this, but it is harder still to *shave.* The captain and officers of the ship have been perfectly polite and kind, and we have had good, solid English fare all the way.

Our passengers are mostly English, Canadians, and Frenchmen—very few Americans among them.

To his Son, Emory M'Clintock.

PARIS, *July* 5, 1854.

I have wished for your company often enough since we left home, but I suppose you would have enjoyed yesterday and to-day with us as much as any we have had, if not more. We left Dieppe at half-past seven yesterday, and reached Rouen at half-past eight. We visited all the chief places of interest in Rouen—the Cathedral of Notre Dame, St. Ouen, and St. Maclon. These are all very old churches, but St. Ouen is one of the finest specimens of Gothic architecture in Europe. The interior is four hundred and forty-three feet long, and perfect throughout, notwithstanding the fact that in the revolution of '93 it was used for a cavalry barracks and for a blacksmith's forge, the marks of which can still be seen. Adjoining it is a beautiful city hall, formerly a monastery, with a beautiful garden; but Napoleon turned the monks out and made the house into a town-hall, and gave the garden to the public. We also went to the old palace of the duke of Bedford, where Joan of Arc was tried, and saw the very spot on which she was burned to death. Altogether Rouen is one of the most curious places we have ever seen. Leaving it at two o'clock we reached Paris at five, and took up our old lodging at Madame Josephs. But I must now stop and bid you good-by, commending you to the care of our heavenly Father.

To his Daughter Augusta.

HEIDELBERG, *July* 18, 1854.

I wrote to Emory last from Frankfort, and hope it came duly to hand. We left Frankfort at five yesterday afternoon and had a lovely ride along the Bergstrasse through Darmstadt to this beautiful town. We got here at eight o'clock, tired and hungry enough. We ordered tea for four, and they soon brought us a lot of nice rolls of bread, eggs, hot water, and tea. Atta made the tea, as she always has to do. They bring you green and black tea in canisters, and a bright kettle of hot water with a lamp under it, and you make the tea to suit yourself. We slept very soundly and had a hearty appetite for breakfast at half-past eight this morning. We then had a nice two-horse carriage, with falling top (costs fifty cents an hour) for us four. Our carriage took us through the beautiful town, first up the river to the *Wolfsbrunnen*, four miles.

The *Wolfsbrunnen* is a fountain, so called because, according to an old legend, a young lady was once torn to pieces there by a wolf. It is one of the loveliest spots you ever saw. They have several little lakes containing trout, and when visitors go they throw little fishes in for the trout to leap at. The trout are very large, some of them weighing as much as ten pounds. We then went up to the old castle of Heidelberg, the largest ruined castle in the world, and formerly one of the most splendid in the world, also. It has been often bombarded, but its final fall was accomplished in 1688, by the French, under Melac, who blew up the strongest towers and destroyed the whole castle as far as they could. One of the walls is twenty feet thick, and yet they blew it down. We bought some flowers from a nice little girl there; I picked a good many more, which we will try to press and bring home with us. It was high time for dinner when we got to the hotel. The courses were, 1. soup; 2. boiled beef; 3. fish; 4. roast beef with potatoes; 5. mutton chops with cauliflower; 6. pudding cakes; 7. veal cutlet with beans; 8. wild turkey; 9. ducks and chickens, with apple sauce; 10. cakes of various kinds, with confectionery; 11. fruits; and some, I think, I have left out.

This is the kind of dinner they usually give at a German hotel for fifty cents. After dinner we rested about an hour, and then Atta and I went down town and did some shopping to hunt little pictures of Heidelberg, which we found very nicely. To-morrow we expect to go to Stuttgart, and the next day to Munich, if mother is able to travel so far by railway; if not, we shall stop all night at Augsburgh, or, perhaps, at Ulm.

To his Son, Emory M'Clintock.

LUCERNE, *July* 30, 1854.

We spent our time very pleasantly at Munich, though the weather was very hot—hot, at least, for this country, though probably not so hot as you have had it at home. The king of Wurtemberg trod upon our heels again, as he came to our hotel (the Golden Lion) and stayed there nearly as long as we did. We had a very fine carriage and horses hired on Saturday, but he had the impudence to hire them for every day after, so that we had them no more. We visited all the principal sights of Munich, of which you have pictures in a little portfolio in the parlor, and you can look them over, and imagine us looking at them. We left Munich on Tuesday 25th, and reached Augsburgh in four hours. There we stayed again at the "Three Moons," but did not get the Napoleon chamber again, as it was taken. But we had rooms, each of which was nearly as large as the college chapel.

Next morning we came to Lindau, where we took the steamer for Constance, reaching that town at half-past five in the evening. There we saw the council hall in which the Council of Constance sat in 1414–18, when John Huss was condemned. We also visited the church in which sentence was pronounced on him, and the stone on which he stood to be sentenced, the cage in which he was imprisoned, and the spot outside of the town at which he was burned. On the whole, it was one of the most interesting spots I have visited. On the next day we came in a carriage to Zurich, a very delightful journey. Here we engaged two carriages for the journey through Switzerland at twenty-five francs a day each carriage. We left Zurich at eight on Friday, and stopped at Cappel to see Zwingle's monument, erected on the very spot where Zwingle was killed. If you don't remember the history of Huss and of Zwingle, you had better read it up in the little Sunday-school histories of them, or in the "Encyclopedia Americana." We stopped at Goldau to dine, and then went up Mount Righi. All of us were on horseback except mother, who was carried up by four men in a big chair. Mag. and mother went down the mountain in the same way. You would have laughed to see them carry "lady-to-London" fashion. It took three hours and a half to go up the mountain, and two and a half to come down, and very tiresome work at that.

The thoroughness and conscientiousness of his editorial work were greatly commended, but there was a difference of opinion in relation to his theory of the conduct of the "Review." Correspondents wrote to him that it was not "popular enough;" his official directors, the Book Committee, advised him that it was "not sufficiently adapted to the practical and utilitarian tastes of the people." They requested him to change its character accordingly. To all such objections he replied invariably that he was not appointed to edit a magazine, or a newspaper; that it was his duty to present to his readers a sound Christian judgment upon the life-questions of the age; and that the "Quarterly" had a distinct work before it as an educator, especially of the rising ministry. In a circular which he sent to the Conferences in 1855, he said to the preachers: "Were my judgment convinced, I should at once alter the plan on which I have heretofore conducted the 'Review;' cut out its foreign Literary Intelligence, refuse all profound discussions of metaphysical and other learned subjects, and fill it with biographical articles and papers on fugitive topics. Such a course would save me much expenditure of thought, time, and labor. But I cannot do this with a good conscience." The best evidence of the correctness of his decision is to be found in the fact, that since 1856—the year when his editorship closed—the "Quarterly" has been conducted on the same general principles which he conscientiously followed.

To a Critic of the "Quarterly."

CARLISLE, *May* 11, 1854.

I thank you cordially for your kind expressions with regard to the "Quarterly," and for your hints in regard to its management. You must remember, however, that if you have no metaphysical turn, others have, and that I must meet their wants. The cultivated young men of our colleges and of the Church will meet with these new forms of speculation inevitably, and it would be very unwise in us to ignore them. The very highest commendations, and from the highest sources, which the "Review" has received under my management, have been given to the very articles which you condemn.

To the Rev. Dr. A. A. Lipscomb.

CARLISLE, *Oct.* 5, 1854.

I think you will find some points well put in Mr. Mercein's book which are commonly slurred over. The Unitarian view of human nature is held unconsciously by many non-Unitarians who cannot reconcile the doctrine of depravity with the high virtue of many un-converted men. Strong and dogmatic assertions wont beat down such a view as this. The novelty and excellence of Mr. M.'s book is, that it shows the necessity of precisely this state of things in order to give probation to such a nature; and that the natural vir-tues and culture which present so strong an objection are, in fact, part of the plan of redemption to reach the depraved soul. I don't remember to have seen this point stated and maintained elsewhere. I have ventured to call your attention to these points, as I would be glad to have the book, as well as the subject, brought strongly to the notice of our preachers, who generally need to be led off in judg-ing any new line of thinking.

In the year 1855 the question of the papacy and mod-ern civilization was before the country, the question which has since grown to be the most important of our time. It was not so well understood then as now. Mr. Joseph R. Chandler, one of the representatives in Con-gress of the city of Philadelphia, delivered a speech in which he denied that the popes have claimed authority over civil rulers as of divine right. He fell into the error of taking the Gallican view of the powers of the papacy as the accepted doctrine of the Church. Dr. M'Clintock replied to him in a spirited letter, published in the "Evening Bulletin" of Philadelphia, which was after-ward expanded into a volume. It was very easy for him to show that the Ultramontane theory of papal power was alone recognized in Rome, and that liberal Catholi-cism had no standing whatever in the pope's councils. Since then the antagonism between Romanism and the modern world has become more pronounced, and the famous syllabus of errors has been issued—a notice served upon the nations of Christendom that no compromise is to be expected. Here, again, Dr. M'Clintock led the way as pioneer in a field of discussion which has now many occupants. His scholarly exposition of the Ultramontane theory of the relations of the Church to the State is just as available for use in the great controversy to-day as it was more than twenty years ago.

In the same year Dr. M'Clintock was elected President of Troy University, which had just been organized by the enterprising Methodists of the interior of the State of New York. In reply to the notice of election, he wrote to the Board of Trustees: " I cannot signify an unconditional acceptance. The state of my health, at present, is such that I could not *now* discharge the duties of the office, and I would not do either the Board or myself the injustice of assuming duties so important and so responsible without a reasonable prospect of being able to perform them faithfully." He continued his connection with the University for several years, but without residence. A very superior Faculty was elected, and some good educational work done, but, unfortunately, its friends lost heart, and the fine property acquired passed into other hands. Dr. M'Clintock outlined a very attractive plan of a complete university, but to achieve it demanded time, money, and the consecration of some one man's life to the task. He was neither young enough, nor strong enough, nor free enough from the claims of other undertakings to permit such a consecration.

He took a deep interest in the success of the Irish

17

Methodist deputation which was first sent, in 1855, to the United States. The deputation had for its object the securing of aid, especially from Irish Methodists in America, for the building and endowment of the Wesleyan College at Belfast. Dr. M'Clintock's attachment to Ireland was very strong. It was the home of his father and mother, which alone was enough to make the "ever-green isle" dear to him. But he had strongly developed in himself many of the finest traits of the race from which he was descended—its warmth and steadfastness of affection, its keen interest in life, and capacity to enjoy life under all circumstances. He loved Irish Methodism very tenderly; his efforts to promote the objects of the deputation knew no limit but the limits of his strength. With its two members, the Rev. William Arthur and the Rev. Robinson Scott, he kept up a frequent correspondence in after years. Mr. Arthur was, during our civil war, his faithful colaborer in spreading through England right views of the nature of our controversy with the South.

To the Rev. William Arthur.

CARLISLE, *Sept.* 25, 1855.

It is of the utmost importance that good foundations should be laid in Baltimore, Philadelphia, and New York, as, after all, whatever is done elsewhere will be trifling to what can be done in those great cities. Pittsburgh should not be neglected. And why can you not, in returning from Pittsburgh, stop here? It is on the way to Philadelphia and Baltimore, and I am sure I can serve your mission if I can get the opportunity of a talk with you about your plans.

Where shall the Baltimore people find you? You should fix on some head-quarters, to which communications could be addressed, and where you could always be got at, indirectly at least. The Book Room, 200 Mulberry-street, New York, would probably be the best place.

The General Conference of 1856 met in a memorable year. It was, as usual, the year of the presidential election, but this election was the first in which the issues between the North and the South were directly drawn. The attempt to establish the slave system in Kansas, as a part of a general extension of slavery over new territory, had roused a spirit of determined resistance. In the feeling which pervaded the free States Dr. M'Clintock shared very fully. He detested slavery, and had risked honor and property in helping the slave. At every fit opportunity, public and private, he denounced the iniquitous proceedings of the pro-slavery party. He believed, however, that the Methodist ministers and people in the slave States, who had adhered to our Church at the time of the disruption in 1844, were entitled to tender consideration. In making their election between North and South they had resisted strong local influences, and had proved their fidelity to ancient Methodist traditions. On the other hand, the excitement which pervaded the nation affected the Church—and Methodism is, of all religious organizations, the quickest to be moved by the surges of popular feeling. There was a demand that the Church should be put in a more decided anti-slavery position, and this could be effected only by a rule forbidding all slaveholding. Such a rule was, in process of time, inevitable; but Dr. M'Clintock was of the opinion that in a few years the *whole* Church would be

ripened for advanced legislation by the natural processes
of its growth.

The General Conference of this year was, therefere, under a pressure from two opposite sides. On the one side
old affections, and the consideration due to a long record
of fidelity, pleaded for forbearance ; on the other, the demand that the Church should stand before the world more
avowedly as an antislavery Church, pleaded for instant action. It was felt on every hand that the whole mass and
weight of this great body must be hurled against slavery,
but the best measures for the hour were questions of expediency on which honest men might differ. It was the
purpose of Dr. M'Clintock to offer a draft of a " New
Chapter " on slavery, declaring that the " general rule "
forbade the buying and selling of slaves, and was in its
spirit opposed to slaveholding, and calling on the Conferences to inform the people accordingly. It would have
served, had it carried, as a " notice to leave " for Methodists who preferred slavery to the Church, and would have
prepared all parties, he thought, for further action four
years later. It cannot be said that this was unwise
statesmanship. Appearing in the debate at a late hour,
when the wish to vote had reached the point of extreme
impatience, he was cut off before he could open the way
for offering his resolution.

With this Conference Dr. M'Clintock's connection with
the " Quarterly Review" closed. The Rev. Dr. D. D.
Whedon was elected his successor.

LETTERS.

I.

NEW YORK, *June* 15, 1856.

It is a beautiful Sunday morning, and I trust you are able to enjoy it. I had two committees up yesterday to ask me to take churches. One, in Brooklyn, offers me $1,800 a year, and they will employ a young man to do all the work I cannot do. If it were in New York I would take it, but I do not want to live in Brooklyn. Mr. Harper offers me the post of literary manager of their publications, but I hardly feel willing to do that as yet. They will give me $1,000 a year to preach one sermon, and have no responsibility, at the new church in Twenty-second-street ; and then Harpers will pay me for reading for them, and I rather think that is what I will agree to. But I shall not decide in haste. I am to preach this afternoon and will therefore stop writing now.

Monday morning.—No time to write, except to say that I am very well ; preached to an immense audience. Church in Brooklyn offers me $1,800, a house, and a horse and carriage. No decision yet.

Mrs. CATHARINE W. M'CLINTOCK.

II.

PHILADELPHIA, *September* 24, 1856.

My head has been worse since my return home, and I am hardly fit to do any thing at all but talk and walk the streets. I don't expect to be able to work for a month. It is a bad look-out for me.

Your letter was very gratifying indeed. Did you receive mine from Jersey City? (1.) Don't go to Freemont meetings *too* often, or neglect any study that should be done at night. (2.) I hope you have not missed prayers, or any other duty, since you have been at Yale. Such punctuality tells not only on your *reputation*, but also on your *character*. If you stick to this, and then master every lesson thoroughly, your way is clear. I should be glad to see Pennsylvania win the field there through you. I hope you make yourself both agreeable and useful to Mrs. Daggett. (3.) Tell me whether you have any trouble about your pronunciation of Greek and Latin—whether it makes any difference.

Revolutions are generally the result rather of undue conservatism on the part of statesmen than of any or all other causes. Take this for your text, and illustrate it by examples from history. By conservatism I mean sticking to old usages, ideas, and laws when it is time to change them ; or, as Carlyle says, trying to wear the old breeches after they have become too small.

Mr. Emory M'Clintock, New Haven.

III.

Philadelphia, *October* 26, 1856.

I am glad to find that you are getting on well with your studies. Don't forget my advice to you about *minute* accuracy in the preparation of each lesson, and about *punctual* attendance on every college duty. With your advantages you ought to take some of the prizes, and I think you can do it.

But the greatest prize of all is that of a conscience void of offence toward God and man. Keep truth and honor in all your relations to your fellow-students. No morality remains when truthfulness is gone. Cherish truth in the smallest statements as well as in the greatest and most important. Acknowledge God in all your ways.

I am not sorry to find you concerned about the election. I feel the same interest, because of the great moral question that is at stake. Every man, it seems to me, of pure and noble instincts, must now be prepared to take the side of civilization against barbarism, of liberty against slavery. The struggle may go on for many years: I hope you and I may both live to do our duty in it like men and Christians.

If Judge M'Lean had been nominated we should have carried him in easily, now it will be a very hard fight. Buchanan promises to be very fair if elected ; perhaps he will, but if he is, the South will try to get up a revolution. God bless you, my dear boy !

Mr. Emory M'Clintock, New Haven.

CHAPTER VIII.

1857–1860.

Dr. M'Clintock as an Orator—Appointed to the Pastorate of St. Paul's Methodist Epis-
copal Church, New York—Great Success in this Position—Visits England in 1857, with
Bishop Simpson, as Delegate to the Wesleyan Conference and to the Evangelical Alliance—
Public Reception at the Wesleyan Mission-House—Reception at Belfast—Kindness of his
Irish Friends—Reception of the Members of the Evangelical Alliance by the King of
Prussia—The King's Attendance upon the Sessions of the Alliance—Entertainment of
Americans in Berlin by Governor Wright—Work upon the Cyclopædia by Dr. M'Clintock
—His many Plans for Literary Work—Effect of Continued Ill-health in Hindering their
Execution.

WE have come to the period of Dr. M'Clintock's
life when he attained to the fulness of his power.
His careful culture had ripened his mind; travel had
added to the stores of his information; his well-defined
opinions had been tested by a large experience of life;
and he now reached a position where all his resources
as a scholar and orator could be best used for the benefit
of his fellow men. Though his aptitudes were so various, he had always regarded preaching as his true vocation, and the kingdom of Christ as the one interest to
the advancement of which all his faculties were pledged.
He might and did enjoy the satisfaction which a well-
won reputation naturally gives, but self-regarding motives were kept by him in subordination to the one con-
straining impulse—the love of his Lord and Saviour,
Jesus Christ. He had consecrated himself to him to

whom he owed all that he was with an entireness which admitted of no divided allegiance.

That so few of his working years had been spent in the pastorate was due partly to the fact that the Church had called him to other duties, partly to the fact that he was disabled by a frequently-recurring affection of the throat, and in part to the fear that full pastoral service would be too much for his strength. He had, too, the student's instinctive dread of the much moving to and fro which is a necessary incident of the Methodist pastorate ; he loved fixed relations, as most favorable to culture, and planned to give himself all possible advantage in carrying forward his literary pursuits. In spite of his plans, however, he made an itinerancy of his own, and wandered up and down the world enough to satisfy the utmost demands that could have been made upon him by John Wesley himself. But whatever his feelings in this regard, they were controlled by his sense of his duty as a Methodist minister; he loyally accepted the itinerancy, and obeyed its requisitions whenever they were laid upon him.

He had a large endowment of the oratorical temperament. The art which is instinctive with the true orator, of magnifying the subject of present interest until it fills his own and his hearers' thoughts, he possessed in its perfection. I have already spoken of his winning presence and graceful action ; but besides these he was master of all the other resources of power which an orator covets. A flow of speech marvellous for its accuracy and finish, readiness in the use of his stores of information, sensibility and the power to kindle sensibility in others —all were his.   He was for many years, however, up to the period on which we now enter, only an occasional preacher.   He had not, except for a brief season when a young man, enjoyed the capital advantage of addressing a congregation of worshippers who looked chiefly to him for guidance, and whose cares, griefs, and frailties were to lie as a burden upon his heart.   In assuming the pastorate of St. Paul's Methodist Episcopal Church in New York, Dr. M'Clintock entered more fully into the work of the Christian ministry; and the drafts made by his position upon his mind and heart were met by exhibitions of eloquence which brought him at once a national fame.

He was an orator, indeed, but he was more.   He was a student, and had the student's preference for slow elaboration of opinion, precision of statement, and rigorous limitation of feeling to the just demands of the subject in hand.   He had his full share of the enthusiasm of the closet, which is kindled by long trains of reflection, and is often suspicious of the quicker and shallower enthusiasm by which masses of men are swayed.   In Dr. M'Clintock the student may have for a time held the orator in check, and delayed the perfect flowering of his oratorical genius.   During all the years over which we have passed his power as a public speaker was ripening with the general ripening of his mind.   In the period from 1856 to 1860 his logic and the great resources of his learning appeared to be fused in the fire of his feeling, and to give him consummate power in the persuasion of men.

The advantages of his position were very great. The Mulberry-street congregation, out of which St. Paul's Church was formed, was made up of choice elements. To it were added other members of high intelligence, chiefly from down-town Methodist churches, who had been carried to the vicinity of St. Paul's by the upward movement of the city's population. He was in the midst of friends, many of them friends of his youth, who had followed his career with affection and pride. Some of them had known him as the ruddy boy-clerk in the Methodist Book Room. He was now among them again, a strong, matured man, tested and proved in long years of public life, loved as it is the lot of few men to be loved, and as genial and as affectionate as in his early days. The Church was welded into unity by the necessities of an important enterprise, and by the consciousness of its growing power. From the laying of its foundation-stone to the completion of its chaste edifice its history was a record of successes. Crowds thronged to attend the ministrations of the eloquent pastor, and the congregation committed to his care speedily took rank as one of the foremost of New York in advancing the interests of the kingdom of Christ.

These were happy years for Dr. M'Clintock. With considerate thoughtfulness his people provided him with an assistant, who relieved him of many of the details of his duty, and divided the Sunday work with him. His preaching here, as all through his ministry, was eminently scriptural. He fed his people, as Jeremy Taylor exhorts, " not with husks and draff, with colocynths and gourds, with gay tulips and useless daffodils, but with the bread of life." He heeded Jeremy Taylor's counsel in another particular also, " not to let discourses to the people be busy arguings about hard places of Scripture." Dr. M'Clintock was too much in earnest for curious preaching, or showy preaching, or contentious preaching, or any preaching that did not set forth Christ crucified as "first, last, and without end." His message was delivered " in simplicity" as well as " in godly sincerity."

The General Conference of 1856 had appointed Bishop Simpson and our friend delegates to the British Wesleyan Conference. The two delegates spent the summer of 1857 in England and on the continent ; Mr. Milburn, the blind preacher, accompanied them, as also did Mrs. M'Clintock and quite a party of friends. Dr. M'Clintock and Bishop Simpson were also delegates to the Conference of the Evangelical Alliance, which met in Berlin in the latter part of the summer. It was not till after the return from this trip that the former entered upon the pastoral charge of St. Paul's. His record of this summer's travel is full of variety and incident.

STEAMER ERICSSON, *Thursday, May* 21, 1857.

We have had a most delightful passage, winds and seas favorable throughout—just enough storm once or twice to give the novices an idea of what the sea can do. It is too rough now to write with comfort, as you may see by the shaky looks of the writing ; but the sky is bright, and the air delicious. Kate has not been sea-sick more than half an hour ; I not at all ; Emory a little for two or three days ; Mr. and Mrs. Marshall and Miss Cameron have had the most of it ; they have kept their berths nearly all the time, and have disdained the humble food on which the rest of us feast daily with so much delight. They nibble crackers, and chew dry toast, and mumhle smoked beef. Mr. Milburn has been full of fun, anecdote, and poetry, and you have rarely seen a pleasanter party than we form around the cahin fire at night, telling stories, playing charades, proverbs, and such like amusements suited to our age and capacity.

An unusual thing on board a steamer is, that we have prayer every night at nine o'clock. First only one besides our party attended, with the Captain and Mrs. Lowber; then one by one dropped in, till now we have nearly all the cabin passengers. Among them are an Irish lady and her niece, Roman Catholics, and they kneel down as decorously as any Methodist among us. So does the surgeon of the ship, who is also a Roman Catholic. Captain Lowber has been every thing that we expected, and a great deal more. To tell the truth, the whole ship has been put at our disposal. I had nearly forgot my throat. Well, I ate some cakes out of the box for my lunch the first day, and that was the last meal at which I appealed to them. I have nice corn cakes and honey for breakfast every morning, but along with them I eat bread and salmon, or any thing else I please. It is astonishing the effect sea air always has on me. I can sing at night without its hurting me, and I think I shall be able to preach when I get to the Irish Conference. At all events I hope so.   ,

LONDON, *May* 27, 1857.

We had a lovely day to reach Liverpool—Friday—as fine a sunset as could be desired, and found comfortable lodgings in the Union Hotel. On Sunday we went to the Stanhope-street Chapel in the morning, where I introduced myself to the preacher, and was most cordially welcomed. In the afternoon I heard a fine street sermon from Hugh Stowell Brown, who is the Beecher of Liverpool. At night Milburn preached very excellently indeed at Stanhope-street, and I prayed the first prayer, and Bishop Simpson the last. The occasion was a very interesting one indeed. Monday we were busy receiving calls, attending to letters of credit, etc., and on Monday night at five Kate and I left in the train for Birmingham, the rest of the party remaining hehind till Tuesday morning. We reached B.

at eight, and had apartments at the Queen's Hotel. Left next morning at half-past nine, and reached London at half-past two. I had to ride a couple of hours to find lodgings. We finally got room for the soles of our feet at the Exeter Hall Hotel, where we have stayed till now.

It is very hard to write long letters amid such constant activity. You come home at night thoroughly worn out, and not disposed to write at all. I wrote one letter from Liverpool to the "Northwestern Christian Advocate," and that is all I have yet sent to the press. I hope to do better in that line by and by.

I forgot to say that Mr. Young, the president of the Conference, called on us to-day, full of offers of kindness and attention.

ROTTERDAM, *June* 6, 1857.

We have gone so fast and done so much that I hardly know how to begin to write to you. First about health : I improve daily in throat—can eat whatever I please, and have utterly discarded arrow-root and cakes.

We stayed in London till Wednesday night, in order to attend a reception given to the deputation at the Wesleyan Mission House, which I will describe by and by. Of course, we were sight-seeing most of the time ; but I cannot go through the descriptions of parks, museums, palaces, etc. All the eminent Wesleyan ministers called on us.

On Wednesday night came off the reception at the Mission House. Some hundreds of ladies and gentlemen were invited for six o'clock. At that hour we went. First we were taken into a room on the ground floor, where refreshments were served ; then up stairs to a fine hall, where hundreds were gathered. Many of these were introduced to us, and we circumnavigated the hall several times. The people seemed very kind, and not a little curious to see us. At about half-past seven the president of the Conference, Mr. Young, called the meeting to order ; and, after singing and prayer, made an address of congratulation, which was very kind and flattering. He then called on Bishop Simpson, who made a very excellent and touching speech. I was then summoned, and I did the best I could.

After me came Mr. Milburn, who interested the audience exceedingly by a humorous account of his "bringing up," and of Western Methodism. Altogether, the meeting was very pleasant and satisfactory.

On Thursday morning we left Wood's Hotel. At twelve we embarked at St. Katherine's wharf in the steamer Leo for Antwerp. I had secured, among other state-rooms, one with four berths for our four ladies, and lo! I found a *valet de place* claiming it for the duchess of St. Alban's and her daughter. Every body seemed surprised that I did not give it up at once; but I simply said that if the duchess had engaged it before I had, she should have it; and as this could not be proved, she did not get it. But by and by the duchess and her daughter came along, and I was quite smitten. She behaved in the most ladylike manner, and expressed the best feelings about it. I then offered her the room occupied by Bishop Simpson and his son, but she got another, telling me she was "equally obliged" as if she had taken it. We had several chats after it, and she was much interested in Kate's health, and in our American trunks. We met again in the Cathedral at Antwerp, and had another talk; but I had not the elasticity of tongue to say "your grace" once during the whole of these talks. It was a very pleasant rencounter, taking it altogether; but I suppose she had not been called "you" so much in the whole course of her life.

Reached Antwerp at twelve on Friday, and went before dinner to see the grand Cathedral of Notre Dame, which contains Rubens's great masterpieces — the descent from the cross, etc., of which I have told you before. Here I decided not to go on to Norway with Bishop Simpson. The rest of us stayed in Antwerp till twelve on Saturday, and then came on to Rotterdam. It was very hot, and we found it a pleasant change from the cars to the steamer in the evening at half-past seven. We passed Dort, where the famous synod was held, and reached the Hotel des Bains, Rotterdam, at ten o'clock. Here your mother and I have two rooms on the ground floor: the first a sitting-room, about fifteen feet square, the back a bed-room, twenty-five by thirty-five, with splendid furniture, ceiling

painted in allegorical designs, and three beds. We went to the
Cathedral to church Sunday morning. The sermon was in Dutch,
(not German,) an hour and a half long. After sermon, the singing
of four thousand powerful voices, accompanied by the grandest
organ in the world, (with sixty-five hundred pipes and ninety stops,)
was one of the most overpowering effects of music that I have ever
listened to.

DIEPPE, *June* 21, 1857.

We were very sorry on reaching Paris to find that Madame Joseph
had moved away, and that we could not find her out. We went first
to the Hotel du Louvre, which is the grandest place of the kind you
can imagine—rooms fit for kings' palaces, and furniture to match.
But as we found it would cost us six dollars or more a day a piece,
we only stayed one night, and then went to the Hotel de Lille et
d'Albion. We are settled here to spend Sunday, in the same house,
and, I think, in the very same rooms, that we had three years ago,
when your dear Atta was along. The very same old chambermaid,
in a crimped cap, that waited on us then, attends to us now. The
rain pours in torrents this morning, and will prevent our going to
church. Our hotel fronts on a basin of the harbor, and on the opposite side of the basin a battalion of infantry is passing, with eight or
twelve drums, disturbing the Sabbath air. After the people come
from church they will occupy themselves in all sorts of amusements.

BELFAST, *July* 5, 1857.

We came from Killarney to Dublin on Friday; rode all the afternoon about the city, and so saw Trinity College, the old Parliament
House, the Custom House, etc. Then mother went out and bought
some things. Left Dublin at half-past eight on Saturday. An el-
derly gentleman, of elegant manners, sat in the same *coupé* with us.
At a certain station he got out, and I heard him say to another gentleman on the platform that " Mrs. M'Clintock had not come." When
he came in again he noticed the name on my writing-desk, and said,
" Why, that might belong to our member of parliament." He told
me that John M'Clintock, Esq., was the member, and showed me

his estate as we passed it, remarking that he was a kinsman. We reached Belfast at thirty-five minutes past one, and were hardly settled in the Imperial Hotel when a deputation came to take me and Kate to Mr. Alderman Mullen's villa, where lodgings were prepared for us. But as we were settled, we stayed. To-day I preached to a fine congregation on 1 Cor. viii, 6, at the Donegal Square Church. After church, Dr. Alfred M'Clintock, of Dublin, who had been to hear me preach, came into the hotel to see us. He was very cordial indeed. He had just returned from Liverpool, where he had been to see his brother, Captain F. L. M'Clintock, sail. This last is the one mentioned in Kane's expedition, and he now sails as commander of the new Arctic expedition. I wish I had seen him before he sailed.

We remain here to-morrow, then on Tuesday go to Antrim, thence to the Giant's Causeway; Wednesday to Londonderry and Omagh; Thursday back to Derry; Friday to Belfast; Friday night to Glasgow. Thus far we have been highly favored in weather, and in the care of Providence, saving us from all accident. My health has wonderfully improved. I preached Friday week, made a speech Monday, another Thursday, preached again to-day, aim to make another speech to-morrow night; and all this without serious harm to my throat.

LONDONDERRY, *July* 8, 1857.

It seems impossible for us to get any letters. All that we have yet had are two. The rest get them in stacks, but Bishop Simpson and I get none. I fear there is something wrong about your mode of directing letters, and I have so stated to Gussie.

On Monday night, July 6, Bishop Simpson preached. I made a speech after him to a large audience in Donegal Square, Belfast. At ten Tuesday we started for Antrim; stopped there till three. Saw the Round Tower there, the most perfect in Ireland, and then went through the domain and pleasure grounds of Antrim Castle. They are very beautiful. At three we took the cars again, reached Port Rush at five, and there took jaunting-cars for the Causeway, whence we returned at half-past six. Spent two hours inspecting the wonders of the Causeway, and then came in and ate a hearty supper, and went to bed on the floor of the sittitng-room, as the bedrooms were all full. This morning took another run to the Causeway in the rain; at ten started in a big carriage and a car. Stopped at Port Stewart, at Mr. Cather's, who had refreshments for us. At one reached Coleraine, where an elegant lunch was prepared for our party. Afterward we walked around the walls of Derry, under the guidance of Mr. Alexander Lindsay and Mr. M'Arthur. The rest have all gone to church to hear Bishop Simpson, and I stayed at home to write.

I forgot to say that the Belfast people made me take three pounds to pay our hotel bill while stopping there. Indeed, the kindness of these Irish people knows no limit whatsoever.

To Miss Jane M'Clintock.

LIVERPOOL, *July* 81, 1857.

I was greatly rejoiced to get the letters of July 14 by the Columbia day before yesterday. It was one of the best budgets I have yet had, and it was certainly quite cheering. The news was all good news, except the story about hot weather. We have had nothing here but cool, pleasant weather; in Paris. Kate says it is warmer, but yet I fancy none of them know any thing of the enormous heats which you must suffer if the summer has fairly set in.

We had our reception-day in the Conference yesterday. At half-past ten the doors were thrown open, and the people flocked in. Bishop Simpson spoke first and grandly. The audience was roused to a high pitch of enthusiasm, and I succeeded in keeping it up during my speech, which was one of the most successful I ever made in my life. We are engaged to dine out every day till we leave Liverpool, and would have, doubtless, for a month, if we could stay. The English are not so quick and warm in their hospitality as the Irish, but it is very good when it comes. We have invitations to spend weeks in Ireland, but I don't suppose we shall be able to get the enjoyment of them.

18

HULL, *August* 4, 1857.

My preaching on Sunday did me good instead of harm, and I left Liverpool at ten this morning to preach here to-night, and to go back to-morrow. As I am pretty tired, and have soon to go into the pulpit, I cannot write a long letter. To-morrow we take leave of the Conference; Thursday go to London; stop there Friday to attend to various matters of necessity about the purchase of books for Troy University; then on Saturday, God willing, we shall be at 217 Rue St. Honoré, Paris.

PARIS, *Aug.* 14, 1857.

I told you in my last how much preaching and travelling I had been able to do, and I bore the rapid trip to Paris equally well. Since I came here I have been chiefly occupied with the purchase of books for the Troy University, and have thus far succeeded very well. To-day was the " inauguration " of the new Louvre—a grand display of troops, some thousands of them, with the emperor and empress in state carriages, and a grand *cortege* of diplomatic carriages, etc. I saw the troops and the cavalry, but I did not get near enough to see Napoleon and Eugenie. Emory succeeded better than I did, as he got near enough to see the royal people very well. I am more glad that he saw them than that I should.

BERLIN, *Sept.* 15, 1857.

We have all sorts of sights of kings and queens, and should have been right glad to present you to them. Last Friday, on the king's special invitation, I went, with about one thousand other people, to visit him at his new palace at Potsdam. He gave us the run of the palace and grounds, with plenty of ice cream, fruits, lemonades, and light wines. We were drawn up according to nationalities. The German usher said, " Americans there ; " and when we were " there " he announced, " English join on to the Americans," which the English did not seem to like very much, but yet they obeyed. The king, a plain old man of sixty-five, came first to the Americans, and seeing Governor Wright, our ambassador, at the head of the column, he said, " My dear Wright, I am so glad to see you, and to see you here." He asked Bishop Simpson the name of his diocese, which the bishop could not exactly answer. Various other sayings might be chronicled, for the old gentleman wended his way down the line, making remarks for about two hours. Meantime the queen talked to the ladies, and when she had done with them we were introduced, whereupon she asked if I were really an American? Altogether it was a great and good thing for a king to do in the heart of Europe.

To-day I saw the sham fight at Spandau—some forty thousand troops—and had the felicity of bowing to the king, to the emperor of Russia, to Prince Gortschakoff, and ever so many more. What was to me far more interesting, I had a long talk with Chevalier Bunsen, who treated me most kindly and fraternally.

GUENT, *Sept.* 20, 1857.

No session of the "Conference of Christians from all Lands" at Berlin, was more interesting than that of Wednesday afternoon, September 16, which was occupied with reports from the lands of the Bible and from Turkey and Greece. When I went into the church I saw the king of Prussia in his accustomed seat in the gallery, listening eagerly with his hand at his ear, to Dr. Dwight, who was giving an account of the American mission, and also of the progress of Christianity and of religious liberty throughout the dominions of the Sultan In the morning there had been a grand display of military manœuvres at Spandau, and a sham battle, with sixty to eighty thousand men engaged, and I had seen the king upon that field with the emperor of Russia, watching the movements of the vast masses of troops. I could not but think that he looked happier and more at home here, in the midst of this "army of the cross," than there amid the noise of artillery and the throng of serried battalions, mimicking war. At all events he sat until seven in the evening, apparently as much interested in the reports of the American missionaries as any clergyman in the body.

Dr. Dwight was followed by Dr. King, of Greece, who gave an account of the mission and the schools at Athens, of which he has been the head for so many useful years. It was a great pleasure to me to meet these two men, whose names have long held so prominent a place among Christian missionaries, and I trust I may be excused for saying, also, that I felt a little national pride in hearing these noble ministers from our own country recounting before this assembly of eminent and learned men from all nations the story of the blessings with which God had followed their labors in those " lands of old renown " to which they had come from the far West, bringing messages of Christian peace and love.

Dr. Schauffler, of Constantinople, had intended also to be present, but the interests of his mission demanded his presence in America. He wrote a letter to the secretary of the Conference requesting that prayer should be offered at the meeting in Berlin at 6 P. M. on Wednesday, on which day, at a corresponding hour, prayer would ascend from a Christian congregation at Providence, Rhode Island, for the same mission. Accordingly, at six precisely, President Kunze rose and requested the Conference and the congregation to unite in prayer for the work of God in the East. The whole assembly, preachers and people, with the king of Prussia at their head, rose as one man, and all seemed to join fervently and heartily in the prayer led by Pastor Kunze. Altogether it was a scene of rare interest. I could not help thinking it even one of great sublimity.

In the evening of the same day we had the pleasure of taking tea with Thomas Farmer, Esq., of England, who, with his amiable family, and the Rev. James H. Rigg, of Stockport, were our neighbors at the Hotel de Russie. Mr. Farmer, as you are well aware, is always ready for every good word and work ; he has taken a great interest in the Evangelical Alliance from its inception, in 1846, and in this Berlin meeting he has been one of the most prominent and useful of the English delegates. On this evening he gathered a number of brethren from all lands to break bread and talk together. It was a happy idea, and we had only to regret that such reunions were not more frequent during the sessions of the Berlin Conference.

I have before spoken of the kindness of the Hon. Joseph A. Wright, late Governor of Indiana, and now American ambassador at

Berlin. He has omitted no possible attention to Bishop Simpson and myself; indeed, I have sometimes been afraid of trespassing too much upon his exuberant kindness. On Monday, the 16th, he invited all the Americans present in Berlin to dinner at the hotel d'Angleterre, and the number sufficed to fill two long tables. Among them were Dr. Dwight, of Constantinople; Dr. King, of Athens; Dr. Patton, of New York; Dr. Baird, the Rev. W. F. Warren, and the Rev. Mr. Eldridge, of New England; Dr. Black, of Pittsburgh; Dr. Nast, and the Rev. L. S. Jacoby. It was delightful in this far-off land to surround a table spread by the bounty of our own ambassador, and to meet so many of our brethren of different denominations, yet all, as Christians and as Americans, seeing eye to eye.

While engaged in his pastoral work and church building, our friend continued the preparation of material for the Biblical and Theological Cyclopædia, with which he had been occupied since 1853. This chief literary product of his life grew upon him and his associate, Dr. James Strong, as it progressed towards completion. In its scope it embraces biblical, theological, and ecclesiastical literature. It was at first supposed to be practicable to compress an epitome of these departments into two large octavo volumes, but the two volumes have grown to six, and will be likely to reach as far as ten. No similar work in English on so comprehensive a plan had before been undertaken, unless we except the translation of Herzog's "Real Encyklopædia," which, unfortunately, was suspended during our late civil war. Dr. M'Clintock brought to this important undertaking great resources of knowledge, the habit of thorough research, an unusual skill in the treatment of the doctrines of philosophy and theology, and a catholic temper. The whole

of systematic theology, of Church history and usage, and
of ecclesiastical biography, came under his observation
in the selection and elaboration of the articles for which
he was responsible. He lived to see three volumes issued,
and was busy with the fourth, when his pen dropped forever from his hand. Dr. Strong, whose entire life has
been devoted to Biblical studies, has gone on successfully
with the task of completing this laborious work.

Regret is sometimes expressed that Dr. M'Clintock has
left behind him no literary product which fully repre-
sents his great talents and various learning. It must
not be forgotten that he died in his fifty-sixth year—an
age which, for a statesman, is counted young, and for an
author, the fit season for the gathering in of the harvests
of life's thinking. Cut off in the midst of his years, large
projects were left by him unrealized. He had made extensive studies in the Pauline writings, and had written
and delivered numerous lectures on the Epistle to the
Romans, which he intended to put to press, but waited
till they could be brought into such form as would satisfy
his critical judgment. He meditated much upon a complete exposition of systematic theology. And if, in early
life, a position at the head of a divinity school, such as he
held during his last years, had fallen to him, this would
have been the work to which he would, most likely, have
dedicated all his faculties. But like a wise man, he did
"the duty that lay nearest to him," and so made his life
fruitful and powerful in every direction.

What was done by him was accomplished under
conditions of health, which would have crushed most

men. After 1848 he never had firm health. Despite fair appearances, the spring within was broken, and he "brokenly lived on." His great spirit resisted and conquered depression, and threw over his life the charm of poetry, love, and joy. I have often rallied him, in a good-natured way, upon his frequent ailments, but since reading his letters and papers the impression has been deepened in my mind that ill-health was for years, with him, a terrible reality; and that he kept on working when others, in his condition, would have pronounced themselves hopeless invalids.

CHAPTER IX.

1860–1862.

Appointed Pastor of the American Chapel, Paris—Cordial Reception by the Congregation—Engages to Correspond with the "Methodist"—Breaking out of the Civil War in the
United States—Patriotic Activity of Dr. M'Clintock—Speech in Exeter Hall at the Wesleyan
Missionary Anniversary—Great Effect of the Speech—Meeting of Americans at the Hotel
du Louvre, Paris—Subscription for Battery of Rifled Cannon—Dr. M'Clintock Translates
and Circulates, in England, De Gasparin's "Uprising of a Great People"—Speech at Meet-
ing of Americans in London, July 4, 1861—The "Trent" Imbroglio—Active Efforts of
Dr. M'Clintock to Remove English Misunderstandings—Correspondence with the Rev.
Wm. Arthur in Relation to Mason and Slidell—His Devotion to his Work as Pastor of the
Chapel—Fruit of his Preaching—Readiness to Serve Destitute and Suffering Americans—
Lending a Hand.

A T the close of his connection with St. Paul's Methodist Episcopal Church, New York, Dr. M'Clintock accepted an invitation to take charge of the American Chapel in the city of Paris. The chapel had been
established by the American and Foreign Christian
Union of this country, on an unsectarian basis, for the
purpose of securing to American travellers and residents
in the capital of France the benefits of Protestant worship.
It set up a distinctive and important part of American
life in a foreign land ; it was a fragment of home which
brought to our countrymen a hallowed Sabbath, and
a simple religious service in their own tongue. Such
eminent ministers as Dr. Kirk, of Boston, and Dr. Pren-
tiss, of New York, had preceded Dr. M'Clintock in the
pastoral charge of the Chapel. It had become a rallying point for Americans in Paris ; hardly a Sunday

passed without the appearance in its pews of some of our countrymen, well known both at home and abroad. The congregation, though continually changing in its composition, was well maintained. On pleasant Sundays it rose, not unfrequently, to the number of three hundred persons, and seldom fell below one hundred and fifty.

On his arrival at Paris our friend was received most cordially by his flock, and immediately addressed himself to his duties. His health being again feeble, he had requested the Rev. Andrew Longacre, of Philadelphia, to take the position of assistant pastor, and found him a most serviceable and affectionate associate. He was met at his entrance upon his work by a difficulty in relation to liturgical and non-liturgical services. There were members of the congregation who had been accustomed to the use of a liturgy, and would have been pained by its omission; others greatly preferred extemporary prayers. Applying himself to the problem before him with his usual readiness and tact, Dr. M'Clintock soon succeeded in effecting a settlement, with which all parties were satisfied. At fifteen minutes past eleven o'clock on Sunday, the morning prayer of the Protestant Episcopal Church was used; at twelve extemporary prayer introduced the sermon; the afternoon service was non-liturgical. All shades of American politics were represented in the congregation, and in the ministers from home who were invited to occupy the pulpit. Dr. Thornwell, of South Carolina, preached for the pastor on one Sunday morning, and Dr. William Adams, of New York, on the Sunday morning following. No effort was spared in the administration of the chapel to make it "a symbol of the essential unity of American Evangelical Christians in all points of the common faith."

Before leaving New York Dr. M'Clintock became associated with the "Methodist," which had just been established, as its corresponding editor. The selection was most fortunate both for himself and for the readers of the paper. Upon the breaking out of the civil war in 1861, he had at once a medium of communication with his countrymen, through which they were advised of the aspects of foreign opinion, and the movements of foreign politicians. He studied the fluctuations of European policy in relation to the United States most thoroughly. The accuracy of his intelligence and the breadth of his views enabled him to furnish the readers of the "Methodist" a series of letters which, to say the least, were not surpassed by any contributed during the war to the American press. In his letters to myself, as editor, as well as in those written to other friends, his over-anxiety in relation to particular events was very apparent; this, however, at his distance from the field of operations, was very natural. But no one could be more confident than he of the ultimate triumph of our arms. His predictions of the length of the war and its varying fortunes proved to be remarkably accurate.

The breaking out of the civil war found Dr. M'Clintock in the very position, too, where he could render the most important service to his distracted country. Had he been at home, he would have been among the foremost to animate his loyal fellow-citizens with tongue and pen. There was, however, an equally important work to be done by intelligent and patriotic Americans abroad. The apparent acquiescence of the people, during the closing months of Mr. Buchanan's administration, in the division of the Union as an accomplished fact—the surrender of Fort Sumter, the loss of Norfolk, the feebleness of the first military preparations of Mr. Lincoln's government, the hesitation of a peace-loving nation to take up arms, the distrust of the future shown by so many—and, on the other hand, the rapidity and decision of the rebel movements, had, taken together, created the opinion in Europe that we had neither the capacity nor the will to maintain the Union by force.

The public opinion of England, at first favorable, veered round, and, led by the " Times," became bitterly hostile. Belligerent rights were almost instantly conceded to the Confederates ; threats were loudly uttered, that if we attempted to blockade the southern ports, the blockade would be broken ; the fitting out of rebel cruisers in English harbors was either purposely not seen or connived at ; threats of armed intervention were rife, and these, no matter how idle, served their purpose in affecting public opinion ; and before many months came the unlucky " Trent " affair, which brought England and the United States to the verge of war. Dr. M'Clintock was one of the men whose qualities show best in such a crisis. He was courageous by nature, and his courage was fortified by Christian faith. His confidence in the triumph of right principles was immovable. He had the scholar's clear insight of the drift of public events, and the scholar's

large and unselfish interest in public affairs. Coleridge
had taught him that "in the knowledge of law dwells
the spirit of prophecy," and he had studied the laws of
moral and political government too long to question, for
a moment, what the issue of our fiery trial would be.
In all the dark period from 1861 to 1863 his voice rang
out clear in its predictions of our final success ; his
-courage made others courageous, his hopefulness gave
others hope.

His patriotism was not, however, of a passive kind.
Instantly comprehending the situation, he struck out a
line of action for himself. He had no official position,
could exercise no official authority, could expect no official recognition ; but he was a citizen, and owed his
country all that it was in his power to do, and that was,
for him, warrant enough. Appreciating the importance
of correcting the misrepresentations of the London
"Times," he availed himself of his opportunity as one
of the speakers at the Wesleyan Missionary anniversary in Exeter Hall, April, 1861, to call the attention
of the Methodists of England to the course of that
paper. He had entire confidence in the honesty and
fairness of Wesleyan feeling in relation to this country,
and he knew the power of Wesleyan public opinion.
The Methodists had come up from all parts of England
to this their great annual festival, and they went back to
their homes with right views of the question at issue in
our desperate struggle with rebellion. How to put a political speech inside of a missionary address might puzzle
most men, but it was done in this instance supremely

well. Dr. M'Clintock found a passage in the remarks of another speaker which served as an introduction of the topic in which he was so much interested, and then proceeded to say:—

The "Times" said, the day before yesterday, just in the words that I will now quote: "The great Republic is no more." Shall I go home, and tell my friends that I don't know whether you believe with the "Times" or not? I am inclined to think you do not; but if you have the slightest disposition to believe any such doctrine as that, let me tell you, "Lay not the flattering unction to your souls." No, I don't believe that Britons will rejoice to see the day when the "great Republic" shall be no more. (Tremendous cheering.)

But, if they shall, let me tell you the day of their rejoicing is very far away. (Cheers.) What sort of a prophet would that have been, who, just at the beginning of the conflict of the American Revolution, when Great Britain was going to fight her rebellious colonies, should have said Great Britain was no more? What would have been thought of the man who would have said, after you had given up the American colonies—a far bigger territory than any you had left at that time—what would have been thought of the newspaper that should have said, at that moment, "The great power of the British crown is no more, the British empire is defunct?" He would have been a splendid prophet, would he not? Suppose, too, that we in New York, editing papers, (and I have tried my hand at that business myself in a religious sort of way,) at the time of your rebellion in the East Indies, should have made use of such an expression as that. I am not afraid of talking about the "Times," because I am not an Englishman; and if we had printed, for two or three days, that Great Britain was no more, and that the diadem was about to fall from the head of Victoria, because there was a rebellion in India, it would have been quite a parallel case. I do not mean to say that this strife in the United States is to end without a loss of some of our territory in America. It may end in that. It may end in the loss of part of that territory, that is to say, the slave-holding part of it ; and are you the men to say, We are nothing because we are not slave-holders ? Why, there was no part of this great " country-man's " speech (a laugh) that you applauded more than that extract from a Yankee Quaker's bit of poetry. (Loud laughter.) Then, as to that great Scotchman yonder, there was not a part of his speech that you applauded more than that about Fanny Forrester, a little Yankee woman, about four feet seven and a half inches high. (Laughter.) No, we are not dead and buried, and what is more, we do not mean to be for a very long time.

Now, let me say to you, Mr. President, and this vast audience of Wesleyan ministers, and good, sensible, intelligent people, do not let your political newspapers, or your politicians, debauch your intellects or morals upon the present exciting American question. For the first time in the whole history of the human race, a people, to the extent of twenty millions, have risen up to say, " We will forfeit our *prestige* before the world ; we will jeopard our name even as a great republic ; we will run the risk even of a terrible civil war, such as the world has never seen ; we will do all this sooner than we will suffer that human slavery shall be extended one inch. (Tremendous cheering.) I am in earnest about that point, and I do not want you to forget it; and if you read the " Times " you will need to remember it.

When I took up the " Times " at breakfast this morning and read the first fifteen or twenty lines, it stopped my appetite for breakfast—I could not get on—I had to vent myself in a few angry words to my wife before I could get my appetite back again. (Laughter.) I had a paper put into my hands called the " Telegraph," which they tell me has a circulation larger than the " Times " now ; it seemed a capitally-written paper, though I did not like the doctrines of it. What did I read in its one article upon American affairs ? This sentence, " Are the Americans going to cut each other's throats about a miserable question of the liberty of blackamoors ? " That, in the city of London !— not in any pro-slavery paper in New York or Charleston, but in the city of London, in a newspaper that is said to be read by more people than the "Times." Now, if you read either of these papers, I hope you will read between the lines hereafter. (Laughter.) So far, at least, as this congregation is concerned, I hope you will not be debauched. We used to think, years ago, we heard voices coming across the great Atlantic, telling us to be brave for the slaves; and three or four years ago, when I was here, I was abused in newspapers printed in the city of London, because I was a pro-slavery man, it was said—not enough of an abolitionist; and we thought that Britain was in earnest in this. And yet, if we were to believe these newspapers, all these professions have been a sham and a humbug, and all our antislavery feeling has been simply fanaticism! God preserve us! for I am sure the newspapers never will. (Loud cheers.)

To the effect upon English Wesleyans of this most eloquent appeal the London "Watchman" bore a generous testimony. "Dr. M'Clintock," it said, "had already the sympathy of many an English heart previous to that bold but most successful challenge which electrified Exeter Hall. Americans will read how he maintained the cause of his country before an English audience, and Englishmen will not despair of the Great Republic, if the contest is to be as he puts it—one between free soil and the extension of slave territory. Whatever our honored friend may have felt, he allowed no shade of sadness or of misgiving to appear in the presence of Englishmen, though he knew that great assembly, at any rate, could be relied upon as the friends of his country and of his Church. The course he took was even more consummately skillful than it was strikingly bold; and we never before saw Exeter Hall in such a tumult of acclamation. The response was just such as became a great Methodist meeting, uttering in a moment of generous enthusiasm its true feeling towards the free United States."

Dr. M'Clintock had another opportunity of expressing his sense of the duty of the hour in a meeting of Americans, at the Grand Hotel du Louvre, on the 29th of May, 1861. His speech on this occasion was full of eloquence and courage, but indicated his opinion that the war would not come to a speedy end. Mr. Dayton, the American minister to France, Cassius M. Clay, American envoy to Russia, General Fremont, Mr. Burlingame, and Mr. Elliot C. Cowdin also addressed the meeting. Dr. M'Clintock took this occasion to do justice to the English people. " I have no fear," he said, " of the grand English nation. Its voice has not yet been heard. When it shall be uttered, it will not be on the side of piracy and slavery. . . . Old England will stand by New England in the battle of Christianity and civilization. I think I am right in this prediction ; but if I am wrong, then I will agree with my friend that the glory of England will have departed forever." To make the issue clear beyond doubt, he published in London the speech of A. H. Stephens, the Vice-President of the Confederacy, delivered in Savannah, March 21, 1861, in which slavery was declared the corner-stone of the new government. Prefixed to the speech was a letter from the Rev. William Arthur, explaining the legal relation of the United States Government to slavery, as defined by the National Constitution. The pamphlet, which was a convincing exposition of our case, was extensively circulated.

The patriotic Americans who were in Paris in the spring

of 1861 did not, however, limit their zeal to public break-
fasts and speeches.   A subscription list was opened, and
quickly filled up, for the purchase of rifled cannon, to be
sent to the Government at home "to be used"—so ran
the statement of the subscribers to the fund—"in en-
forcing the laws and upholding the Constitution of the
Union."   It became a serious question with Dr. M'Clintock how to procure the money needed for such expo-
sitions of the merits of our cause as would help to correct
the errors of English opinion.   His friend, Mr. Thomas
N. Dale, one of the principal supporters of the Chapel,
who had returned to New York, raised there, without
delay, a considerable sum and remitted it to him.

With this money Dr. M'Clintock published, in London, De Gasparin's timely book, "The Uprising of a
Great People," translating it himself.   Americans cannot
forget the impression produced by that eloquent plea for
our Union, both in America and in Europe.   Even in
circles where it did not convince, it checked the formation of hasty judgments.   It lifted our cause far above
the level of a political strife, and presented it as a struggle for the preservation of the best elements of civilization in the New World.   "We *are* concerned," wrote
this brilliant Frenchman, "in the American crisis.   Not
simply because we may have friends, or trade, or property
in America, but, above all, because *our* principles and *our*
liberties are there at stake.   The victories of justice, on
whatever soil they may have been gained, are the victories of the whole human race."   With De Gasparin Dr.
M'Clintock corresponded during all this gloomy period.

19

When the unlucky capture of Mason and Slidell brought forward De Gasparin again, as our advocate, Dr. M'Clintock translated and published his "Word of Peace on the American Question," and circulated it as extensively as possible throughout England.

Our countrymen in London had almost determined to let the fourth of July, 1861, pass by without any observance, but fortunately better counsels prevailed. The more sagacious felt the importance of declaring to the world on this day that Americans had confidence in the future of their country, and bated not one jot of heart or hope in upholding its fortunes. About one hundred and twenty assembled in the Colonnade Hotel. The Rev. Dr. Wm. Patton presided; the Hon. and Rev. Baptist Noel represented the English Non-conformists. Dr. M'Clintock, in his address, made prominent the distinction, which was always present to his mind, between the *real* and the official England. "It is," he said, "because we love England that we are anxious to hear kind words from England. Sorrowful as are the circumstances attending our national anniversary on this occasion, never on any happy fourth of July at home, never in those halcyon days of peace, have I been prouder of my countrymen; for they have shown fidelity to great principles, to the memory of Washington, and to the heritage of freedom which God has given them. They are fighting because they have a flag which has been dishonored, a constitution that has been trampled upon, and a history that has been thrown to the winds. They have grand memories which the bulk of the community have never forgotten, and a nationality which they mean to maintain. They are fighting now to show that they have a government which all the world shall recognize in the end. I have no doubt on which side the victory will lie, and am now prouder and more hopeful of my country than ever; and I am sure, too, that in her heart of hearts England is prouder of it than she has ever been."

These were the words of a brave and Christian spirit, and there was an England prepared in due season to receive them. But the danger, great at all times during the war, of foreign complications, became imminent when Mason and Slidell were taken from the English steamer Trent, by Commodore Wilkes. The English Government could not believe that Commodore Wilkes acted, in arresting the commissioners, without instructions, and they concluded at once that Mr. Seward meant either war or a menace of war.

During this critical period the Rev. Wm. Arthur and Dr. M'Clintock corresponded rapidly in relation to the intentions of the American Government. The former was in communication with leading English statesmen. It was agreed at a consultation held by our leading representatives in Paris, that Mr. Thurlow Weed should go over from that city to London and have an interview with men whom it was important to set right. Mr. Weed took with him a letter of introduction from Dr. M'Clintock to Mr. Arthur, which was of great service, as will be seen further on. Here, as all through the war, Mr. Arthur showed himself a devoted friend to the United States. He was, and is, an Englishman in every fibre of his nature, but he was also a lover of liberty, of right, and of peace. The letters which passed between him and Dr. M'Clintock during the Trent negotiations do honor to them both. The two friends might on many points disagree, but they could not for a moment distrust each other's sincerity.

PARIS, SUNDAY NIGHT, *July* 1, 1860.

It is now about half-past two o'clock, or perhaps three, in New York, and you are getting ready to go to the communion at St. Paul's. We have been twice to church. The first service was at half-past eleven o'clock. Mr. Longacre read prayers and preached, and he and I administered the communion. It was nearly two o'clock when we got home. At half-past three I preached on Romans xii, 1. The gown rustled a little at first, but I soon forgot it entirely. There were many home faces: Mr. Corbitt, Mr. Newman, Mr. and Mrs. Wright, and perhaps twenty others. It was not St. Paul's; I could not see your faces, so near the pulpit, and always so kind and loving. But I tried to preach a plain and earnest Gospel, and I think a good impression was made. Mr. Longacre has won golden opinions, as, indeed, I knew he could not fail to do. There is a great field here to till. If we can only make the different denominations to harmonize quietly, I think we may look for great success.

The church is a little larger than our chapel—perhaps one third—and will seat some six hundred persons. I hope to see it full.

We landed at Havre on Wednesday morning last at 8 o'clock, and had a delicious breakfast at the Hotel Frascati. It took me till four o'clock to get the luggage through the Custom-house, and to have the passports viséed. At six we set out for Rouen, and reached there at eight o'clock, thus dividing the journey to Paris on account of the baby. The little swinging cradle attended us all the way, and was an object of great interest to the officials at the Custom-house and railways. Men in soldier clothes would look at it, make it go, and laugh. It seems to be a new invention here.

We reached Paris at five o'clock, Thursday, and found our old apartments at the Hotel de Lille et d'Albion. A great part of our time since has been spent house-hunting, but we have not decided on anything yet. We hope to be settled next week, but it is uncertain. There are to be immense parades this week, at the funeral of Jerome Napoleon, who now lies in state at the Palais Royal. The crowds visiting him are so great that we have not been able to get in yet, and I suppose we shall not.

O! dear, I wish you were as near us as you are to the parsonage. Perhaps you are in heart and feeling, if not in person. At any rate we feel quite near you. But God, our trust, is nearer yet; may he protect you and yours, and grant you all temporal and spiritual blessings in Christ Jesus!

To Mr. Fletcher Harper.

PARIS, *July* 80, 1860.

Our domestic establishment goes on nicely, but we are not yet permanently settled. At the end of two months we shall leave our present home, unless the landlord comes down in price. In this last case we shall stay where we are.

I trust Mr. Longacre and I will be able to make the American Chapel go. At all events we shall try. Can't you help us? Can't you give Dr. Murray room in the "Weekly" or "Monthly" for a short account of the chapel, stimulating Americans to rally around it? All means must be used to accomplish our end of building it up.

I have sent an installment for the dictionary, and shall send small parcels by each steamer, to run as little risk of loss as possible.

Now I pray you sit down at once as soon as you get this and reply to it. Tell me all your household news. Remember me most affectionately to Mrs. Harper, your sons and daughters, and don't let the grand-children forget me.

To Mr. C. C. North.

PARIS, *August* 4, 1860.

Our new order of worship will go into force next Sunday. I hope it will succeed fully. Nearly every body here is satisfied, now, that things look so prosperous with the existing order. But we look for hearty co-operation from all sides hereafter. Each side gives up something for the sake of harmony. So we must all do in this world.

Mrs. M'Clintock is somewhat better than when I wrote last. My own health seems to be constantly improving. I have had to keep on the run since I have been here, and this activity, with the cool, bracing weather we have had all the time, has done me great good.

To Mrs. Dr. A. S. Purdy.

Paris, *August* 14, 1860.

Your letters are like springs of water in a dry and thirsty land. The minute account you give of Church matters is just exactly what I want to get : and no one else will do it but you, so please continue to " walk by the same rule and mind the same thing."

My jaw opens nearly as well as ever; my general health is better than it has been for years—thanks to the cool weather and constant out-door exercise. We have not yet had a hot day : warm clothes, overcoats when driving, two blankets at night. On no day yet have we been able to keep a window in the house open, or to wear summer clothes of any kind.

How often I wish the doctor could come in to take a quiet rest, chat, and smoke. How often after our meetings we wish for your happy and loving face to cheer us up. But we must do without these blessings ; thank God for what we *have* enjoyed, and hope for reunion in the future, both in this life and in the next.

We have not yet decided whether to stay in our present quarters or to move. But we must settle it this week, after that we shall feel more like living. It is very comfortable where we are, but $1,600 is a large price for two floors, and it makes a big hole in a salary of $3,000.

Dr. Adams preached for me last Sunday morning. It seems like home to have the pastors of Madison Square and St. Paul's in one pulpit together. We are all to spend this evening together at Mr. Faulkner's, (the ambassador,) who, with his family, are among our most devoted adherents at the Chapel.

To Mr. C. C. North.

PARIS, *August* 29, 1860.

I send this sheet to show how our programme goes. We omitted by accident to insert, "Under the control of the American and Foreign Christian Union," but that will be inserted in the next that are printed. Circulars will be sent weekly to all strangers, according to the list of arrivals. I have to attend to these matters myself, with Mr. Tucker's help. I hope to get some of the young men trained to these duties, and to general deaconship. Three persons have offered themselves for Church membership. I shall procure a book, put their names down, and take all others that offer. Pray God to bless the American Church in Paris! It is a pity that the word *chapel* was used at first.

To Mrs. Dr. Purdy.

PARIS. *September* 8, 1860.

Though I have answered your letter I write again. I suppose that before this can reach you, we shall get another from you—at least I hope so. It seems a long time to wait for letters. Don't always wait till you get them from me before you write.

We had not settled upon our new home when I last wrote. I have given Dr. Purdy a sketch of it which will let you see exactly how we are situated. It is clean and comfortable, but by no means grand. Still I am sure you would enjoy coming to visit us in it; and we should give you the best bed, the best board, and the best of everything in the house. When will you come? When will you let the doctor come if you cant't both come together? It is now nearly three months since we left you—it seems like a year. Part of this feeling is doubtless due to the many novelties of life here, to the multitude of people we have seen, the new acquaintances made, etc.; but a great deal of it is owing to the *want* of the dear friends we have left behind us. We are too old (the truth must be spoken) to form new ties rapidly. And then our new friends here, though kind and good, are not Methodists, and that is a great bond of union missing. A

Methodist preacher can make friends readily among Methodists, but not so readily elsewhere. Nevertheless you must not understand me as hinting that we are not kindly received. The very reverse is the case. There are only too many invitations out. To-day, for instance, I must go out to dinner at half-past six P. M. and not get home till ten ; and I should greatly prefer to spend the time by my own fireside, and writing a better letter to you. So also we have visits from many American travellers. Thus far, among them all, there have been no St. Paul's people but Mr. Pine, the artist. He lunched with us last Sunday. Mr. Newman is to preach for us to-morrow morning, and Mr. Longacre will preach in the afternoon, so that I shall have a day of rest—only reading prayers in the morning.

Sunday afternoon.—I was interrupted yesterday. This morning I read prayers and Mr. Newman preached on the " Millennium." This afternoon Mr. Longacre preached on " Occupy till I come." We have had a very good day, but I always feel strange on Sunday night when I have not preached at all during the day.

I thought a good deal about your father yesterday. Pray don't fail to give my best love to your mother and sister when you see them. As for your own household, I take it for granted you always give all our kindest love when you hear from us, for we always mean to send it. Do tell the young people to write to us ; and for all your little folks, don't let them forget us, or grow out of their former selves before the Lord allows us to go back and see them. Perhaps some day we shall all sit together around your table, as of old ; if not, may we all unite around our Father's table in heaven !

Your letter gave us more church news than we have had from any other quarter. Don't stop in the good way, but give us just such another budget as often as you can. If you were here we should get up a class of young ladies for you, and I am sure you would do them good.

It is now dinner time, and I must stop. O dear ! if we could have one of the St. Paul's Sunday evenings, and have the doctor and you with us, and the children together ! Well, let us thank God for the blessings we have had and still have.

To Mr. C. C. North.

PARIS, *September* 10, 1860.

After a great deal of trouble and loss of time, we are at last comfortably settled in our home. Please direct letters, 10 Rue Balzac hereafter, instead of care of J. Munroe & Co.

Your kind letter of August 8th was a great comfort to me. I have also had a very kind one from Dr. Campbell, who says "there is no doubt the arrangement about services will please the Board." I hope soon to hear of their action confirming what I have done.

Last Sunday we had grand congregations. Brother Newman preached in the morning. Dr. Keith, of Scotland; Dr. Thornwell, of South Carolina; Rev. Mr. Armstrong, of Nashville; and several Roman Catholics, were in the congregation. In the afternoon Longacre preached a noble sermon on "Occupy till I come."

I find a vast deal of running to do to visit strangers. It takes a deal of time and cab-hire; but it is good for the Church and good for my health. I am better, on the whole, I think, than I have been since 1850.

PARIS, *January* 7, 1861.

A happy New Year! and may you have it such in spite of panics, disunion, and civil war. Here we cannot think it possible that madness will so far prevail among you as to break up the Government.

I have good news from the Chapel—Mr. —— partook of his first communion on Christmas day. A great change has been going on in him for some months, and he is now living for the glory of God. This blessed result is due largely to Mr. Longacre, who has been greatly useful to him and his family.

A work of grace is going on in the hearts of other persons here— some men of mark. We thank God and take courage.

· I shall stay here as long as the signs of success are as encouraging as they now are, and as long as my purse will hold out. The outlay, however, is more than I can stand under, with my family claims; and · I have so informed the gentlemen who support the Church.

My knee still continues bad. I cannot walk, but am able to ride to Church, and preach sitting on a stool.

To Mr. Lemuel Bangs.

PARIS, *January* 8, 1861.

Are you scared out of your wits in New York ? One would think so to judge from the papers. If, as the telegraph reports to us to-day, Mr. Buchanan has allowed Fort Moultrie to be given up, you have doubtless, ere this time, sought to have him impeached. The French press, like the English, is terribly severe on the South. The slaveholders have no friends in this world except in the Northern States of the American Union. Should the secession be finally achieved, there will still be cakes and ale, and ginger will continue "to be hot i' the mouth." Therefore I pray you, of all things, not to be frightened. If things get so bad that I can draw no more money from New York, I must pack up and go home, bag and baggage. It will be pleasanter to starve there than here.

PARIS, *February* 18, 1861.

Your political news is not very encouraging ; but nations, like individuals, must have their trials. Their length of life depends on their force to grapple with difficulties and overcome them. If the Government maintains itself, all will be well ; if not, there will be anarchy for years. But it can hardly be possible that the men of the North, no matter of what party, will let the Government go down ; or, what is the same thing, let it remain what Buchanan has made it —a mere pretence.

The feeling in France, as well as in England, against the South is really terrible. No journal in France, except the *Pays*, has dared to argue in favor of slavery. We are very anxious here about ministers and consuls. London, Liverpool, Paris, and Havre should all be filled with vigorous men. Things will be left in a sad condition, I fear, by some of our present diplomatic and consular agents. The English and French Governments are willing to do right, but the American ambassadors, who talk to them, are either not Union men at all, or are very timid ones. I hope these posts will be promptly and well filled by Mr. Lincoln.

Our church was full yesterday, in spite of the number that have gone home.

PARIS, *March* **30**, 1861.

We are in a state of great anxiety and uncertainty about affairs at home. The news of the surrender of Fort Sumter and Fort Brown has just reached us. The first feeling was that of shame and indignation that the great Government of the United States should be brought to such a pass as this. We are not proud *now* to call ourselves Americans. It may be that our pride needs punishing, and that God intends to humble us in order to raise us up again. Some people here say that the next news will be that you have surrendered the Government at Washington to Jefferson Davis, and have all become his submissive subjects.

But I drop this painful topic. The spring has been lovely here for a month. The shrubs are all in green, the earlier flowers are all in bloom, the birds wake us early with their singing. In spite of all troubles and sorrows it is spring time in our souls, too. God blesses his word, preached poorly enough, but in faith and love. Souls have been blessed under it. I thank him for the fruit which I can see ; I have no doubt, that, in his mercy, there is a great deal which I cannot see. In this respect I thank God for sending me here. With regard to my health, also, I have great reason for gratitude.

Mr. Longacre has been in Italy for a month past, and I have had full charge of both services each Sunday, with no one even to read a hymn for me. As I have to read prayers at a quarter past eleven, and sing, pray, and preach at twelve, it is nearly equivalent, with the afternoon service and sermon, to three sermons a day. Yet I have been able to do it all without any injury to my throat, thank God ! It may be that I shall be able to return home strong enough to take full charge of a Church, and if so, my highest ambition will be gratified. My knee improves very slowly. I can walk about half a mile, but still have to sit in preaching.

To the Rev. Andrew Longacre.

LONDON, TUESDAY, *April* 30, 1861.

It has been an incessant stream of dinners, teas, breakfast meetings, sermons, and speeches, so that we could not write. . . . Dined on Tuesday, with about fifty people, at Mr. M'Arthur's ; on Saturday with about twenty at Mr. Lycett's. Heard Punshon, on Wednesday, at Great Green-street : and sat in a great draft which gave me a sore throat. Spoke at 4 P. M. in Exeter Hall, after the people had been sitting there from ten o'clock—more politics than missions in the speech. The principal result of my efforts is the sore throat aforesaid, which, I fear, will not leave me till we get out of the cold, dull London air. After the dinner Dr. Hoole, Mr. Arthur, and I got into a clarence and drove out to Richmond, ten miles, to dine with Mr. Hall, Mr. Farmer's son-in-law. It was really one of the grandest dinners I ever saw. The English people are all right, thus far, in feeling, on the American question. But they are awfully ignorant of American facts. A very intelligent gentleman asked me if Massachusetts was among the seceding States ! Even Dr. S. seemed to think the tariff question had as much to do with the rebellion as slavery. I have tried to set them right.

To Mr. Lemuel Bangs.

PARIS, *May* 16, 1861.

I am working very hard just now, rapidly translating Gasparin's " Un Grand Peuple." But I suffer for want of money. My correspondence and writings of every kind are heavy. I could do a great deal more if I had free command of money. If any of your patriots, or committees, can help us, I will do all that is possible with the press here and in England.

PARIS, *May* 30, 1861.

The Government does not seem to appreciate the absolute necessity of giving everybody something to do. So much enthusiasm will certainly spoil unless people are kept busy. Turning back volunteers and disbanding regiments don't seem the thing—especially when the crack Seventh has only enlisted for thirty days. Our meeting at the

Louvre yesterday was a grand success. Dayton has raised himself greatly here by his speeches. Fremont also spoke nobly—as, indeed, did everybody; even your humble servant did his best. The enthusiasm frightened the Frenchmen who were present.

I feel tempted to go home by every steamer. Did I not think I am doing more good, both in Church and State, by staying here, I should go in the next steamer.

To his son, in Germany.

LONDON, *April* 80, 1861.

As for your proposition to go a soldiering, I like your pluck very well, and if I had five sons, or even two or three, I should probably feel it my duty to say yes. But as you are my sole masculine heir in this world, I do not think it your duty to go, or mine to let you go. I am growing older, if not old, and am not very robust. In the order of Providence you may have yet to take care of me and of your sisters. Others can go who are differently situated, and there will be plenty of such. You and I, perhaps, can serve the country as well here as if we were to go to the wars. I laid down some pretty strong meat for them at Exeter Hall, as you will see in the report, if it is full.

PARIS. SATURDAY, *May* 18, 1861.

Between you and me and the post, I fear a re-action at home before hot weather, if the troops are kept simply on the defensive. I fear, too, that the men in power have not brains nor experience enough for the emergency. But I may do them injustice; and if the war goes on, men enough with brains enough will spring up. England continues to act shamefully. Won't we pepper and salt 'em with sarcasm after the war is over! Won't we show up their Pharisaical anti-slaveryism? Mr. Langdon gave last night (for the guns) 1,000 francs; Emmet, 1,000; Curtis, 500; Warden, 2,000; Strong, I think, 2,000; M'Clintock, 100; Longacre, 50; Wendell, 500, etc. They will probably get 15,000 more from persons not present. If this letter were stretched out it would fill two sheets. God bless you! Write oftener.

PARIS, *May* 31, 1861.

I send you *Galignani*, containing an account of the American meeting, and the latest telegrams. I wrote the resolutions for the meeting : hope you will like them. I also made a speech, but, as I did not write it out it could not be given in to the paper last night as the others were. It was a grand meeting. Mr. Dayton sat on the right of the president, I on his left ; Fremont next to Dayton, Cassius M. Clay next to me. I like Clay amazingly, and the liking seems to be mutual. He has one of the sweetest and most benevolent faces I ever saw—quite different from the truculent being the southern papers make him out. Dayton made a grand impression ; I think he will make the same impression on the emperor. If he had a good secretary of legation who knew French, he would get on very well indeed.

To Mr. C. C. North.

PARIS, *June* 19, 1861.

Of course, in these times, the Chapel has caused me a great deal of anxiety. Many of our pewholders have gone to America, and few have come to take their places. Yet our congregations are as good as ever. This is caused by the number who come in from other parts of Europe, to be nearer the news from home, and to be ready to go home if necessary. These persons do not take pews, but it is a blessing the Chapel is there for them. Thus far the treasurer has been able to pay my salary punctually every month out of the receipts, but I have no idea this can last.

I shall need to be away in England two to four Sundays at least during the summer. I consider the Chapel my first duty, and patriotism the next. Thus far I have sought to do my whole duty to both, and God has given me more physical strength than I had, to do the duties that have fallen on me. I shall not give up the Chapel unless Providence clearly indicates that it is my duty to do so.

To his Son, Emory M'Clintock.

PARIS, *July* 8, 1861.

The *Times* contains a short account of our breakfast. As you see it, I did not post it to you. The *London American* of this week will contain a full account, and you will get it. The meeting was a great success, and did much good in England. Noel's speech was really grand and statesmanlike. Everybody in England is trying to prove how friendly they have been to us all along. They are right in feeling, but most of the people are so ignorant of foreign affairs that the Government can make them believe anything. At present I think the Government is all right. I think Adams suits them very well. He is a cold, cautious man—very much of an Englishman himself—and really will do more good there than a man of more impulsive nature could do.

PARIS, *July* 15, 1861.

The newspapers lead us to believe there is a chance of a compromise with the rebels. I hope not, if it be an arrangement which will make it necessary for us to go through all this trouble again in a few years. It ought to be settled now and forever, after all the sacrifices we have been compelled to make.

PARIS, *July* 27, 1861.

Bishop Janes has spent three days of this week here. He was all for my going to West Point before he left America, but since he has been here, and has seen the new ambassadors at our different posts, nearly all of whom have heard me preach and know me personally, he thinks I ought to stay here.* The question will be settled in a few weeks one way or the other.

The bishop enjoyed his stay here hugely. His brother Edwin and Dr. Jacoby were with him, and I rode about with him all the time, showing him the sights.

" Gasparin " makes a neat little volume. I would send it by post, but as you will return so soon it is not worth the postage. It must do good in England. The *World* credits me with writing an able article in *L'Ami de la Religion*, which was really written by Delavile, an able lawyer here. I am sorry for this.

---

* The chaplaincy of West Point had been offered to Dr. M'Clintock, but after consideration the offer was declined.

I am amused, and at the same time pleased, by your anxiety that I should not give much time to politics. In the first place the preservation of the Government is not politics, in the ordinary sense of the word. If the Government is lost, all is lost—family, Church, property—everything. In such a crisis as this I hold it the duty of every man who has any influence, to use it on the side of law and order. If not, the wicked will prevail: God's law and all justice will be trampled under foot. In the second place, I have not given so much time as you think, even to this great duty. I have never neglected my duty to the Chapel in any degree. I have been absent but two Sundays for months, and but once from prayer-meeting, unless when my throat was too sore to go. I am thankful to say that my health enables me to do these duties without inconvenience. I have preached twice the last two Sundays, besides reading prayers, without injuring my throat. The congregations are remarkable, considering how many have gone home. Bishop Janes thinks I had better stay here. His ideas of the importance of this work are greatly increased since he has been here. I will stay, if it be possible, in spite of our anxious desire to see you all.

I am rejoiced to learn that you are growing in grace and faith, and in the comfort which faith brings. Our religion is meant to make us strong in such times as these. It is not provided merely for calm weather. Faith sees the sun behind the clouds. Brother Jacoby was talking with me the other night about the German missions, of which he is the head, and of the probability that money from home would fail. "But," said he, "I am not afraid about that. It is the Lord's work, and the money will come somehow." He lays all his care upon the Lord, and sleeps quietly. Can we not all do this ? I am glad to trust in God. During all the fears and anxieties which our home troubles have brought—and, in some respects, the anxieties are greater for us so far away than for you at home—I have never lost a night's rest on account of them. But I cannot help much sorrow of heart over this wicked and causeless war. To think of friends ruined in circumstances, of many gone to the field of battle and to death, of the arrest of religious activities and missionary movements ; these things, apart from my own personal losses, which are, perhaps, as heavy in proportion as other peoples', are enough to pierce one through. Judge M'Lean told me five years ago that all this was plotting in the South, but I could hardly believe him. Now it has come to pass before our eyes. But nations, like individuals, must, it seems, in the order of the Divine government, have their trials and purifications. No nation in history has escaped. This is our trial. I believe God will bring us out of it purer and better than we have ever been. This is the time to believe in him as the divine ruler of nations and of men.

VERSAILLES, September 4, 1861.

We left 10 Rue Balzac on Monday—sending our goods to the new house, and the family to our summer resting-place in Versailles. We have a grand old apartment on the third floor containing ten rooms, thoroughly furnished with old style French furniture — everything comfortable and nice. No carpets: some of the floors are waxed, others are tiled, but all as clean as a pin. Clocks in almost every room —and very elegant ones, too—writing desks, and, in fact, every convenience. I really think this plan of apartments would be very successful, if once fairly introduced, in the American cities. We have the gardens of the palace to walk in, and the park to ride in, whenever we feel rich enough to pay thirty cents an hour for a carriage. I should have gone to Geneva this week to attend the Evangelical Alliance, but my knees got so tired with the moving that I must give them a week's rest.

We expect to hear by Sunday that Washington is taken by the rebels. There is great incapacity somewhere ; but it will all come right by and by. I have no fear for our country in the long run. But what an account will the men have to give who have made this wicked rebellion for the purpose of extending human slavery. I fear there can be no peace in America while the cause of all our troubles remains untouched.

20

To Mr. Lemuel Bangs.

PARIS, *October* 12, 1861.

Emory, I am sorry to say, has made up his mind to go to the wars. In view of his *physique*, of the fact of his being my only son, of his talents and prospects which fit him to work better for usefulness to his country and the world in other lines than the military, I do not think he ought to go. But he is of age, and must decide the question for himself. I have written to the War Department, sorrowfully enough, asking a commission for him. I really hope they will not grant it, and that something else will turn up to employ him. I fear he will be invalided upon three months service, if not killed. But the will of Providence be done. He has studied military books with his usual rapidity of apprehension, and could probably pass an examination to enter M'Clellan's staff, if he could get a chance. Importunity, I suppose, secures such things, and importunity alone, with sufficient influence from members of Congress. The adhesion of the Orleans princes will bring up that whole party, which is very powerful in France, to our side of this great question even more decidedly than they have yet been with us. If Prince Napoleon comes home with good impressions, he will carry with him one wing of the Napoleon party. As for the emperor himself, he has always been with us. But Thouvenel is very ill informed on our affairs. What a pity it is that Mr. Dayton cannot talk the question over with him ! The *Times*, you see, has moderated very much in tone. Lord John Russell declared to an American gentleman privately, last week, that they had not the slightest idea of breaking the blockade, or of interfering with us in any way.

PARIS, *November* 15, 1861.

Our Church goes on wonderfully well, in spite of the number who have left for home in consequence of the war. The congregations are excellent—better, even, for the last few weeks, than they were before. If my knee would allow me to do pastoral visiting, I should feel more happy in my work : but, as it is, I try to do my duty as well

as I can, and am not unhappy. But if the way were open how gladly would I go back to St. Paul's to work among so many friends, and
praying friends, who would hold up my hands when they incline to
hang down ! I hope the time will come when our Discipline will be
less stringent on the point of a preacher's stay in a place ; but it will)
probably not be in our time.

I see that Mr. Matthias has gone home. He was my first presiding
elder, and I have always had a warm feeling toward him from that
day to this. I trust his family is provided for. We are all passing
away ; may we be gathered together in our Father's house above !

The war, I suppose, will last two or three years at least. I hope
the northern people are making up their minds to that—for if they
do not they will be likely to be disappointed. Patience and perseverance are the great lessons they require to be taught. I trust the end
of the war will be, at least, the beginning of the end of slavery, which
has caused the whole trouble. God bless you all !

In order to show more clearly the meaning of Dr.
M'Clintock's letters in relation to the Trent trouble,
much of the correspondence of this date between him
and the Rev. Wm. Arthur is here inserted. These two
friends saw the misunderstanding which was working
mischief in the minds of leading men of the two nations,
and labored assiduously for its removal.

The Rev. Wm. Arthur to Dr. M'Clintock.

November 29, 1861.

I have no heart for public affairs just now ; but seldom as I agree
with the *Times* its money article of to-day, seems so exactly to express the universal feeling of this country that I send it. As I always said, if your people are determined to make an enemy of England they can. People here would hate a fight begun when your
hands are full ; but if you force it on, it will be such a one as was
never seen. This has always been my testimony, and you may rely

upon it. The idea of war with you is odious to our people ; but if
your Government only shows a desire for peace, I have no fear of
ours.

The Rev. Wm. Arthur to Dr. M'Clintock.

November 30, 1861.

I cannot mention names, but I know upon as high legal authority
as can be, that the *Times'* account of the opinion of the law officers
is perfectly correct. The view taken is this : The American Government is as well versed in the law of the case as any one ; their later
writers are the best ; and if Commodore Wilkes acted on instructions
in taking the law into his own hands, his Government means war.
The law authorities have no shade of doubt or difference on the question, " Did Wilkes, or did he not, take the case out of the hands of
the law and settle it by violence ? "   I do not speak on second-hand
information here.

As to political feeling in the highest quarters, it is to avoid a fight
if possible ; but a strong fear prevails that Seward wants to force
England into it.   On what this is grounded I don't know ; but on
two things you may rely : That we will offer no provocation, will
make no grievance beyond what loyal opinion decides to be such, and
will for such firmly insist on reparation.

Dr. M'Clintock to the Rev. Wm. Arthur.

PARIS, *November 30, 1861.*

It is of vital and pressing importance that I should get an immediate answer to the following question :—

" Does the British cabinet really believe that Mr. Seward wishes
to have war with England, and that his measures are intended to
provoke it ? "

If you can, through any of your friends, get an answer to this that
may be relied on, you will do more good than you can well conceive.   I do not wish my name mentioned, nor will I mention yours
in return.

The converse question, " Whether the British cabinet really mean to push us to the wall?" I suppose cannot be answered. But if I can get a sure answer as to the first, (and I see no reason why not,) it will go a great way, perhaps, toward preventing things from rushing into war between America and England—a war which would thrill the master of evil with Satanic joy.

The Rev. Wm. Arthur to Dr. M'Clintock.

December 2, 1861.

My Saturday's note would show you that not only politicians but lawyers take the acts of your Government as meaning a hostile intention. It is most seriously believed on all hands that Seward wishes a war. Why, again I say, I do not know.

As to our Government wishing a war, it is out of the question. Not one of its acts gives countenance to such an idea. Neither glory nor gain could result to us.

Personally I no more believe that your Government wishes a war than ours, but I can hardly find a man to agree with me. Some busy power is making each believe that the other is a secret enemy. If reasonable proof could be given to influential men that Seward does not desire to make capital out of hostility to England, it would do great good. Commodore Wilkes has done more for the South than ten thousand Slidells and Masons could have done, as far as feeling on this side is concerned. Would it do any good if I had an introduction to your minister here?

Perhaps I go too far in saying that *all* believe that Seward really wishes war, most do; but those who know better, and look deeper, may think he only wishes to make capital out of a show of menacing us, and this is, to *men*, the more offensive supposition of the two.

Dr. M'Clintock to the Rev. Wm. Arthur.

Paris, *December 2, 1861.*

Try to look at this grave question calmly—even amid the tempest which has been got up in England. Put the two following points together—both taken from the *Times* you send :—

1. The money article says, that "even on points where there is but

a small doubt in their favor, that doubt should be conceded to the Washington statesmen."

2. An article signed "Templar," on page eight of the same *Times*, cites Sir W. Scott as laying down that "you may stop the ambassador of your enemy on his passage." An article signed "Senex," on the same page, gives the same point more at length.

Is not the "*small doubt*" here? But instead of the "small doubt," there are precedents by the score in British usage, and citations multitudinous to be taken from English law-books, in favor of the procedure in the case of the Trent. The *Star's* quotations from Dr. Phillimore are alone ample to furnish a complete vindication of it. If the newspapers are correct, your law officers have decided that Wilkes "ought to have taken the Trent into port for trial." And on this punctilio, great and magnanimous England proposes to join the slaveholders against us, and to strike us to the earth when we are too weak to resist her!

You have several times reproved me for my prediction of last winter. My only error, it seems, was in the time I allowed. The intervening months have been spent—you know it as well as I—in poisoning the British mind against us in base perversions of the ground and causes of the rebellion. In a word, in preparing the public mind of England to sustain the Government in striking us when the first plausible pretext should come. Now it *has* come.

You are stronger than we are, and could do us more harm than we could do you, even if we were united. Now that the slaveholders are fighting us, you can crush us. But will not the shame of such an alliance cause your ears to tingle when you hear of victories? And when you have subdued us, established the dominion of King Cotton, and have fixed the yoke of the slaveholding oligarchy firmly upon the necks of our people, will the achievement be one to be proud of? Will England stand, then, at the head of Christian nations? Will God be glorified thereby? The laurels to be won in forcing the priest party on poor, distracted Mexico, will fade before the greater honor of forcing the slave power upon the prostrate United States.

God bless you and your country, my dear friend ! If we have war, and it lasts five years or ten, I shall never cease to love you, to thank you for the great services you have rendered us, and to pray for you, even on some night when your ships may be bombarding my old home in New York.

The Rev. Wm. Arthur to Dr. M'Clintock.

LONDON, *December* 4, 1861.

May God bless you ! Thanks for your letter, which will not be useless. There is one word on which I seriously differ from you— "punctilio." I hope Com. Wilkes meant the difference between arresting the ship and judging her, as in our favor, and always say so ; but it is one of the most cherished distinctions in our executive proceedings. We give every policeman the right to arrest a person accused, and carry him before a tribunal ; but let the highest police officer in the land assume to deal out justice and he will soon be dismissed.

As to Fairfax, I am inclined to agree with much you say. As to Wilkes, all was the most studious insult. His shotted guns, his live shell, his armed men, his bare cutlasses, convinced every sailor I have heard speak that he deliberately meant to provoke war. So persuaded are they of it, that those who do not believe in the Government wishing war, suppose that he must be at heart a secessionist. If one thing is certain under the sun, it is that the day before the news of Wilkes's movement reached us, the universal feeling in England was satisfaction that we had succeeded in being neutral, hope that complications were now impossible, and congratulation that our commerce and money market were daily showing themselves superior to the influence of the war. Our papers acted badly, very badly, but the idea of a war was far from the heart even of the *Times.*

Many thanks for the extract from the *Herald.*

The Rev. Wm. Arthur to Dr. M'Clintock.

The French papers are full of sensational news, and I venture to say that the scrap you send was never read a second time by any one here—no one saw it. Our men were full of the conviction that Seward intended, by deliberate insult, to bring on a war, and lay on us the blame of recognizing the South. I think they now see a little more clearly; but as a specimen, I saw a letter from a peer in the country, requesting his nearest friend to tell the Government that he had good information to the effect that the real destination of the armada was the West Indies, and Port Royal a mere feint. People here have striven hard to reconcile themselves to the prospect of a war, but cannot; and if your Government makes amends, there will be more jubilant feeling than for many a day, though sober, as will, in the other case, be the sorrow.

Weed is a noble fellow, and will do great good. He is the right kind of a man for our folk.

Would to God that your North had had the generosity to say from the first England will be our friend, instead of flinging constantly in our faces your belief that we should make defensive and offensive alliance with the South! Common policy taught the South to do what good feeling, without it, might have taught the North; what both combined ought to have done.

The feeling here is less for war every day, still all are ready if they must; and if this passes over I believe the incident will do much to make us understand each other.

The God of peace bless you and America!

Of the service rendered by Dr. M'Clintock and Mr. Arthur to Mr. Weed in his mission, Mr. Weed gives the following interesting account in a note to me: "Three days after I reached Paris, in November, 1861, news was received that Messrs. Mason and Slidell, Confederate commissioners, had been taken from the Trent, an English ship, by a United States' war steamer. That news occasioned great excitement both in England and France. After a consultation between Mr. Dayton, the American

Minister, Mr. Bigelow, our Consul, Archbishop Hughes, and General Winfield Scott, at which Dr. M'Clintock was present, it was deemed proper that I should proceed immediately to London. Before leaving Paris Dr. M'Clintock handed me a letter of introduction to the Rev. William Arthur, remarking that I had better deliver it as soon as convenient after my arrival in London. Remembering the earnestness of Dr. M'Clintock's language and manner, I lost no time in calling upon Mr. Arthur, whom I found at the Methodist Mission House, of which he was secretary. My reception was very cordial. Mr. Arthur, while putting on his hat and coat, expressed great apprehension that the Trent affair would occasion a war. It was important, he said, that I should immediately be made acquainted with the Hon. Arthur Kinnaird, and other influential friends of the North. Taking a seat with me in a cab, we were driven to Pall Mall, where I was introduced to Mr. and Mrs. Kinnaird, both of whom sympathized warmly with our Government, and entered promptly upon measures calculated first to avert war, and next to correct the erroneous views, so widespread in England, of the causes of our Rebellion. I was indebted to Mr. Kinnaird for early introductions to Lord Palmerston, the Earl of Shaftesbury, and other distinguished personages. As a member of Parliament I found him an efficient friend of the Union during the Rebellion. I was several times in Paris during the eight months we were abroad, always finding in Dr. M'Clintock a devoted friend of the Union, upon whose intelligence and advice I could safely rely."

To Mr. T. N. Dale.

I send by this mail Saturday's *Opinion*, containing an article of mine signed ———, and also yesterday's *Opinion*, with notice of the article in the bulletin. Don't mention my name in connexion with these articles. I am to keep *l'Opinion* posted hereafter. I have also just translated Gasparin's new pamphlet, and sent it to London to be printed. In truth I have been working so hard recently as seriously to hurt my nervous system. Yet one must not spare himself in these times.

To Mr. Lemuel Bangs.

I have nearly written myself into a fever on this quarrel with England. If we get out of the scrape I hope I shall have contributed to it by what I have written and printed, both in England and here. I hope you will give up Mason and Slidell. Such an affair as this Trent is the only one on which the English aristocracy could have fired up the masses against us, and they have used it with fearful skill and success. If we deprive them of this issue, and they try another, they will fail, unless, indeed, it be another of the same sort. Moreover, even in France, the opinion prevails that our Government dare not resist the mob. To give up the rebels would put down this cry: even English lies could not cover up or pervert so great a fact, for which all the world is listening with open ears.

If the war *does* come, I shall have to go home at once, I suppose; and my feelings lead me to go. It is a terrible tension of the nerves to await the arrival of the steamers. Yet there never was a time in which it was so important to the country for me to be here, as it will be after war breaks out. I have greater means of influence now than ever. If things are rightly managed France will take our side within six months after war breaks out. But *will* things be rightly managed? We had the threads all in our hands then, but Mr. Seward could not be prevailed upon to use them. *Now*, he sends Hughes, Weed, M'Ilvaine, and all such, but it is, I fear, shutting the stable door after the steed is stolen. Half the expense last spring would have kept him in the stable.

To the Rev. A. Longacre.

PARIS, *December* 20, 1861.

Your letter of the 7th inst., from Cairo, arrived yesterday. You were in blissful ignorance, when you wrote, of the state of warlike madness into which our friends on the other side of the channel have lashed themselves. It has somewhat subsided now, but the state of things is fearful to behold as among a Christian people. All their fine preachings to us about the "sin of fighting" are suddenly ended. The point of honor—national pride—is, for England, more than philanthropy. Especially when behind the point of honor lies a want of cotton and a dread of republicanism. Yet the whole heart of the people is with us. The people may be led or driven by the aristocracy into a hateful war, but it has not come to that yet. We believe and hope that Lincoln will give up Mason and Slidell, or propose the arbitration of the Emperor Napoleon. The London *Times* and *Herald* insist upon it that England will not agree to the latter proposition, but I do not think Palmerston will dare to refuse it. It is said that the queen is opposed to fighting us, some say the Prince of Wales also, but it is hard to find out the truth these days.

I have just translated De Gasparin's new pamphlet to print in London. I fear, however, it will fall on unwilling ears.

Americans in Europe felt very keenly the manner in which the country was often wronged by the telegrams sent through the Atlantic cable. The editorials of the English and continental papers were based upon the cable reports; the corrections of the cable news, which came later by mail, as a rule, went unnoticed. It was evident that if the dispatches from this side were imperfectly, or carelessly, or unfairly made up, the effect, in a time of such overwrought excitement, could not be other-

wise than hurtful to our country abroad.   Dr. M'Clintock
called attention to this subject, first of the agent of the
Associated Press in New York, and next of the department of war at Washington, with the result of putting
all parties on their guard.   The incident was not in itself
important, but is an example of the vigilance with which
he watched the influences that were every day mould-
ing European opinion.

Let it not be supposed, however, that he became so
absorbed in the service of his country as to forget or
slight his duty as pastor of the American Chapel.   Far
from it.   Never was his preaching more direct than during his ministry in Paris.   He speaks gratefully of its
fruit in the conversion of some of his hearers.   His assistant, Mr. Longacre, having returned home in the spring
of 1862, he assumed himself, from that time, the entire
Sunday labor, preaching twice, and reading in the morning the Episcopal service.   Nor did he forget Christ's
word, "I was in prison and ye came unto me."   There
is in his collection of letters one from the American minister, the Hon. W. L. Dayton, to the Prefect of police of
Paris, which runs thus: "The bearer of this note is the
Rev. Dr. M'Clintock, the pastor of the American Chapel.
I respectfully ask, in behalf of such of his countrymen as
may be confined in the prisons of Paris, that he may be
permitted to visit them when and as often as his counsel
and services may be desired by them respectively."   For
one American, in prison on a serious charge, he interested himself greatly, visiting the authorities, and finally
appealing to the emperor in his behalf.

A little incident of his Paris life is very characteristic. One of our missionaries in India, the Rev. J. T. Gracey, who was under great obligations to a surgeon of the British army, wished to present his benefactor a scarce scientific book, which could not be had in the East. He wrote to Dr. M'Clintock asking him, if it were practicable, to find and purchase it. " Amid all his other cares and duties," says Mr. Gracey in a note to me, " he put himself to no small pains to secure and forward it, and as I took it unbound, he would not accept any thing in payment for it. The deep sympathy which he had with our foreign mission force was the explanation in part of his kind attention to my demands." A well-known American writer, Edward Everett Hale, in one of his brilliant fancies, sketches the plan of a club, propagating itself over the world, two of whose cardinal principles should be, "to look up and not down, and to lend a hand." In such an association Dr. M'Clintock, by a natural and easy process, would have become head and chief. If he had had a hundred hands he would have lent them all, in help and service, to his fellow-men. " To look up and not down, and to lend a hand," were the sum and substance of his philosophy of life.

LETTERS—1861 TO 1862.

I. TO DR. M'CLINTOCK.

I.

War Department, Washington, D. C., *Sept.* 16, 1861.

MY VERY DEAR SIR:—Your letter of the 28th ult. was very welcome, proving as it does your intense interest in our great struggle.

I have written to the President of the American Telegraph Company a special letter on the subject, and as I know all his sympathies are on our side, I am satisfied he will remedy the difficulty in regard to the telegrams made up for Europe. When I hear from him I shall take pleasure in letting you know what he says and what he has done.

You ask several questions. I reply: Martial law practically has existed at Washington for six weeks. The provost marshal (General Porter) is arresting traitors day and night.

The wealthy people at Washington whom you suspect are giving aid and comfort to the rebels are rather hard to find now, as, thanks to the vigorous measures of General M'Clellan and General Porter, they have either been caught and sent to Fort Lafayette, or have packed up their trunks and gone to parts unknown. Believe me, with warm regards to your family,

Your sincere friend,   JAMES LESLEY, JUN.

II.

War Department, Washington, D. C., *Oct.* 21, 1861.

DEAR SIR:—Your favor of the 3d inst. is acknowledged with much pleasure.

I am very much gratified in being able to give you the satisfactory intelligence that arrangements have been definitely made to transmit the proper kind of telegrams to the English press. This matter has required considerable judgment to arrange, but by the aid of the Secretary of State, and the Assistant Secretary of War, it has been finally accomplished. I think there will be no more cause for complaint hereafter. With kind regards to your family,

I remain your sincere friend,   JAMES LESLEY, JUN.

II. FROM DR. M'CLINTOCK TO HIS FRIENDS.

I.

PARIS, *July* 81, 1861.

You see that I mean to keep you in debt, for letters at least. But, like the New York merchants, I have decided on a cash business—thirty days the very longest date, and you have had much more than that time on my last. Please pay up promptly. The difficulties which the war necessarily brings must fall upon you in common with others, and must make demands upon your time also. But it will relieve your mind to write. I am sure you will find my prescription good.

If possible, our anxiety here is greater than yours at home, for we get our news all in a lump, and not gradually, in driblets, as you do. The last steamer brought us the accounts of M'Clellan's victories, and of the advance of M'Dowell's column. I pray God that the great preparations of the Government may cause the southern army to disband without fighting, so that our country's soil may not be saturated with fraternal blood. What an account will the men have to render who have undertaken to destroy the mildest and best Government the world ever saw! But this is our time of trial. I trust the country will come out of it like gold tried in the fire.

Bishop Janes has just left us. His three days' visit was a blessing to us all. His view of the importance of my work here, in the American Chapel, has greatly changed, and he now urges me to remain some years—in view not only of the work of God in Paris, but all over the continent of Europe. I have not yet decided whether to return this fall or not: it will depend on letters to arrive in a week or two. In this, as in all things, I hope to act simply as Providence dictates.

A. V. STOUT, ESQ., NEW YORK.

II.

PARIS, *December* 10, 1861.

MONSIEUR:—Your letter of December 2 arrived at a moment when I was worn out with writing to England and America about the Trent affair. Moreover, my secretary is ill, and has been for two weeks. Nevertheless, I wait for him no longer, but write to you in English, not trusting my own French for such a purpose.

I had anticipated your wishes in writing to America. My hope is that this dreadful evil of war between England and America may be averted, and I am straining every nerve to that end. But the public opinion of Britain has been so shockingly perverted and demoralized by the " Times," and other journals, that I cannot say that I expect peace to subsist long, even if war does not grow out of the Trent affair. Good men in England abound, and many of them have stood by the cause of truth and justice from the beginning ; but their number is small compared with those who, for political or commercial reasons, are determined to take part with the slaveholders.

The New York journals are very moderate in tone on the Trent trouble. The "Patrie" has some new canard every night. No confidence whatever can be placed in its *dernières nouvelles.* The " Débats " has had some noble articles this week.

I have just received your second letter. To-morrow I shall go to Levy's and get the proof sheets, if he has them ready, and will endeavor to meet your wishes as to the translation for England promptly.

May God bless you for your earnest and active sympathy for our cause ! God is just. Even if England goes to war with us in aid of the slave cause, all is not lost.

I am, with the sincerest respect and regard, M. le Comte,
Your obliged,

M. LE COMTE DE GASPARIN.   JOHN M'CLINTOCK.

III.

PARIS, December 20, 1861.

DEAR GENERAL :—I beg you to listen to me one moment. There is war in America, not merely rebellion. Your war must be conducted on established principles, or our Government will take rank with Austria and Naples.

Privateering is as legitimate as war on land, except for nations that have accepted the Paris decisions of 1856. If you hang one of the privateersmen you alienate all European sympathy. The Liberals all over Europe are with us now ; but they will drop our cause at once if you do this thing. The Liberals are likely some day to be " rebels " themselves against tyranny here : and they will not sustain you in establishing such precedents.

The honor of our Government is much more at stake in not waging vigorous war, and in not using all legitimate means of harming the enemy, than in such points of etiquette as hanging privateersmen, refusing exchange of prisoners, etc. The rebels are at war with us, and at tolerably successful war, too. Let us beat them in war first, and the rebellion will fall of itself.

I beg you to understand that I am not simply expressing my own views, but those of the best informed Americans and Frenchmen whom I meet.

For the sake of the honor of our country, and of republicanism— for the sake of liberal principles all over the world—I adjure you to use your influence to prevent the hanging of any of the privateersmen. May God have you in his holy keeping !

GENERAL SIMON CAMERON, Secretary of War, Washington.

IV.

PARIS, *December* 27, 1861.

REVEREND AND DEAR SIR :—I have requested Messrs. S. Low, Son & Co., to send you a copy of De Gasparin's " Word of Peace," which I have just translated. If you think, with me, that its circulation will do good, pray send to Mr. Low and get copies to distribute to any persons of influence you may choose. I have directed them.

I do not believe that God will allow unprincipled men to get up a war between England and America.

Of all the miracles of modern days, the success of the " Times " in persuading Englishmen to believe that Mr. Lincoln's Government desires war is the greatest.

Your prayer at Exeter Hall has gone to the ends of the earth ; and, what is more, it has, I trust, reached the ears of Him who heareth prayer. May God bless you !

THE HON. AND REV. BAPTIST NOEL, London.

21

V.

Paris, January 2, 1862.

A happy New Year! May 1862 be better for your and for our country than 1861 has been!

We are still on the *qui vive* for the settlement of the Trent business, hoping that Providence may save us from the folly and peril of a war with England. Even now I have no certainty that this letter will reach you, as the English steamers do not pledge themselves to sail beyond Halifax.

I have been doing what I could. De Gasparin wrote a powerful pamphlet on the Trent trouble, which was published in Paris. He urged me to translate it for England. I did so, and it has had, I think, great effect there. Arthur has written a noble article for the January number of the "London Review." I have had it printed as a pamphlet and circulated in England. If this affair blows over, I hope that a better state of feeling will grow out of it between England and America; and I hope, too, that you will fortify Portland, Newport, New York, Delaware Bay, the Chesapeake, and the Lake harbors, in such a way that John Bull will get the worst of it in case of war hereafter.

It is not to be disguised that we are losing ground in Europe every day. The rebels spare no money or talents on the press here: our Government leaves the whole matter to individual effort. Our want of military success at home is believed to prove our want of military skill, and France, as well as England, is laughing at our vaunting as contrasted with our doing. If this winter passes away without decisive operations, you need not wonder if France and England recognize the slave confederacy in the spring—nor need you complain of them for so doing. The commerce of the world can't wait ten years to let the American people learn the art of war.

All pretty well—chapel flourishing. If we have war with England, however, most of the Americans will go home, and therefore we shall go, too.

J. A. Wright, Esq., Philadelphia.

VI.

Paris, *April* 8, 1862.

MY DEAR FRIEND:—Nothing is heard of all over Europe but Merrimacs, Monitors, iron-clad steamers, etc. Vessels are coating with iron in every country which puts a ship to sea. We have fairly got the start of them, and, I hope, will keep it. The English, you see, take all the credit of the Monitor, calling it a clumsy piracy on Coles's plan of cupola ships. They will next declare that Stevens's iron battery, begun twenty years ago, is pirated from some English invention. By the way, I take credit to myself for urging our Government last year to complete Stevens's ship, though the urgency was in vain. I hope it will be done promptly now. With two or three such ships, built a year ago, you might have taken Charleston, Mobile, and New Orleans long since, saved thousands of precious lives, and millions of money. The late news — Columbus, Newbern, Manasses, Beaufort—has, for the present, put the rebel sympathizers here in bodily fear, and even the "Times" has dropped its slaveholding clients. But if you meet reverses the whole pack will soon be in full cry again. The British aristocracy is not converted to our side, it is only disappointed, and disappointed to the heart's core. I do not trust the British Government a pin's weight more now than I did a year ago, and hope our Government and people will not be put off their guard by the lull of English abuse, caused only by our victories.

Your letters have done more good than you can readily think. They have furnished me with facts and arguments which I have used, not merely in meeting the assaults of our enemies, but also in strengthening the nerves of timid friends. How many people there are in this world who require others to hold them up! I have had several American correspondents during the war, but your statements have been more full and accurate, and your predictions more correct, than any that I have received. No passage of Scripture is oftener verified than this: "Be of good courage, and God shall strengthen thine heart." To him that hath shall be given. A bold facing of peril clears up the mind, and enables it to work vigorously against the evil; while a trembling man loses his mental and his moral vigor. But I did not mean to preach a sermon.

My health has been very poor for several weeks—cold, influenza, diarrhœa, and rheumatism in my ancle, which, added to the trouble in the knee, has made locomotion almost an impossibility. Yet I have missed but one Sunday in six months at the Chapel. Within the last week I have begun to get better, and hope soon to have at least my ordinary health again. We have had a great deal of sickness in the family also, but all seem to be mending now. Bishop M'Ilvaine is here: I asked him to preach for us, but he had engaged both Sundays to Mr. Lamson and Mr. Forbes. He preached for Mr. Lamson on Sunday morning. I had an idea that it would make a good deal of difference in our congregation, but it did not — we had about as many as usual.

The new Wesleyan Chapel, near the Boulevard Malesherbes, is going up rapidly. They have church, school-rooms, bookseller's shop, and pastor's residence, all under one roof, yet presenting a fine architectural appearance. It is a great pity we had not adopted such a plan at first. But as it is we must try to get the Evans lot, and fix the American Chapel on immovable foundations by building on it. Then, and then only, will we be strong and safe. If I could see this thing done before returning to America, I should go back happy and contented. The suggestion in your last about the legation, strikes me as just the thing. Of course I have not mentioned it, and shall not until the time comes. If we now had a good, pleasant room, we should have a full Sunday-school. One part of the Rez-de-Chaussée might be a reading-room, stocked with American journals, reviews, etc., thus making it an attractive place for Americans, young and old. The scheme is perfectly feasible if we can only get the money. But for the war we could have had it.

We hope to hear, by each steamer, that the Senate has adopted the House resolutions as to compensated emancipation. Why in the world is the bill for freeing the District of Columbia delayed? It is a shame to civilization that the capital of the United States should have a slave in it for another hour. Nor does any constitutional or legal barrier stand in the way to justify delay. With that measure accomplished, and the president's recommendation adopted, it will not be long till Delaware and Maryland are made free States.

T. N. Dale, Esq., New York.

VII.

Paris, *October* 27, 1862.

Your letter of the 10th, with enclosed draft for £26, has just arrived. I need not say that I am touched by the kindness of the unknown friends you allude to. Pray convey my sincere thanks and acknowledgments. Had the letter arrived six weeks ago I should have gone at once. But *then* there was a minister here, very acceptable to our people, who would have been willing to remain and preach for me during my absence. Now he is gone, and there is no chance of my getting any one to fill the pulpit in my absence.

That would be reason enough if there were no other. But there is another. My health has run down very much within the last month or two, afflicting my head especially. If I were in New York now, I could not stand the excitement of public services, and so my going would be of no use. Moreover, suffering as I am from rheumatism, I could not undertake two winter voyages.

My first thought was to return the draft for £26; but seeing there would be a loss in that, I retain it. Please pay the amount back, and charge it to me on account. You will owe me that much, according to my account, by December.

I need not say how much pleasure it would give me to take a look at you all. But at present I must not think of it. Unless I devote this winter, or a good part of it, simply to rest and recruiting, I fear my health may be utterly broken up. I shall write just as little as possible.

Rev. Dr. G. R. Crooks.

VIII.

Paris, *December* 2, 1862.

I succeeded yesterday in purchasing the " *Rapport Général sur les travaux du Conseil D' Hygiène,*" etc. It is unbound. It occurs to me that you would desire to present it handsomely bound. I await your order in that respect before sending it. I have paid for the book sixteen francs. To bind it well in half morocco will cost ten or twelve francs more; or, with gilt edges, about fourteen francs, bringing the total cost up to thirty francs, or about £1.4.6. You can remit the amount in francs, by draft on Paris; or in sterling, by draft on London. Be good enough also to indicate by what mode of conveyance you desire the book sent. I am glad to render you this slight service. In case you, or any one else connected with our missions, shall ever need anything from Paris, pray command me.

The prospect at home is better, I think, than it has been for some months. The war, I hope, will be ended by next summer, and freedom established throughout the land. May God grant it!

Rev. J. T. Gracey, India.

CHAPTER X.

1862-1864.

Dr. M'Clintock's Habitual Interest in Political Affairs—The Scholar in Politics—Effect of his Activity upon his Countrymen in Europe—Prosperity of the Chapel—Respect of Europe for "Monitors"—Tribute to the Memory of the Rev. Dr. Bangs—The United States *is* a Great Nation—European Opinion of General M'Clellan—A Detachment of Lee's Army Enters Carlisle—Anticipation Eight Years Before of such an Event by Dr. M'Clintock—Notice to American and Foreign Christian Union of his Purpose to Return Home—Review of his Pastorate in Paris—The Rev. Andrew Longacre's Sketch of Dr. M'Clintock's Personal Life—Making Sunshine for All—Charity for Men, and Faith in God.

THOUGH devoted by his choice, and by the obligations which he had assumed, to the ministerial calling, Dr. M'Clintock had been all his life deeply interested in national politics. He believed the moral integrity of the State to be as vitally important as the integrity of the individual. He could not be deluded by the sophistry that a commonwealth composed of moral beings can exist for ends in which morals have no place. It was his opinion that the State should be served by citizens of the purest character and highest culture, and he deplored the separation which has been going on for so many years between the best classes of American society and its political administration. He by no means considered it his duty to confine himself to watching and praying while political managers took the country far on the road to destruction. Nor could he be warned off by the clamor which, despite our sufferings, is popular still, that scholars are not sufficiently practical to deal with political

issues.   He had learned from Lord Bacon that "it cannot but be a matter of doubtful consequence if States be
managed by empiric statesmen, not well mingled with
men grounded in learning."   Dr. M'Clintock claimed a
place for the scholar in politics, and, true to his convictions, struck strong blows for the right whenever he saw
a fit occasion.

The sneers that scholars, in serving the State, are
not supple and worldly-wise, were treated by him with
the contempt which they deserve.   His teacher, Bacon,
had reminded him again, that "although men bred in
learning are, perhaps, to seek in points of convenience
and accommodating for the present, yet, to recompense
that, they are perfect in those same plain grounds of religion, justice, honor, and moral virtue, which, if they
be well and watchfully pursued, there will be seldom need
of those other, no more than of physic in a sound and
well-dieted body."   Few Americans were better versed
than he in the Constitution of the United States and its
history.   He could cite its provisions with a readiness
which often silenced an over-confident debater.   He was
heart-sick of the reign of empirical statesmen and empirical statesmanship, and longed to see the day when the
most capable citizens should be called, not exceptionally,
but as the rule, to places of public trust.

His vigorous activity during the war, therefore, was
not out of the line of his habitual conduct.   To a friend
who gently chided him for his great zeal in the national
cause, he replied: "The family and the Church can only
exist under the wing of Government: if that is gone, all

is gone. With these views it appears to me to be the duty of every man to use his influence to sustain the Government which protects him." While, therefore, he was never betrayed into an act unsuitable to his position as a Christian minister, he let it be known to all that his voice, pen, and means were unhesitatingly given to the service of his country. The effect of his energetic exertions was felt and recognized by Americans all over Europe. The Rev. Dr. Hurst, who lived at Frankfort-on-the-Main during our late civil war, wrote from that important continental centre: "Unless one has been in Europe, and even lived here, and come in contact with some of the Americans who reside abroad, making Paris their head-quarters, but yet circulating for pleasure or improvement from country to country and city to city, it is extremely difficult to comprehend the magnitude of Dr. M'Clintock's services. There was not a United States consulate in Europe where his influence was not felt in behalf of the country's struggle for integrity, and probably not an adult American living here, or in the countries around the Mediterranean, whom his words, spoken in public or private for the national cause, and reproduced in the 'Galignani' newspaper, did not reach."

During the dark period from 1862 to 1863 he was abundant in hope, though often depressed by the reverses of our national arms. He still, however, worked on, writing, speaking, cheering the faint, and pouring out his overwrought feeling in his correspondence with friends at home.

To Mr. C. C. North.

PARIS, *January* 7, 1862.

We are still full of anxiety and excitement about the Trent trouble. We expected a settlement of it by the Europa, but her news is not decisive. If it were not so serious a matter, it would be amusing to read the comments of the New York papers, and such speeches as Hale's, in the Senate, talking of Napoleon III. anxious to avenge Waterloo, etc. I fancy the receipt of Thouvenel's dispatch has changed all that. Napoleon is determined to keep the English alliance at any cost, and he will never join us against England, unless driven to it by French public opinion. Unfortunately, not only French public opinion, but the opinion of the whole continent, is against us in the Trent matter. If we must fight England, as appears not unlikely, let us wait till we get a case in which the world will stand by us. But I hope that after this Trent business is settled a better state of feeling will arise in England. Had our Government taken the proper means to enlighten public opinion in France and England during the last four months, we should be in a very different position now. Arthur deserves the thanks of every American. He has worked nobly, and with great success, too, especially since the Trent imbroglio began.

In reviewing the year at the Chapel we have great reason to thank God. In spite of the vicissitudes of the time, our congregations are as good as ever, and we are gradually gathering Americans in who have never attended before. I never had more attentive hearers, though I never preached plainer or more direct sermons in my life. Last week I had an earnest letter of inquiry—the cry of a convicted soul. Recently several southern families—from Mobile, Charleston, and Savannah—have taken pews. The great drawback upon my comfort and usefulness has been my knee. It has hindered me from pastoral visiting, as going up and down stairs is the worst thing for it, and most people here live up three or four pairs of stairs. My own apartment is on what would be the third floor in America, and when I go up and down it twice a day, it is as much as I ought to do, without further trial of the knee. As yet I can only walk a short distance, so that my visits have to be made in cabs, and the expense is too great to allow a constant use of them. All this has hindered my pastoral service, greatly to my sorrow; but I have done the best I could, and must leave the result with God.

To Mr. T. N. Dale.

PARIS, *January* 18, 1862.

Emory goes to secure a position in civil or military life. He has promised me to seek a civil position first, in some of the lines for which his education would so thoroughly fit him. Failing in that, he will seek a military post. My fear is, that his constitution is not strong enough to bear the fatigue. But Providence will direct.

The rendition of Mason and Slidell has made us all happy. The Trent papers cover Lincoln and Seward with garlands. England has thus given up a claim of right to take persons out of neutral ships, about which we have been contending with her for half a century. Thank God!

To Mrs. Dr. A. S. Purdy.

PARIS, *January* 80, 1862.

The pressure of public and private griefs has affected my health a great deal of late. I could doubtless bear all things better if I could take necessary out-of-door exercise; but my knee continues to forbid that, and of course the physical organization obeys the physical laws, and suffers. I have lost a great deal of flesh, going back rather to the size and weight at which you knew me when a boy, than to that of my later years. Whether this is a bad sign or not I do not know, but yet it is very comfortable to be well cushioned with fat. It shields one's nerves, and wards off many a blow at sensitive points. But you must not think I am going to sticks, or that I have given up to low spirits. I cannot be insensible to the public troubles of the time, to the fearful state of our country, to the private sufferings of my family and friends. All these things pierce me to the heart. Yet I retain full confidence in God, and have never yet seen the day in which I could not "cast all my care" on him.

I sometimes think our situation makes us more nervous about the

war and its results than you can be at home. You get news every
day, but we are kept on the stretch from week to week, waiting the
arrival of the steamers, and when they do come we tremble to open
letters and papers for fear of bad news.   We are now waiting most
anxiously, for the last news was, that a general movement would take
place. God deliver our distracted country!

If God will, we shall remain here at least until the spring of 1863,
as all the indications of Providence point out this as my post of duty.
As long as these indications remain the same, I shall stay. Pray that
my work may be owned and blessed of God.   I often yearn to see
you and all my dear friends on the other side of the water; but
homesickness is not wholesome for body or soul, and so I check it,
and try to be as happy and contented as possible.

To Mr. Lemuel Bangs.

PARIS, *March* 29, 1862.

The springs of Wildbad, in Germany, it is said, will cure all my ailments, but I can't go there till June.   This illusion, you see, is, therefore, good for three months.   What a blessed arrangement it is, that
we have one illusion thus after another, to keep up our spirits, and
to carry us on through life.   It is a proof of immortality: there *will*
come a time when hope shall be realized.

So M'Clellan has let the rebels escape him.   His star is waning: I
hope he will be able to brighten it up again soon.   The Monitor and
Merrimac have awakened more attention in Europe than Manasses,
simply because people are interested here in the question of iron-
plated ships.   The English begin to think that if we can build Monitors in one hundred days, it would not be so easy to crush us, even
with "Warriors."   The old heroic stories of wooden walls will do
now for stories, like the tournament battles of the Middle Ages.

All Europe is thrilled with the proposal to initiate compensated
emancipation.   It is the true issue and end of the slavery question.
Push it all you can.

I feel the homesickness coming stronger upon me now that Emory
has gone.   Moreover, my health is leaving me all the time.   I fear I
am trying to do too much.   Yet I am not willing to leave this post

so long as it clearly appears my duty to stay here, as it now does. The spring is, with us, beautiful and delicious. The chestnut and the locust trees are full of leaf, and the cherry trees are flowering. We are several weeks in advance of New York in the spring. Politics were very fiery here a few weeks ago, but they have quieted down —plenty of arrests. My American papers were nearly all opened at the post-office last week—the first time it has happened since I have been here. My London " Star " has only been permitted to reach me two days out of six. These are signs of timidity, even in this strong Government—really a very good Government, too.

PARIS, *April* 29, 1862.

I hope your prognostications as to the state of your father and mother's health will not be realized, and that this letter will arrive in time to convey my cordial, affectionate, and reverential regards and sympathies to them. Take it all together, in spite of their share of the common evils that afflict humanity, and their endurance of some of· the uncommon ones, their life together has been a singularly happy and successful one. Most of the aims of life they have achieved —the very highest aims they have achieved fully and successfully. Now they are going down to the grave with gray hairs—crowns of glory—and attended by "honor, love, obedience, troops of friends " —most of all, with the light of the city of God gleaming brightly out for them beforehand in their living and dying faith. And for you it is a rich inheritance, the treasure of their good lives and their good name. God bless them both, if they are living, with the richest outflow of his grace in their last days !

We are waiting, tremulously, the news by the Niagara. It is expected to bring us reports from M'Clellan.

To the Rev. Andrew Longacre.

PARIS, WEDNESDAY, *May* 7, 1862.

The last part of your letter has affected my feelings very much. My own fear always has been, with reference to you, as to all others that come under my influence, that the flagrant weaknesses of my character must do more harm than any virtues I possess could do

good. If it be otherwise, I thank God for *overruling mercies*, as
Cromwell would say. It may be a comfort to you to know that your
presence with us has had a most excellent effect upon our entire
household, and that you leave us bearing the affection of each and
all away with you. If you can drop a line from Liverpool before you
sail, do so. God send you a prosperous and speedy voyage !

To Mr. Lemuel Bangs.

PARIS, *May* 20, 1862.

Your grand old father has gone to his rest at last. His end was
indeed a euthanasy—just such as was to be expected after such a
life. Seldom have the ends of life been so completely accomplished
as in his case. His career is now *totus, teres, atque rotundus.* What
a legacy for you ! what a memory for the Church and for the country ! What a thorough *man* he was—so tender, and yet so strong ;
so fervent in his love, and yet so honest, and even hot, in his indigna-
tions ; so clear-headed, and yet so confiding. I consider it one of the
blessings of my later life that it was spent at New York at a time
when I could see so much of him : I now only regret that I did not
see more. Nor have I any better consciousness than the belief that
I enjoyed his affection and confidence.

Make my kindest regards and most cordial sympathies to your
mother, who, in spite of all appearances, has thus been allowed to
see how men in all lands are honoring the memory of her husband.

The news from home is all cheering, so far as it goes. The English press hides its real import from the people as much as possible,
disparages our military successes, and does everything it can to bol-
ster up the rebel cause and to prolong the rebellion. How fearful
is this wickedness, wrought, too, at the expense of the poor manu-
facturers of Lancashire. I have just returned from Yorkshire, where
there is little distress, as that is a woollen region. The politics
of Yorkshire are strongly liberal, and we have very many friends
there. But the ignorance of the middle classes is astounding. They
believe anything they read in their morning paper, and their knowledge, thus obtained, is dogmatically asserted in conversation. But

I found a great change in six months: not, indeed, any increase of good feeling toward us, but much less arrogance, much more respect. Monitors and armies will probably teach John Bull manners yet. Arthur is now on his high horse. All his views and predictions are coming out right—just as we knew they would, and as most of the preachers in England believed they would not. He had to "run a muck" last winter for his Americanism, but it's working round now.

We are all on the *qui vive* to get at the bottom of Hunter's proclamation of freedom. I suppose it will turn out that he anticipated Mr. Lincoln's order a little. But I am more and more satisfied that the rebellion will never be effectually suppressed without the abolition of slavery. God will work it all out.

While working with the prodigious energy here described, Dr. M'Clintock was so lame from the affection of the knee, of which he speaks repeatedly in his letters, that he was almost entirely disabled from walking, and was compelled to sit on a high chair or stool while preaching and conducting the other services of the American Chapel. He was advised to try the waters of Homburg, and went thither for a month's rest in the latter part of June, 1862. Learning late on the evening of July 3 that the Americans in Frankfort intended to celebrate our national anniversary, he went over on the morning of the Fourth, and listened with great delight to the addresses of his countrymen there assembled. Being himself called on, after the representative of Her Britannic Majesty to the German Confederation had spoken, he said in the course of his address to the company: "His lordship has informed you that the United States bids fair *to be* a great nation. Permit me to inform his lordship that the United States *is* a great nation." Of the patriotic spirit of our consul-

general, Mr. Murphy, who presided on the occasion, Dr.
M'Clintock was in the habit of speaking in terms of the
highest praise.

To Mr. Lemuel Bangs.

PARIS, *September* 10, 1862.

We have just received a lot of confused telegrams about Bull Run,
Manasses, Centreville, and Leesburg, from all which we gather that
our brave fellows are fighting now the fields that M'Clellan ought
to have fought last December! and with what result we know not.
God grant that the next news may not be the capture of Washington! But, on the other hand, there seems to be a grand chance for
our generals to destroy the whole rebel army, if they will only em-
brace it. To help crush us, on this side, comes the president's colo-
nization speech, telling the negroes of the South, in substance, that
they have no choice but slavery or exile! At all events that is the
way it will be represented to them, and that is the way it is represented to Europe.

I made several speeches in London last week, and tried to do some
good. I found plenty of religious sympathy, but, as for political sympathy with us, in England, it does not exist, except in a very few noble
souls far ahead of the times. Arthur keeps in his high place, and looks
down with pity upon his mistaken brethren. But even he thinks our
Government has failed to meet the occasion: that we have had an
army of heroes led by—not a donkey, but a military pedant.

We have recently been cheered by the sight of some Methodist
preachers—De Hass, Foster, Keeler, Vincent, and Haven. You
can't imagine what a pleasure it is to see their faces. We see plenty
of other people, and plenty of other preachers, but the Methodist
sympathy is a very strong thing.

To the Rev. Andrew Longacre.

PARIS, *September* 30, 1862.

Your letter seems to imply that I wished you to become an apostle
of amalgamation. I must have expressed myself very unfortunately.
I do not see the connexion between getting rid of the feeling of caste

on the one hand, and admitting negroes to social equality with whites on the other. There is no social equality in England, yet there is nò caste. I should oppose amalgamation, even with Chinese; but I should not treat Chinese as though they were pariahs, notwithstanding. All these minor points would regulate themselves if we once do justice to the negroes. It takes all one's Christian patience to get on with our English friends. But, then, how much we ought to love and honor Arthur and the rest, who behave so nobly. They have fought, and are fighting, against a tremendous public opinion.

I have just received a letter from Arthur, which I send you as a specimen of the way in which our military affairs look to the friendliest eyes here : "Surely it is for some great purpose that Providence has denied the North a general. M'Clellan is a mere engineer, with confidence in plans, guns, and trenches—none in men. He would ruin a hundred armies after he had organized them. I don't know what to think of Pope. I did think him the best man on the ground, but the last affair looks all against his generalship. If they will only march and act, they must, however they fail, at last succeed ; but men who never stir till they have to repel an attack, are ten times worse than enemies. It is the strong giving the weak all the advantages of a better position." More truth than poetry in this I fear. Our congregations at the chapel continue large. A number of southerners come, even secessionists.

Paris, October 28, 1862.

I hope it will increase your respect for me when I tell you that yesterday, October 27th, was my forty-eighth birthday. No bells were rung, no bonfires lighted, not even an extra bit of *pain d'épice* was bought for dinner. A number of our friends, indeed, gathered in the evening, and we gave them tea and cake. as usual; but, alas! they came, not because it was my birthday, but because it was Monday. After all, perhaps, the people were right. What is the use of rejoicing, at least in a worldly way, because one is a year older?

I have not been very well for a while ; but I have no right to complain as long as I can preach twice on Sunday, even though the preaching be not very vigorous. We have had quite a deluge of English friends and English weather for the opening of their new chapel. Poor souls—every service almost has been reached through torrents of rain, and O, the mud ! I intend, if God will, to give myself a good rest from writing and from work, except my parish work, for some weeks or months, if so be I may get stronger thereby. In all things, however, I am content, satisfied, and happy, knowing that all things work together for good.

To Mr. J. D. Wendel.

Paris, December 2, 1862.

You see that I write upon the anniversary of the *coup d'état* of 1852. The emperor has kept his place longer than the people thought he would. But his imperial crown is not made of roses—or, if it be, there are plenty of thorns among the flowers. I hope, however, that his Government is in no immediate danger.

The removal of M'Clellan has caused a good deal of stir here, as at home. The preponderance of approbation is greatly in favor of the act. The general sentiment is that, no matter what his talents, a man who has had command of so great an army for nearly eighteen months, and was found at the end of that time nearly where he was at the beginning, ought to be superseded by a new hand. It is to be hoped that Burnside will be more successful. The secessionists here do not approve of the change of commanders at all.

I preached on Thanksgiving Day from Psa. cvii, 31, and endeavored to show the many grounds of thankfulness we have, even amid the civil war. They are not few. Even now there is more freedom, quiet, prosperity, and security for life and property in the northern states than in any European country. It is not safe, nowadays, to walk London streets even by daylight—or by the dim fog-light which passes for daylight there. People are knocked down, choked, robbed, and half-killed, at all hours of the day, in the most public thoroughfares. If all this were to happen in New York, what lectures the "Times" would give us on the "blessings of Democratic government !" And in France, stories of plots, of risings of workmen, strikes, of suppression of news, etc., are the order of the day. The present condition of our people is one of the sublimest things in history, and is a complete vindication of the superiority of republican institutions with all their perils.

The congregations in the chapel have kept up excellently. People are very poor, however. Exchange at 1.46 makes even rich people poor—of course poor people are poorer yet. But there is no suffering from want, thank God ! and until there is suffering no one knows what poverty is. I should be glad to get back home, to see the dear old land, and to see all the friendly faces again; but Providence seems to will that we should stay here some time longer.

To Mr. C. C. North.

PARIS, *December* 15, 1862.

I do not know whether you are in debt to me or not ; but you will be, at all events, when you receive this letter.

We have had a great deal of illness in our household during the last four months, and have kept quite a hospital. But amid it all we have been a cheerful, happy, and contented household. " No changes of season or place have made any change in our minds." God's mercy is ever the uppermost theme of our hearts and of our songs. I thank him that he has given us this crowning blessing of contentment, and of resignation to his blessed will.

The year's work at the chapel has been also an occasion of great thankfulness. I have lost, I think, but three Sundays from illness, and have always preached twice a day, except when I have had the help of visiting brethren ; and my health is better, I think, at the end of the year than it was at the beginning. Our congregations have kept up steadily, and are as good now as at the best times of prosperity. I have received several persons into the Church on profession of faith. Last week I baptized two young ladies. I have heard of fruit to the word, in many instances, to the glory of God. We have had no disputes or bickerings, no questions about forms of worship, or about anything else. As one of the good signs, we have a number of southern people regu'arly worshipping with us, though they hear the most earnest prayers every Sunday for the authorities of the country, and for the triumph of the good cause.

The indications of Providence are that I shall remain here for an-other year at least. I have been, and am, happy in my work, but I will not disguise from you an occasional homesickness, especially during the dark days of the civil war. But here again I am satisfied that, so far as my own feeble efforts go, they have been, perhaps, more useful to the country on this side of the water than they would have been on the other. Some day I hope to have the privilege of talking with you over all these matters.

We are to have a series of meetings this week at the Wesleyan Chapel and at the American Chapel, which will, I hope, be produc-tive of good. I wish we could see your face and have your help here, for a time at least.

To Mr. Lemuel Bangs.

PARIS, *February* 20, 1863.

I have been greatly edified and comforted within the last few days by reading the " Olive Branch, by Matthew Carey, Bookseller," 1815, 8vo. It gives full accounts of the evils of the times, party spirit, etc., with documents, and is, as nearly as may be, a mirror of the present state of things, only now all is on a bigger scale. The thing that hath been is the thing that shall be. And as we came out of the difficulty then, so, by the blessing of God, I think we shall now. The election of Morgan, and the general results at Albany, are, on the whole, very encouraging. Public opinion in England is getting right from *below.* The ruling classes are very angry, but they can-not arrest the rising of the popular tide. It will overwhelm the abet-tors of reheldom and slavery by and by. As for France, Poland and Mexico absorb all its faculties. Appearances now indicate a war be-tween France and Prussia ; but no one can judge by appearances, or even by the promises of the present French government. Our men at Washington will be surely duped if they trust to words; acts are the only reliable thing.

LEEDS, *March* 6, 1863.

The Emancipation Society has changed the face of things in England very much. Indeed, one would not believe that so great a change could be so soon effected. Seward's reply to the French proposal has filled us all with exultation. We hold up our heads with the old American feeling.

Upon hearing that a detachment of Lee's army had entered Carlisle, in June, 1863, Dr. M'Clintock makes this entry in his diary:—

"*Monday, July* 13.—The rebels are in possession of our old home at Carlisle. I suppose I shall get no more rents from that quarter this year. Eight years ago, in that very house in Carlisle, I told my wife that it would be an unsafe residence in case of the outbreak of civil war, which was sure to come some day, and that therefore we should leave it. We did leave it. Many laughed then at the idea of civil war, but we upon the border knew better."

General Early, who took possession of the town, gave the people a great fright by recklessly shelling it, and sending men, women, and children to the cellars of their homes for refuge. It should be said, however, to the honor of the Confederate officers, that they used special care to protect the college. Some of them had, most likely, in the days of their youth, shivered, on many a winter morning, in the chill air of its high-ceiled chapel, had been familiar with its long stretches of hallway, and had been governed by the routine of its life.

The prediction, in this instance, of what was likely to come, is an illustration of Dr. M'Clintock's habitually clear outlook upon public events.

Mr. J. D. Wendel.

PARIS, *August* 18, 1863.

Our trip to Homburg was very beneficial to us all around. As you will have learned, we have really had an American summer. Thermometer ninety to one hundred degrees; grass all dried up, streams running dry, trees almost leafless, etc. The Bois looks like an American forest of the middle of August. Yesterday brought us relief—a little rain, and a change of thermometer from ninety to seventy-five degrees. You may imagine how we rejoiced in it.

We have had the pleasure of enjoying American company of the Methodist sort—which I think about the best sort—recently. Mr. Elliott and family and Mr. Oliver Hoyt have been here for a week past. Governor Wright is expected to-day or to-morrow.

The war goes on as fast and as well as Providence allows. That is my comfort amid all discouragements. It will end, I do not doubt, in the downfall of rebellion and slavery. Then we shall have permanent peace. The emperor of the French is doing in Mexico what his reputed uncle did in Spain — preparing the overthrow of his dynasty. I do not think the boy Napoleon will ever sit upon his father's throne.

To Mr. Lemuel Bangs.

PARIS, *September* 21, 1863.

We were all a good deal broken down in health in the early summer. To recruit, we spent four weeks in Homburg, and then in England.

Every one is nervous about war between France and America. The French people do not want it, and it will be a fearful risk for the emperor to run. I have the chance of knowing that he has recently been giving special attention himself to American affairs, and not depending so much upon what Slidell and other people tell him. If the elections in Pennsylvania and Ohio go for the administration, I do not think he will even help the rebels. As for any moral consideration having weight with him, or with the British Government either, that is entirely out of the question. Our Dahlgrens and

Parrotts are the only arguments that have any weight with these people, and they have a great deal of weight.

I feel a stronger yearning for home than ever. When we do come it will probably be to seek some quiet spot where I may preserve my health of throat in spite of the climate.

I have just heard that the Government has forbidden the Imperialist papers here to attack the American Government as they have been doing. This is very significant, and I trust it is the omen of a decision in the emperor's mind to let us alone. If there be a war, it will be a very fearful thing for us all, but not necessarily destructive to us. Indeed, my faith in the destiny of our country, and in the goodness of God, is as firm as ever, if not firmer. Believing that *he* is with us I cannot be afraid, no matter who may be against us. In public affairs, and in private, I can fully trust in his kind and benignant providence.

To Mr. C. C. North.

Paris, *October* 29, 1863.

By this steamer I send notice to Dr. Campbell that I must resign the American Chapel next spring. I give notice thus early that there may be ample time to provide a successor. My term of house-rent ends April 1–15, and at that time, or thereabouts, I wish to leave. It is thought that a few months in the English climate may be beneficial to my wife's health, and we shall, therefore, probably remain in England until the autumn. The brethren at St. Paul's have kindly intimated their wish that I should serve them next year, in case the bishop appoint me. But I do not feel myself strong enough to assume the full charge of such a society. They need a man in full physical, as well as mental, vigor. I have not either.

By the time of our return I shall have spent about four years here. They have gone rapidly and happily. The Church has prospered, and is now prospering, beyond all my expectations. Had it not been for the sectarianism of a few extreme Episcopalians, who are trying, under Mr. Lamson's impulse and guidance, to get up a separate American congregation, we should have all the Americans in Paris worshipping together. As it is they get very few. The largest part of our pew-holders are yet, I think, Episcopalians; and none condemn this sectarian effort more than our best Episcopalian members. There is no more need of a second American Church here than of a separate "confederacy" on American soil. I trust that neither enterprise will succeed.

My relations to the people have been always most pleasant. I have never had one single word of difficulty with the committee, or with any member of the Church or congregation. Greater kindness, or greater confidence, I never found in any church. I shall leave with regrets and grief on many accounts. But duty to my family requires me now to return home. I trust that when the eternal reckoning shall be made, it will be found that the Divine blessing has not been wanting to my humble labors here.

To complete the picture of Dr. M'Clintock's life in Paris, the Rev. Andrew Longacre, his assistant in the charge of the American Chapel, has written the following description of its personal features:—

"The pastorate of the American Chapel was at that time unlike any thing elsewhere. It had been, and still was, the only American Church in Paris. Christian people of all denominations made it their home—of all classes in society also, and of all shades of politics, and that when the country was breaking out into civil war. In the crowded congregations of a Sunday morning were expatriated families from Mississippi and Georgia; permanent residents of Paris born in Boston or New York; the families of business men representing the great houses of the large cities; people of wealth and leisure who made Paris their home for one or more years, and always the ever varying stream of passing travellers. There, with a form of worship which had been settled in a spirit of generous concession, all happily united — Episcopalians, Presbyterians, Baptists, Methodists, each finding some trait of his own preferred forms. I am not aware that so broad and comprehensive a union was ever attempted elsewhere.

"In that world-centre, in face of the dominant Romanism of France, this testimony of a united Protestantism was peculiarly valuable. It would have been asking too much to expect that the members of each Church, fresh from their own modes of worship at home, would be perfectly satisfied with the modified and adapted services there in use. To carry it on so as to secure the sincere support of all, called for a rare combination of piety and tact and good humor. This Dr. M'Clintock happily possessed, and with this his universal culture, his remarkable personal and social attractiveness, and his charm as a preacher, which none failed to own, united to bind his flock to him, and together, in cordial interest and co-operation.

"His preaching was, perhaps, never more highly appreciated than by his Paris congregations. They kept the elegant chapel in the Rue de Berri filled, and listened with a marked interest to his sermons—clear, scholarly, earnest as they were, and brightened with the flashes of a fine fancy and noble bursts of inspired oratory. There were hearers among them to whom his words became an undying impulse for good.

"The actual outbreak of war in America carried off from the chapel many of the southerners. Until then they

had been among his warmest friends, and even afterward
some of them lingered in the congregation in spite of
his well-known loyalty to the Government.   One accomplished girl from South Carolina, whose father was minister to Spain, he had the happiness of receiving into the
Church by baptism.   Many he visited as pastor, comforting the sick and burying their dead.   Later, when the
cutting off of communications with home had brought
many of them to want, they turned to him with a confidence that was nobly justified by his untiring efforts to
relieve them.   To the honor of our countrymen, it may
be said that he found the hearts and the purses of the
most loyal Americans open to all such appeals.

   "Soon after he had taken up his residence in Paris, he
adopted the custom of giving one evening in the week
to the reception of all who chose to call upon him.
These little, free, cheery reunions he greatly enjoyed;
as did all who shared in them.   His house was
common ground, where all who came laid aside the
real or fancied distinctions insisted upon elsewhere.
The passing traveller here met the American Parisian,
who seldom visited his native land; active men of
business, ministers on their vacation, students of art,
of medicine, or of theology, men of leisure, mingled together, while now and then a chance visitor from England succeeded in provoking and amusing all the rest by
his unaccountable inability to understand American affairs.   Paris itself Dr. M'Clintock appeared thoroughly
to enjoy.   The climate, the mode of life, the superb city,
then robing itself in the unparalleled splendor of the

second empire, the immense energy of its internal improvements, the treasures of art, the grand libraries, and the living intercourse with men of letters from all parts of the world—all were delightful to him.

" He gave much of his time to his work on the " Cyclopædia," employing on it a regular assistant. His correspondence with America was as much an enjoyment to him as a labor. It acted as a perpetual stimulus, requiring a quick and broad observation of all that was going on around him.

" With the growing power of the rebellion he became intensely absorbed in the great interests at stake, and he worked with all the means at his command to give just views of the strife to the people of France and England. For this purpose he made several visits to London, pressing the true issues upon his most influential friends there. His speech, much more political than any thing else, which he made at the annual Wesleyan missionary meeting in Exeter Hall, in 1861, made a profound impression. He had the Count de Gasparin's book, " Le Grand Peuple qui se Reléve," translated and published in England. He was in the thick of all gatherings of Americans in Paris for the encouragement and aid of the Government at home.

" Now that the excitement of those events has so long been a thing of the past, it seems strange to recall it. But we felt it keenly then. Almost every foreigner we met treated us Americans precisely as if we had failed in business. There was pity for us, sometimes polite, but always mingled with an evident inward feeling of satisfaction. There were few even of our friends who did not share the

sentiment which the eloquent Mr. Punshon expressed at
the memorable missionary service I have referred to, when
he said that he wished the American flag no more harm
than to be divided, so that the stars might be all on one
side and the stripes on the other. They could not see
that a rent flag, like a rent nation, was not two but none.

"Dr. M'Clintock never doubted for a moment the ultimate triumph of the Government. His hope was the
most confident of any man's I knew at the time, and he
used to say, laughingly, what a 'crowing time' he meant
to have in visiting England after the war. How far his
visit in 1869 met this wish I cannot say. He may
have found little occasion to speak of the past, for our
good friends there are now as happily oblivious of their
former wishes for the success of the rebellion as if they
had never had a doubt of its final suppression.

"The remembrances of Dr. M'Clintock, which I value
more than these, lie within a narrower range. I was permitted to be as near to him as I ever got to any man,
and I never knew one who bore the close scrutiny better,
or whose wealth of mind and character made the intimate acquaintance a greater satisfaction. His wide and
varied culture, his universal knowledge, were fixed quantities in all intercourse with him. But there was never a
shadow of assumption or of condescension. He was a
master in acquiring, as well as in giving, information, and
both were done instinctively, and were woven into his
every day talk in the most natural way in the world. He
gathered something from every one, and his tact made
the dullest show at his best. His common talk was thus

a most delightful going to school, a school where the lessons were not tasks but plays and pastimes. He treated with respect even the smallest fragments of truth or of fact, but he had small patience with guesses. He would worry a chance statement with a good-humored pitilessness till he had got at its modicum of truth, and that he accepted. One great charm of his home-life was his bringing every thing that interested him into the family conversations, to be talked over and argued and tossed, sometimes in fun and sometimes in earnest, from side to side. Reading the French newspapers, he would extemporize translations of articles that struck him, more admirable, we thought, than his more studied efforts.

"His temperament was wonderfully buoyant and hopeful. Notwithstanding previous illness and long periods of a half invalid condition, no one had ever less the spirit of a sick man. In all affairs, public and private, he never failed to see the bright side. Pecuniary losses were borne without a word of repining. Little annoyances were dismissed with an imperturbable good humor. He had a great faculty of enjoyment. The good things of all sorts that came he got the full worth of, and he seemed to enjoy scarcely less much that never came at all. Things beyond his reach were thus made to minister to his gratification. For instance: his invalid habit compelled him to continual abstemiousness in diet, yet he would talk over the pleasures of the table with the gusto of an epicure. He made sunshine for us all, and he made it out of every thing.

"In all his life at home there was an ever present and

unfailing considerateness for the wishes and needs of others. The busy pen could be laid down for hours that he might read by the bedside of the sick. Lame himself for many months, no arms but his own would be permitted to carry the invalid from room to room. The time for a walk was not when he chose it, but when it suited some one who would not have enjoyed it without his companionship.

" His charity in judging others was the most unlimited I have ever known. No unkindness to himself seemed to find lodgment in his remembrance. He saw good in every body, and of that and that only would he speak. Indeed, in taking his opinion of men it was always necessary to allow ample margin for this persistent blindness to their faults. He left it for others to be simply just; he was all mercy.

" In the inmost sanctuary of all, depths not often opened to the gaze of any one, he kept a firm and childlike faith in God. He had, when I knew him, long passed the era of conflict with doubts. Scepticism in all its forms had been met and overcome, and he had come now to be " as a little child," the true heir of God's kingdom. His unquestioning trust in the goodness and care of God was the underlying rock of his hopeful and happy spirit. His charity, too, was grounded in his religious convictions. When we would sometimes question its reasonableness, he justified it by the mercy of God and the Christian law of love. Without a taint of sectarian bigotry, he was, nevertheless, in doctrine and in his views of practical piety, a very sincere Methodist. There was nothing in our received theology which he did not accept heartily. In his family he upheld the old time simplicity of godly living, of avoidance of extravagance, and of doubtful amusements. The gayeties of Paris were unknown to them save by report.

" It would be understood almost without the saying, that toward myself personally Dr. M'Clintock showed the kindness of an elder brother. My interests seemed to be as dear to him as his own. From all appearance of dictation or control he shrank as if by instinct. If he advised it was as if he were the younger and I the elder. He cheerfully opened my way for such opportunities of travel as came to me, doing double duty himself, and urging me to take full time."

LETTERS.

I.

PARIS, *February* 12, 1862.

Better late than never. It is never too late to mend. Accidents will happen in the best regulated families. You see I give you occidental proverbs for your oriental aphorisms. You see, too, that they form the prelude to an explanation of my long delay in answering your letter.

The facts are on this wise. I received your last letter just as I was setting out from home, to be gone a month. I gave it to a French friend, *au courant* with such things, to make the necessary inquiries and report to me. On my return at the end of the month I moved my household to a new abode, and thus kept my study topsy-turvy for a fortnight more. When things got to rights I looked for your letter but could not find it, forgetting, entirely, that I had given it to the friend aforesaid. He, also, was taken ill in the mean time, and was confined several months. I renewed my search repeatedly through every drawer, portfolio, and desk in the house, but, of course, in vain. At last I determined to ask all possible questions about Chinese type, even though I had forgotten the *points* of your inquiry, as I had only glanced at them in the haste of departure. One day my sick friend reappeared, and I questioned him as to his knowledge of Chinese type. "Why," said he, "you gave me a letter on that point in the autumn—I made the inquiries—but your absence and my illness drove it out of my head." Here was an *éclaircissement*. He brought me the letter on his next visit, and I now answer it! I have made this long and valid explanation simply to clear myself of negligence. I assure you that my mind was uneasy about it all the time.

Well, after all, I can give you no useful information about Chinese type. All of that sort of thing in Paris belongs to the *imprimerie Impériale*. When anybody wants Chinese printing done they do it, but they will not sell types, matrices, or anything else. One set they have already sent to China for the use of the Jesuits, and that is all they will send. So you see that, for all the good of the thing, I might just as well have written you a friendly letter long ago in reply to yours, and left type, matrices, etc., entirely out of the question. And perhaps, after all, when this reaches China you will be on your way to America.

THE REV. DR. WENTWORTH.

II.

PARIS, *April* 19, 1862.

Your letter of 7th was very welcome indeed. You do not mention mine of October last. I directed to Black Rock, not knowing any other address. In it I suggested a Paris winter for you, but it is too late for that now. Our spring and summer suns would probably be quite as serviceable to you, and as pleasant to Mrs. Scott. I wish we had space in our apartments to make you comfortable, but every nook in the *flat* is occupied. I can't afford a self-contained house in these war times. But if you should entertain the idea of trying the desired change of climate, which you can secure by merely crossing the Channel, and will give me notice, I will secure suitable lodgings for you, and we will all exert ourselves to make Paris as agreeable as possible to you.

My ailment in the knee still continues. I can walk but little, and have to preach sitting, like a cardinal. Moreover, a similar rheumatic disorder has seized my ankle. My general health, of course, suffers from the forced confinement. So one pin of our tent is loosened after another. How wisely and kindly our heavenly Father prepares our changes for us. All is right which he ordains.

My son returned to America several weeks ago, and has, probably, by this time entered the army, for which, however, he has not sufficient health. My daughters are pursuing their studies with great success here. The little one is a great comfort and joy to us all.

The public troubles of the last two years have, of course, distressed me. I have lost, I think, not less than twenty pounds' weight in that time. But my faith and hope have never failed. God can never allow the cause of rebellion *and* slavery to succeed. We are all very sorry indeed that our cause has been so little understood and appreciated in Britain, and that English statesmen, of all parties, seem to agree in desiring our country to be divided. At the same time we are the more thankful to William Arthur, and other noble souls like him, who have struggled against the tide, and have, indeed, under God, saved us from the fearful issues of a war between England and America. Heaven grant that these two great Protestant powers may never cross swords with each other in anger.

April 21.—I have been hindered from finishing this. We just have the telegram of the fearful battle at Corinth. I hope the details will prove less bloody than the first reports. The next steamers will doubtless bring us news of M'Clellan's first movement on Richmond, where the resistance is expected to be greater than anywhere else. But the backbone of the rebellion is completely broken, though it will be a twelvemonth more, I fear, before all is over.

I pray God that your health may be restored, and that you may be filled with all spiritual grace and comfort. May God have you in his holy keeping! Pray let me hear from you again soon.

THE REV. BISHOP SCOTT.

III.

PARIS, *April* 30, 1862.

The last reports from America are all of a gloomy tone. We await the news from Yorktown, the Merrimac, and Corinth, with profound uneasiness. The strain upon the nerves, in this expectant state of mind, is greatly intensified by the length of the intervals between one steamer and another. At home you get *some* kind of news every day; here we are often six days without a syllable. Of course the whole pack of detractors of our institutions in England and France are in full cry again upon us. If we meet a mishap at Yorktown there will be a tremendous effort made to get a recognition of the Slave Confederacy from France and England, and I think it will be successful. Gladstone's speech, considering the man from whom it comes, is the worst blow in the face we have yet had. The abolition of slavery in the District, however, arrives just in time to increase mightily our moral hold upon the English and French masses. If our Government would employ the same means of inflaming the press that the rebels do, we could soon create a public sentiment that would render any interference impossible, either on the part of France or England.

To O. TIFFANY, ESQ.

CHAPTER XI.

1864-1870.

The Afternoon of Life—Signs of Bodily Decay—Formation of the European Branch of the Sanitary Commission—Invitation to Return to St. Paul's Church, New York—Trip to Rome—Taking Leave of Paris—Reception by Friends in New York—Offered a Public Dinner by Leading Citizens—Failure of Health—Retirement to the "Brown" Farm, near Philadelphia—Chairman of Central Centenary Committee—Great Success of Centenary Work—Mr. Drew's Offer to Found a Theological School—Opening of Drew Seminary under the Presidency of Dr. M'Clintock—Removal of Dr. M'Clintock, first to New Brunswick, and then to Madison, New Jersey—Interview with President Johnson at Washington—No Rest for Us in this World—General Conference of 1868 and Lay Delegation—Work on the Cyclopædia—Trip to England in the Summer of 1869—Continued Decline of Health—Letter to Fletcher Harper—Attack of Fever, March, 1870—Last Words, and the End.

IT was now with Dr. M'Clintock the afternoon of life. There are afternoons so long that they overpass the fixed boundaries of the day. The sun lingers in the sky, and suffuses the earth with a mellow radiance, which adds, with a new aspect, another glory to the visible world. It makes in its lingering almost a second day, which, if less brilliant than the first, is a more perfect image of calm and peace. Dr. M'Clintock knew that the evening time had come to him. Though by no means old as years are reckoned, he discerned plainly enough that his life was coming to its close. He understood what the signs of bodily decay meant. To one of his correspondents he confesses, though without complaining, that his constitution appears to be breaking up. In their tone his letters are less hopeful, than they were in former years, of a future of energetic working power.

He is looking much to the end, and speaking of it, too, but always in terms that befit a Christian faith. His trust in a divine Providence becomes more conspicuous in his correspondence with intimate friends. He still believed that rest and care would give to his life a long afternoon. But it was otherwise ordered; and though he lived his last years, upon the record of which we now enter, usefully and successfully, yet it was with a growing sense of weariness, until at length—his tasks all about him—he ceased at once to work and breathe.

Despite, however, the disadvantage of failing strength, these years were the most effective of his entire career. His life in Paris had made him widely known to his countrymen, and had increased public confidence in him. He had illustrated his energy in an entirely new sphere of activity, to the surprise and gratification of patriotic Americans. Before resigning the pastorate of the chapel he took part in forming a European branch of the Sanitary Commission, becoming its chairman. The announcement of the creation of this branch was received, with great satisfaction by Dr. Bellows, the president of the Commission at home. He wrote to Dr. M'Clintock: " Your movement is the first organized attempt to collect and centralize the efforts of our countrymen abroad in the support of our work, and it therefore merits and calls forth our special and grateful acknowledgments." Dr. Bellows also suggested that the European branch should be represented at the Sanitary Fair in New York, for which preparations were making on the most extensive scale, in the spring of 1864.

In relation to this subject Dr. M'Clintock wrote him the following letter :—

We regret exceedingly that the call for "works of art" for exhibition at the Metropolitan Fair was not made sooner. Had there been three months' notice, or even two, Paris would have been very well represented, both by American and French artists. But just now, all the artists are preparing for the French Exhibition, which opens in a few weeks. All that we can hope to do is to get minor works, not engaged for that exhibition. Nevertheless, a good deal will be done.

In the latter part of 1863 Dr. M'Clintock's devoted friends, the members of St. Paul's Church, New York, invited him to occupy again the pulpit which he had filled from 1857 to 1860 with such pleasure and profit to them all. In view of his broken health he hesitated to accept this call, but finally consented upon the assurance that an assistant would be provided to relieve him of the more fatiguing part of his duty. He began without delay to make preparations for his return home. Before leaving, however, he made a short trip to Italy.

To Mr. Joseph Graydon.

PARIS, *October* 10, 1863.

Allow me first to say, that no service in the Church at home could be more agreeable to me than that of St. Paul's ; nor do I know of any other in which, with my present knowledge, I think I could be more useful. On the point, then, of my willingness to serve you, if able, you may be perfectly assured.

But it is due both to the Church and to myself that I should say frankly, that I do not consider myself strong enough to take the work at St. Paul's, nor do I see any likelihood that I ever shall be. You ought to have a man in full physical force, capable not only of the Sunday work, but also of the week-night meetings, and of steady and protracted work when necessary. Were I to undertake this, I should, in all human probability, break down in it, and that result would be as bad for the Church as it would be for myself.

As to the other plan, of having two ministers, it works well enough in other denominations, but in our peculiar system there are difficulties in it, which you understand as well as I.

Taking every thing into the account, therefore, I think it best to say at once, without waiting for the result of your joint meeting, that I am not able to undertake the charge of St. Paul's.

You are quite at liberty to read this letter to the brethren, if you see fit to do so. And, at the same time, I beg you to assure them of my undiminished regard and affection. I shall never forget their kindness to me; and, if the way were open, I should rejoice to give them my services, such as they are.

When we do return home, I think it must be to the quiet of a retired place, where I may be able to do some service to the Church by my pen, and by such occasional preaching as my strength will enable me to do. At present I am, thank God, able to preach twice, and do all the work of the American Chapel here. But the building is comparatively small, and the work in every respect much lighter than at St. Paul's.

To Miss Maria Emory.

Rome, January 28, 1865.

We expect to leave here on Saturday, January 30, to reach Marseilles on Monday or Tuesday, and to get home on Thursday or Friday. I will write again from Marseilles.

The last five days have been lovely—warm, dry, bright, everything that could be wished. We have made good use of them, invalids as we are. At a party at Dr. Gould's on Monday night I made a little speech for the Sanitary Commission, and they are going to send a table of Roman articles for the fair at New York. There is to be another large party to-night to further the Commission, at which I am to speak.

If I could be away from home another Sunday we could see Naples and Florence; but as I have not heard from Dr. Vannest, I, of course, must return at the time specified. The steamers leave also on very unfortunate days for us, namely, Sundays and Wednesdays, and Wednesday is too late to reach Paris by Saturday. But we are thankful to have seen and enjoyed as much as we have. We had invitations to a large party at Rogers, the artist's, last night. but could not go.

To the Rev. Bishop Ames.

PARIS. *February* 8, 1864.

My only fear has been that my health would not justify me in undertaking the charge of a Church like St. Paul's. But the brethren have so kindly agreed to relieve me of all undue labor, that I have no plea, in conscience, for declining to go to the work if appointed to it.

My engagements here hold me until the 15th of April, or thereabouts, so that I shall not be able to reach New York until the latter end of that month, or the first of May. I shall thus be deprived of the pleasure of attending the Annual Conference, which meets two or three weeks earlier.

The Danish-German war has begun. For months I have looked to that point as the spot where the general European war, which is inevitable. must break out. Its spread may be arrested for a time, but it must come.

To Mr. John W. Graydon.

PARIS, *February* 13, 1864.

We reached home last week, and both Mrs. M'Clintock and I much the better for the trip. My rheumatism did not allow me to put on my ordinary boots, and I saw the chambers and galleries of Rome in a pair of white Russian boots with black tops, and lined with sheepskin, which were the wonder of all beholders. In one of the great ceremonies at St. Peter's, where the Pope was borne on men's shoulders, with all the cardinals in procession, the attention of the throng of spectators was divided between the spectacle and my boots. Since reaching home I have come down to the leggings worn by ordinary men. It is, of course, a humiliation, but I bear it well.

The pain still remains in my left arm, and a little in my chest, and is quite trying. With this exception we are all well.

The weather was very cold in Rome during part of our stay there, and the winter has been, up to yesterday, very severe here. Indeed, this seems to have been the character of the winter all over Europe, and still more in America.

The people at home seem to have an idea that the war is nearly ended. I do not share this notion. I fear that Longstreet will get Knoxville, and if he does the war will be prolonged for a twelvemonth; unless Grant means to let him take it, and then fall on his flank or rear and cut him off. But I do not really think the war can end until 1865.

The British Government has plainly been brought to reason. They will have to pay for all the damages by the Alabama. The " Times " of day before yesterday has an article preparing the public mind for the step. England dares not enter into any European war while this question is unsettled.

Dr. M'Clintock left the American Chapel with many regrets. His associations with his congregation had been very happy. "No word of complaint of my poor services," he writes in his Diary, "has reached me during my stay, and friends have been wonderfully kind." A valuable testimonial, bestowed with a touching delicacy, expressed to him the affection of the people whom he had served. The Americans in Paris, and elsewhere on the Continent, felt his departure very much. "I hope," wrote the American Minister to Italy, the Hon. George P. Marsh, "that you are not going to leave your place long vacant. I know from many sources that you have been most useful there, and I do not know where a man like you can do better service to all good causes in which you are interested." In making the preparations for returning his health quite broke down again. His son, who was then United States' Consul at Bradford, England, was sent for to help him. "April 8," (1864,) he writes in his Diary, "left Paris with family, so feeble that Emory had to lift me almost into cabs and out. Got on board steamer at Dieppe at eight P. M., and fell asleep by nine on a sofa; slept till six A. M., when we were in New-haven; first sleep without anodynes for a fortnight. Stayed in London till Monday. April 20, sailed from Liverpool in the 'Scotia;' health much restored by the trip. Parsonage all ready for our occupancy on our arrival, May 2."

It was a joy indeed to be in his old home once more. He had helped to plan the St. Paul's parsonage, had watched it as it grew towards completion, and had spent in it delightful months. Upon his arrival in the city he was not only greeted most affectionately by his congregation, but received marked attention from many eminent men. His fellow-citizens of New York offered him a public dinner as a token of their appreciation of his services to the country. "We have observed," they say in their letter of invitation, "with pride and pleasure your zealous and effective labors in enlightening public sentiment abroad in regard to the principles involved in the great contest, now, as we hope, happily drawing to its close, and we cannot doubt that the result of those labors will be manifest, for many years to come, in a much better understanding of our government and people on the part of the nations of the old world." This invitation was acknowledged most gratefully, but declined.

Dr. M'Clintock threw himself with ardor into the work he loved so well, the preaching of the Gospel, but found soon that his health was not equal to the duties of his position, and after a year he retired to seek repose. He rented the "Brown Farm," at Germantown, near Philadelphia, where he could, when he wished, exchange his pen for a hoe, watch the growing of his fruit, and occupy himself with the little nothings which beguile the hours of an invalid's day.

To the Rev. Professor M'Cabe, Delaware, Ohio.

NEW YORK, *June* 18, 1864.

Your letter was like your call, cheering and exhilarating. Ever since I first saw you I have felt a warm attachment to you. Throughout all our Church controversies, I have kept my personal attachments above and apart from all the petty strifes of the hour. I know that good men form different opinions of the same thing from different points of view, and I have been too earnest an abolitionist all my life to quarrel with even extreme men, though I might weep over what I thought to be their errors in hurting the good cause. All your kind expressions are thoroughly reciprocated ; I feel in my heart, though not in my flesh, as young as ever. Does not this continuing youthfulness of the affections give us a glimpse of what heaven, what immortality is ?

As to church power, I have never sought it in any form or shape. Had I been so minded. it would have been easy, I think, to go with the majority at Indianapolis and Buffalo, but my judgment and conscience would not allow me to do this. I remain of the same mind ; rejoicing in our national triumphs, rejoicing over every successive blow dealt the monster which has caused all our woe, but yet satisfied that we should have been in a very different position, nationally and ecclesiastically, in Maryland and Virginia, and that we should have saved thousands upon thousands of invaluable lives by a different ecclesiastical course. Since the Rebellion our Church course has my hearty approval, and all this controversy, thank God, is ended.

The "Methodist" has, in my judgment, done more to educate the middle region to antislavery ideas than the "Advocate" did, or even could do. Moreover, for twenty years I have longed for an independent Methodist paper, loyal but firm. My residence in Europe has confirmed all my fears of the dangers of ecclesiastical corporations. Nothing but free criticism can save them from rotting. We Methodists are but men ; therefore I think the "Methodist" will live and ought to live. There must always be men, in every ecclesiastical and political body, who shall work for the best good of the body, without holding the form of power in it. I am content to be one of these men in our Church. All that I have of intellect, of culture, and of position in the world, I give to Methodism, because I believe Methodism to be the best form of American Christianity. But if Methodism does not want me in any of what are called the posts of power, I am not only content, but thankful and happy. It makes me shudder to see men eager for these posts, with all their responsibilities. I know that I am unfit for nearly all of them, and my Master knows it better than I do. It is He, doubtless, who has directed all my goings, for my own good, as well as for that of the Church.

To Mrs. Dr. Purdy.

GERMANTOWN, *May* 30, 1865.

I have been out hoeing and pruning till I have got all heated up, and come in to cool myself a little. I use the rest time in writing to you. We are all rustics : our old clothes are turned to good use. Our cow is doing well, and we have as much milk and cream as we want. We have only twelve hens, and some are setting, so that we do not get as many eggs as we ought to have. We had a duck and drake, belonging to some neighbor, we do not know who. The duck went to setting on a lot of eggs, and the drake wandered around the premises, doing mischief in general. So we just cut off his head to stop his cutting up. Our peas are coming up nicely ; strawberries are just ripe, and if you don't come on you wont get any of them at all ; cur-

rants and gooseberries make nice pies, but are not ripe enough to eat
otherwise ; cherries are growing plump and red ; cabbage is coming
to a head ; our bay horses, Tom and Jerry, are both strong and very
merry ; we have also a gray, whose name is Jack, very slow in har-
ness but very good to back. We have not bought a dog, nor are we
quite sure that it's best to get one—they are so hard to cure of madness
when they're bitten. But our cat is a beauty, you may be sure of that
—a regular tortoise-shell, which, I am told, is the finest style of cats.

She is not bold, but will, by and by, without doubt, be able to
run all the rats out of house and stable. Gussie, Maria, and Annie
are out doors picking strawberries, to do which they must get on all
fours, a job I don't like much for more than one reason : my head
don't better by stooping, nor my chest such squeezing as you get
when you try to pick up things from the ground. If God helps this
year I hope to get round, and then I shall try to do all that I can to
work for the Church, for God, and for man. As it is I am very little
good to any body but myself, my wife and my small children, and a
few of my friends, among whom I am sure I may class the residents
of Fourth Avenue below Twenty-second-street, New York, who, if
they have as much sense as they used to have, will soon get into the
cars and come to Kensington Station, where we shall meet them with
a carriage, and bring them out to the Brown Farm.

To his Son, Emory M'Clintock.

GERMANTOWN, August 8, 1865.

The weather has been very hot, but is a little more tolerable now.
My health has continued to improve on the farm. We are sorry to
leave it, but our funds are not strong enough to give the price asked
for this place, beautiful as it is. We shall not remove to New Brunswick till next spring, and meantime will go on with building and
other improvements there to make it suit us.

The Harpers are going on with the Dictionary again, and it gives
me all the work I care to have. I hope it will pay some day, but am
doubtful of getting all the money back I have spent on it, to say
nothing of the time and labor.

I have preached but twice since I left St. Paul's, and intend to keep quiet till the hot weather is over. It is, as I tell you, cooler weather now; but the thermometer on my table, in the coolest place I can find to write—that is, in the front hall—is between seventy and eighty degrees. Not so very cool after all. The crops will be very great, in spite of all croakers. The reconstruction of the South goes on, but not well—thanks to the want of statesmanship which kept us four years at war, and which will now keep us ten years in hot water. But, perhaps, big statesmen would be the death of us. Slowly, but surely, the true democracy prevails in this land, and will prevail in all lands, England included.

To the same.

GERMANTOWN, *December* 24, 1865.

A happy Christmas! The ground is covered with snow, the air is filled with sleety rain--too stormy a day for Kate and me to go to Church. Maria, John, and Annie went off, however, in the big carriage. The evergreens on the lawn in front are fretted with silver; the meadow beyond is like a vast counterpane newly bleached. In doors all is quiet, warm, and cosy. Aunt Jane, who is just recovering from an attack of illness, which brought her so low that she was not thought likely to live half an hour, lies on the sofa in the parlor reading the "Methodist." Mother lies on the sofa in her bedroom reading the "Independent." I sit in my sanctum, with one window looking north over our beautiful lawns and fields, dotted with firs and elms, to the woods on Cassadav's farm, which limit the view on that side. The west window gives a wider stretch. On that side the lawn begins to slope rapidly some twenty yards from the house to a deep meadow, which rises again beyond in a gentle slope to a hill at the west end of the farm, behind which, again, is another rising slope, the view ending in a belt of wooded hills a mile away. All this is better than the view in Rue de la Plaine, or in Fourth Avenue.

I returned from New Brunswick on Friday. They are getting on slowly with the house; but it will be ready for us in March. The outside is gray, with rich brown trimmings; observatory or belvedere on top of house with a view of thirty miles, and the Raritan mean-dering through it. So you see we shall be well off, if we live to get there, during the few remaining years of our sojourn upon earth. It will not be long before all these cares and pleasures will come to an end, and I look for a better home, where some day, in your turn, I hope to see you coming in.

To the same.

GERMANTOWN, *Dec.* 80, 1865.

Just received your letter. I am not surprised very much, nor am I overmuch sorry. It is, perhaps, quite as well for you to come · home, and there is nothing to grieve over at all.

N'importe; if yours by next steamer puts out the idea that any thing *can* be done at Washington, I shall go on and try it. But I do not see that any thing *can* be done without a fight, and that would hardly pay.

We shall get into our new house in March, and be ready for you in case you come home; all well. There will be plenty of ways for you to use your time and talents here; this being at the mercy of officials is poor business. So don't fret about spilled milk, and don't go to calling it *cream*, now that it *is* spilled.

To the Rev. William Arthur.

GERMANTOWN, *January* 80, 1866.

Being in Washington this week, I got Grant's and Seward's auto-graphs for you. I could not get to Chase's house, but will secure his anyhow by letter. I told Grant that we Methodists had pre-emp-tion rights in him, and he talked of his old class-leading father with reverence, regretting that he himself is not "in full connection," to use his own phrase. He will not withdraw the troops from the South till all is pacified; so he assured me.

I had a long talk with Johnson. He declared to me that if the southern people abuse the negroes he will use all the power of the Government to protect them; but he said also that he believed to give them the suffrage would bring on an immediate war of races after our troops are withdrawn. I told him I had ventured to predict, in a speech in England three years ago, that this Rebellion would be put down, and no man hung for political crime. " Yet," said he, " we must show that treason *is* a crime. As to bloodshed, I remember that He who was most offended, and who was strong enough to put all the offenders to death, himself died for them." It was said with feeling, too.

To the Rev. Dr. T. V. Moore.

GERMANTOWN, *February* 20, 1866.

On reaching home last night I found your letter of 14th, and the familiar handwriting gave me a throb of pleasure. But what on earth makes you fear that the war and its works can affect our hearts; you did not make the war, nor did I. It had to come, and its work is done. Let the dead bury their dead. Do you remember our talks in Richmond in 1857? You told me that if Seward should be elected in 1860 there would be secession, and we both agreed that if secession, then war; and you gave as the reason that young men ruled the politics of the time. But I hope to talk these things over with you quietly, and will not write of them. My health is so broken up that I am resting on a farm. I have purchased near New Brunswick, N. J., and we remove thither in a few weeks.

My son, J. Emory, is in England, where he has been for several years. My daughter, Augusta, was married last November, and so our family is reduced. Tell me of yours. Shall you come North shortly? I cannot put into a letter what I should like to say about your European trip, not half, nor quarter. But if there is no way of seeing you, I will write, of course. Two points I may mention now : 1. It will save much money to go direct to Bremen, as the fare is (or was) as great to Southampton as to Bremen, and then take England on your return, sailing home either from Southampton or Liverpool ; 2. You may calculate, roughly, on spending $4 to $5 (gold) per day, from the time you land in Europe till you leave it, supposing that you stay at hotels, say for one hundred and fifty days, seven hundred and fifty dollars. But it may be done for less, with care and economy. I did it once for less; in other trips more. Of course, I spent nothing on opera tickets and the like, nor is it probable that you will. But write and let me know if I shall see you personally; if not, I will write my ideas fully and send to you.

You are mistaken, I think, in supposing that "many here feel a change" from the war. I have never seen man or woman whose private friendships or affections have been modified. Many and many a time I have thought of you and your wife and little ones, and longed to hear from you. God bless you and them!

The General Conference of 1864 had prepared a comprehensive scheme for the celebration of the Centenary of American Methodism in 1866, and had created a large committee of ministers and laymen to carry out its directions. The committee met at Cleveland, Ohio, in February, 1865, and after drawing up a schedule of objects for which the gifts of the Church should be asked, appointed a central committee of six persons to organize the work of benevolence, and to enlist the people in its support. Of this committee Dr. M'Clintock was chairman.* The committee gave to the Centenary nearly two years of unremitted attention, and had the satisfaction of seeing their labors crowned with a success which outran their most sanguine hopes. The contributions of the people for all objects rose to the sum of $7,000,000; local and general interests were successfully harmonized, and at the close of their work the committee received the thanks of the General Conference, which met in 1868. Dr. M'Clintock was never more efficient than

* The members of the Committee were—Ministers: J. M'Clintock, D. Curry, G. R. Crooks; Laymen: James Bishop, O. Hoyt, C. C. North. The Rev. W. C. Hoyt was made Secretary.

during the period of his connection with the Central Committee. His address, delivered at the great meeting held in St. Paul's Church, New York city, January 25th, 1866, was one of the most powerful that he ever delivered.

Early in this year it became known that Mr. Daniel Drew contemplated appropriating a large sum for the founding of an educational institution. Dr. M'Clintock and the writer were requested by the Central Committee to wait upon him and to learn his intentions. In a very brief but agreeable interview Mr. Drew informed us that it was in his mind to devote two hundred and fifty thousand dollars to the establishment of a theological school, stipulating only that it should be located in the place of his birth, Carmel, Putnam County, New York. Even this latter condition was subsequently waived by him when it was found that another place would be more satisfactory to the friends of education in the Church. All was done in the simplest and most unostentatious manner. It was understood that Mr. Drew wished Dr. M'Clintock to be the first president and organizer of the seminary, and in due time the latter became president. Mr. Drew subsequently went beyond his original pledge, and charged himself with the obligation of bestowing a half million of dollars for the founding and equipment of the institution. If his recent financial misfortunes (in which he has the sincere sympathy of every lover of education) have disabled him from fully carrying out his benevolent purpose, it should not be forgotten that his first promise has been fully redeemed.

24

Drew Seminary, which was finally placed at Madison, New Jersey, is now in possession of lands and buildings of the value of two hundred and fifty thousand dollars, and has received from its founder in all over four hundred thousand. The appreciation of the value of Mr. Drew's benefaction has been shown in the readiness with which others have come forward to supplement it, and to give perpetuity to the school which bears his name.

The seminary was formally opened on Nov. 6, 1867, in the presence of a large assemblage, drawn from all parts of the territory occupied by the Methodist Episcopal Church. It was a bright and balmy autumn day, a day of good omen. The exercises, though occupying the morning and afternoon, (with a collation intervening,) held the undivided attention of the company. In his explanation of the nature of the work about to be undertaken Dr. M'Clintock said : " It is its design to furnish instruction in theology in the widest sense of the word, and in the sciences subsidiary thereto, and especially in the doctrines and Discipline of the Methodist Episcopal Church, with a view to the training of the students to be preachers of the Gospel and pastors in the Church." He believed it to be of the last importance that the students should be educated to be preachers, (not readers of sermons;) a provision was therefore inserted in the Constitution, which required the " professors, both by their instruction and by their personal example, to aid the students to form habits of ready and effective expression *ex tempore*, to the exclusion of the use of written discourses." Young men at once flocked to the school, and have continued to fill it to the entire extent of its capacity to accommodate them.

Upon leaving Germantown, our friend purchased a farm near New Brunswick, N. J., to which he gave the name of " Embury." His house faced the Raritan River, towards which its grounds sloped. Here he busied himself with building, draining, sowing, and planting, and, bating the discomforts of moving his household goods, he enjoyed his outdoor life greatly. But he groaned over the labor of carrying his library from place to place. In October, 1861, he thus sums up pathetically the annoyances he had endured to that time from his many changes of abode : " Spent morning arranging books, papers, etc., in library : very irksome work. I have had it to do eight times since 1848—once at J. City, 1848 ; New Brunswick, 1851 ; Carlisle, 1853 ; Irving Place, 1857 ; St. Paul's Parsonage, 1859 ; Rue des Ecuries, Paris, 1860 ; Rue Balzac, 1860 ; Rue de la Plaine, 1861. The vexation and annoyance of these changes is excessive ; destruction and loss of books very costly. The itinerancy does not suit men whose pursuits require a large library. It must be modified or such men will shun it. Just now I am only half living, so far as books go. I brought from New York to Paris but about one thousand volumes, leaving several thousand behind."

He had been too busy for some years to keep his diary with regularity ; but the entries in the early part of 1866 are unusually full :—

Monday, January 15. — Left home (Germantown) at 9 ; drove to Philadelphia in two-horse carriage with Jane and Kit, and left

Prime-street station at 11 : 30. On train, talked with General Owens about the war ; gave me some graphic sketches of battles ; after Malvern Hill we could have been in Richmond in a few hours if M'Clellan had not been too timid. Reached Washington at 6 P. M. in a driving snow-storm.

Tuesday, January 16.—Creswell and I went to see General Grant ; very affable and pleasant. He said it was impossible for us to withdraw our troops from the South, and would be for a long time. "They would cut each other's throats." I asked him whether native Americans were less docile and subordinate as soldiers than other races. "Not at all; their individuality is great, but does not interfere with subordination, and they make, therefore, the best soldiers. They know what they fight for, and know also that men can't fight in bodies without subordination." "All our soldiers yet in the field are clamorous to be mustered out : that is our difficulty of keeping troops in the South." Creswell asked him if he had said 50,000 American troops would beat any other 50,000. "No. But I do say that with 50,000 of the men who marched down Pennsylvania Avenue from the war, with their officers, from sergeants to generals, I would undertake to fight any 75.000 European troops, with their officers ; our's having had their three years' discipline." Altogether his talk was very sensible and thoughtful.

Wednesday, January 17.—At 10 A. M. Senator Creswell accompanied my brother and myself to see President Johnson. Many were waiting, but the senator took precedence. The President received us most cordially. He is about my size, dark complexion ; talked of his health and eyes, which trouble him. Creswell told him the object of my visit. I said, "We (that is, Methodists, not as politicians) desire to support your Government, as it is our Christian duty to do so. But we are befogged by what we hear of the difficulties between you and Congress." He smiled and said "I will talk frankly and fully," and went into a long statement of the principles of his Government. "We must look at facts," he said over and over again. I told him we wanted to know his views as to the protection of the four millions of human beings who were made his wards by emancipation.

"They shall not be oppressed while I am President. I will protect them to the last atom of the power of the Government." He dwelt upon this at full length. Then, as to negro suffrage, he said : "If I were satisfied that suffrage was the best thing for the protection and advancement of the negroes, I should give it to them. But with my knowledge of the 'poor whites' of the South, I am satisfied they would butcher the negroes sooner than vote with them." He dwelt on the need of time. "The South has advanced in sentiment in one year more than the North in twenty. Give them more time."

I do not agree with him as to suffrage. It could have been given in a month after Lincoln's death, and would have been accepted. With the ballot the negroes would have been protected effectually. The President said, "I must think for myself; but if I can be convinced I am wrong, I think I have sense and self-command enough to change my course." This talk went on about three quarters of an hour, when the Secretary of the Treasury came in with the Canadian delegates about reciprocity. We then got up, but still the President kept us standing about a quarter of an hour more. I was greatly surprised at his urbanity, and even his affectionate way. I had not looked for it. He impressed me as a man very strong within his sphere of thought and knowledge. But I did not get the sense, in his presence, of a superior atmosphere, so to speak, as I did in Lincoln's. Lincoln's mind seemed greatly more susceptible, and more comprehensive—ready to get at truth from any quarter, and to assimilate it.

Monday, January 31.—Finished article "Arminianism" for Dictionary. Read for it Bayle, Cunningham, Nicholls, Ebrard, Neander, and others.

Wednesday, February 2.—Rose at 7:20; made articles "Arnauld," (3), and "Arnold of Brescia" for Cyclopædia.

April 13.—Left our house, at Germantown, March 25, and stayed at Mr. Bishop's, New Brunswick, till April 12, waiting for house at Embury Farm to be ready. Every thing in confusion as we enter. The year 1866 was devoted chiefly to the centenary work of the M. E. Church, I being chairman of the Central Committee. For this service I neither asked nor received any remuneration.

Friday, June 24.—Sunday, preached in chapel of St. James, New Brunswick, on Matt. vi, 2. I have now preached for St. James' congregation every Sunday since April 22, as they have no stationed minister, without remuneration of any sort.

July 18.—Continued as pastor of St. James until spring of 1867

In March, 1867, finding that Mr. Drew's centenary gift for theological education was not likely to be consummated soon, unless I agreed to accept the presidency of the seminary to be founded by him, I agreed to do so—my salary to commence in the spring of the year. The purchase of the Gibbons estate was consummated in June. My work, for seminary, from March till November, consisted of, 1. The organization and plan of instruction; 2. Arrangement of Board of Trustees and meetings thereof for organization; 3. Study of all European catalogues for purchase of books through H. B. Lane, agent.

In November broke up my beautiful home on the Raritan with great reluctance, and removed to the Gibbons mansion. Sold part of my furniture, Mr. Drew agreeing to give me what furniture I needed out of the Gibbons house. Spent autumn of 1867 in organizing the seminary, which opened in November, and the troubles of that autumn and winter, with delays of workmen, with seminary work, with buildings, etc., no mortal can know.

The discomforts of moving were speedily overcome and forgotten, and once settled in the Gibbons mansion, Dr. M'Clintock's life went on very happily. It is a house of princely proportions. The spacious library suited him perfectly; the broad porches afforded him exercise in stormy weather, and the grounds, covered with young forest trees, gratified his sense of the beautiful in nature. Yet it cost him an effort to break up his New Brunswick home. In establishing it he had made one more effort to attain his ideal of a union of out-door activities with

study. He writes almost pathetically to his daughter:
"There seems to me to be no rest for us in this
world." He was like a bird, he said, that had no nest.
But his habit of looking at the humorous side of every
situation served him well here, and his correspondence with his family soon ran on in the old delightful way:—

To his Daughter, Mrs. Augusta Longacre.

NEW BRUNSWICK, *Sunday, June 2,* 1866.

. It is a sort of rainy day, but we have all been at church, except
mother, who is not well enough to go yet, and Emory, who could
not find the key of his trunk in time to get his best coat out. Anne is
in New York visiting her aunt, a visit which has kept her in a flutter
for a fortnight. She had a party there yesterday afternoon. I am
to fetch her home to-morrow; all are well. Emory has been up at
Carmel for a fortnight, surveying the grounds for the new college;
he got back yesterday.

We are afraid that if you do not come here soon you will not
come at all. Emory wants you while he is here. So you see the
propriety of hurrying up your arrangements as rapidly as possible.
We have not finished the outside of the house yet, but the inside
is as neat as wax, and we want you to see it while it is nice, and
has the new shine on. Moreover, it will burst out hot one of these
days, and then it wont be so nice to you.

The building at Carmel will take a year, or a year and a half, to
complete, so that our going there is a thing of the future. All will
be ordered right. I have found it so thus far in my pilgrimage, and
expect it to be so to the end, whether the way be rough or smooth.
Let this be your way of thinking and feeling, and you will find life a ·
much better thing than if you fret about its uncertainties. God bless
you! Do write oftener.

To the same.

NEW BRUNSWICK, *March* 27, 1867.

It is Sunday morning; the first rest Sunday I have had for many a long day, and I am enjoying it greatly. I did not get up till after eight, and decided not to go to church at all, not that I am particularly unwell, but simply jaded, and feel that a good rest will be welcome. So I take part of my pleasure in writing to you. On week-days it is nothing but write, write, all day long. What with the Dictionary, of which the second volume is in progress, and the Drew Seminary, and the winding up of the Centenary, and my own private affairs, and the New Brunswick Church, and all my European correspondence, I am literally fagged out when night comes. By the way, the Drew Seminary is organized, and we are in correspondence about the Faculty. It will begin in September, and by that time we shall remove there. There seems to be no rest for us in this world.

Every thing here is arranged to our heart's content, and we must pull up stakes and leave it. Arthur wrote me some time ago that we must not build *nests* for ourselves here, but just find a good twig to rest on, and hop to another. We have been *twigging* all our lives, and appear likely to keep at it to the end. At the end, we trust, there is a house, not made with hands, prepared for us in heaven. It is hard for us to go to Carmel, and the earthly inducements are not great; $2,500, and house (not built yet) near a little village of three hundred people, and near nothing else but the blue lake and the eternal hills, and our heavenly Father. We shall have almost no company but the Faculty and our friends who visit us. That wont trouble me, as my books and work are full company, so long as I have health; but it will not be well for Maria and mother.

One point of morals before I close. The Chinese have kept up organized human society, with an immense population, for thousands of years. I think this singular longevity is due to the doctrine of filial piety, which penetrates the national life. Now, I do not want you to set up votive tablets in your drawing-room, and burn incense before them to the shades of your ancestors, Irish or Indian. But I

want you to consider whether it is right for you to leave us for weeks
without a scrap of writing from you? You now owe mother two
letters, and Maria one. I know all about your health and your mani-
fold duties. But with all that, you could write a letter, longer or
shorter, once a week, and I shall not consider you up to your duty,
much less to your privileges, until you do that thing. Take it seriously to heart. All join in love to James and the baby, with kisses.
I hope change of air will cure that "rash" infant.

In the year 1868 Dr. M'Clintock was a delegate to the
General Conference which met in Chicago, and advocated
the admission of the laity to that body in a speech of
great power. He had been for years an outspoken sup-
porter of this change in the polity of the Church, but did
not live to see it consummated. The time has hardly
come for writing the history of a movement which peacefully closed a debate of fifty years' duration. One of Dr.
M'Clintock's latest published essays was a tract on Lay
Delegation, written while the popular vote was pending,
and giving a reason for "the faith that was in him."

He felt his burden of work during these last years to
be very heavy. His Cyclopædia demanded unceasing attention; the organization of the seminary and the teaching of his classes, and his correspondence, taxed all the resources of his strength. In addition to this work done
on secular days, he preached nearly every Sunday, supplying during the last months of his stay in New Brunswick the pulpit of St. James' Church in that city, and in
1868-9, in association with Dr. Foster, the pulpit of St.
Luke's Church, New York. In the spring of 1869 symptoms that he understood warned him that he must seek

rest. He closed his house, and with his family went over to England again, the England he loved so well.

To Mr. Fletcher Harper.

LEAMINGTON, *July* 25, 1869.

Thus far our journey has been very successful and happy. My health is wonderfully mended. Mrs. M'Clintock has not improved so much, but yet she is in many respects better. All the rest of the party are very well indeed. We spent nearly four weeks in London, where we had nice lodgings at the West End at a moderate price. I saw our friends, S. Low and J. Low, Junior, frequently. They are very little changed. We have had a fortnight here, seeing all the beauties of Warwickshire, and having an excellent home in a furnished house. In a day or two we go to Derby, (Chatsworth,) etc., and thence to York. After that a fortnight in the Lake Country will finish our trip. The weather has been the perfect English summer which Hawthorne describes—three or four days only have been too hot for comfortable walking. The average thermometer indoors has been seventy degrees.

I am deeply thankful to God for the opportunity of this trip, which has given my system rest just when perseverance at work during the hot weather at home would probably have put an end to all earthly labors soon. But the end cometh for us all, when no man can work. Our friends leave us—by and by we shall be old, and before long we, too, shall be gone. God grant that for you and me the change, when it comes, may only be the happy passage to the presence of our God and Saviour, which is the true aim of good living here! And, in the mean time, may you and I, old friend, do our work cheerfully, looking for that blessed hope.

I wish that you and Mrs. Harper were with us, though I know well that duty keeps you at home. I have heard, with pain, a rumor that your brother, John, has been seriously ill. I hope the story is untrue, or, at least, that he has recovered. Make my cordial salutations and sympathies to him, and also to your brother, Joseph Wesley. The old times come up to me as I write, and the old faces.

To his Sister, Miss Jane M'Clintock.

SCARBOROUGH, *August* 8, 1869.

I wrote to you from London, and Kate wrote from there or from Leamington. But we have no letter from you since we sailed. I begin to fear that you have been ill, but hope it has not been so. You are generally, however, so good a correspondent that your silence is always suspicious.

We all went to the Primitive Methodist Church this morning. The congregation was very large, and the whole services was old St. George's over again — except that there was a good organ and very fine singing. The amens and shouts here just such as we used to hear in Fourth-street. The preacher was not a Primitive, but an eminent Wesleyan. He adapted his sermon, however, to his audience, with great skill and tact.

We have improved in health more at Scarborough than anywhere else, and all wish we had come here sooner. We can only stay to the end of this week, as we are engaged to be at Mr. Darlington's by the fourteenth of this month. After that we go to the English lakes, and sail from Liverpool on the eight of September in the Colorado. We have given up our trip to Ireland, chiefly on account of the extra expense in which it will involve us.

Living in lodgings is very comfortable. I wish the plan were adopted in America. It would be very nice for people of moderate means, as you can make the expense just what you please.

The British Conference is sitting not far from here, but as I came away for my health, I have not been near it, nor do I intend to go.

To his Sister, Mrs. Joseph Graydon.

KESWICK, *August* 26, 1869.

Your letter was very welcome. I had written you another letter, but it seems to have lost itself.

We have been here now five days, and the last two have been the warmest we have had in England. The thermometer has reached seventy-six degrees in a sunny room indoors, and outdoors the sun

has been too hot for me to walk out in the middle of the day. Our
visit at Netherwood was one of the best parts of our trip: everybody
in the house, servants included, was full of kindness, and everything
was done, indoors and out, to make our time pass agreeably. We
had a splendid day at Bolton Abbey.

I climbed to the top of the hill, and had a ramble among heather
on the moors for the first time in my life. We are in excellent quarters here, at the Keswick Hotel, and have seen most of the lions.
Maria and Bella went to the top of the Skiddaw on ponies, and came
back well tanned and freckled. Kate and I have confined our excursions to regions practicable for wheel carriages. The only drawback
I have had has been rheumatism, which is now passing away.

To-morrow we leave here for Bowness: stay in that neighborhood
till Tuesday, and then go to Liverpool to prepare for sailing.

We can hardly yet realize that Mrs. Elliott is gone, and that we
shall see her kind face no more. I think she is one of the best illustrations I ever knew of the power of personal kindness to make
friends and to disarm enmity.

This trip was, as his letters show, enjoyed greatly, yet
on his return he was but little stronger. His step
was slower; indeed, the old alertness of movement was
wholly gone. The brave, cheery spirit, the genial interest in men, women, children, and in life for what it
brought him every day, were not changed—as to these
he was the same as ever. He took up his work in
the autumn where he had dropped it in the summer,
and went on with it though he knew that his strength
was ebbing away. His friends knew it, too, for its
signs were plainly visible. In lecturing to the students during the winter of 1869 he would occasionally drop the thread of his discourse, and be for a moment or two unconscious of their presence. Still he

preached on alternate Sundays at St. Luke's, though so feeble that a carriage was needed to carry him to and from the church. One of these last Sundays was spent at my house; in the afternoon a walk was proposed to the Central Park, a few blocks distant. He had only reached it when he begged to be taken back. This outcry of weakness made us all feel sad enough. Yet during the day, and on like days, he was, when sitting in the house, so full of wise and playful talk, and so capable of enjoying whatever others enjoyed, that a stranger would not have supposed him an invalid. It was only when he rose and moved that the exhaustion of his vitality became painfully visible.

The last letter from him that has come into my hands, written only twelve days before his death, was addressed to his friend, Mr. Fletcher Harper. I have hardly dared trust myself to speak of his long friendship with the Harper Brothers, so trustful on both sides, and so honorable in them all. As his years increased, his heart turned back to the old times when he and they were younger. The letter is such a one as fitly closes Dr. M'Clintock's varied correspondence :—

To Mr. Fletcher Harper.

MADISON, N. J., *February* 20, 1870.

It was a great grief to me that I could not go to the funeral of your brother, Wesley. For ten days I have been confined to the house by inflammation of the windpipe. I am better, but yet unable to go out. Twice I fixed days to go to Brooklyn during his last weeks of life, but both times was prevented by storms.

When I was a young preacher I was occasionally invited to preach in

New York. You may remember that you several times walked with me
to church on these occasions. But Wesley did it several times, also.
During this illness he has been in my mind a great deal, and somehow
always in connexion with these walks, as if the intervening time were
nothing. Two features impressed me then, and they have remained
associated with my thoughts of him ever since—his wisdom and his
kindness. Boy as I was, he seemed much older—certainly he was
very much wiser. His shrewd nature, his sagacious insight, his habit
of observation of preachers and preaching, enabled him to give good
advice ; and he gave it so kindly that you hardly knew or felt that he
was advising at all. Then his criticisms upon the sermon, reaching
not simply to its structure and to its form, but to its spiritual aims
and worth, and always given with so much judgment, and with a
sweet kindness, that made them seem more like praise than criticism,
did a great deal, I remember, to enlighten me upon my own duty
and work.

Not many months ago, dear friend, I wrote you on the death of
your brother, James. We are all tending to the same bourne—I trust
to the same heaven. Of all the successes of your brother Wesley
his greatest was that he kept his religious life and his simple faith.
In those last bright weeks in Clark-street, the light which made his
sick-room so cheery and so beautiful a place, was the light, not of
earth, but of heaven. It would have been the same if he had died
a poor man ; but that he kept the faith, to die so beautifully, as a rich
man, this was indeed a wonder of success in the highest sense of the
word.

It cannot be very long before the summons will come for you and
me. There are few men living for whom I have so strong a personal
affection as for you. I wish that we lived nearer to you, and that I
could see you oftener during these swiftly passing days before the
sunset. But, as this cannot be, may God grant us his abundant peace
to spend these days in his fear and love, that we may be reunited
with all that are dear to us in the unchanging life above !

Ever your friend,   JOHN M'CLINTOCK.

There was still hope felt that he would rally from his prostration, as he had rallied so often before. But on the third of March, 1870, the telegraph summoned his friends in haste to Madison. They went fearing the worst. He had been seized with fever, and when we arrived was wholly unconscious. The felicity that had marked all his days attended him even in dying, for the friends of his boyhood, his youth, and manhood were with him. At a late hour the company, save the chosen watchers, separated for rest, cheered, too, by a faint gleam of hope. Shortly after midnight he awoke once more to consciousness, and recognized his son, and his colleague in the seminary, Dr. Foster.

" Foster, is that you? I am very sick, am I not?"

"Yes," was the answer, "you are very sick, but we have hope that you may recover yet."

" No! no!" said the patient, "but no matter what the event, it's all right." And pausing for a moment as if meditating, " It's all right, all right."

These were his last words. In the early morning a messenger bade us hasten to the sick chamber. Before it was reached all was over. Dr. M'Clintock breathed no more. The heart that had through so many years responded to every generous impulse was still.

CHAPTER XII.

Tributes to the Memory of Dr. M'Clintock: From Dr. W. H. Allen—Bishop Janes on the Elements of his Power—His Early Life, by Mr. T. A. Howe—Mr. C. C. North on his Industry and Organizing Talent—The Rev. William Arthur's Recollections—The Young Professor, by the Rev. Dr. Deems—The Hon. John Bigelow on Dr. M'Clintock's Life in Paris—His Social Qualities, by Mrs. Mary S. Robinson—The Rev. Dr. Hurst on his Helpfulness to Young Americans in Europe—His Leading Mental and Moral Traits, by the Author of this Memoir.

I SHALL not attempt an estimate of Dr. M'Clintock's character, for it has been sufficiently portrayed in the passages from his journals and letters contained in this memoir. It was a character transparently clear. There were in it no dark and hidden passages which the light never reached. All was with him as open as day. He had nothing to conceal, for, with his utmost strength, he tried to live an upright, manly life. Nor is it needful to dwell upon the tenderness with which loving hands committed all that was mortal of him to its last resting-place. It will be more fitting to gather together the many tributes paid to his worth by his friends, and out of them weave a wreath, to lay upon his grave :—

"Since the death of M'Clintock, so many beautiful and, in the main, truthful notices of his life, works, and character have been written—the best and most discriminating of them by *Alumni* of Dickinson, his former pupils—that to one ambitious of fame it would almost seem worth while to exchange life for such abounding praise.* If the beatified spirit were sensible of earthly eulogy, our choicest expressions of admiration would not add a feather to that eternal weight of glory, nor a drop of blessing to those joys which it hath not entered the mind of man to conceive. But while our plaudits cannot penetrate the ear of death, nor our incense stir its torpid brain, every just eulogium is an incentive to those who survive. It is an exhortation and a promise —go thou and do likewise, and thy name no less than his shall be a memory and an example.

"M'Clintock, like Goethe, was 'many sided,' and, like a fortress, every side had its salient angles. Hence the photographs of his character vary with the focal distance of the lens, the quality of the light, the *posé* of the sitter, and expertness of the operator. While in all of them we recognize the man, we fail to find in any one of them all the man. I shall attempt no exhaustive analysis. I propose nothing more than a sketch, with rude pencil but loving hand, of a few of the more prominent and obvious traits of that distinguished man, as at my point of observation and in the light I had they appeared to me.

"The youngest of our corps, he quickly made himself felt as a power among us, and gave early promise of the breadth and depth of attainments which subsequently made him eminent. His perceptions were quick and clear, his grasp of new thoughts firm; every faculty of his mind moved with the velocity of the electric cur-

* From Dr. W. H. Allen, President of Girard College, and formerly Dr. M'Clintock's colleague in the Faculty of Dickinson College.

rent.   He was remarkable for a kind of intellectual *élan*,
and charged upon the subject before him with the abandon of an assaulting column in battle.   Enthusiastic in
the pursuit of knowledge, he acquired it with prodigious
rapidity, and his tenacious memory let nothing escape.
He could prepare a sermon, write a review, learn a language, or master the details of a scientific treatise in less
time than any man I have known.   I remember that
when pressed for copy, he wrote an article for the
'Methodist Quarterly Review' in a single day, which
filled twenty-two pages of that periodical—and this in
addition to his regular work as a professor.

"But his intense mental activity taxed beyond healthful endurance a physical constitution naturally robust.
While midnight oil may lubricate the mind, it poisons
the body.   The laws of our vital being cannot be violated
with impunity.   In the earnestness of his work, our
friend exhausted his strength, and was frequently compelled to remit his labors to recover his health.

"Physiologists assert that the maximum ratio of brain
to muscle in the animal world has been reached in man ;
and that any marked excess in that ratio is abnormal,
and a cause of early death.   Thus the popular belief that
precocious children die young is confirmed and explained
by science.   But M'Clintock had a head as large as
Daniel Webster's, poised on a body half its size.   How
so small a frame could support so vast a dome for fifty-
six years, is a problem which may puzzle physiology.
Although that frame was hewn from the toughest tim-
ber, squarely jointed, stoutly braced, compact in every

mortice and tenon, its parts needed frequent repairs to prevent the superincumbent weight from crushing to ruin the whole structure.

"Dr. M'Clintock's transition from the chair of mathematics to that of ancient languages was so easily and gracefully made that he seemed to be equally at home in both departments. Though he was not a man to bury himself in numbers, quantities, and dimensions, until he ate, drank, wore, talked, and dreamed mathematics, and breathed no atmosphere but equations, differentials, and integrals, or until imagination, sentiment, and sense of beauty were so dead and dry within him that, like a mathematician we read of, he could lay aside Milton's 'Paradise Lost' with the question, 'What does it prove?' yet I have always deemed it fortunate, both for himself and the Church, that he entered the field of literature. This afforded wider scope for his talents, and accorded better with his tastes and aspirations. His translation of Neander and his connexion with the 'Methodist Quarterly Review' gave breadth and depth to his theological studies, made him familiar with German thought, and the exhaustive methods of German research, and added to his rare qualifications for the great work which will be an enduring monument of his industry and learning.

"In the pulpit, M'Clintock was sound in doctrine as held by our Church, courteous to other denominations, catholic in spirit, convincing in argument, rich in illustration, persuasive in eloquence. Learned without a display of learning, pleasing without effort to please, he spake from a full mind and warm heart to minds and hearts that responded in sympathy with his own.

"On the platform, ready, bright, strong, the right word in the right place, he fastened the attention of his audience to the sentiments he wished to inculcate, sometimes by an apt comparison, sometimes by a suggestive metaphor, and often by sallies of wit and humor, which shot forth like coruscations of the aurora borealis, in ever-varying hues and shapes, and threw over his subject a playful and shimmering light.

" In social life, frank, genial, simple-hearted as a child, transparent as crystal, with no assumption of dignity, no consciousness of superiority, alive to all human emotions and sympathies, his conversation now shone with the rich, soft hues of the opal, now flashed with the brilliant light of the diamond.

His sympathy with the poor and defenceless assumed the form of a broad philanthropy. There is a kind of philanthropy which overlooks the naked and hungry at its own door, but sends clothing and food to the Feejees and Hottentots to be seen of men, and to blazon its name in the newspapers. But M'Clintock's great heart had room for the near as well as the remote. Like the wise king of old, he 'considered all the oppressions that are done under the sun: and behold, the tears of the oppressed; and they have no comforter. And on the side of their oppressors there was power; but they had no comforter.' He resolved to be their comforter. He stopped not to count the terrible cost of word or deed in behalf of an unpopular cause, in a misled though honest community. He knew that legality is not always right; and that in every conflict between human law, which may be wrong, and divine law, which is always right, the power of man is on the side of what is legal, while on the side of right is the power of God.

"Some who are now present may remember the day when the cry, 'Down with M'Clintock!' rang through the college campus, and young men, frantic with rage, were ready to tear him in pieces, or hang him to the nearest tree. He was charged with instigating a riot to rescue a fugitive bondman from his pursuing master. If the charge could be sustained, he would be held responsible before the law for the sad consequence of that riot —the death of a man.

"When the brave Colonel Shaw fell, with many of his soldiers, in the unsuccessful assault on Fort Wagner, a flag of truce was sent for his body. The commandant of the fort replied, 'We have buried Shaw with his niggers.' In the indictment of the Carlisle rioters the name of John M'Clintock was included in a list of twenty-nine. It was a feeble attempt to bury John M'Clintock with his negroes. But as the fame of Shaw has outlived the petty insult, so has the fame of M'Clintock. He was acquitted. The sober second thought of the students succeeded their passionate excitement. They who had shouted 'Down with M'Clintock!' became afterward his personal friends, and he still lived.

"The services which M'Clintock rendered to his country during his residence in Paris demonstrated his ardent patriotism, and their value can hardly be overrated. In

the dark days of our calamity, when men's hearts began
to fail them for fear, he breasted the tide of foreign
prejudice, and, with arguments that could not be answered, sent forth through all channels of communication
with the public to which he had access both in France
and England, did much to aid the accredited agents of
our Government in preventing the recognition of the
Confederate States by those two great nations.

"The Christian public of all denominations has been
gratified with the announcement that the ensuing volume of the great "Cyclopedia," for which, in connexion with Dr. Strong, he had been fifteen years collect-
ing materials, needs only a revision to prepare it for
the press. If the forthcoming volumes shall fulfil the
promise of the three already published, the work will be
a splendid monument of Christian learning and research,
which will perpetuate the names of its authors and add
to the reputation of the country. And when Biblical
and theological scholars of whatever sect or creed shall
rise from the study of its pages, they will say, ' Servant
of God, well done ! ' "

_____

"One of the first elements of his power, and one of
the principal sources of his successful life, was his earnest spirit.* His ardor was quenchless, and his energy exhaustless. Whatever he undertook he accomplished ; he could not fail. In his youth he aspired to a
collegiate education. Have it he would, and have it
he did. And when he received his parchment he did

* From the Funeral Address of Bishop Janes.

not receive it as a bill of divorcement from books; it was only an inspiration in the pursuit of eminence in scholarship. While a professor in Dickinson College he was more of a student than any undergraduate in the institution. It was the burning of the midnight oil that gave him his greatness and position. This resolute will, and persevering effort for Christ, may be seen in all the labors of his life.

"Another reason of his success was found in the systematic manner in which he employed his time. His was not a hap-hazard life. His had a time for devotion, for general reading, for study and writing, for social life and general action—a time for every thing. It was this systematic effort that enabled him to turn to the best account every fragment of the day, and to win such a wide reputation.

"Another reason of success was the simplicity of his plan, the oneness of his purpose. We have a right to state that he had an eye single to the glory of God, and that he sought to promote that glory by advancing the interests of humanity. His eye being single, his purpose being a simple one, his whole life was one of candor, frankness, and openness. He was just as ready that his opponents should know what he intended and was doing, as that his friends should know. He, therefore, never lost the confidence of any one. I have known him from childhood, and I say, before this congregation and God, that I never knew any thing of him that was dishonorable. He was as careful of the interests of another as of his own, and he was jealous of all that pertained to the glory of God. Because he was thus devoted, and his motives pure, his actions were always understood, and nowhere was this seen to greater advantage than in the sacred desk. He sought in the simplest and plainest of language to present the doctrines of our holy religion. He ascribed originality of thought, so far as divine truth is concerned, entirely to God. As a man, as a Christian man, as a minister, as a man to whom the Church had committed many of its interests, we remember him with gratitude and with love. I feel that no one will say we exaggerate the merits of our deceased brother; but every one will retire from these services to-day, and think that his character has not been fully set forth. I shall offend no one in saying, we have in the Church no one left superior to him."

———

" My personal acquaintance with him* commenced on his coming from Philadelphia to New York to take a position in the Book Concern, then in charge of Messrs. Emory and Waugh. My own position was that of chief clerk in the Book Department. Young M'Clintock had that of book-keeper and general assistant to Mr. Waugh, who up to that time had kept the books of the Concern as the associate of Dr. Emory. On his coming from Philadelphia his appearance was very youthful; in fact, he was but a boy, and he would have blushed to be called any thing more. When Mr. Waugh saw him he fairly expressed his surprise by saying he had supposed

* From Mr. Timothy A. Howe, his fellow-clerk in the Methodist Book Room.

him older. John, however, took the position assigned him, and soon gave satisfactory evidence of his ability.

"He was very winsome in his manners and appearance. His round jacket and close-fitting clothes were well adapted to show off, even at that time, a splendid figure. His countenance, fair and ruddy, was very attractive, while so sensitive was he that the slightest personal allusion to him would mantle his checks and forehead with crimson. He had the privilege of a home in the family of the late Rev. Samuel Merwin. The influences there thrown around him were well suited to make a deep impression on a mind so sensitive as his; they were, in fact, only a continuation of the same influences under which he had hitherto lived in his own father's house. His regard for Mr. Merwin was very great. He loved him much, and well he might, for Mr. M. was a wise and judicious counsellor, and, while seeming to make himself an only equal of the young, he at the same time would be imparting the most useful lessons of instruction. And religion, as exemplified in Mr. Merwin's family, was ever attractive.

"The late Rev. Dr. James Floy was a fellow-clerk in the Book Concern, and in memory of our then bachelor days we three, afterward for many years, as opportunity offered, had our annual dinner at some appointed place, at which none others were allowed to be present. The following notice now lies before me:—

"'DEAR SIR: The annual dinner will take place, if you have no objections, on Wednesday, and the company will meet at the office of —— at 3 P.M. Yours in fraternity, J. FLOY,

"'MONDAY, *September* 22, 1850.'" J. M'CLINTOCK.'"

" But these friends of my youth have passed away, and
I am left alone to my 'annual dinner' in remembrance
of them."   _____

"At the General Conference of May, 1868, in Chicago, we lodged at the same hotel.*   Often in his room, I
observed that, in addition to his Conference labors, which
were enough for two ordinary men, he spent hours of each
day in examining proofs of his great work—' The Cyclopædia of Biblical, Theological, and Ecclesiastical Literature '—the proofs being sent daily by mail.   In connection with the Drew Theological Seminary, it has been
my privilege, as a trustee, to observe the same remarkable
industry and fertility of resource.   As the trustees have
met from period to period, it was not needful to bring
to our meetings any resolutions or suggestions, for Dr.
M'Clintock, as President of the Seminary, was always
ready with every point carefully arranged for our discussion and adoption.

The last display of his energy and capacity was seen in
the formation of the Board of Education, where, as on
other occasions, he appeared the master spirit.   Out of
twelve trustees appointed by the late General Conference, nine were present in New York in December, 1869,
among whom were found some of our ablest ministers
and laymen.   In a day spent in discussions which were
to consolidate the whole movement and send it forth organized for its work, M'Clintock shone conspicuously in
amplitude of suggestion, in scope of comprehension, in

* From Mr. C. C. North, of New York city.

vigorous application, and broad sympathy for the chief object of the movement—the education of young men for the ministry. This was probably the last business-meeting he attended in the interest of the Church. In preparing documents for publication, it devolved upon the writer to visit Dr. M'Clintock at Madison on Wednesday evening, February 16. He had been suffering with a disorder of his throat, and had for a week been speechless. That evening he recovered his voice, and was enabled to greet me with his accustomed urbanity. We spent two hours after tea in revising the 'proofs' of the documents we were to send forth to the Conferences, and with his usual facility he crossed a sentence here and altered a word there, until the whole matter was finished, when he said: 'Now, let us visit the ladies.'

"And now for an hour he was full of vivacity, and entertained us with remarks on furniture and household matters, on expenses in Paris, and on his literary labors. Among other things he said: 'I have come to believe that I am a modest man.' 'Why?' I said. 'Because,' he replied, 'so many persons have issued books on the life and character of St. Paul, while for years I have had a pile of manuscript on the same theme which I have not ventured to give to the public.' Alluding to his losses of property during the period of his residence in Madison, which to most minds would be serious and depressing, he said: 'These things have not cost me the loss of a moment's sleep, nor on account of them have I experienced even the pain of anxiety.' A few days after this conversation I heard of his illness—not then thought to be fatal—a few more, and word came that there was little hope ; on Friday, March 4, all doubt was removed— the noble man had fallen ! "

———

" Dr. M'Clintock's death to me is one of those events that mark a stage in one's relations and memory.* It alters, more than one could believe, in a case where personal intercourse was so slight, one's mode of thinking as to men and affairs in your country, in the world of letters, and in American Methodist activities. From the first time I met him in London, in, I think, the year 1850, he drew me toward him with a joint force of heart and brain rarely met with. During my visit to America this force had added to it that of most winning, personal kindness, and noble services to the cause of Methodism in Ireland, which I was happy to see espoused by one whose help was powerful.

" Had I never seen him again, I should have till death held him in memory among rare men, as I do several others whose acquaintance I then made. But subsequent visits of his to Europe, and especially his residence in Paris, put it in my power to see more of him than of any other of my American friends.

" From him I had, during a visit to Washington, gained much light on many of the more obscure aspects of the problem of slavery, especially in its relation to the Free States and the central Government, bearing on points clear enough to Americans, but scarcely understood by one in a million in Europe, and yet necessary to an intelligent

* From a letter of the Rev. William Arthur, London, England.

view of the conflict which was then shaking the Congress
in anticipation of the time when it would shake the bat-
tle-field. This was one of the things which most helped
me early to see through misrepresentations which were
spread here on all hands by Americans accredited with
the highest positions and name, and, as a matter of
course, generally received. The ardor with which he
entered into the cause of his country in the day of the
great struggle, while he was so far from home, was only
part of his nature and habit, but certainly if ever man
burned and toiled to serve a great cause he did.

"I feel as if I hardly saw him in London last summer,
for at the time I was ill, and scarcely able to talk or
enjoy society. One could not feel much surprised at his
death, for he always struck one as a man not merely deli-
cate, but liable to menacing illness. Still, he sprang up
again so quickly, and returned to work with so much vigor,
that one almost felt as if the physical resources of his constitution shared in the abundance of his mental ones. I
valued his "Cyclopædia" before, but now it has a touching
claim upon the heart in addition to all its claims upon the
mind. I often envied his stores of learning, and seldom
parted from him without ' more keenly than of wont ' feeling a regret which through life has been habitual with
me, and often made me shrink to a distance from men
whom I desired to know, namely, that the incessant
activity which has been called for by my allotted share
of public service had left me destitute of much furniture
which else I should have stored up and greatly prized.

"Many will, through the 'Cyclopædia,' be assisted in

gathering up some part of his stores, and will also through
it inherit some fruit of his power."

" I shall never forget the first impression made on me
by Professor M'Clintock.* It was the summer of 1836
when he arrived at Dickinson College to take the chair
of mathematics. I had just entered my Sophomore year,
and was not sixteen years of age. Professor M'Clintock
was not seven years older than myself, and he had come
to teach our class and the three older classes what we
regarded as the most difficult portions of the curriculum.
He was a small, well-built, lithe, wiry, florid young man,
with a disproportionately large head, which seemed sur-
charged with brains. His eyes had a flattened appearance, as if they were inadequate to let out the fire of his
mind, doing that work very partially because they were
preoccupied with inward speculation. They appeared to
have work of their own, and were not quick at carrying
errands from his mind to the mind of the beholder. So
to me it seemed that his intellectual brightness illumined
other features more than his eyes. The play of his lips
was particularly interesting; his mouth was expressive
in many senses.

" As an instructor, the largeness of his gifts and the
wealth of his acquirements were against him. His intellect was so rapid that it could not sufficiently sympathize
with the tardy movements of slower minds. To members of the classes whose mental operations resembled

---

* From the Rev. Dr. C. F. Deems, pastor of the Church of the Strangers,
New York, and an alumnus of Dickinson College.

his own he was a delightful leader; and even in the eyes of those who were less able to follow him, and to whom, therefore, he could not be so useful, he was nevertheless splendid.

"Sometimes a man's friends misjudge his work. Perhaps as a general thing the toilers of the brain do their best in the sum total of their efforts. But it always seemed to me as if the intellect and learning of Dr. M'Clintock might have made some contribution to literature which should have had some more direct and powerful influence on the progress of human thought than Cyclopædias, translations, sketches of Methodist ministers, the analysis of Watson's Institutes, and Greek and Latin school books. Useful as all these are, they seem to belong to intellectual drudgery.

"In 1860, when about to return to America, I found him established in Paris in charge of the American Chapel, and working on the Cyclopædia. In his study I looked over the sheets of the article on the title 'GOD,' which showed more labor and painstaking than it exhibits as printed in the Cyclopædia. I ventured to make the suggestion stated above. His reply in substance was that he did not have my estimate of his capabilities of becoming by any culture a very effective preacher; that he felt his calling to be literature, which he wished to follow in the way best calculated to establish the Redeemer's kingdom; that he had taken up from time to time what seemed to him most needed to be done, which he could do probably as well as any other, and which no other seemed inclined to undertake.

"After all, a man does more by his character than by his actions. What a man does by tongue and pen may be partly computed by close and intelligent observers; but what the impulses, imparted by his life to those in near and remote connection with him, continue to produce, can be known only to God. A lightning stroke leaves a mark in the riven tree, but who can trace in the flower and fruits of garden and orchard, and in the health and beauty of men and women, the influence of the gentle yet powerful electric agent which pervades the earth, hiding, yet working every-where? So the life and character of our revered preceptor—Dr. M'Clintock— stimulated thousands of young men, of whom hundreds have given a healthy stimulus to many others who will keep his memory bright and sweet and fragrant for the coming generation of scholarly Christians."

——

"During the period that I knew Dr. M'Clintock most intimately,* dark clouds, which seemed to be charged with a great public calamity, were hanging over us, and absorbed our attention and thoughts so completely, that incidents and traits of character which, under other circumstances, might have proved 'a joy forever,' left a comparatively transient impression. Our correspondence, never very considerable, is at present inaccessible to me. During his residence in Paris he was a frequent correspondent of the late Governor Seward, and in that correspondence, which I am sure will be most cheerfully

* From the Hon. John Bigelow, Secretary of State, New York, late American Minister to France.

placed at your disposal, you are likely to find many precious memorials of his earnest and noble nature.

"My personal acquaintance with the doctor commenced in Paris, soon after the first and most humiliating battle of our late civil war. He had gone there to avail himself of the libraries, and other rare facilities of that great metropolis, in the preparation of the 'Cyclopædia of Biblical, Theological, and Ecclesiastical Literature,' with which he proposed to enrich the literature of the Christian Church. He had consented to add to his literary labors the pastorate of the American Chapel in Paris, and that became the social centre of a very considerable proportion of his country people at the time sojourning in that city. As a parish clergyman he was greatly esteemed. Though called to a society in which there were very few strictly of his own communion, he made himself eminently acceptable to all the church-going portion of his countrymen. His house was always one of their favorite resorts, and his cheerful and fruitful conversation one of its chief attractions. He was besides as hospitable as a bishop.

"There was no American in Europe more absorbed in the fortunes of his country, then engaged in a deadly struggle with the enemies of its own household, nor more ready to spend and be spent in her defence. With pastoral and literary employments more than sufficient for his strength, he was constantly occupied, through the press and by personal intercourse, in enlightening Europeans in regard to the causes of our civil war, and the magnitude of the interests at stake upon the result of it;

26

in correcting the delusions sedulously and successfully
propagated by our enemies ; in strengthening the faith
of such patriotic Americans as were desponding, and
in developing unwonted zeal and energy in those who
were not.   He never dishonored himself.   By personal
intercourse, also, he exerted a very seasonable influence upon a very influential section of French society,
and was one of the quiet, but by no means unimportant, agencies under Providence for organizing the
strong popular hostility in France to the Imperial
policies in America.   When he returned to the United
States his loss to the Church, as well as to the general society of Americans in Paris, was universally deplored.   He was a representative American of whom
all were proud, whom every one knew personally, and
whom all regarded as their friend and, in need, their
trusty counsellor.

" Dr. M'Clintock possessed a vigorous and commanding nature, which was commended to the world by singularly genial and captivating manners.   He was learned
far beyond the average of his profession, and his mind
had been equipped, and his character strengthened, by a
large and instructive intercourse with the world.   As a
pulpit orator he was always edifying, and not infrequent-
ly eloquent ; and his crowning virtue, the religion that he
taught and practiced, was a religion that united and har-
monized, not a religion that separated and antagonized,
his fellow-creatures.   He was ' liberal ' in his theology,
for the dews of his charity fell upon the just and the
unjust ; but he held no opinions about which he was in-

different, or about which he allowed others to think him indifferent."

_____

"My earliest recollections of my dear and honored friend are of his occasional visits to my parents, and of the pleasure derived from them by my mother especially, whose wit and gayety of spirits were invariably kindled by the exuberant vitality and vivacity of her guest.* As a child, I was won to him because he retained all the freshness of childhood ; while I could but be impressed at the same time with his manly acquirements, and pre-eminently with his affable and charming manners as a gentleman. With what wondering awe did I note his intelligence, that was interested, apparently, in every thing ! To me he seemed actually to take cognizance of every thing, so that in after years I was not in the least surprised to hear a distinguished German scholar say : 'Ah! your Dr. M'Clintock was a genuine scholar. Actually he knew some things that I didn't know !'—this with the air of one who makes an assertion, hardly credible. Neither when my husband submitted to his examination a small compilation of hymns and tunes for social meetings, something of a novelty in our Church at that time, was it surprising to me, who knew his versatility and working capacity, that he found leisure amid pastoral and literary labors to hear the tunes, and to make many fine suggestions, some of them requiring research on his part both for hymns and tunes. No burdens seemed to oppress his capacious mind, no tasks were too diverse for his multifarious activity.

* From Mrs. Mary S. Robinson, daughter of the Rev. Dr. A. Stevens.

"In the spring of 1863 we found ourselves in Paris, lodged in an obscure apartment in the Latin quarter. One morning I heard a cheery voice pealing through the dark little entry: 'Why don't you let your friends know you've come hither? What's the use of being so awfully exclusive?' etc., and the doctor's rosy, genial face shone into the dull room from the door-way. He allured us to his dinner-table the same day, and I clearly recall his discriminating conversation on French architecture and other arts, and on French life and manners. His admiration was warm for the brilliant people among whom he was living—a people whose finer traits are in accord with those of his own Irish temperament.

"Here, as every-where, he was conscientiously systematic in the employment of his hours, devoting a certain number daily to study, to exercise, and to society —becoming thus, by turns, preacher, pastor, *littérateur*, statesman, and man of the world. This rigid adherence to system in every thing is the only possible explanation of the variety of detail and the aggregate amount of his labors. His sermon on Sunday, at the American Chapel, was elegant and effective, as were all his pulpit efforts. Yet on such occasions I could but think he was less powerful as a preacher than he might have been had his united energies been directed to this single end. All that he did was well done, confessedly. Yet in the two or three professions he followed, any one of which is vast enough to absorb the widest culture and the utmost of native ability, the efforts of his genius were undoubtedly hampered by its own versatility—as it was, however, his pastoral office was dear to him. He once referred in conversation to some overtures that had been made toward his appointment as ambassador to the French Court. 'I told ——,' he said, 'I would rather be a minister of the Gospel, than minister to any empire under heaven.'

"In Paris, as elsewhere, he was harassed by infirmities of health. Several times, during the sermon I have alluded to, his face flushed, and he was forced to pause a moment, being almost overcome by a rush of blood to the head. The injury to his knee-joint also oppressed him painfully. Yet these seemed scarcely to impede the ordinary activities of his life. He adhered to his routine, and accomplished more than most persons do in good health.

"When, a year or two later, I entered the parsonage of St. Paul's, New York, he greeted me with his customary salutation, taking both my hands in his with cordial pressure, and asserting with rapid emphasis his pleasure at seeing me. How many can recall that salutation, quick, *empressé*, yet most natural — the two-toned cadence of a sympathetic voice, whereby the sociability and sweetness of the speaker's heart made itself heard. As by an electric chain, the person greeted was instantly put *en rapport* with the greeter. This first moment gave one the right to claim him as one's intimate friend.

"At Madison, where I visited him occasionally, his versatility and energy were brought into full requisition. Every detail pertaining to the seminary, from securing its potatoes, and examining in the rudiments the youth

who composed its earlier classes, up to recondite lectures and elaborate Cyclopædia work—all received his
personal attention. What a head was needed for this
amassing of labors, what wise distribution of time and
force, no one can conceive who did not hear from his
own lips something of his method. He reminded one
of those great generals who allow no detail of fort, field,
or camp life to escape their vigilance.

"In the afternoon of the day of one visit we drove
over the beautiful uplands whose horizons are vailed by
the tinted mists of the Kittatinny Range. Precious instruction fell continually from his lips, while ever and
anon he leaned forward in quick gesture to kiss his little
daughter, sitting opposite. I thought his nervous energy
found relief in this affectionate way, precisely as that of
a boy expends itself in sudden shiftings and ever-recurring
motion. This was the last time I saw him in life. Never
had I been more deeply impressed with the harmony of
his nature, the beautiful equilibrium of his brain and his
heart, and with the extraordinary development of both!
Among the hundreds gathered about his bier, I am sure not
a few mourned, as I did, the loss of an intimate friend.
'He knew how to sympathize,' said one of his Church
members to me in that sad hour; 'when the tidings came
of my son's death in the East Indies, he was the first of
all my friends who came to comfort me.' Genius, in the
ordinary acceptation of the word, he had in generous
measure. But the flower and crown of all his gifts, that
which cast resplendence on all these, was his genius for
loving and for winning love!"

"No American visiting Paris since Dr. M'Clintock's pastoral charge of the American Chapel,* and coming within the circle of American families represented by the congregation, has had to wait long for grateful testimony to his unfailing spiritual care of a flock standing in peculiar need of it. It was because he comprehended the dangers attending the path of Americans, and particularly the young, in a foreign land, and knew well how to place on their guard those who came confidingly within reach of his counsel, that his memory is now cherished by the members of the American Chapel at Paris with no less attachment than by the larger parish in New York, from which he had come and to which he returned.

"His official visit to the British Wesleyan Conference in 1857 was the beginning of an honored relation that increased in attachment during his subsequent residence in Paris, while his sympathy with Irish Methodism, as exhibited by his attendance at the Conference, and his labors at home in behalf of the Irish Fund during our centenary year, repeatedly found public recognition; and it was but natural that when the new Wesleyan College in Belfast, under the presidency of the Rev. William Arthur, was to be dedicated, Dr. M'Clintock should be invited (though unable to accept) to come from America and take a leading part in the exercises.

"He did not live to see acknowledged in Europe the full merit of the 'Cyclopædia' on which he had labored with the unwearied enthusiasm of the real scholar—that

* From a Letter to "The Methodist" by the Rev. Dr. Hurst, President of Drew Theological Seminary.

could not have been expected before completion of the work—but he was not without testimony from the seats of German learning that the magnitude and success of the undertaking was appreciated, as much so as could be expected while the great task was yet unfinished.

" There are many young Americans now attending the German universities who received from him their first impulse toward these fountains of foreign thought, and some have already given expression to their keen sorrow at his loss.   But the great lesson of his life for the young, here and at home, will not be thrown away—the joy of work, the intensity of Christian life.   Whatever his labors were—and he knew how to labor in more ways than are often given to men—the chief object of life with him when overtaken by death was what it had been years before, when he wrote: ' We shall all have work enough to do in preparing the ministry of the next generation. God help us to do it well!'"

" When I have thought of the possibilities that were in him, I have found myself wishing that he were not so various, so many-sided, so occupied with multifarious in-terests.*   I have mentally asked, Would not the product of his life be greater if he were to concentrate himself? But truth is, his heart was as big as his brain—loving, tender, with sympathies running out in every direction, and carrying his mental energy after them.   Whatever interested human kind interested him.   To this breadth

* From an article by the author of this memoir, printed in the " Meth-odist " March 12. 1870.

of his sympathies he owed the social power which spread such a charm over his life.

"But what shall I say of his simple, earnest piety, which rested with childlike confidence on the fatherly care of God; of his nice sense of right, which stood guard over all the inner springs of action; of his abounding charity, which would see only the better side of men? He abhorred cant in religion and in every thing else, and would have none of it. Whenever he spoke of his Christian life, it was always in the fewest and plainest words. And so, coming to and seeing the end, he announced his readiness with the utmost composure.

"Had Dr. M'Clintock been asked the secret of his success in life, he would have promptly answered, 'Work.' One of his first college addresses was a panegyric upon labor. He believed in hard, earnest, downright toil, and relied solely upon it. He had great talents—talents such as are rarely given to men, but never deluded himself with the expectation that they could be made effective without untiring exertion. He built himself up laboriously—built wisely on solid foundations, and kept on building till the fabric stood before the eyes of men conspicuous for splendor and beauty.

"His mind was not so much creative as judicial. He was essentially a critic. To investigate, and to sum up the results of investigation in a clear, condensed statement, was a habit which had become to him second nature. In these mental processes he was aided by the rapidity with which he would track the information of which he was in search. No matter in what or how many volumes hidden, it could not escape him. That his mind tended to encyclopedia came necessarily from the largeness and variety of his acquisitions. In theology especially, nothing less than the survey of the whole circle, and that from the centre, would satisfy him.

"And so he appeared before us a complete, well-rounded man, certainly the foremost scholar of American Methodism ; in eloquence, the peer of the most eloquent ; in gentleness, love, and goodness, well-nigh incomparable. He owed much to nature, for ' the elements were kindly mixed up in him ; ' much to culture, to which he faithfully dedicated himself ; but most of all to the grace of our Lord and Saviour, which wrought mightily in him. The highest eulogium we can pronounce upon him is that he was a good man. Better this than all learning, than all eloquence ; for ' whether there be tongues, they shall cease ; whether there be knowledge, it shall vanish away ; but love abideth forever.' Having in life been Christ's, he is Christ's now by a closer tie, and so dwelleth with him eternally."

THE END.   .

www.ingramcontent.com/pod-product-compliance
Lightning Source LLC
Chambersburg PA
CBHW030824110726
47900CB00006B/1736

* 9 7 8 3 3 3 7 1 4 9 7 8 9 *